by nancy thayer

the
summer we
started over

nancy thayer

the summer we started over

a novel

ballantine books

new york

Copyright © 2024 by Nancy Thayer

All rights reserved.

Published in the United States by Ballantine Books, an imprint of Random House, a division of Penguin Random House LLC, New York.

BALLANTINE BOOKS & colophon are registered trademarks of Penguin Random House LLC.

LIBRARY OF CONGRESS CATALOGING-IN-PUBLICATION DATA
Names: Thayer, Nancy.
Title: The summer we started over : a novel / Nancy Thayer.
Description: First edition. | New York : Ballantine Books, 2024.
Identifiers: LCCN 2023056257 (print) | LCCN 2023056258 (ebook) |
ISBN 9780593724002 (hardcover ; acid-free paper) |
ISBN 9780593724033 (ebook)
Subjects: LCSH: Young women—Fiction. | Sisters—Fiction. |
LCGFT: Domestic fiction. | Novels.
Classification: LCC PS3570.H3475 S876 2024 (print) |
LCC PS3570.H3475 (ebook) | DDC 813/.54—dc23/eng/20231211
LC record available at https://lccn.loc.gov/2023056257
LC ebook record available at https://lccn.loc.gov/2023056258

Printed in the United States of America on acid-free paper

randomhousebooks.com

2 4 6 8 9 7 5 3 1

First Edition

Title-page art: dachux21 © Adobe Stock Photos

For Dinah Fulton
friend of my heart forever

acknowledgments

Dinah Fulton is the most glamorous person I know. She's also kind, generous, beautiful, and hilarious. I met her when my first novel, *Stepping,* was bought by Doubleday. Dinah drove from Willliamstown, Massachusetts, to New York City to take me to lunch to celebrate at the famous 21 Club. A year later, when *Stepping* was published, Dinah looked at the plain black dress I planned to wear to the pub party. "Oh, God," she cried. "You can't go like that." She loaned me a diamond chain necklace to wear with the dress. That is the kind of thing Dinah does.

More than that, she brought me to Nantucket for the first time.

More than *that,* she introduced me to Charley Walters.

And more than that, she is the bravest, strongest-willed person I know. She has succeeded in doing what few people can do, and she's done it day by day, every day.

My *real* Dinah is not like my character Dinah Lavender, except, perhaps, for being knock-out beautiful and irresistibly warmhearted. I love you, Dinah Fulton. Thank you.

Love and thanks to Jill Hunter Burrill, Deborah and Mark Beale, Mary and John West, Tricia and Jimmy Patterson, Melissa and Nat Philbrick, Gussy Manville, Sofia Popova, Martha and Chuck Foshee, Antonia Massie, Denice Kronau and Michael Reitermann, Annye Camera, Mary Bergman, Jess Toole, Dr. Paul Roberts and Dr. Jamie Roberts, Charlotte and Tom Kastner, Gerilyn Brewer and Henry Mueller, Martha and Charley Polachi, and as always, Curlette Anglin. Thanks to Angela Giles, who is very wise for someone so young.

Special thanks to the infinitely brilliant Misty Jump and Aimee Marx of the Batavia Public Library, who make reading fabulous! And thanks to Sammy Aquiar and Ann Scott, and all of the librarians at the Nantucket Atheneum.

Nantucket Book Partners, along with Mitchell's Book Corner and Nantucket Bookworks, is my home away from home and only a five-minute walk from our house. Wendy Hudson and her crew do wonders for writers and readers, and both shops are fabulous worlds to visit. Christina Machiavelli is my go-to for information on new books, and I'm grateful for our literary chats. Tim Ehrenberg is an amazing force for books and authors. We're lucky to have him on this island.

On the mainland (which is what we call the country thirty miles across the sea from us), Titcombs Bookshop on Route 6A is another superstar store for both readers and writers. Thanks to Elizabeth Merritt, Fran Ziegler, Vicky Titcomb, and Rae Titcomb, who host brilliant book events and remember what each person likes to read. Thanks also to Bank Square Books, Bethany Beach Books, Browseabout Books, and bookstores large and small.

My books wouldn't be what they are—they just wouldn't *be*—without the hard work and perceptive eye of my editor, Shauna Summers. She is my guiding light and sometimes my emergency flare. Huge thanks to Kim Hovey and Kara Walsh for steering the literary ship through shifting seas. Allison Schuster, Karen Fink, Emma

Thomasch, Jennifer Rodriguez, and Mae Martinez: What would I do without you? Thank you.

Special, enormous, and multi-colored thanks to Belina Huey, for designing my beautiful book covers.

Meg Ruley is my friend and agent, and I'm grateful for her every day. Jesse Errera, Logan Harper, Christina Hogrebe, and the entire Jane Rotrosen Agency has my gratitude for their skill and support.

Love audiobooks? So many of my friends use audiobooks, and I'm delighted that Brilliance Audio has so many of my books available.

Thanks to Chris Mason for my website, which has all my books listed and all my news flashed on the home page. And huge thanks to Christina Higgins, my talented and creative virtual assistant.

My family is my inspiration and my delight. I couldn't do anything without my clever, handsome husband, Charley Walters. I'm delighted (most of the time!) by news flashes about the real world from my son, Josh Thayer, and his husband, David Gillum; my daughter, Sam, and her partner, Tommy; and especially from my grandchildren (whom my friend Jill calls the Vowel Children): Ellias, Adeline, Emmett, Annie, Arwin, and now Avery.

I get such great energy and wisdom from my readers! A quick hello (and a good review!) brightens my day. I'm delighted to learn what my readers think, but more than that, I simply love the connection with everyone out there. I sincerely love you. It is you I'm writing for and I'm grateful to you all.

the
summer we
started over

one

Eddie Grant was surprised at how well her life had turned out, especially given what an eccentric family she'd come from.

Here she was, twenty-eight years old, living in Manhattan and making a six-figure salary as a personal assistant to the famous and beloved romance writer Dinah Lavender. Eddie got to travel with Dinah, eat at posh restaurants with Dinah, wear fabulous clothes, and meet fascinating people.

And the work she was paid for? She made reservations at restaurants, booked airline tickets, chose between USPS and FedEx when mailing off Dinah's giveaways, and fixed Dinah's computer when it confused her, which usually involved little more than turning it off and back on. She knew how to hem a dress in a pinch, help correctly sign documents, post photos on social media, answer Dinah's hundreds of emails, and keep her shelves of books—the ones Dinah had written, over a hundred and growing—in order. Eddie had created a list of essential phone numbers for Dinah: her editor, her agent, her publicist, her stylist, her therapist, Luigi's Fine Liquors, and Big Tony's Pizza. She'd added them to all three of Dinah's cellphones so that all Dinah had to do was push a button. She'd consoled her when a character in one of her books died, and only once had she reminded Dinah that *Dinah* was the one who decided his fate.

Dinah worked hard, tapping away at her computer, pacing the floor at night talking to herself about what her heroine should do next, weeping in a perfumed bubble bath because she didn't like her newest book's cover. When Eddie first applied for the job of personal assistant, Dinah had stipulated that Eddie live with Dinah, because the writer often worked night and day. Dinah lived in a handsome apartment on Park Avenue. She had people who cleaned and cooked for her, but they didn't live in. She had friends to dine out and go to the theater with, and she received loving letters and emails from readers around the country, but she didn't seem to have anyone special in her life.

Eddie had her own gorgeous bedroom and en suite bath. When Dinah had appointments or lunches or dinners, Eddie had free time to visit the Met or the Guggenheim, to see a movie or go out with friends, but she would often simply lie in bed reading. She had a walk-in closet filled with silk, cashmere, Hermès, Ralph Lauren, and Kate Spade. True, many of her clothes had been bought by Dinah *for* Dinah but she'd tossed them to Eddie before even wearing them. The two women were more or less the same size, although Dinah's figure was substantially more hourglass.

Dinah was in her forties, and Eddie wondered why the writer had never married.

Maybe, Eddie thought, just maybe, Dinah, like Eddie, had fallen in love with a man who wanted more than she could give. Maybe Dinah was traveling all over the world and writing three books a year so she didn't have time to think about the love that might have been.

The love that might have been—now *there* was a Dinah Lavender title.

But Eddie had promised herself not to think of Jeff.

Instead, Eddie thought about her sister, Barrett, who wanted Eddie to come home to Nantucket for a few weeks. And Eddie *wanted* to go. *So much*.

First of all, Barrett was finally going to launch her shop, Nantucket Blues, on Memorial Day. It was a huge, exciting undertaking for Barrett. The summer residents would be flocking to the island, and so would the tourists. It would be an enormous help to Barrett if Eddie was around to assist by simply being there. Moral support, Eddie supposed it was called. They'd always been there for each other. Eddie could also help with their father, a handsome, intellectual man who had been so weakened by sorrow that he'd escaped to a farmhouse on Nantucket, brought his daughters with him, and hid himself away writing a book Eddie wasn't sure he would ever finish.

Also, Eddie hadn't had an actual vacation in two years. As luxurious and glamorous as life was with Dinah, Eddie still missed home. She missed walking on the beach at sunset and munching a Downyflake doughnut and exchanging glances with Barrett when their father said something hilariously bizarre. She missed sitting on the back porch with a cup of warm coffee in her hands while she sweet-talked the horse, who would nicker with pleasure to hear her voice but canter away if Eddie tried to touch her.

On the other hand, Jeff was there.

Jeff was her age—twenty-eight—an island man who owned his own small but successful contracting business. He was tall, handsome, and funny. He read books almost as voraciously as Eddie did.

They met because of a book he bought.

Eddie, her father, and her sister had just moved from western Massachusetts and the memories there. They'd settled in a big old farmhouse on Nantucket. Eddie found a job immediately, working as a clerk at Mitchell's bookstore. Located in a historic brick building at the corner of Orange Street and Main, the shop was cozy, bright, and filled with books for every age. Eddie knew something about books—she was passionate about reading, majored in English lit in college, and after graduating, worked for a year in New York, interning with an editor, which was Eddie's dream job.

Or was it?

She'd been trying to figure that out when her mother left and her brother, Stearns, died, and the family fell apart. Eddie had given up her New York job to return to Williamstown and help her sister and father. Like them, she needed to be near her family to have the courage to continue. Helping them helped *her* keep up her courage.

After that terrible time, her father had resigned from his professorship at Williams College and sold their large and cluttered colonial house near the college observatory. Eddie and Barrett held secret whispered meetings and decided they had to move with him. They had to help him start again, and that would help them start again, too.

The chaos of packing and moving helped mask their grief and provided a much-needed sense that they were doing *something*. The moving van, the ferry crossing, and the choice of rooms in the big old farmhouse, all that was healing. Still, their father remained despondent, hiding in his office, intending to write a book, and buying countless books for his research as if they were drugs.

It had been spring by the time they were settled in the house, and businesses were hiring. Barrett worked in retail and waitressed all day and babysat when she had time. Eddie took a full-time job at the bookshop. She felt the pressure of her age weighing on her—she was twenty-five, and ready to start her *real* life, if only she could decide what that was.

One day Jeff walked into the bookstore, a tall, tousle-haired man in carpenters' pants and a dark blue rugby shirt.

Well, now he looks interesting, Eddie thought.

He stopped walking. She couldn't stop staring at him. She smiled. He smiled back at her, nodding as if accepting something.

Eddie said, "Hello."

Jeff said, "Hey." Coming closer to her, he announced, "I'm here to buy a book."

"That's good. We've got books. Lots of books." She waved her hands like a magician's assistant to demonstrate the shelves of books all around them. *Settle down,* she ordered herself. *That's not possible,* her lovestruck self replied.

He took a few steps closer. "I need a gift book. Like a book of photos. Of Nantucket. For my father."

"Where does he live?" Eddie asked.

"On Pine Street."

"Oh, Pine Street on the island?"

Jeff was standing next to the counter with the computer. "Yeah, I know it seems odd to give him a book of photos about Nantucket when he lives here, but . . ."

Eddie leaned on the counter, gently pushing a pile of books aside. "I think it's wonderful. It must be amazing to live in a place you love so much that you want a book about it."

"Nantucket's special." He cocked his head. "You must be new here."

He'd missed a spot shaving his smooth, tanned, beautiful neck. She wanted to reach out and touch it. "I am. New here. We just moved here two weeks ago."

"We?" He drew back slightly.

"Oh, no, not that kind of 'we.' I'm not married. I moved here with my sister and my father. We moved to the farm off Hummock Pond Road."

"Nice." He was tall, broad-shouldered, blue-eyed.

She took a deep breath. "I'm Eddie Grant."

"I'm Jeff." He held out his hand. "Jeremiah Jefferson, actually, but

Jeremiah makes me seem like a prim old Puritan wearing a hat with a buckle on it."

"I doubt that anything could make you seem like a Puritan," Eddie said, and shook his large, warm, callused hand.

Another customer entered the shop, an older woman with hair like a frozen meringue.

Eddie forced herself to be professional. "Our coffee-table books are upstairs. Lots of gorgeous books about Nantucket."

"So I should go upstairs," he said.

"You should."

"Could you come with me? I mean, to help me choose?"

She nodded toward the other customer. "I need to be here."

"Okay. I'll be back."

"I'll be right here. I won't go away," she told him.

"He's not exactly leaving for the moon," Meringue Woman snapped from her spot in the nonfiction aisle.

Eddie straightened her shoulders. "May I help you?"

"Just browsing," the woman replied.

Eddie managed to maintain some kind of poise as the man went up the stairs to the second floor. The shop had other customers, and Eddie attended to them happily, knowing the man had to come downstairs sooner or later, and the other clerk was on her lunch break.

He came down after a few minutes, carrying a heavy coffee-table book about Nantucket.

"Beautiful book," Eddie said, ringing up the sale and putting the book into a paper bag.

"Beautiful," Jeff had agreed, his eyes meeting hers.

"Would you like a bookmark?" she asked.

"Sure. And I'd like to take you to dinner tonight." As he reached for the bag in her hand, his hand touched hers, and he kept it there.

He was steady, and warm, and confident, Eddie thought. She wanted to turn her hand over and slide her palm against his. Of course that would mean she had to drop the book, and she wouldn't do that.

"I'd like to go to dinner tonight," she told him. "I get off work at six."

"Good," Jeff said. "That will give me time to show you some of the island."

At six o'clock exactly, Eddie stepped out from the bookshop onto the sidewalk. The sky was still light, the trees lush with new green leaves, the window boxes spilling over with flowers.

"Hi." Jeff was right in front of the shop, leaning against his truck. "Ready to go?"

"Absolutely!"

Jeff held the door open for her and she slipped inside. He got into the driver's side, and the cab was filled with his wide shoulders, long arms, handsome face. Being that close to him was exhilarating. *Is it too soon,* Eddie thought, *for me to throw myself on him?*

"Have you spent any time at Madaket?" Jeff asked as he backed out onto the cobblestone street.

"No. We've been to Surfside Beach a few times, but we've been too busy getting settled to see all of the island."

"Good. I'm taking you to Madaket. It's the western end of the island."

"Sounds good," Eddie said. She was insanely attracted to him in an urgent, visceral way. Madaket. The moon? She would go anywhere with him.

"Why are you named Eddie?"

Eddie laughed. "I'm Edna, actually. My father named his children after his favorite poets."

"Edna St. Vincent Millay," Jeff said.

He knows about poets. She said, "That's impressive! Do you live here year-round?"

"Absolutely. I was born here. I grew up here. I went away to college, and I worked in Boston for a few years. But I missed the island, so I returned. I can't decide if that's a sign of strength or weakness." He kept his eyes on the road.

"Strength or weakness?" Eddie thought about it. "I suppose that's the way men would put it. I guess I would say that I have to choose between being responsible and being . . . free."

"You must be the oldest child," Jeff said.

Eddie glanced over at him. "How can you tell?"

"The oldest child feels responsible. The younger child feels he has to measure up to the powerful older child, especially if he's male."

"Ah. You must have a brother."

"I do. And I'll never measure up to him."

Eddie joked, "What is he? A Navy Seal?"

"Actually, he's an Army Ranger," Jeff said.

"What? Really? Wow. You're right. You never *will* live up to him. Do you have a younger sibling?"

"Nope. And thanks for that vote of confidence."

They laughed together.

"The truth is," Jeff continued, "he's my hero. He's four years older than I am. We used to fight when we were kids, but whenever I got in trouble, he had my back."

"Were you a troublemaker?"

"Nah. Not a real troublemaker. I was a clown, mostly. Until I got into high school and realized that I'm better looking than he is."

"Probably humbler, too," Eddie said.

"Actually, yes. I *am* humbler than he is. He's got a powerful ego. He likes competition, traveling, surprises, being tested."

"And you don't?"

"I don't. I'm a pretty traditional guy. I'd like to have a life like my parents have. Live on the island, marry the woman I love, have a couple of kids, spend time with friends."

Anxiety nipped at her. Before she had time to think it through, she added, "What about reading books?"

"Books are part of my life. Always will be." Jeff pulled into a small parking area. "We're here."

She jumped out of the truck and followed him along a sandy path and up a high dune.

"Oh, wow."

From here, she could see a long beach stretching into the distance, the blue ocean gliding up onto the shore, gentle waves breaking into white fans.

"Beautiful, right?" Jeff said. "Believe me, it's seldom this calm. We're on the ocean side of the island. The waves can be ferocious out here. I'll bring you out sometime when we've got some wind."

He'll bring me out here sometime? He was already planning another time to be with her? Her knees went weak. She stumbled.

He caught her arm. "This dune is steep. It will be nice and flat down by the water." He held her hand as they slid down the dune, and he didn't let go once they were on the shore.

They strolled down the beach. The sun dazzled the water with colors. It was warm, and the air smelled like heaven.

"Let's sit," Jeff suggested.

They settled on the sand a few feet from the tide's reach with their arms wrapped around their knees as they watched the waves.

He studied her face. "Tell me about your family."

"Well, there's my sister, Barrett—"

"Elizabeth Barrett Browning," Jeff said.

"Score. You must have majored in English."

"History, actually. So . . . Barrett?"

"Barrett is my younger sister. She's working hard to pile up money so she can have her own business on the island." Eddie lifted a handful of sand and let the grains trickle through her fingers. How could she talk about her brother to a man whose brother was an Army Ranger? "My younger brother, Stearns—"

"Thomas Stearns Eliot," Jeff said.

She smiled at him. "Right. Um, Stearns died in a motorcycle accident last year."

"I'm sorry." He said nothing else, did not press her for details.

"Thank you." Eddie cleared her throat. "Anyway, now, it's just me and Barrett and my father. And a dog, Duke. And Duchess, a horse that came with the farm."

"You must have bought the MacKensies' place," Jeff said. "I remember meeting that horse. Although I suppose 'meeting' isn't the right word. She wasn't interested in me."

"She's not interested in anyone. Honestly, she acts as if she's too good for the rest of us."

Jeff leaned back on his elbows. "Why did you all move here?"

Eddie wondered how much she could tell him without frightening him away. But he was easy to be with, and if he felt even a fraction of what she felt, he would be seeing her again.

"My father was an English professor at Williams. My mother left my father. Divorced him. She'd never enjoyed the whole mommy-and-wife business. My sister was taking courses at UMass, and Dad suddenly announced he was selling our house and moving us to Nantucket. I was working in New York, and I quit my job to come home and help." She shrugged. "It's complicated."

Jeff didn't seem fazed by her eccentric history. "What were you doing in New York?"

"I worked as an assistant to an editor's assistant. Basically, I was an errand girl. But I've always wanted to work in publishing, so I took the job, even if it was on the lowest rung."

He studied her face. Returning his gaze to the sea, he said, "I never wanted to live here all my life. I thought I'd move off and do something amazing. But I did move off. I lived in Boston for a few years. When I came home to see my parents now and then, I realized I prefer the island life. Now you, Eddie, your family, must have some kind of money, if you could afford to buy a house and a piece of land on Nantucket. I don't have that kind of money. Most people who grow up here don't have that kind of money. I live with my parents now, but they were smart. They bought a piece of land for me out at Tom Nevers Head when I was born and I'm building a house there. Working *hard*. Especially in the summer when I won't be able to see you as often as I'd like."

"Oh," Eddie said lightly, "you want to see me again?"

"Yes, and not only in the bookstore."

Eddie thought every cell of her body was actually sparkling with pleasure. "We can meet tomorrow evening."

"I don't think I can wait that long." Jeff leaned toward her and softly, lightly, kissed her lips.

Her breath caught in her throat. "Wow. What was that?"

"Basically, just a sign to show you I'm a gentleman. If I acted on my instincts, I'd do a lot more."

Eddie shivered. "If I acted on *my* instincts, I'd let you."

All that summer, and into the fall, Eddie was with Jeff whenever they found time in their busy lives. They sat in the seclusion of the shadowy dunes at Madaket, watching the sun set in a showgirl explosion of color. They kayaked to Coatue to picnic and swim. They held hands while watching movies at the Dreamland. Jeff showed Eddie his apartment over his parents' house, and they made love, and it was *love,* sweet, urgent, and undeniable, like sunrise and the surge of the ocean. They talked. They spoke about his parents, his brother, Jeff's college football team. Eddie told him about Stearns and Dove and her father.

Eddie told Barrett about him.

"I want you to meet him," Eddie said. The sisters were doing the dishes. "But I also don't want him to meet you."

Barrett tied a dish towel over her head, peasant-style, bugged out her eyes, and made her two front teeth protrude like a rabbit's. "We're not good enough for him?" She purposefully drooled as she spoke.

Eddie laughed. "No, silly. I just don't want him to think . . . that we're serious about each other."

"But you are serious, aren't you?"

Eddie looked away. "It's puppy love."

"You are way too old to be a puppy," Barrett remarked.

"Okay, then, it's summer love. Island love. It won't last. Anyway, Barrett, you know I'll never have children. Jeff's someone who would be a great father. Just not with me."

Barrett touched Eddie's shoulder. "You don't really mean that, Eddie."

"I do," Eddie said. "I absolutely do."

One night in March, when the clouds made a blueberry sky and the ocean was darker and somehow threatening, its heavy waves rearing up and crashing down, Eddie and Jeff lay on his bed after making love. Eddie was drowsy and dreamy, her body satisfied, her mind blissed out.

Jeff lay next to her, spooning her, his arm over her waist, his warm breath against her neck.

"I love you," he said.

Eddie whispered, "I love you."

"I want to marry you," he said.

Eddie froze. She'd thought this might happen, but she hadn't thought she would have to give him up so soon.

Now, while he couldn't see her face, she said, "Jeff, I can't marry you. And you shouldn't marry me. I can't have children."

"Why not?" Jeff's voice was calm, reassuring. "Is it . . . something physical?" Before she could respond, he said, "We can adopt."

"It's not physical. It's . . . it's the way I am. I don't want to be a mother. I would be a terrible mother." Eddie pulled away from Jeff's arm. She rose from the bed and hurriedly dressed in the clothes she'd cast off hours before. "I have to go."

Jeff rose and pulled on his shorts. "I don't understand."

"I'm sorry." Eddie put her hand on the doorknob.

Jeff reached out and clasped her wrist. "Is it the book thing? New York? You don't want to stay at home with a baby drooling on your shoulder? You want the glitz and speed of the city?"

Eddie hung her head. She closed her eyes. She had told him why she didn't want to be with him. It was as if he hadn't heard.

"Yes," she whispered. "That's it. That's the reason. Let me go, Jeff."

He withdrew his hand. "I'll drive you back."

Three days later, a New York contact texted Eddie about a romance writer who needed an assistant. Eddie sent her résumé to Dinah Lavender. She did a long FaceTime interview with the writer. A week later, Eddie left the island and flew to New York and her new life.

Standing in Dinah's Manhattan apartment, Eddie thought of Jeff. They had fallen in love so fast. They'd spent every day and night together as often as they could. They'd been bonded, joined together so completely, as necessary and essential as the shore and the sea. They had wanted to be with each other forever. But Eddie had left, and Jeff knew why. And they both knew she would leave again.

But, Eddie reminded herself, she wasn't returning to Nantucket because of Jeff. She was going to the island to help her sister.

She had to talk to Dinah.

Thais had made a large and complicated dish of chicken pad Thai that evening. Eddie set the table in the small morning room, smoothing out a fresh Irish linen tablecloth, and laying out the Spode Buttercup dinnerware, which seemed to be Dinah's favorite. She poured white wine into the stemless wineglasses, and set a small pot of yellow primroses in the middle of the table. The room was bright with sun in the morning, but by evening, the light was dimmed, and gentle on the complexion.

Eddie walked down the hall and tapped on the door of Dinah's study.

"Dinner's ready."

"Oh, thank God!" Dinah shoved her chair away from her desk so quickly she nearly tipped over. "I'm right where I should be. I know what Ace will be doing tomorrow. Could you research the rarest sports car made in England in the 1960s?"

Eddie walked toward the hall, tapping notes onto her phone as she went.

Dinah wore jeans, sandals, and a Versace shirt with ruffles at the neckline and wrists and gold bangled earrings that swung and shivered with her every move. Her black hair was so thick and heavy that she had to wear three barrettes to hold it up when she wanted it twisted back and out of the way. As she spoke, the ends of the twist waved above her head like black feathers. Sometimes just looking at Dinah could make Eddie motion sick.

Eddie opened the lid on the bowl and ladled the pad Thai onto Dinah's plate, and then onto hers. As they ate, Eddie asked Dinah about the book she was working on, because Dinah's mind was always filled with whatever book she was working on. Dinah seemed to believe she was writing a documentary, and she fretted anxiously if a character had to go to jail or give birth to a baby without medical help. Eddie listened, seldom saying a word, but Dinah always thanked her at the end of the meal for helping her sort out some of her characters' issues.

"Dinah," Eddie said, after taking her last sip of wine. "I had a call from my sister today. I need to go to Nantucket to help with my father."

"Is he ill?" Dinah asked, blotting her lips with her linen napkin.

"Not ill, really. He's depressed. He has been ever since . . . my mother left."

"Shame." Dinah had little interest in the problems of others unless they were compelling and explosive enough to give her ideas for her books. "I suppose you could pop up for the weekend."

"I need to stay longer than that." Eddie kept her gaze on her employer, an unspoken message that she wasn't going to back down.

"Oh, dear. How long?"

"At least a month."

"A month? I can't do without you for a month!"

"Sure you can, Dinah. We can talk and text and email and I can do everything virtually, the way most things get done these days."

Dinah's hands flew to her mouth as if she'd been given a bad medical diagnosis. "But who will I go out to dinner with?"

"Liz. Sara. Emily." Eddie named Dinah's editor, agent, and publicist. "They have all been begging you to go to lunch or dinner with them."

Dinah shook her head. "No. Not for a month. I'm at a *crucial* place in my novel."

"Dinah, you are always in a crucial place of a novel." Eddie was surprised at the strength of her convictions. "I haven't had a vacation in two years."

Dinah argued, "But we've been to Paris! To London! To Hawaii!"

"That's right, Dinah. *We* have been. I've never gone off on my own."

Dinah sniffed. "I see. I hadn't realized my presence was so distasteful."

Eddie took a deep breath. "Dinah, stop. I know that deep down you are a really kind person. You know that *right now* we are not in one of your books. I'm a real person with a troubled father and a sister who needs me. You will be just fine here. I'll bet you've got a dozen contacts who would wine and dine you."

Dinah sweetened her voice. "What if I gave you a raise?"

Eddie laughed. "Dinah, I have to go. I'll call you every day. Now you go choose a movie and I'll make us hot fudge sundaes."

Dinah froze for a long, dramatic moment.

Then she asked, "With sprinkles?" Dinah grinned, letting Eddie know she was well aware of her little girl act.

"With sprinkles."

Eddie wrote in her journal that night. She hadn't written in it since she moved to be with Dinah. Her time in New York had been so busy, crowded with work and play and fabulous restaurants and theater. She'd shot photos with her iPhone instead. Now she realized that those photos were all about the surface. She hadn't caught her deepest thoughts, and now she needed to write in her diary to delve into her extremely confused soul.

> *Barrett is so brave. So certain. My desires, my life plan, my vision of the future wobbles like a tower of Jell-O compared to Barrett's confident decisions.*
>
> *I think of my mother now, and it always hurts to think of her— how little pleasure she took from being our mother, how little interest she had in us—and I'm afraid that I'll be that kind of mother, resentful and erratic.*
>
> *I don't want to be a mother. I shouldn't be a mother.*
>
> *I won't be a mother.*
>
> *My most secret, most haunting dream of my future is, at the best, fantasy. It is completely unachievable. I must harden my heart against sentimental longings. I think of Jeff as the love of my life, but I must be the love of my life, even if it breaks my heart.*

two

In the farmhouse on Nantucket, Barrett made a peanut butter, lettuce, and mayonnaise sandwich and put it on a plate, covered by a napkin. She taped a note for her father on the top: *Your sandwich is under here. Your favorite kind!*

She moved around the kitchen, putting away the clean dishes from the dishwasher, scrubbing the counter and the spacious old porcelain sink. She washed her hands and leaned against the sink, rubbing hand lotion into her skin, exactly the way her mother had done every day and evening before she went away.

Eddie had also gone away, for two whole years. But she'd promised she'd come back in May, to help with Barrett's shop opening and with their increasingly dotty father. Eddie often sent money, enough to pay for a new water heater or storm windows on the east side of the house. Mostly Eddie had sent wonderful, usually useless, gifts from Paris or

Tuscany or wherever Dinah Lavender took her. But Barrett needed her sister here, now.

"Buck up, buttercup!" Barrett said to herself. She tapped her leg. "Come on, Duke. Let's go feed the horse."

Duke, their sweet rescue dog, went to the back door, his black and white tail wagging. The odd-looking dog was a happy creature, pleased to go with anyone, or curl up anywhere, preferably next to a person's warm body, and snooze.

Together Barrett and Duke walked out into the May morning. Spring could be fickle on Nantucket. Today the wind was playful and the sun shone bright, unobscured by clouds. They walked to the small barn, originally built in the 1800s to shelter animals and store bags of grain, and now not used for very much at all. Although it stood strong and steady, it had an air of emptiness. And it *was* empty, except for the few bales of hay and oats kept over the winter to feed the arrogant horse.

Duchess had come with the farm when William Grant bought it three years ago. Actually, it was in the terms of the sale that the horse remain on the farm, because the relatives of the owners who had died didn't want to take the time and trouble to find someone to buy her, and they assured the Grant family that the horse was very happy here and would be no trouble. They had been right. The horse was no trouble. But also wrong, because she certainly didn't seem happy. She was a buckskin bay with chocolate mane and tail, sixteen hands, beautiful and standoffish. The first year Barrett lived here, she'd tried her best to befriend Duchess, and as a new girl in town, she could have used a good frien.. on the island. But the horse would bolt if Barrett tried to touch her. When Barrett held out a carrot or an apple, the horse would approach warily, extending her head and sniffing, her rubbery nose touching the apple, then snatch the apple with her huge horsey teeth and race off to the opposite end of the field.

Gradually, Barrett made human friends and stopped spending time with the horse. That first year, Barrett and Eddie were frazzled, doing

ten things at the same time, unpacking boxes, buying groceries, cooking meals, trying to stir their father into a semblance of life—after all,
he was the one who had moved them here! But their father had sequestered himself in his office on the first floor near the kitchen. He was,
he said, working on a book. He wandered the house day and night,
eating whatever was around, not interacting with his daughters. His
only pleasure seemed to be ordering used books from literary internet
sites and receiving them in the mail. Eddie stayed for the first year, settling their new, smaller, family into the farmhouse and working at the
bookshop. Barrett waitressed at night, worked in retail all day, and
babysat when she had time, to save up money for her shop.

"Good morning, Duchess!" Barrett called. "The sun is shining, it's
almost summer, and I'm going to open my shop in one week! I've got
to stop mooning around. Eddie will come home and deal with Dad,
and I'll get rich for all of us."

She knew that wasn't true, that she'd get rich, but she did have high
hopes for her shop.

When they moved to Nantucket, Barrett had quickly realized she
could make serious money here in the summer. She took as many jobs
as she could, worked hard, and made friends. She took business
courses virtually for two years, and at the same time she continued
working. She had a dream and she made a rational plan.

Barrett had made friends and gradually become comfortable in her
life. That, she thought, was saying a lot. For that, she thought, she
deserved some kind of medal. Her brother had died, her mother had
left them, her father had retreated into his books, and after a year on
the island, Eddie had left to work with Dinah Lavender. For Barrett it
had been sink or swim. There had been days and weeks when she
wanted to stop struggling and collapse in grief. But the horse and dog
and her father needed feeding, and friends invited her to beach parties, and really, it just wasn't in her nature to give up.

Who was she? Barrett thought during those odd transitional years.
She wasn't a genius like her brother had been, and thank God for that.

She wasn't a scholar like her father. She didn't run away from her problems like her mother. She didn't want a glamorous life like Eddie.

Most people have parents or teachers to advise them. Barrett lived in her dreams. She wasn't crazy. She did well in school and had fun with friends. She watched television with her father. She kept up on current events.

But at night, trying to sleep, she slipped into a dream world, a day-dream world, an emotional sanctuary. It was as if she were inside an egg, a robin's egg that was a beautiful blue inside as well as outside. The egg was as big as the universe, and over the years she imagined rooms that were like oceans she could float in. A room made of the sapphire of the island's hydrangeas. A room as transparent as sea glass, and one as deep indigo as the ocean at night. The blue of flame, the blue of ice. The blue of the summer sky.

By the time she was twenty-three, she knew that she wanted to own a shop on Nantucket. It would be called Nantucket Blues. She was building her future on dreams, but she had saved most of her money while she worked on the island, and she had enough to rent a shop on Lower Main Street, in the small courtyard of shops like Aunt Leah's Fudge.

It was a good location. People passed it on their way to and from the Hy-Line. It had a large display window and a small back room with a table for wrapping gifts and unwrapping deliveries. She'd rented a credit card machine and invested in a touch screen cash register. She wanted to make her dream come true at last. And she was prepared, and could handle both things—business and dreams.

She would open the door to Nantucket Blues on Memorial Day weekend.

Her front window was ready. On the right side was layered a pile of cashmere sweaters in dreamy spring and summer colors—aquamarine, turquoise, azure, and sapphire. In the center, a pair of expensive co-balt blue vases were surrounded by waves of blue and white silk, the background for earrings, necklaces, and bracelets fashioned into scallop shells, lightship baskets, starfish, mermaids, some inexpensive, some pricey. Picture frames adorned with tiny dried flowers, translucent jingle shells, dried blueberries, and ribbon faced the street along the left side. The frames held pictures of happy families on Nantucket beaches. The photos were spectacular, because her friend Cath was an island photographer, and this helped both Cath and Barrett. Notebooks with heavenly blue covers. Finally, a large white antique pitcher tempted the eyes with its bouquet of Nantucket's showgirls, giant blue hydrangeas. Most of her items had been handmade by Nantucket crafters or judiciously bought at estate sales on the island.

Eddie had said, "Care Bear, Nantucket Blues is a great idea. But I worry that the shop won't be successful and you'll lose all the money you worked so hard to earn."

"Eddie, stop. I'm making my dream come true. How many people can say that?" Eddie was older and wiser and more sophisticated, but this summer Barrett felt strong. She knew people came to the island for the sun and the beach, but they also came for the time to dream. "Can you?" she challenged.

Eddie had taken a moment to respond. "I suppose I sort of can. I've always wanted my life to be about books."

"There are so many ways for a life to be about books," Barrett reminded her sister.

Eddie, usually so sweet, snapped, "I'm *fine,* Barrett." Regretting her cranky response, she added, "I just don't have everything figured out. Dreams don't just pop into your heart in complete detail."

Mine did, Barrett wanted to say, but she diplomatically said, "I'm sure you're right."

Eddie could have flown into Nantucket. She absolutely could afford to. But she took the fast ferry for the crossing over Nantucket Sound to the island. The boat was packed with people headed to the island for Memorial Day, the start of summer. She stood at the railing with the wind in her hair as she left one world for another.

The boat docked with a sturdy bump against the wharf and soon, with much clanging and banging, the crew positioned the metal ramps so the passengers could single-file down to the brick sidewalk.

Eddie's heart lifted as she set foot on the island. It *was* beautiful here. She'd forgotten how sweet the air was. She walked toward the crowded baggage claim area, glanced up, and tripped over her own feet.

Standing only a few yards away was Jeff. She hadn't seen him for two years, but he still looked like everything she'd ever wanted.

Eddie was stunned. Instead of fighting through the crowd to the luggage carts, she froze, staring at Jeff as if he were a vision. She shouted—the crowd was noisy—"What are you doing here?"

"Hello, Eddie," Jeff said, with his slow sweet smile. "I just put my grandmother on the boat. What are *you* doing here?"

Had he gotten taller in the two years she'd been away? Was that even possible? She didn't think so, not when he was almost thirty. But his shoulders were wider, and his entire body was more . . . more *there* . . . than it had been before.

She wanted to kiss him.

She had never stopped wanting to kiss him.

She forced herself to be sane, or at least act that way. "I'm coming home for a few weeks, helping out while Barrett opens her shop. And to check on Dad. How are you?"

"I'm good. Hey, let me drive you home."

"Oh." Alone with him in his truck? She was so not ready for this. Eddie stumbled over her words. "Right, fine, yes, thanks."

"Excuse me!" a woman said, as her corgi pulled on its leash. "We need to get by."

Jeff asked Eddie, "Which bags are yours? I'll get them."

"Oh, the navy blue suitcases in cart forty-seven. There. I put ribbons on the handles so I could spot them."

Jeff shouldered his way to the carts and lifted off her two roller bags. "Follow me," he told Eddie.

She nodded. She followed him.

He looked amazing from the back.

As he hefted her suitcases into his truck, he said, "You look good."

Her heart pounded. "You, too." Was he going to kiss her, right out on the parking lot of the steamship terminal, with all sorts of people coming and going?

Was *she* going to kiss him?

"Thanks." Jeff opened the passenger door of his Dodge Ram pickup truck and held out his hand to help her up. Her skirt rose as she stepped up into the truck, and she hoped he noticed.

Jeff came around, got in, and started the truck. "Going home?"

"Yes, home. How are you?"

"I'm great. My guys and I are building houses as fast as we can hammer. Making big money and building big muscles." With a grin, he flexed his arm.

"Impressive."

They buckled into their seats. Jeff slowly wove his way into the traffic.

"So. You're a city girl now." He kept his eyes steadily on the road.

"I am. But I do miss Nantucket." Eddie couldn't think straight. The attraction between them was as intense as it had been two years ago. She was still crazily in love with Jeff.

"You haven't come home very often."

They were almost to her house. Trying to be flippant, she said, "You noticed."

Jeff jerked the steering wheel to the right, pulled over to the curb, and put the truck in park.

Turning to face her, Jeff said, "Eddie, did you think I wouldn't notice? I love you. I didn't say that lightly. I meant what I said. I'm never going to stop loving you."

She ducked her head, hiding the sudden tears in her eyes. "I love you, too, Jeff. Just as much. But I told you why I can't marry you."

"Maybe you need to see a counselor. A therapist."

Eddie put her hands to her face. She took a deep breath. "Jeff. Right now I need to go home."

"Got it." Jeff put the truck back in gear and drove.

They didn't talk for the rest of the ride. Jeff turned right and right again, and there they were, at the long, crushed-shell driveway to her family's home.

The house was a traditional farmhouse, white clapboard, a front porch with two rocking chairs, four first-floor windows, four second-floor windows, one half-moon window on the top floor. A wooden fence began behind the house, starting at the barn and running off into the distance. Yellow daffodils and pink tulips filled the gardens next to the house, and fruit trees were flashing their flowers.

"Looks like a greeting card," Jeff remarked.

Eddie nodded. "It really does." Emotion surged over her, almost taking her breath away. How could she have left?

Their dog, Duke, raced up to the truck, barking, wagging his tail, jumping with joy.

Eddie stepped down from the truck. Jeff carried her suitcases to the porch, and she followed him.

"Thanks for the ride." She paused. "Could we, I don't know, get together for coffee sometime?"

"Sure. Sometime."

Eddie thought he was going to kiss her, but he hurried down the steps, into his truck, and tore out of the driveway, leaving her standing there alone.

She took a moment to regroup. Her emotions were all over the place.

———

Three years ago, their father suddenly bought the small farm on Nantucket and moved them there. The clear, clean air of the small Berkshire Mountains town where they'd lived for years had seemed to Eddie to be clogged with the gray of ashes. When her father told her they were moving, she understood why.

Eddie knew that their father hoped this would be a way to distance them from the residence of a tragedy, to live where no one had known her brother, where they could start their lives anew.

Eddie had quit her city job to stay and do what she could to help. Barrett had been about to graduate from college. She needed support, stability. Eddie had gone through the packing of what they wanted and the trucking off to a charity shop of what they didn't want. Eddie had been the strong one for the family, what was left of the family. She'd bought a used four-wheel drive Jeep. She put delicious food on the table for them at normal hours and did the laundry and threw out the flowers that had been sent and later wilted and died.

And this house, this farmhouse, such an odd place on a resort island, like a Laura Ingalls Wilder book set in Saint-Tropez, had been clean and bright and welcoming. The floors were wide-board pine, freshly stained to a butterscotch shine, and the windows were large, letting the sun brighten the air and everything in it. The rooms were spacious, some wallpapered in pleasant old-fashioned flower designs, all of them with freshly painted marshmallow white trim. The kitchen had a large porcelain sink and a Garland six-burner gas stove from the fifties. They put a large, oval-shaped rag rug in the middle of the room with a new oak kitchen table with six matching chairs.

The property had been excitingly strange, not at all like the stony Berkshire Mountains, and not like Nantucket's golden beaches, but rich with thick grass laced with wildflowers, and next to it, at the end of the driveway, a small, handsome barn. It had a loft full of hay so sweet-smelling Eddie wanted to chew on it, and a floor of large unpainted wide boards that made a satisfying clopping sound when you walked over it.

She'd stayed for almost a year. She bought a used Jeep for herself and gave her newer Jeep to Barrett. She painted rooms, washed windows, bought groceries, and cooked dinner. She worked at the bookshop six days a week. Sometimes, she missed New York and her life there. Still, she went to the beach with Barrett, and to the movies, library lectures, concerts, any event where her sister might make friends. She tried her best to coax their father into joining them, but he remained in a kind of walking coma, dealing with the loss of his son and his wife by arranging books on the shelves in an order that only he comprehended. Eddie knew they had to give him time.

She'd met Jeff.

And now, here she was, after two years away. She took a deep breath and walked toward the house.

three

Eddie tried the front doorknob, and of course, it turned and opened because no one ever locked it. She pulled her suitcases behind her and went into the front hall. The house was quiet. A new bookshelf had been added. It was filled with books, and it ran the length of the hall, and all the books, she could tell, were her father's. Leaving her suitcases—she'd take them up to her bedroom later—she walked toward her father's study. For a moment, she stood in the open door and took it all in.

The large room was filled with light from the two long windows in the back wall. Her father's desk and his sagging old leather reading chair stood where they always had been, and an old table was next to them, piled with books. All the walls were stacked with books, so that the windows were framed by shelves and gave a sense of being re- cessed. In the past two years, her father had obviously acquired more

books, and she could tell he'd arranged them in a sensible order—
biographies here, literary criticism there, novels leaning dangerously
in the corner.

Her father stood in the midst of it all, holding a book in one hand
and muttering to himself. He wore baggy khakis, an old college sweat-
shirt, and sneakers. He hadn't shaved for a few days and his blond-
brown hair was still a shaggy, handsome mop.

"Hi, Dad," Eddie said.

Her father pushed his reading glasses up to his forehead and
smiled. "Darling, have you seen my biography of Charles Lamb?"

Alarm lanced Eddie's heart. Was her father senile at fifty-five?

"Dad?"

"Oh, wait," William said. "Eddie! That's you! You're home! I didn't
know you were coming home!" He set down his book, crossed the
room, and hugged her. "Let's go to the kitchen, have some tea, and
catch up. Now where's your sister? She'll be thrilled to see you."

Relief washed through her. Her father wasn't senile. He seemed
almost like his old self, kind, loving, enthusiastic about life. She followed him into the kitchen, where the counters, the stove, the round
oak table were shining clean—Barrett's work. In the middle of the
table was the antique ironstone bowl, filled with bananas, apples, and
pears. Barrett's touch there, too. In the midst of a house full of books
and confusion, the kitchen was serene and welcoming.

William filled the Keurig with water and popped a pod in. "These
are recyclable," he told Eddie quickly, before she could ask. "Ha!" he
laughed. "Look out the window."

Eddie leaned over the porcelain sink and saw the red barn and the
long spill of land beside it, rolling slightly all the way to the woods
that separated it from the winding road through the new housing de-
velopment. The horse was trotting, shaking her mane, chasing after
Duke.

Before Eddie could speak, William said, "It's a game they play.
Duke nips at the horse's heels and runs while Duchess chases him.

Don't look so worried. They like each other. Think of it as occupational therapy."

"That's great," Eddie said. "I'm glad the horse has finally made a friend."

"You want a drop of milk in your coffee, right?" William opened the refrigerator door and took out a carton of milk.

"Yes, thanks." Eddie sat at the table, pleased that her father remembered how she liked her coffee and wishing she could ask him to remove his reading glasses from his forehead. The lenses caught the light and reflected it haphazardly across the room. It was unsettling. But she didn't want to say one negative thing during this precious time with her father.

William put her cup in front of her and sat at the table with his own cup in his hands.

"Now, tell me everything," he said. "First of all, why are you here? Are you still working for that writer? What's she like? Her books seem . . . *lighter* than what I would choose to read."

"Dad, she's wonderful and so are her books. I'm here because I haven't had a vacation in two years."

"But, Eddie, you've been to Paris!"

"True, Dad, but I went as Dinah's employee. I wanted some time to myself."

"And you came home." William smiled. "You could have gone anywhere but you came home. I'm so glad."

For a moment, Eddie was a little girl, safe in her father's arms. "I want to see if I can help Barrett with her shop."

The smile vanished from her father's face. "I'm worried about Barrett. Well, not Barrett herself, but her shop. You know she saved money for years, working long hours when other young people were out at beach parties. I hope she can make a go of it."

"I know." Eddie sipped her coffee. Hot and rich. The brand they'd used forever. Dunkin'. "And what about you, Dad? What about your book?"

"It's going very well, actually. Wilson put out a new biography of Charles Lamb this year and it's a brilliant book, just brilliant. Your Dinah Lavender would love Charles Lamb! You know his sister killed their mother, right?"

And here we are, Eddie thought, wandering through her father's thoughts about the lush and leafy maze of poetic history.

She tossed back the rest of her coffee. "I want to see Barrett and her shop. I'll carry my bags up to my room, but I won't take time to unpack. I plan to stay here for a month, more or less."

She rinsed her cup, set it in the drainer, and left the room before her father could say more. Once he got started on his favorite subject, he could go on for hours.

As she lugged her suitcases up the stairs, she couldn't help knocking into piles of books. This was nothing new, the books on the stairs, but when she entered her bedroom, she was shocked to see towers of books leaning against the walls, the end of her bed, the sides of her chest of drawers. A narrow path led through the books to her dresser. At least there were no books on her bed.

She used the bathroom she shared with her sister, smoothed her hair and put on lipstick—she might run into old acquaintances and she wanted to look good. When she got downstairs, she found her father back in his study. This wasn't the time to talk to him about his books. She'd wait and gang up on him with Barrett.

She went out to the back porch. There, in the shadow of the barn, was her trusty old Jeep. At least she hoped it was trusty. She checked the hook by the back door and was relieved to find the keys. There had been times when her father had used a car key as a bookmark. Barrett had added fat rubber toy buoys to their key chains.

"Bye, Dad!" she called, and stepped out the back door and down the steps to the yard. The horse and dog were at the other end of the property. The barn door was closed. Her father's Land Rover sat in the driveway. She settled in, adjusting the seat, fastening her seatbelt, checking her hair in the rearview mirror.

She was nervous. Or tired. Or overexcited. It had been a lot, seeing Jeff again, so soon, so unexpectedly, when she stepped off the ferry. And then her father, who seemed good, but all the books, so many more books than when she left, were worrisome.

How brave Barrett was, to remain on the island, to open a shop here. Her baby sister, only twenty-six years old, opening a shop. Making her dream come true.

Barrett had made her own OPEN and CLOSED signs. Sky blue background, white lettering, and pale imprints of shells, mermaids, and gems. The sign was turned to CLOSED because she still had work to do, but the overhead lights were on while she unpacked the white paper bags printed with NANTUCKET BLUES on the side. It would have been cheaper not to have the bags printed, but her friends told her it was a good investment. The bags would serve as walking advertising. She'd ordered three different sizes, for jewelry, housewares, and sweaters.

She was on her knees behind the counter when someone knocked on the shop door. For a moment, she hesitated. The door was locked, and no one could see her from outside, so she could wait down here behind the counter until whoever it was got a clue, saw the sign that was hanging right in front of them, and left. She hated turning people away before she'd even opened her business.

"Barrett! It's me!"

Barrett jumped up so fast, she hit her elbow on a shelf. That was her sister's voice!

She raced around the counter, across the small room, and tried to pull the door open, then remembered she'd locked it. She turned the lock, opened the door, and crowed triumphantly.

"You're here! You're really here! Oh, my God, you look so fancy!" She threw her arms around Eddie and squeezed until they were both breathless.

Eddie returned the hug. She pushed Barrett away, holding her shoulders with both hands. "Let me look at you. Barrett, you're so pretty."

Tears of happiness rolled down Barrett's face. "Have you been to the house yet? Where's your luggage? Did you take a boat or a plane? Are you hungry?"

Eddie laughed. "Let's go inside. I want to see your shop."

Had she ever been happier? Barrett wondered. She took her sister around the small shop, her heart racing. Eddie looked so sophisticated, with her dark blond hair styled in a short spiky cut and her black leather ankle boots and her sleek black dress. Her makeup was flawless, and did she have false eyelashes carefully woven into her own?

And oh, God, please let her approve of the shop. It was way too sweet for Eddie, who'd never met a mermaid she didn't dislike, who read books instead of playing with dolls, who had always been and would always be older, smarter, more sophisticated, and prettier than Barrett. Okay, maybe prettier was the wrong word. Maybe more beautiful, more elegant, more fabulous.

"I *love* your shop," Eddie said.

"You do?" Barrett burst into tears. "Sorry, sorry to be so emotional, it's just that I'm so happy you like it."

"It's a clever idea, such a range of blues in such a range of items. There's no other shop like it here. I think you'll make a fortune. Please. Enough with the tears. Let's take a coffee break."

"Oh! I don't have a way to make coffee here—"

"Great! Now I know what to buy you for a shop-warming present."

Barrett said, "Oh, Ed, you don't have to buy me a present! I mean, I can afford to buy a Keurig. I just hadn't thought about it."

"Well, too late. I'm on the case now." Eddie took Barrett's arm. "Let's go to Born & Bread."

Barrett forced herself to take a few deep breaths as she went around her shop, checking that any electric appliances were off. She locked the door and they set off walking through town to the coffee shop. It was busy, but not crowded. The season hadn't started quite yet. They chose chocolate croissants and coffee and settled at a table by the window.

"Have you seen Dad yet?" Barrett asked.

"I did. On the bright side, he was dressed. On the worrisome side, the first thing he did when he saw me was to ask where to find a biography of Charles Lamb."

Barrett squinched up her face. "Oh, Eddie!"

"It's all right. He suddenly realized who I was. It doesn't seem like things have changed much with him. He's still obsessed with the book he's writing."

"I know." Barrett dipped her head for a moment. "He doesn't play tennis or work out at a gym, although in the off-season he sometimes takes Duke for a walk on the beach."

"He used to be so active. Maybe he needs anti-depressants."

"I don't know, Eddie. Dad's lost his son, his wife, and his job."

"He *chose* to leave the college," Eddie pointed out.

"Still. It's a lot. He does email his old friends, but he needs to make new friends."

Eddie reached over and held Barrett's hand. "Don't worry. I'm here. I'll help deal with it somehow. But let's not talk about that. Tell me, who are you seeing? Anyone special?"

Barrett almost cried anyway, because Eddie held her hand and tried to cheer her up. Eddie was one of God's *can do* creatures who hated being sentimental, so she must be seriously upset about their father.

Barrett shrugged her shoulders. "No one special since our last phone call. It's okay. I see friends I used to work with, but I had to finish some online business courses, and with the house, and getting the shop ready, I haven't had time."

"No one special for me, either. I go out a lot, with Dinah. She's always got mobs of beautiful people around, but in the city, it seems everyone is too busy climbing some kind of career ladder to really get involved. I've had dinner with a few men, gone to an art exhibition or cocktail party. You know. I've told you everything. But I'm not looking to settle down. Are you?"

"Good grief, no!" Barrett answered. "But, Eddie, I'm only twenty-six. You're twenty-eight. You're almost thirty!"

Eddie dabbed her napkin to a bit of chocolate on the side of her mouth. "Guess who drove me home from the ferry."

Barrett's eyes lit up. "No."

"Yes. He had brought his grandmother to the Hy-Line. He offered to drive me home, so . . . I said sure."

"How is he?" Immediately, Barrett imagined her sister married to Jeff, pregnant, living on the island where Barrett could see her every day.

"Good." Eddie changed the subject. "I'd rather talk about you."

Barrett said, "What a great idea! Hey, listen, I'm truly grateful you're home for a while. I want this shop to be a success. I plan to be there every day, all day, starting during Memorial Day weekend. I can't continue as Dad's maid, chef, and chauffeur, and his book hoarding is out of control—"

"I know. I'm sorry I haven't been back more often," Eddie said. "Maybe I can convince him to clear out some of the books. I'll do the grocery runs and all the cooking while you're running your shop. When I go back to New York, I'll hire a part-time cleaning company for the farmhouse."

Barrett turned her spoon over and back, hesitating.

"What?" Eddie demanded.

"It's just . . . I missed you so much."

Eddie squeezed her hand affectionately. "Come on. I'll walk you back to your shop. What time do you get home?"

"If I can get stuff more organized, I'll be there by six."

"Great." Eddie stood up. "See you at dinner tonight."

"That sounds wonderful." Barrett stood, too, and hugged her sister. "I'm *so* glad you're here!"

Eddie drove out to Bartlett's Farm to buy some irresistible treats and a cartload of spring flowers to cheer up the inside of the house and put in the window boxes. She sang as she headed back to the farm. She knew Barrett had tried her best, but her younger sister was just too sweet to be bossy enough to get their father out of the house and into real life. Tonight, dinner out at a local, low-key restaurant. Tomorrow, a lecture at the library. Next, friends for her father—and a boyfriend for Barrett had to be waiting out there somewhere! Eddie smiled. She could do it all. She hoped she could do it all in a month.

As she pulled into the driveway, her cell buzzed. Dinah. It hadn't been even twenty-four hours since Eddie left New York. But Eddie was in a good mood.

"Hi, Dinah!" Eddie put the car seat back and got comfortable. Dinah never had a little bit to say.

"Eddie. Someone's stalking me."

Eddie rolled her eyes. "Dinah, calm down. Why are you whispering?"

Dinah hissed, "Because I don't want anyone else to hear."

"Okay. The doors are all locked?"

"Yes. And Sara is here."

Eddie rolled her eyes again. At this rate, they'd get stuck like her mother used to predict when she crossed her eyes as a child. Sara was Dinah's agent, and even more take-no-prisoners than Eddie.

"Honey, if Sara's with you, you'll be fine."

"She can't spend the night."

"Where is Sara now?"

"Out buying Scotch. She says she'll have a couple of Scotches with me and I'll sleep like a baby."

Eddie swore under her breath. "Dinah, hard liquor often makes you sick. It gives you headaches. Sometimes you throw up. Remember? Just drink wine, okay?"

Dinah's voice strengthened as she burst into tears. "Oh, Eddie, please come home! I can't remember all this stuff when I'm writing! You know the ladies in my book drink sherry!"

"I can't come back, Dinah. I just got here. Look, I wrote down the information you need on the notepad by the kitchen landline. Ask Sara to go over it with you."

"Fine, but honestly, Eddie, I'm afraid this guy will find a way to sneak into my apartment. I can't stop imagining what could happen."

Eddie spoke calmly. "Your life and your books are two different things, Dinah. Remember, you've got extra bolts on all your doors. Locks on your windows. A state-of-the-art alarm system. Plus, your favorite doorman, Jorge, will be there, and he would never let a stranger into your apartment."

"But—"

Eddie interrupted. "Dinah, why do you think you have a stalker?"

"Remember the book signing I did last week? At Barnes & Noble? And the man in the camel-hair coat who bought three books?"

"That's hardly stalking."

"Wait a moment, please! Yesterday, when Sara and I went out for lunch, the same man came in a few minutes after I did. He sat at a table behind me. He was looking at me. And this afternoon, when we went for a walk down Fifth Avenue, he was across the street."

"Dinah. Dinah, slow down. First of all, he couldn't have known what time you'd go for a walk, or what streets you'd walk on. Maybe he lives in your area."

"When we were having lunch, Sara said, 'Don't look now but you have a fan.'"

"That's probably exactly what he is. A fan. An admirer." Eddie spoke with humor and affection. "Come on. You can't believe that a stalker would wear a camel-hair coat."

"They do in my novels!"

"Right. And we've talked about this before. Your novels and your life are two completely different realities."

"I know that! But this man is not imaginary. Eddie, if you don't come back, I won't be able to sleep and then I won't be able to write, and I'll miss my deadline, and everything will be a mess!"

Eddie heard genuine alarm in her employer's voice.

"Dinah, I'm not coming back for a month. We've talked about this. I thought Sara was planning to spend the night."

"One of her kids has the flu. She has to go take care of him." Dinah whimpered. "Never mind about me."

"Okay, Dinah, here's a plan. You feel safe in hotel rooms, right? Why don't you go over to the Ritz or the Waldorf Astoria and get a room. Not a suite. You don't want too much space. Just one really nice room without a connecting door. Spend the night there. You'll be safe."

Dinah began to cry, her sweet breathy cries, as if she were a doll with the air being squeezed out of her.

Eddie stayed strong. She knew Dinah wasn't faking her fear, and she had so much sympathy for her. Yet the more sensible voice in her head said, in a sarcastic tone, *Get a babysitter*.

It wasn't such a bad idea. All the babysitter had to do was sleep in the guest room, or maybe on the sofa near the front door.

Dinah sniffed. "Sara's back."

"Good. Listen, ask her to spend the night with you after she's got her child settled. Or she can bring him to your place. They can both sleep in the guest room."

"Fine." Dinah's voice went all haughty. "I'll be fine. Don't worry about me."

The phone blinked off.

Eddie sat in the car for a moment, wondering if every person alive was crazy, and if so, did that mean she was crazy, too? Probably. Seeing Jeff at the boat had knocked her off-balance, that was certain, but she hadn't had time to process it yet.

four

Today Eddie believed she could conquer the world.

Last night she had taken Barrett and her father to dinner at Cross-winds, the restaurant at the airport that summer people never went to because it wasn't expensive enough. They'd ordered cocktails and pineapple ginger shrimp stir-fry, and several men had come to the table to say hello to William. They hadn't seen him in a while, they said. Where had he been? They wanted to ask him to join their men's Winter Group, but they hadn't been able to find his email, and it didn't matter now because they were facing summer, but they'd be in touch with him come fall. When they got home, Eddie and Barrett went into his office, woke his computer, and saw that their father still used his college email address. Eddie set up a new account for him.

"What do you want the name of your account to be?" she asked him.

Her father came and leaned over her shoulder as she sat at his desk, tapping away on his laptop. "I don't know. Professor Grant?"

"Dad." Eddie shook her head. "You're not a professor anymore so get over yourself."

Barrett agreed. "She's right, Dad. Do you think Lindsay Kellogg uses 'retiredtransplantsurgeon@gmail' as his address?"

The three of them discussed possibilities that became sillier and sillier and they laughed together, and for a moment they were a family again, until Eddie ruined it by saying, "How about vaguelysenile-bookhoarder@gmail?"

"Not funny," Barrett said.

"But true?" Eddie nudged her sister.

"I'm not a book hoarder," William protested.

"Sorry, Dad. I'll bow out. I've got to go to bed." She kissed the top of his head and pecked a kiss on Barrett's cheek. It wasn't until she got to the top of the stairs that she realized this was the first time in two years that she'd been frank and forthright about her thoughts, because no matter what, her father and sister would still love her and couldn't fire her. She had this job—daughter, sister—for life. Nothing said family like an honest argument.

She was tucking herself into her familiar bed when Barrett knocked on the bedroom door and stuck her head in.

"He's calling it WGrant400," Barrett said.

"Why the '400'?" Eddie asked.

"He said it was a tribute to the French film *The 400 Blows* about a teenage boy."

"Oh, dear." Eddie took a moment to let thoughts of their brother rest in the atmosphere.

Barrett lifted the mood. With a big smile, she said, "Thanks for tonight, Eddie. Dad was so happy." She came into the room, bent over the bed, and hugged Eddie tight. "I love you."

"Love you, too," Eddie replied.

Barrett left the room, singing quietly, an old habit of hers. Eddie turned off the bedside light, pulled up the covers, and closed her eyes.

Immediately, she wondered when she'd see Jeff again. Her forbidden pleasure.

Barrett didn't even wait to eat breakfast. She rose early, dressed, and left the house before someone could ask for coffee or toast. She jumped into her red Jeep, which was dented and scratched on the outside but had four-wheel drive—necessary for the beach—and a large hatch area so she could pick up and deliver packages. She parked in her se-cret spot near Commercial Wharf by the town pier and walked the few short blocks to her store.

She couldn't stop thinking about Eddie, how great it was to have her back home, how quickly she'd gotten their father to connect with the world, and how it seemed all of Eddie's clothes were black, which might be fine for New York, but not for summer on Nantucket. She decided to stop in at Murray's Toggery on her way home and buy Eddie a present. A T-shirt? No. Sweatshirt? Way no. She'd find a silk navy blue button-down.

She had just gotten settled in her shop when Eddie called.

"I can't find available cleaning people," Eddie said.

"Good morning to you, too, Eddie. I know you can't. It's summer. No one is available. Trust me. No one."

Eddie was quiet for second. Then she said, "Well, I am."

Eddie stood in the middle of the kitchen with her phone in her hand. How had Barrett kept the house this tidy all by herself? Not that it was actually neat and dust-free, but the kitchen and downstairs bath were bright and shining, thank heavens for that. It was the other rooms that had been neglected. Eddie wandered through them, understanding why they were so dusty and chaotic. Every room had stacks of books rising from the floor, teetering as if on the brink of falling. Books were piled on the lovely old chintz sofa, on the matching armchair, on the coffee table, and even in the fireplace which hadn't been used in years. The dining room table was clear of books at the end closest to the kitchen, but piled with towers of books at the other end. The old mahogany buffet had stacks of books on the top and the handsome family silver trays had been pushed under the buffet, as if in hiding. She didn't need to go into her father's study. She'd seen it yesterday and it was a sight she couldn't forget. Besides, her father was in there, working.

She climbed the stairs. Her room was crowded but most of the books needed to go. Barrett's room was a dream of sanity with its two beds, desk, dresser, and slipper chair all book-free. The bathroom was clean and had only a small pile of books in the corner, on a small table near the toilet. The guest bedroom, where no guest ever slept because they'd never invited one, had, not surprisingly, bookshelves against all four walls, floor to ceiling, spilling over with piles of books rising from the floor like colorful stalagmites.

Finally, she opened the door to her father's bedroom.

Oh, dear.

His room was like a giant maze of books, with a clear but narrow path to his bed, his dresser, his closet, and his bathroom.

Eddie stood in her father's room and was very, very, sad.

She took a deep breath and left the room She went down the stairs and into her father's study.

"Daddy. What's going on?"

William peered over his reading glasses. "Good morning, darling."

Eddie removed a pile of books from a chair and set them on top of another pile of books.

"Dad, I think you really have become a bit of a hoarder."

William nodded. "Yes, I suppose you're right." With his forefinger, he moved his reading glasses back in place and bent to his book.

Eddie lifted a book from one of the piles.

"*The Doors of Perception* by Aldous Huxley. You don't need this book. Let me take it to the Seconds Shop."

William actually smiled. "Eddie, that book is absolutely necessary for my research. You know that Coleridge and others used laudanum and morphine. Huxley's book is—"

At least she had his attention. She picked up another book. "*The Magnificent Chicken?* How does that fit into your subject?"

William scratched his head. "I haven't decided how to work that in yet, but I'm sure many poets, or their wives, kept chickens. Also, we live on a farm. I think we should have chickens. Think of the eggs."

"Really." Eddie skewered him with her gaze. "We have a horse. We have a dog. Do you ever feed them?"

"Well, no. Barrett does that."

"Ever take Duke for a walk?"

"Sometimes."

"What does Duchess eat in the winter?"

William looked nervous. "That's not in my purview."

"Your *purview*. Dad, you aren't teaching any longer. You're—"

She paused. She almost said, *You're using books to hide from the world.*

But why *shouldn't* he want to hide from the world? Three years ago, his son died and his wife left him. He'd probably used up all his optimism and energy moving them here from the town where they'd remember Stearns at every street corner, school, and café. Her father had done what he could. He'd done all any father could.

"I need to think about this," Eddie said.

"That's nice," William replied, and returned to his book.

Eddie went to the kitchen and sat at the table, lost in memories.

The Grant home in Williamstown was a handsome brick house in a charming neighborhood with winding roads and mature trees. Their father taught English at a small but prestigious college in a storybook town. Their mother was beautiful and unhappy. She didn't enjoy being a mother, which she considered menial work. She was dissatisfied with her social position in the college town and always angry because her husband earned so little money. In desperation, she decided to be an artist, and set up a studio in the attic.

The three Grant children were stairstep children: first Eddie, next Stearns, one year younger, and Barrett, one year after that. They were a close little trio, because they seldom saw their mother, which was okay. Their presence never made their mother happy. Once, when she took them shopping for school shoes, she paused in front of a store window displaying a satin dress with a rhinestone buckle.

"I would look stunning in that," she told her children. "And if I didn't have to buy so much for you three, I could buy it." Her shoulders drooped as she left the window.

The children were stung and anxious. Was their mother going to cry here in the mall?

Sabrina didn't cry. But she stared down at their faces and said, "Don't ever have children. They will ruin your life."

After that moment, after they had their school shoes and had returned to their house, after their mother escaped to the attic and her art, the children understood what would help make their mother happy.

Eddie became the taskmaster who told them to take baths, do homework, brush teeth, eat vegetables. Barrett and Stearns grumbled at her, but they always did what she ordered. Eddie worried about them constantly. Why was Stearns spending so much time alone in his room? Why couldn't she make better dinners than boxed macaroni and cheese? One morning, on her way out the door, Barrett said she needed a parent's signature on a form giving permission for a class trip. She'd forgotten to ask her father, and he was at the college now. Would Eddie get in trouble for faking their mother's name? (She didn't.) But it was an enormous responsibility. She never wanted to do it again.

Thank heavens for the Fletchers.

The Fletcher family moved into the large, classic Victorian next door with a turret, a wraparound porch, and stained-glass windows. They were wealthy and glamorous. Mr. Fletcher was an officer in a bank. Mrs. Fletcher sold real estate and drove a dark green MG convertible. When Sabrina Grant saw it, she burst into tears.

"I'll never have anything like that," she cried.

Stearns had tried to console her. "I'll buy you one when I'm older, Mom."

"Sure you will," his mother had said bitterly and went up the stairs to the attic.

The Fletchers had one child, a gorgeous little girl with blue eyes and a waist-long tumble of white-blond hair.

Dove.

Dove Fletcher was a year younger than Eddie and a year older than Barrett, exactly Stearns's age. She was magic. It wasn't just her enormous house where the four played hide-and-seek for hours, or the little cottage her parents had built especially for Dove in the back garden. It was her imagination, her sparkling energy, her happiness. The rainiest day was a delight for Dove. She invented entire worlds where a cup became a chalice and an umbrella became a sword. Inside with Dove, Eddie, Barrett, and Stearns became superheroes with capes and masks, or doctors with a ward full of sick baby dolls, and it wasn't just that Dove's parents had given her doctor kits, it was the stories Dove invented, enclosing them all in their own realm. Outside with Dove, they slipped like spies through the neighborhood, leaving secret codes inside tiny porcelain boxes they'd purloined from the Fletchers' attic and chalking signs on the trunks of trees. In the winter, they made snow people and an entire snow house for the four of them to live in, even though it was a tight squeeze and snow drifted onto their noses.

On summer nights, when they crawled into the backyard tent Stearns had put together, they ate marshmallows and ginger snaps and made fun of their teachers and planned to run away from home, all of them together, in a VW bus like the one in *Little Miss Sunshine*. Stearns liked to make graphic novels about the four of them. They all had enormous heads and tiny stick bodies, but it was amazing how he could make each face look like the real thing. He gave them adventures. All four of them riding a missile to Mars. All four of them floating in space with cosmic vacuum cleaners that sucked the excess carbon out of the Earth's air. All four of them in a personal submarine blasting down to the ocean floor to meet creatures never known before to mankind. He gave each character a name. Eddie was *Nice*. Barrett was *Funny*. Dove was *Beauty*. Stearns was *Genius*. The sisters agreed that Stearns *was* a genius, and for the first time they became aware that Stearns had special feelings for Dove.

When they were older, their mother took a job at a fine jewelry shop. Sabrina was much happier and even less interested in the responsibilities of motherhood. It was understood that the Grant kids would spend after-school time at the Fletcher house, even though Dove's parents weren't always around.

Eddie, Barrett, and Stearns spent countless hours in the Fletcher rec room, watching DVDs, eating chips and cookies, playing video games, singing and jumping around to the karaoke machine. Dove's parents never complained when they left the rug littered with Cheez-It crumbs or candy wrappers. The Fletchers had a housekeeper who came three times a week when they were at school. When the four were in their early teens, they did their homework together in the rec room while Stearns lay on his stomach on the floor, reading graphic novels.

Occasionally, they helped themselves to the Fletchers' liquor cabinet, tasting not only gin and vodka but crème de menthe and cognac. Dove had become an expert in refilling the bottles so her parents didn't notice, but Eddie, Stearns, and Barrett hated the liquor. It burned. It tasted like fingernail polish remover. They favored chocolate milk and sinful Cherry Cokes.

For years, the four were an informal club, and if they'd had a motto, which they didn't, that would have been too cheesy, plus there were four of them, not three, it would have been "One for all, and all for one."

As they grew older, the relationships changed, shifting slightly. Stearns was brilliant. His mind raced through lessons and lectures and books. He aced his tests and worked Rubik's Cubes under his desk while listening to his teacher. He clowned around in class to disguise his boredom. Dove's father told Eddie that Stearns would either win the Nobel Prize in physics or be the next Robin Williams.

By fourteen, Stearns was also heartbreakingly handsome. He shot up to six feet and let his butterscotch hair fall around his face like a rock star. He was a wizard with computers. He helped friends troubleshoot their video games and laptops, and when he was fifteen, he was hired for the weekends and evenings by a computer shop in North Adams. When he had time to hang with his sisters and Dove, it was always Dove he sat next to. His gaze lasted longer on Dove's face than on his sisters'. Dove's face shone with a special light when Stearns entered the room.

"Do you think Stearns *really* likes Dove?" Barrett asked Eddie one evening. "I mean—*that way?*"

"I hope so," Eddie replied. "They could get married and she'd be part of our family."

One afternoon, the Grant sisters came home from school to find Stearns's bedroom door locked. The first time, they tiptoed away, assuming he was sleeping, maybe with a flu. The next time, they banged on the door and called his name.

When Stearns opened the door, they saw Dove in his room. Sitting on his bed.

"You guys!" Eddie stood just inside the room, too surprised to know what to say.

Barrett tried not to laugh. "Stearns, you have lipstick all over your face."

"We're talking about homework?" Dove said, her voice rising on *homework,* as if she was asking a question.

"This is cool," Eddie began awkwardly.

Barrett added, "But you won't pay attention to *us* anymore."

Stearns reached out and took Barrett's hand. "Come sit down. Let's talk."

The four sat cross-legged on the floor, the way they did when they played poker or Monopoly.

Eddie folded her arms over her chest defensively. "So what's going on?"

Dove patted Eddie's arm like a mother soothing her baby. "You guys, everything is changing. You're going to college in September, Eddie, and then I'll go and then Barrett."

"What about Stearns?" Eddie realized as she spoke that she hadn't noticed where her brother was applying for college, and she experienced a sudden stab of guilt, before remembering how she'd been too busy cooking dinner, doing laundry, cleaning the bathrooms, because their mother was never around.

"I'm taking a gap year," Stearns told her. "I've got a sweet job at a computer company in Troy. I'll make a ton of money. I may not go to college." He smiled, embarrassed, adding, "I may not finish high school. But I'll make enough to help you both pay your tuitions."

"But what about Dove?" Barrett asked. "Are you *with* Dove?"

Stearns sounded serious when he answered. "I'm with Dove. Totally. I'm saving up for a bike so I can get to Amherst to see Dove."

"You get Dove." Barrett spoke slowly, realizing what that meant. "I don't know if I'm jealous or happy."

"Come on, Barrett, it's not like this is a shock," Eddie said. "We've known they'd be together for years. But she's still ours."

Stearns put his arm around Dove's shoulders and pulled her against him. "Maybe mostly mine."

Slowly at first, and then suddenly, like an iceberg cracking and plunging into the sea, their lives as they had lived them for years vanished.

It was March, Eddie's final year in high school. Stearns was a junior, acing classes effortlessly, and Barrett was a sophomore.

During lunch period, Barrett got a text from Eddie.

Have you talked to Dove today?

Barrett answered: *No. What's up?*

Not sure.

Barrett and Eddie kept in touch all that day. They each called and texted Dove, but she didn't answer. They decided she must be sick.

When Eddie and Barrett got home from school, they saw a moving van in the Fletchers' driveway. Mr. Fletcher's BMW wasn't there. Mrs. Fletcher's MG convertible wasn't there. Dove's antique red Mustang was there, but not Dove.

Barrett hurled herself up the steps and through the open door of the Victorian house. Most of the furniture was gone. She ran yelling Dove's name through the house, but saw only heavy-muscled moving men lifting the remaining boxes from Dove's bedroom and TV room and rec room.

When Eddie entered their own house, she found their mother talking on the phone. She held up her finger—*wait.*

"You won't believe this!" Sabrina said when she put her phone down. "Mr. Fletcher has been arrested for embezzling money from the bank. They've lost their house, their cars, *everything.* Jeanine Fletcher will have to sell her jewelry!"

"Have you talked with Dove?" Eddie asked.

"You're so sweet, worrying about your friend." Sabrina picked up her purse and hung it on her shoulder. "Got to run."

"Where's Stearns?" Barrett asked.

Sabrina shrugged. "God knows."

Barrett was crying. "What can we do? We *have* to see Dove!"

"Girls, I know you were good friends with Dove. This will be an opportunity for you to make new friends." Sabrina tweaked a twist in her hair. "I've got to get back to work."

The sisters called and texted Stearns, but got no answer. Finally, when he came home from work, they tackled him at the front door.

"Where's Dove?"

Stearns was flushed, his eyes desperate. "I haven't heard from her since yesterday. I've called. She doesn't answer. I've texted. She doesn't reply. I don't know where she is. Probably hiding because of this mess with her parents. I don't know why she would hide from me."

"Oh, Sterny." Eddie's heart hurt for her brother. "Oh, honey." She hugged him. "She'll get in touch with you. You know she will."

"Yeah." Stearns pulled away. "I'll let you know."

For weeks, the local news focused on the Fletcher embezzlement and arrest.

Trees budded and blossomed. The sweet fragrance of mown grass drifted in the air. A new family moved into the Fletcher house. The Brooks family had two small children, and soon Barrett was babysitting for them. It was odd to be in the big Victorian, with completely new furniture and curtains, but it was all right. It would have been so sad to be in rooms that reminded her of Dove. Eddie left for college. Stearns continued to attend classes and work at the computer shop. His parents were astounded at his salary. It was a new world for everyone.

One day at school, Barrett heard a group of girls in the corner of the hall, humming like a hive of bees. She heard Dove's name mentioned.

She elbowed her way into the group. "What about Dove?"

"OMG, Barry, you should see her!" Skye Becker gushed. "She's *wrecked*. She's like totally drunk and hanging out with some older guys and—"

"Where was she?" Barrett demanded.

"At the baseball field, no game, just Dove and some men and a zillion cans of beer. They were throwing their empty cans into the middle of the field!"

"That's so sad," Tara said.

Barrett caught the school bus, begrudging every laboriously slow mile the driver went. Her mind was on fire. Eddie had her car in Northampton but their father walked to the college, so his old Volvo station wagon was in the drive. Barrett snatched the keys from the kitchen corkboard.

The high school playing fields were out of town on Route 7. Barrett drove carefully, never speeding, and soon she was there. The football team was out, running, barking, scrambling after balls.

No sign of Dove or men or beer cans. Barrett waited for an hour.

That evening, when Stearns returned home, Barrett met him at the door.

"Have you heard about Dove?" she asked.

"Yeah, I heard." Stearns brushed by her, took the steps two at a time, and slammed the bathroom door shut. A minute later, they heard the shower running. Barrett called Eddie.

"Why hasn't she called us?" Barrett asked Eddie. "How can she live without us?"

Eddie was thoughtful. "You've seen the news. Dove's life has been tornadoed. Her dad's going to prison, they've lost their house, Dove must be traumatized. She'll get in touch with us when she's ready."

Their lives rolled on, school, friends, homework, TV, TikTok. Summer. Eddie entered her freshman year at Smith. When Stearns was fifteen, he was hired for the weekends and evenings by a computer shop. Fall came. Christmas came. A new year came.

Spring came. One early April day as Barrett was leaving school, Curt Waterman, who thought he was Kurt Cobain, drove slowly past the school in his convertible. Dove was sitting in the passenger seat.

Barrett raced over. She would have thrown herself in front of the car if necessary.

"Dove!"

Dove looked terrible. Her skin was gray, she had circles under her eyes, and she'd lost so much weight she was skeletal.

The convertible top was down. Barrett threw herself over the car door and hugged Dove.

Dove froze. "Hi, Bare."

"Dove, where have you been?" Barrett demanded.

"It doesn't matter," Dove said.

"Bye, girly," Curt said, and peeled off, back onto the road.

"DOVE!" Barrett yelled.

Dove didn't look back.

That night, Barrett sat at the table with their father, mother, and Stearns. If Sabrina hadn't bothered to cook a meal, at least she was eating with them. The family lived on pizza and tacos, but Barrett was glad to have the four of them together. Having their brother at the table was almost miraculous.

"What have you been up to, kids?" their father asked.

Barrett said, "Oh, Dad, I saw Dove today. She doesn't even look like the same person. She looked terrible."

"Where was she?" her father asked.

"In a car with Curt Waterman. He drove by the school with Dove in the front seat, as if he was showing off a trophy." Barrett paused. "She smelled like she'd showered in Scotch."

Their mother sighed. "I've heard that she's . . . developed a serious drinking problem. Poor girl."

Barrett needed Eddie with her. "We have to *do* something."

Their father shook his head. "I don't know what we can do. Her parents don't respond to my calls or texts."

Sabrina sighed. "I always thought that family wasn't as perfect as you children thought they were."

———

Summer arrived. Eddie came home and the sisters worked for a children's camp in Vermont. Two guys were counselors there, too. Kit and Peter. During the long hot, bright days, while they hiked up the mountain, or did art projects in the great barn on a rainy day, Eddie and Barrett knew they were transitioning into adulthood, birds flying out of the nest, leaving home. This was the last time they would feel like children, running joyfully with the little kids, past the flower garden and the vegetable garden and into the clear, cold stream bubbling down the mountain. They watched the children carefully and taught them about frogs and mushrooms, five different types of knots, how to make slime.

They didn't hear from Dove, and they never saw Stearns, although he texted from Troy to ask how they were.

Barrett started at UMass Amherst. Her grades weren't great, but she didn't really care. She let herself be carried along by life's tide.

A year passed, and then another. Eddie graduated and went to New York to work as an assistant in a publishing house. Barrett attended classes, dated a bit, and worked at a farm stand after school and on weekends. She saved her money and wasn't sure why, except that it gave her comfort. Stearns continued to attend classes and work at the computer shop. Their mother worked longer hours at the jewelry shop in Pittsfield and their father taught an extra course in English literature and it was as if they were *all* growing up, changing, becoming more particular in themselves and less part of a family.

In October, Stearns came by the house.

Halloween was near. The moon was full, the trees half-stripped of leaves, and the air was pure and bracing. Eddie was home for the weekend. She and Barrett were in the family room watching *Stranger Things*. As usual, their mother wasn't home. Their father was in the living room, watching the History Channel.

They heard their father open the door.

"Girls," he called. "Come to the living room."

For a moment, the sisters couldn't make sense of what they saw.

Stearns had always been tall, but he'd grown a few more inches and added weight and muscles to his body. He wore canvas trousers and a clean shirt.

Stearns was a *man*.

Next to him sat Dove.

Dove.

She was radiant. Her blond hair was held back in a low bun, curls escaping, all glossy and clean and lovely. She wore jeans and a white T-shirt and a thin gold chain around her neck.

Barrett burst into tears.

Eddie walked close and pinched her beautiful old friend. Not hard, just enough to have Dove's skin between her fingers so she could believe Dove was real.

She didn't even try to be subtle as she sniffed the air around Dove.

Dove cracked a sideways smile. "Yeah, I'm sober. Have been for months."

"We missed you," Eddie said, her voice splintering with emotion. "We missed both of you."

"Thanks, sis." Stearns gave Eddie an awkward hug. "We missed you."

"Can you stay for a while?" their father asked.

"Yeah, awhile," Stearns said.

Eddie put her arm around Barrett, who was red-faced and trembling. Awkwardly, as if they were new to sitting on furniture, they sank onto the sofa.

Stearns had been promoted to a full-time junior-level job at the computer company. He would make more money than his father made as a college professor.

"I'm so proud of you," their father said. "You've found work you love." He added happily, "And you will be close enough to come home every so often."

Dove was going with him. She planned to attend a community college. They'd live in Stearns's apartment in Troy, which wasn't that far away, Stearns said, just a drive over the Taconic Trail through the mountains and up past Albany.

When Dove was asked, she told them that her parents were okay. Her father was in jail, but would probably be out in a year. Her mother had moved to Florida to live with a friend. A male friend, Dove added with a sardonic smile.

Yes, she said, she'd been living with Stearns for the past six months.

Yes, she said, it was Stearns who found her, brought her to live with him, and got her sober.

"Maybe," she said, "*maybe* we'll get married."

"What?" Barrett blinked in surprise. "Married? But, Dove, I don't understand. How could you do all this without even telling us? We always told you *everything*! You always told us everything! We were your best friends. *We* could have helped you get sober! *We* wouldn't have let you get drunk in the first place!"

"Things change," Dove said softly. "Sometimes things change really fast. I didn't know my father had lost all our money and was a crook. I didn't know my father would go to prison. I didn't know we would lose our house. My mother vanished and never gets in touch with me. I lost everything. I am sorry. But I was stumbling in the dark for a while."

Eddie leaned forward and spoke quietly. "Okay, then, Stearns. Why didn't *you* tell us? Why didn't you tell us something, anything, at least that Dove was alive?"

Stearns shrugged, looking apologetic. "Come on, Eddie, you know how you are. If I'd told you she was okay, you two would be demanding to know how I knew, and where did I see her, and why wouldn't I take you to see her? And you would have been freaked out if you'd seen her when she was getting sober. It was not a pretty sight."

"But she did it with you," Barrett said accusingly.

Their father, usually so easygoing with his family, spoke up. "Stearns,

it was wrong of you not to tell us. Dove was almost part of our family.
Still, we're all glad that Dove found help with you."

Later, for days and weeks, Eddie and Barrett would talk and talk and
try to understand why Dove hadn't come to them when her family
life exploded. Eddie and Barrett wouldn't care that her father had
skimmed money or that the Fletchers lost their house. They would
have supported Dove in that crisis. But Dove had just *abandoned* them
for that druggie Curt Waterman. She hadn't cared a thing about the
sisters. Or maybe it was simply that Dove had been too deeply shocked
by the huge changes in her life. She'd lost her place in the world. And
Curt Waterman had reached out and grabbed her.

But Stearns had saved her. *Stearns.*

They should have known. It was great for their brother that he had
Dove, but it hurt that Dove and Stearns had such an enormous secret.
But, they consoled each other, they were all older now, all headed into
their new lives and really, it was a good thing that Stearns and Dove loved
each other. Dove would really be part of the family when they married.

A few days before Thanksgiving, their parents sat them down in
the living room and with a brisk formality, their mother announced
that she was divorcing their father. Sabrina had rented an apartment
in Pittsfield. She and her friend Abel Kuiper, the owner of the jewelry
store, were leaving for Amsterdam in the spring to learn more about
diamonds.

"I have a good eye for gems," Sabrina said. "If I hadn't had children, I could have gone somewhere in the jewelry world."

"Where would you have gone?" Barrett asked.

Sabrina rolled her eyes at her daughter's innocence. "I mean, I
could have been *important.*"

Barrett and Eddie studied their father's face closely, looking for a
reaction.

William caught their looks. "It's okay," he told his daughters. "Sabrina and I have talked about this. We'll be fine here. I'll continue teaching—"

"And I'll live the life I've always wanted," Sabrina said.

The girls weren't surprised that their mother was leaving them. Their mother had been leaving them for years. They didn't feel as betrayed by her as they had felt with Dove.

That Christmas, their father went with them to choose the biggest, tallest Douglas fir they'd ever had. He hung the lights and they decorated the tree and bought presents. Eddie flew home from New York with her luggage full of gifts. The sisters read recipes and planned a feast and bought several bottles of a good champagne. They didn't receive so much as a Christmas card from their mother, but they hadn't really expected to get one.

Stearns and Dove drove over the treacherous Taconic Trail to Williamstown and spent the night before Christmas at the Grants' house, Dove and Stearns sleeping in his old bedroom.

Christmas Day, Stearns and Dove gave three small boxes to William, Eddie, and Dove, insisting that they open the presents at the same time.

Eddie got a pair of booties. Barrett got a small white cap. William got a small silver spoon.

William said, "I don't understand."

Barrett screamed and jumped in the air.

Eddie burst into tears.

The baby would be born in April. No, they didn't know the gender. Yes, Eddie and Barrett could be aunts *and* godmothers.

Robert Joseph Grant was born early in Albany on a snowy March night. Stearns, exhausted and exuberant, called his father and sisters and sent videos of the tiny baby boy lying next to his mother. Dove beamed a brilliant smile at the family, and invited them to come visit in a week or so, when she wasn't so emotional.

"Keep sending us videos," Eddie begged. "He changes so fast!"

But after work, Eddie called Barrett and they shared their fears. They'd heard that new mothers could get depressed, overwhelmed. Would that jeopardize Dove's sobriety? No, they decided. Dove would be fine. Everything would be fine.

They made plans for Eddie to come home for Easter to see the baby.

The police came to the pretty Williamstown house on a cold April night. Barrett was in bed, reading. Her father was in his study, reading. Eddie was in New York.

The sound of the door knocker startled them both.

William wore old sweatpants and a flannel shirt. Barrett wore yoga pants and a T-shirt.

It was odd, Barrett thought, as the police, in their uniforms, entered their house, odd that she and her father were dressed so casually for this important event, a visit from the police.

Stearns had had a fatal accident on his motorcycle speeding on the Taconic Trail. No one was with him. No one else was involved.

Barrett and her father called Eddie. She drove home from New York that night. The three of them wandered aimlessly around the house, making tea, pouring Scotch, setting the glasses and cups down untouched.

William called Dove. He asked her to come live with them in the Williamstown house.

Dove let out a bark of a laugh. "In the house where Stearns grew up? Next door to the house where my family was evicted? Oh, no, please don't ask that of me."

Dove sounded odd when she told William that she thought yes,

Stearns would approve of cremation and scattering of his ashes over the Taconic Trail. She sounded like a bad actress reading a part.

Eddie and Barrett called Dove on speakerphone. "Then we'll drive over to Troy. We don't want you to be alone now."

"My uncle and aunt are here," Dove replied. "They flew in from Colorado. They're helping me . . . get organized. I'm going to live with them in Denver."

"But the baby!" Barrett protested. "Our baby!"

"I need to start over, Barrett." Dove sounded sad but sober. "I need to get away from so many difficult things. I love you all, but it's too much. The past is too much. I want to start over fresh now that my baby is here."

"But what about us?" Eddie asked, choking on her tears.

"I don't know," Dove replied, and her words seemed weighed down with heavy stones, so that she hardly could speak.

The memorial service was short. Dove did not attend. She was in Colorado with her aunt and uncle. Their mother did not attend. She emailed William that she couldn't bear it. But several of the men who worked in the computer company came, driving over the winding treacherous Taconic Trail, wearing suits and wool overcoats. Several of Stearns's school classmates attended, and many of the high school teachers. Later, William, Eddie, and Barrett climbed Mount Greylock on a blustery, cold day and released Stearns's ashes into the wind.

"It's strange," their father confessed as they were driving home, "all my life I've told my students they would find consolation in their reading. But I'm unable to read now. I stare at the television. I go for walks. But I can't read!"

"Words," Barrett said bitterly. "You think words can explain everything."

Her father said, "No, Barrett. I know they can't."

five

Standing in the Nantucket kitchen, Eddie thought how a person can never know what a day might bring or how quickly life can change. She closed her eyes and breathed deeply. A therapist had told her that she couldn't change the past, but she could live more thoughtfully in her present.

Opening her eyes, she found herself staring at a shelf of self-help books that had been her mother's. Why were they here? Their mother and father were divorced. Sabrina was with another man. *She* had obviously helped *herself*. Her father had obviously unpacked these books three years ago when they moved to the island. He wouldn't ever look at them. He should get rid of them. He should—

Eddie had a brilliant idea. Such a wonderfully practical idea that she wanted to applaud herself.

She hurried back to her father's study. William sat frozen, elbows on the desk, head in his hands.

"Daddy," she said gently. "I have an idea."

William lifted his head and smiled at Eddie. "Tell me about it."

"We should turn the barn into a used bookstore."

Her father frowned. "You're just trying to move my books out of the house."

"True. I am. Now listen. We can put up shelves in the barn and you can organize your books and clear out some room in the house."

William pushed away from the desk, rose, and stretched his back. "Eddie, no one will buy my old books."

"Do you have a problem with that? If no one buys them, you'll still have them, right?"

Eddie could tell he was intrigued but also worried. Wanting to give him space, she moved away from his desk toward the window with light shining in between the stacks of books. From here she could see the paddock and the barn.

"It's a nice idea, Eddie," William said at last.

"Think of all the space," Eddie said, pressing her point. "Dad, imagine it. We could put all those self-help books in the barn."

"Those self-help books were your mother's." William nodded sagely. "They can go."

Eddie smiled. "Yes, and her books on knitting, and potting, and beekeeping, and playing the guitar."

William reminisced, "She had so much enthusiasm for her new hobbies. For the first few weeks. Then she'd lose interest. Remember when I said I was glad she hadn't tried to take up the piano?"

Eddie's smile turned bittersweet. "She got really mad at you. I remember that well." Quickly, while she had her father's attention, she said, "Look, Dad, you have so many duplicates."

William nodded. "True, but in many cases they're different editions. I like the different covers, and introductory essays. You know, it's possible to tell a lot about how our culture has changed by reading the introductions to various novels."

"I understand," Eddie said, softly, calmly. "But, for instance, look at all your James Fenimore Cooper books. They take up three long shelves."

"Oh, no. The Coopers stay." William was firm. "Cooper wrote his rather romantic novels in the early eighteen hundreds, not long after Wordsworth, in England, wrote his poetry."

"But look at this." Eddie carefully removed from the shelf an old paperback edition that had come apart. Clumps of pages fell out. She caught them, treating them reverently, and held them toward her father.

"Um, have I made any notes in the margins?" William asked.

Eddie looked. "No." She pulled out another book. "I'm sure you're not including Hawthorne in your book."

William shook his head. "He was an awful man. He hated women. I have only kept his books because of the time in which he wrote. Although . . . I should keep one set because they are part of the literary canon . . ."

Eddie quickly scanned the shelves and removed five duplicate copies of several Hawthorne novels. She pushed the remaining books together and pointed to the empty space on the shelf.

"Voilà!" she said, excited. "Now you can shelve your books by Catharine Maria Sedgwick and the other early American female writers."

"Oh, that's a good idea." William started to continue but stalled. "But we don't have any shelves in the barn."

"Then we'll have some built!" Eddie countered, full of delight. She was a genius, she absolutely was.

"Yes, of course," her father agreed. "Let's ask Jeff Jefferson to help us. I've heard he's a good carpenter and a good guy. Do you think we could get Jeff to build them?"

"Oh, um, well." Eddie hadn't been prepared for this suggestion. Her father had met Jeff when she and Jeff were dating. He'd liked Jeff, and Eddie wanted her father to be comfortable about moving the books. It wasn't about her need to see Jeff. Really.

"You know what? I'll call him right now."

———

In her shop, Barrett sat on her tall stool behind the counter, working on her laptop. Her bookkeeping worksheets and all the other business records were in place. She needed to work on her social media and publicity. She had already made accounts at Instagram, Facebook, and Pinterest. She scrolled through her phone to find the photos of her merchandise she wanted to spotlight. She started with the jewelry, editing her photos, cropping them and using filters to highlight.

She was concentrating on a silver and labradorite necklace when someone pounded on the door. Glancing up, she could tell that the person was male, so it wasn't her sister, just some impatient guy who couldn't be bothered to read her sign plastered across the top of her window saying: OPENING MAY 29.

She ignored him.

The pounding continued. It was irritating.

Barrett slid off her high stool, walked across her shop, and opened the door. "Can't you read?"

Immediately, she wished she hadn't been so shrewish. The guy was about her age, tall and handsome, with thick blond hair and blue eyes. Her mind said: *Go away!* Her body said: *Please come in.*

"Sorry," he said. "I'm really sorry to bother you, but I just landed on the island and it's my sister's birthday today and if I don't take her a present, she'll never let me forget it." The way he talked, dressed, and looked told her this guy was from money.

She should have shut the door in his entitled face. She didn't. "Um, haven't you noticed there are other shops that are actually open?"

"Maybe, but that sweater you have in the window? My sister would love it so much and I've never seen anything like it."

Okay, Barrett thought, that was a point in his favor. The sweater lying on the shelf in the window was hand-knitted in shades of hyacinth and blue by a Nantucket woman. Her trademark smiling whale swam just above the left breast.

"It's expensive," Barrett warned the guy.

"It's for my sister," the guy repeated.

When he spoke, he smiled. It was a great smile.

"We're not officially open." Barrett hesitated. She was having trouble thinking clearly. "But come in. Since it's your sister's birthday." She moved to the shelf and picked up the top sweater. "This comes in three sizes."

"She's small," the guy said. "Like you."

"It's three hundred fifty dollars."

"Okay, do you take credit cards?"

"We do," she answered. "Um, come over to the counter."

As she transacted the sale, she forced herself to focus. *My first sale, and a big one!*

She handed him the receipt and couldn't help saying triumphantly, "You are my very first customer."

"Cool. Do I get a medal or a ribbon or something?"

"No medal, but I'll wrap it for you since it's her birthday."

"That would be excellent. Thank you."

Barrett reached under her counter and brought out a folded box, tissue paper, wrapping paper, ribbon, and Scotch tape.

He held out his hand. "I'm Drew Fischer. You probably got that from my credit card."

She shook his hand, finding the action slightly embarrassing. But she was a businesswoman now. She told herself to grow up.

"I'm Barrett Grant, after Elizabeth Barrett Browning. My sister is named after Edna St. Vincent Millay—she's Eddie."

"Barrett is kind of cool," Drew said. "Eddie . . . a little more unusual."

"My sister has the personality for it," Barrett assured him.

"Does she live on Nantucket, too?"

Barrett carefully pulled the dark blue ribbon over the package, and tried to form the bow, focusing on not wrinkling the ribbon. "Well, no and yes. I mean she's here now, but she's been living and working in New York."

"That package looks nice," Drew said.

"Thanks." Barrett smoothed it out. "Here you are. I don't have any gift cards yet, but you can buy birthday cards at the pharmacy."

She handed Drew the box.

"Nice ribbon," he said. Then he laughed at himself. "*Lame.* Um, Barrett, I'm not as idiotic as I seem. Could I take you out for dinner sometime? Or lunch? Or coffee?"

What? "Well . . . How long are you going to be on the island?"

"I work in Boston, but my family has a house here, so actually, I could be here a lot."

"Oh." He was a summer person. That made her wary. She never wanted to be anyone's milkmaid to his lord of the manor. Still, Drew was nice. And very nice to look at. "Sure, I'd like to go to dinner or lunch or coffee."

"How about tonight?"

"Sorry." Barrett was genuinely sorry. "My sister just got here from New York. I need to spend more time with her."

"Your sister, Eddie, right?" Drew paused. "How about Thursday night?"

"Okay. Um . . . that works. Thursday night."

"I'll pick you up at six?"

"Okay. I live on a farm with my father."

"A farm? There's a farm on Nantucket?"

"Several farms. We don't farm, actually. We have a dog and we kind of have a horse, but she's aloof."

"Horses can be that way." Drew smiled and held out his phone. "Could I get your number?" Barrett put her information into his phone.

Drew took it from her. "Got it. See you."

"See you," Barrett echoed.

After Drew left, Barrett called Louisa, who had knitted the beautiful sweater, to tell her she'd already sold it and needed more. She unpacked more inventory, filled out more tax forms, checked the shop's website, watched crowds of people stream off the ferries. She knew they would be settling in for the summer, stocking up on groceries, taking the first walk of the summer along the beach.

Barrett checked her phone. No storm was coming, but it was late afternoon and she had done pretty much everything she could to prepare her shop for the grand opening.

She'd made a sale!

Louisa had told her she had more sweaters ready. Barrett decided to stop by and pick them up on her way home. She always enjoyed a nice chat with Louisa, who knew everything about the island.

It was almost six when Barrett entered her house. She stopped in the front hall. Something was different. Something was—something delicious was in the air.

"Eddie?" she called.

"In the kitchen."

Barrett set her things on the front hall table and hurried to the kitchen. Eddie was at the sink, rinsing her hands.

"What's that smell?" Barrett asked.

Eddie wore a pair of ancient jeans and a loose sweatshirt. "Roast chicken. It won't be ready for ten minutes or so. Sit down. Let's have a glass of wine. How was your day?"

"Have I entered an alternate universe?" Barrett looked around, eyes wide. "Roast chicken? Dinner rolls? Vegetables? What's happened?"

Eddie laughed. "I guess you did all the shopping and cooking for the past two years. It's not fair for you to work and cook, too. Sit down. I'm drinking Chardonnay. Is that good for you?"

"Yes, please." Barrett slid into a chair. Smiling shyly, she said, "Guess what. I made a sale."

Eddie lit up. "That's great, Barrett! Congratulations."

"Also," Barrett confessed, "I'm going out with the guy Thursday night."

Eddie frowned. "Really? Is the guy nice?"

"No," Barrett shot back. "He's got zits and fangs."

"Sorry. Tell me about him."

"He knocked on the door of my shop today. He wanted to buy a sweater for his sister's birthday. I sold it to him, and wrapped it, and we kind of chatted, and he seems pretty great. He asked me out, and I said yes."

Eddie tapped her fingers against her lips. Barrett hated when she did that.

Eddie asked, "Is he a summer guy or a year-rounder? What's his name?"

"Drew Fischer. He's from off-island, but his family has a house here. I haven't seen him around before."

"Fischer." Eddie pulled her phone from her pocket and tapped. "Here he is." She held the phone for Barrett to look at. "His family owns a 'small' pharmaceutical company. Wait." Eddie tapped again. "Last year the company's sales were over two billion."

Barrett shrugged. "I'm just going to dinner with him." She changed the subject. "Did it go okay with Dad?"

"More than okay." Eddie set a glass of wine in front of Barrett and took a chair next to her at the kitchen table. "Ready for this? I convinced Dad to move some of his books out to the barn. We're going to open a used bookstore!"

Barrett broke into laughter. "Eddie, no one will buy Dad's old books!"

"Maybe, maybe not," Eddie conceded. "The important thing is that they won't be in the house any longer."

"Ooooh, Eddie. You're a genius." Barrett lifted her wineglass. "Here's to you."

Their father came into the kitchen. "Something smells good."

"Sit down, Dad," Eddie said. "I'll pour you some wine."

William sat. "I've been thinking."

"Oh, no," Eddie joked. "That's a bad sign."

Their father laughed. Barrett gawked. Her father was laughing? A miracle.

William asked, "Barrett, has your sister told you about our plans?"

"She did say something about a used bookstore in the barn, but—"

"It's a great idea, isn't it?" William seemed more alive, happier. "I will enjoy choosing which books I can part with. And, Eddie, while you've been busy, I called Jeff about the bookshelves. He said he'll come over here tomorrow morning to talk with us and look over the barn to see how it could be done."

"Dad, that's wonderful!" Barrett said.

Sounding like someone deep in thought, Eddie mused, "Jeff will be here tomorrow. Great that he can come so soon." She rose from the table and became terribly busy at the stove.

six

The next morning, Eddie woke early. She pulled on jeans and a sweat-shirt and quietly went down the stairs and out the door. Duke followed her and Duchess strolled up to the fence and nickered softly. The sun was strong, but the morning was still sweet with early mist and air cooled by the sea and the night. She closed her eyes, leaned against the warm wooden barn door, and let herself breathe. She hadn't had this for two years, this simple, unhurried unfolding of the day. She heard the mourning doves and felt the sun warm on her back. The gentle purr of one of the island's small planes flying in from the Cape feathered the silence and disappeared.

How old was this barn? Eddie wondered. Had it once been filled with cows and horses mooing and neighing and tossing their heads and kicking at the stalls? Had the horse that came with the farm ever had companions shelter here with her in a storm?

In the city, it was easy, Eddie thought, to live a fantasy life. With her iPhone, she could present a carefully edited view of herself, as someone clever, posh, even glamorous. Dinah certainly presented a cultivated front, a combination of expensive clothes, diligently coiffed hair, personalized makeup, and laughter, sometimes real, sometimes forced. Many of the people Eddie met in the city were living the lives they *wished* they had, striving to become the elite, enviable legends they were crafting.

Not that Eddie thought that was bad. It was another way to live, and it meant something different to everyone, those all-night bashes around a swimming pool on a penthouse skyscraper, the dinner parties at the latest sensational restaurant where the bill ran into the thousands, leaving the theater at midnight with the glitter of neon blitzing the air.

She'd enjoyed that life. At first, Eddie had nearly worshipped Dinah Lavender, and in time she and Dinah became true friends. But now that she was back on the island, she was happy to be here, where the barn's wide boards reminded her of how deep time was and the sun's expansive light warmed her and made her whole.

What kind of life did she want?

Did she want to return to the city, to the flash and the hurry and the crowds? Could she possibly want to stay here? She knew she wanted books in her life. She knew she cherished being able to see her sister and father every day. And the island sparkled around her like a treasure chest sparkling with gold and diamonds.

She decided to settle for today, now, as she was, home and happy. Maybe high on the sweet salt air, but whatever, she'd take it.

She returned to the house and got breakfast ready: eggs, bacon, and fresh squeezed orange juice. When she opened the kitchen window, the trills of birdsong floated in on the sweet air. She'd forgotten how delicious Nantucket water was, coming from a glacier melted centuries ago.

"Look at you, sis," Barrett declared, coming into the room. "You've become an island girl."

"I'm ready to meet with a carpenter about the barn." Eddie wore clothes she'd left behind when she went to New York, jeans, a T-shirt beneath an open blue button-down, and sandals.

"A carpenter?" Barrett teased. "Please. Don't you mean Jeff?"

"Do you want breakfast or not?" Eddie lifted the plate, holding the bacon away from Barrett.

"All right. I'll be good." Barrett poured herself a cup of coffee and sat at the table. "How does it feel, being home?"

Eddie set their plates before them. "I like it, of course. I have to get used to it. Life with Dinah is . . . faster paced. Fabulous dining, theater, opera, bookstores, art museums." She ate a bit of bacon and sighed. "I know people who say they're vegetarian, except for bacon."

Duke, sitting next to the table, wagged his tail and whined pitifully.

"No bacon for you, Duke," Barrett said.

The dog whined again and let his head droop almost to the floor.

"You are such a fake," Barrett said to Duke, and gave him a piece of bacon.

Eddie's phone chirped. She glanced at it and said to Barrett, "I've got to take this. I'll meet you outside." She hadn't taken Dinah's last few calls and she wasn't keen to take this one. Dinah had sent many texts. She was still worried about her stalker.

"Eddie, I don't know what to do!" Dinah whispered.

"Good morning to you, too, and why are you whispering?"

"Thais is here, preparing lunch and dinner, and she has a key to the apartment."

"You gave her the key, Dinah. She's cooked for you for years. Dinah, come on. Don't tell me you're worried that Thais will give the key to your stalker."

"No, I trust her. But what if the guy jumps her and pulls her into an alley and hits her and goes through her purse?"

"Dinah, are you writing a thriller now?"

"What? No. I'm worrying about a perfectly possible realistic attack. I'm not thinking of myself, I'm thinking of Thais."

Eddie had gone through many crises with Dinah before. Ups and downs in her love life, of course, and freak-outs about a cover for her newest book or fears that no one would like it. She knew when Dinah was just being dramatic, and this wasn't it.

"Have you alerted the police?" she asked.

"Eddie, you know they can't do anything about it. They can't stand in front of my building twenty-four hours a day."

"Why don't you hire someone? A private detective slash bouncer? Someone who could frighten away your stalker?"

"I could do that, but I still wouldn't get any sleep."

Duke nudged Eddie's knee, staring at her with his sweetest expression. When Eddie didn't give him her last bite of bacon, Duke barked, once.

"What was that?" Dinah asked.

"That was a dog," Eddie said. She gave the bacon to Duke. "Maybe that's the answer. Maybe you should get a dog to protect you."

"I'm going out to the barn," Barrett called.

"Who was that?" Dinah asked.

"My sister, Barrett," Eddie said, and as she said the words, she knew exactly what Dinah was going to say next.

"You have a dog and a sister. I wish I had a sister. I don't think I'm ready to train a dog. If I came to stay with you for a few weeks, I would be safe, and my stalker would give up and go away."

"Dinah—"

"I wouldn't bother you. You're working for me remotely now. You wouldn't even have to talk to me. And . . . I could . . . I could walk your dog for you! I'd stay in my room, reading. You've told me about your house. You have lots of bedrooms."

Eddie spoke firmly. "Dinah, it is going to be chaos here. We're having bookshelves made in the barn and we're going to move a lot of books from the house to make a used bookstore."

"Oh," Dinah cooed. "That's so romantic!"

"Romantic?" Eddie echoed. "We've got a house crammed full of books." As soon as she spoke, she knew nothing else she could say would entice Dinah more. She quickly changed tack. "Dinah, what will happen when you marry someone or I get married? I can't live with you forever." She glanced out the window and saw a pickup truck pull in. "I have to go. Call Juliet. Hire a private detective. Speak with your doormen."

"Eddie . . ."

"I'll call you later."

Eddie pocketed the phone and hurried outside. Barrett was by the fence, talking to Duchess. As she walked to the barn, the sweet smell of hay centered her.

"What are you doing?" Eddie asked Barrett.

"Waiting for everyone. Dad's out front. I can't believe Jeff agreed to build the bookshelves. He's gotta be slammed with work."

"Hey."

Eddie turned. Jeff was walking toward them. He wore a clean T-shirt, canvas work pants, and a baseball cap.

"Hey," Eddie said in reply. She almost reached up and kissed him. She wanted to.

"So, bookshelves, right?"

"Are we mad?" Eddie asked.

Jeff stepped closer to her. "Yes, *you're* mad. But I've always thought you look sexy in a bookshop."

"You, too." It was the most Eddie could think to say. She could feel the heat of his body. He smelled of Irish Spring soap.

Barrett said, "Here's Dad."

Their father strolled up to the barn, talking with another man.

"Good morning, everyone," William said. "Girls, this is Grady, who works in construction, and plans to help us with this, um, enterprise."

"Grady Manchester," the man said, and nodded curtly. He was probably in his fifties, but he looked older than their father, with his sun-wrinkled face and slight limp.

The five of them walked around the barn. Grady grunted now and then and scribbled something in a notebook.

They walked out of the shadows to stand in the warm sunlight.

Grady said, "You've got a space here about sixty by ninety. I can't see how you'd need sixty feet of shelving. A good thing: They've brought electricity into the barn so you don't have to go through the nightmare of having a trench dug. How are you going to do the lighting? And you need to figure out how you want to insulate the space. Do you want to heat it or cool it? Do you want a toilet and sink? I think these walls will easily hold bookshelves. They're old wide-board pine. You couldn't get boards like this these days. This end of the barn has a decent floor, wide boards again. But they're old and splintered so you might want something better. The bookshelves will be the last structure to worry about. Oh, and you should have a normal door built into one of the barn doors because you won't want the big doors open all the time to the elements."

When Grady paused, the Grant family stared at him as if they had to decide how to get a missile to Mars.

Jeff said, "Hang on. Wait a minute, Grady. We don't know if this shop will draw any customers. Used books? Maybe a few bored people on a rainy day. Could we think about this on a much smaller scale? Have you seen the book bins in the children's library in town? You know, like record stores used to have so people can sort of paw through them. Maybe we could build some of those and get some books out here before summer's over and then see where we are. It may not be worth doing all the work that you've been so good to tell us about."

"Well." Grady rubbed his nose and looked around and said nothing.

Barrett perked up. "Jeff, I like your thinking. The floor here is good enough to walk on. We could have bins of books and advertise on Instagram and Facebook, and if we could get it done in time, we could open the shop in June and have two or three months to see how it goes."

Their father spoke up. "I agree, Barrett. Grady, we're grateful to you for spelling this all out for us. It seems like a difficult and demanding task. I vote we have bins made and get books out here as soon as possible to see if we've got anyone on the island who wants used books. If we do, Grady, we'll call you for some remodeling."

Grady nodded sagely. "I told Jeff I thought you were all crazy for even considering a used bookstore. We can get all the used books we want from the Take-It-or-Leave-It shed." He turned to go.

"Grady, come in and have a cup of coffee and a muffin," Eddie suggested.

Grady snorted. "On a day like today? I've got a hundred construction jobs waiting for me." He tipped his Red Sox cap and trudged away.

William turned to Jeff. "You'll come in for coffee, won't you?"

Barrett and Eddie watched the two men walk back to the house.

"Let's give them a minute," Eddie suggested.

Together the sisters walked to the fence and looked out over the field of new grass threaded with daisies. Duchess came close to the railing. Barrett stroked her velvet nose. She reached into her pocket and held out a carrot. Duchess gently picked it up with her huge teeth, snorted, and walked away.

"I wish we could ride her," Eddie said. "She lets us near her, but gets freaky if we try to put a saddle on her."

"I know. We did have a vet come out about a year ago to trim her hooves and check her over. She didn't put up a fuss. She let the vet walk right up to her, take her by her halter, and tie a rope to the fence. I stayed next to her, patting her, talking sweet talk, but later, when I tried to put the saddle blanket on her, she pawed the ground and walked away."

"We need a horse psychiatrist," Eddie said.

"Sure. We'll pay him with the proceeds of the sale of the books." Barrett turned around and leaned on the fence.

Eddie glanced toward the house. "Barrett, seeing Jeff makes me wonder if I made a mistake, going to New York instead of staying here."

Barrett wrapped her arm around Eddie's waist. "You know, Eddie, I watched Jeff while we were talking about the bookshelves in the barn. I saw how he looked at you. Are you two getting back together?"

"No. Definitely not. Oh, I'm still in love with him, Barrett. I didn't expect to feel this way, but when I saw him at the ferry, it was like my heart woke up from a long nap. I felt all flushed and hopeful and energetic. But Jeff and I want different things in life. That's why we broke up. Plus, how can I leave Dinah? She's got swarms of people around her, and yet she's the loneliest person I know. She doesn't seem that way because she does so many signings and talks and goes to parties and events. I think we've become close. I think she relies on me. I feel sort of guilty being away from her. I worry about her." Eddie paused. "I want . . . I want to be careful with people."

The sisters stood in silence for a moment. Then Eddie put her arm around her sister's shoulders.

"We'll figure it out. Right now, let's go join Dad and Jeff."

They entered the house through the kitchen and found the men sitting at the round oak claw-foot table, drinking coffee and talking.

Their father said, "Have some coffee. Join us. Jeff said he'll bring out some cardboard boxes we can put the barn books in and he'll help carry them out to the barn. You girls can sort them. Books are heavy to carry, you know."

"That's wonderful, Jeff," Barrett said. "Thank you."

"You're welcome." Jeff started to rise. "William, it's been great chatting with you, but I've got to get to the construction site. I'll probably see you tomorrow."

"See you." Eddie smiled at him, and their gazes clicked, making her heart tumble around in her chest.

Barrett said, "Dad, isn't this cool? We're going to have a bookstore!"

William laughed. "It will take months getting your 'bookstore' started."

"Not if we start sorting right now." Barrett stepped into the pantry and brought out an armful of brown paper bags from Stop & Shop. "We don't have to wait until the racks are built. We can get quite a few books into these bags."

William asked, "Barrett, what about your shop?"

Barrett gave her father a great big smile. "All done, except for the last-minute things. I'm so organized I'm rearranging."

Eddie cooed, "Come on, Daddy, this will be fun. You'll probably find books you didn't know you have."

"I wouldn't be surprised." William followed them into the dining room.

"Look!" Eddie held a book high. "James Beard's *Hors D'Oeuvre and Canapes*. It was published in 1999. Dad, have you ever *once* used this book?"

"It was your mother's," William said.

"When did our mother ever make hors d'oeuvres to serve at a party?"

"Point made." His grin was wicked. "Maybe you girls would like to have it. We could give a party here . . ."

Eddie snorted. "Right, that could happen. First of all, there's not enough room for a party. This is out."

Barrett laughed. "Eddie, look—a Thomas Kinkade engagement calendar!"

William grinned again. "Those are *really* not mine. Your mother liked his pictures."

Barrett lifted out an armful of Kinkade's books. "Someone will enjoy these." She tucked them into a brown paper bag.

Slowly they added other books. *Learn to Sail in a Weekend. Quilting for Fun. Scuba Diving for Beginners.*

Stacked neatly together beneath the long table were at least two dozen hardback novels by Barbara Vine and Ruth Rendell.

"Look, Dad," Barrett said. "We can put these in your bookstore and some mystery reader will be thrilled."

"Fine."

"Well, these are definitely Mom's." Eddie lifted up a stack of books about diamonds. How to value diamonds. Elizabeth Taylor and diamonds. A history of diamonds.

"Maybe I'll keep them." Barrett took them in her arms.

"Really?" Eddie raised her eyebrow at her sister.

"You're right," Barrett said. "They should go."

Eddie turned to her father. "Do you want to send them to her, Dad?"

William rolled his eyes. "She's in Amsterdam. I don't think she needs them."

The girls continued working, carefully checking each book title and suggesting some to their father. They struck gold when they found an entire set of the 1995 *Encyclopaedia Britannica*.

"Remember how you used to explain stuff to us by reading from these?" Eddie asked their father.

"I do. Those were good old days." Before they could react, he said, "And we've all got many more good days to come."

By noon, they had moved several bags of books and had dust in their hair. There were spaces in the bookshelves like gaps between a seven-year-old's teeth. They stretched, groaning at their complaining muscles.

"Dibs on first shower," Eddie said, and raced up the stairs.

Barrett shook her shirt and watched the dust drift in a ray of sunlight. With Eddie here, everything seemed easier.

"Come into the kitchen, Dad," she said. "I'll make you some lunch."

"I'm not really hungry," William said. They'd discovered an ancient tome—ancient for their family—titled *Great Poems of the English Language*. It had been given to their father's grandmother by her aunt. The cover was falling off, but many pages had been dog-eared, and William sat on a chair with the book on the dining room table, reading the selected poems and nodding to himself.

"Yes, yes," he said every so often. Or, "I had forgotten this."

Barrett went into the kitchen and made three tuna fish and tomato sandwiches, covering two plates with paper towels. She ate her sandwich standing over the sink. She was worried about her date with Drew. Although *worried* wasn't quite the right word. She was unsettled. She was twenty-six years old and living with her father. On Nantucket, that was normal. Real estate was crazy expensive on the island, and she knew she'd never have enough money to buy her own place. But was she weird for being so glad that Eddie was home? Had their brother's death and their mother's desertion made Barrett unable to start her own life? Plus, Eddie was almost thirty and not attached to anyone, and their father was handsome, but he didn't have a woman in his life.

Barrett was attracted to Drew, but he might be smug or boring. She resented the time she spent thinking about him when she should be focusing on her shop.

Still, this summer would be interesting.

seven

What kind of restaurant would Drew take her to? Barrett wondered. What should she dress for? The old money people never wore designer clothing or flashy jewelry, unlike the new money people who wore their wealth like blinking neon signs. But Barrett wasn't rich or poor. And she wasn't an islander or a summer person. She'd lived here long enough to be considered a washed-ashore, and for heaven's sake, she was a grown woman, she should wear whatever she wanted. The late May nights could still be cool. She decided on a flowery dress, a long cashmere cardigan, and a long cashmere scarf. Layers were always good for the spring. She coiled her hair up into a messy chignon, added small diamond ear studs and only a touch of lipstick and eyeliner. Rich or poor, it didn't pay to wear heavy makeup if you might go swimming or boating. No blush or mascara could hold up to the ocean and its breezes. Best to be honest about yourself from the start.

Barrett snorted. She was only having dinner with the guy. During

the years she'd lived here, she'd learned one sure thing about herself:
She wanted to live on this island for the rest of her life. The ocean
captivated her. It was eternally mysterious and compelling. A good
long walk by the ocean often solved her problems and lit up a path she
hadn't known was there. She'd made friends here, and she didn't want
to leave them. They *got* her, the adult Barrett, the real woman. She
didn't want to live with her father all her life, but she did have a vague
plan in the back of her mind about building a small house at the other
end of the property, or turning the barn into a house where she could
live and have her own life but still be helpful to her father. Although,
she had to admit, her father was still young enough to meet a new
woman and start his life over. She hoped that happened for him.

How did Eddie do it? How did she manage to extract herself from
the family crash site? Barrett had heard a hundred thousand times
how much fun it was to live with Dinah.

*Oh, look, now we're in Paris! Oh, wow, we saw Florence Pugh on
the street, but I didn't snap a pic because we don't do that in the city.
OMG, Dinah just bought me a pair of pink Manolo Blahnik pumps
($1,200)!*

The crackle of gravel in the driveway alerted her. Drew was here!
Barrett blew herself a kiss in the mirror and hurried down to the front
door. Eddie had promised to keep their father in his study, discussing
Wordsworth or Coleridge, whatever, so that William wouldn't come
wandering up to Drew and babble about daffodils.

Barrett came out on the porch just as Drew stepped out of the car.
It was a Jeep convertible, not a Lamborghini or even a Mercedes. He
wore a blue button-down, no blazer, so Barrett had dressed just fine.

"Hi," she said, skipping down the steps and over the slate path to
meet him.

"Hi," Drew said back.

His eyes were almost robin's-egg blue. Could that even be possible?
He was shorter than she'd remembered, but very handsome.

"You look great," Drew said.

"You, too." If she'd had longer eyelashes, she would have fluttered them.

"I thought we'd go to Town," Drew said. "They've got a good menu. Have you been there?"

He opened her car door and held it as Barrett slid inside. "Yes, I love it. They have great cocktails."

Drew got in and started the car, looking over his shoulder as he backed out.

Barrett asked, "Do you spend every summer here?"

"I wish." Drew flashed her a smile. "I used to, when I was a kid. Now I'm too busy working to live here all summer."

"You're from Boston?" Barrett prompted, wanting to know more.

"Right. I'm the CFO for the firm's Boston branch. We've always summered on Nantucket and spent holidays here. I go back and forth."

Drew was quiet as he navigated the narrow one-way streets. He parked on Broad Street, a short walk to the restaurant. They chose to eat inside because the May evenings could be chilly, and soon they were tucked into a quiet table in the corner.

After they'd ordered drinks, Barrett asked, "Did your sister like her sweater?"

"She did. Very much. For once she approves of my decision."

"For *once*?" Barrett laughed. "I get it. I have a sister, too."

Conversation paused while the waiter set down their drinks and took their order.

Barrett unfolded her napkin, wondering if she should ask him, and then thought she might as well find out about his soft spots now. "Is your sister hard to please?"

"No. Janny's actually adorable. We all spoil her." Drew smiled. "She talked her way into getting the bedroom facing the ocean. I face the street."

It seemed only natural for Barrett to ask, "Where do you live on the island?"

Drew paused before answering, as if wanting to be careful with his reply. "Our summer house is on the cliff. The large old shingled house with roses all over one side."

"Oh." *Eddie was right*, Barrett thought. *He's from* that *wealthy family.* "I know which house you mean," Barrett said. "I love that house."

Drew turned the conversation back to her. "You said you have a sister. How do you two get along?"

Barrett sipped her drink while she considered how to answer. "Just fine. We're different, even though we're only a couple of years apart in age. She's ambitious and sophisticated and . . . she likes to go at a faster pace than I do. But I love her, and I admire her."

"Any other sibs?"

Barrett paused. This was not a good time to mention Stearns. "No. Our parents are divorced. My father was a professor at Williams College, but he left to write a book."

Drew looked impressed. "Nice. He must be brilliant. And your mother?"

Barrett shook her head. "She left us about four years ago. It's fine. Motherhood was never a pleasure for her. We think she's in Amsterdam now."

"Wow," Drew said. "That's huge. Do you miss her?"

"Truthfully? Deep in my heart, I wish she'd been a more loving mother. But I get it." She paused, wondering again if she should mention Stearns. No, she decided. It was too sad, and she wanted to be happy right now. "She loved my father, but she has a wanderer's heart. She was a good enough mother when we were young. Now we're grown. She's set free. I'm happy for her."

The waiter appeared and set their first courses in front of them.

"My mother is the opposite of what your mother sounds like." Drew paused to dip a piece of crusty bread into the sauce around his mussels. "She's super-traditional, glued to routine, and she's done the iron-hand-in-the-velvet-glove bit all my life. I love her, of course. I respect her. But sometimes I wish she'd go away."

"I get that," Barrett replied, with a sad smile.

Drew said, "Tell me about living on the island."

Barrett told him about moving here from Williamstown, how she'd worked two jobs and saved enough money to start her store.

"Of course, living with my father means I don't have to pay rent, but in a way, taking care of him is like a third job. I buy groceries and cook and keep the house clean. Also, when we bought the house, it came with a horse, that was part of the deal, because the horse is . . . not difficult, but *sensitive*. She won't let us ride her. It's like we're engaged in a very lengthy courtship. I put hay and corn out for her all winter and keep her water trough full and brush her once a week. She's sort of like another dog. Our real dog is named Duke."

"What jobs did you work here?" Drew asked.

"Ha!" Barrett said.

She leaned toward him, entertaining him with tales about cleaning houses and waitressing. Drew had tended bar when he was in business school, and suddenly they were exchanging stories about crazy or obnoxious patrons, and they were laughing together, and Barrett felt like she had known Drew all her life.

They lingered over dessert and coffee, still talking about their recent histories. Barrett slowly being accepted by Nantucket people. The things Drew had done on the island when he was a child. Which beaches they preferred, their favorite spots on the moors. The parties friends gave in the summer that lasted all night long.

Afterward, they strolled around town, checking out the store windows, all decorated for summer. As they crossed the cobblestones on Main Street, they bumped shoulders, and Drew took Barrett's hand, and they walked together, holding hands.

They sat on one of the benches in the library's garden as the night fell around them. The air was cool and fresh. The trees in the garden were in full blossom, providing a delicate screen from the sidewalk. From across the street, laughter and music floated.

"Are you seeing anyone?" Drew asked.

"No. Since we moved here, I've been too busy to date seriously. I've made some good friends, but no, I'm not seeing anyone." She studied him. "Are you?"

"I've got a busy social life in the city, but—" He interrupted himself. "Gak. *Busy social life*. I sound like I'm presenting my résumé. Let me start over. I'm working eighty hours a week, and I have a few women friends, but no one special. I haven't wanted to make time for anyone special."

"But you came to Nantucket," Barrett reminded him.

"Yes, for my sister's birthday." He paused. "I have a feeling I'll be coming to Nantucket more often."

"That would be nice," Barrett told him.

A group of giggling tweens rushed into the garden, chattering past Barrett and Drew, breaking their mood.

Drew stood. "Enough talk about families. Let's go look at the boats in the harbor." He held out his hand.

Barrett took it, rose, and together they strolled toward the harbor. It wasn't the high season yet, but several small yachts and deep-sea fishing boats bobbed in their moorings. When they walked to the end of the dock, they were surrounded by stars reflected in the dark water.

Barrett knew Drew was going to kiss her, and he did. Gently, he touched his lips to hers. He cupped her face in his hand and pulled her body close to his as their kiss deepened. He was an excellent kisser, in a sort of paint-by-numbers way. How many women had he kissed in his life? And why should it matter to her? The thought crossed her mind, as swift and bright as a firefly, that Drew considered kissing a competitive event in some kind of romantic triathlon.

Why was she thinking instead of feeling?

Clearly, she was out of kissing practice.

It was almost midnight when Drew took her home. He stopped at the end of the drive, out of range from the porch light.

"I have to go back to Boston tomorrow," he said. "I'm here only for my sister's birthday. But I'm due some time off. I'll come back as soon as I can."

"I hope so," Barrett told him.

He leaned toward her and they kissed lightly.

From the house, Duke began to bark.

"See you soon." Barrett slipped into the house, glad that it was quiet and everyone else had gone to bed. She wanted to be alone with her thoughts.

At midnight, Eddie was in her room, scrolling through her phone, texting New York friends. She'd spent an hour on the phone with Dinah, praising her for her bravery, assuring Dinah she was safe. At last, she heard a car in the drive. Barrett, coming home from her date. She rolled off her bed and went to her window to look out. Drew kissed Barrett before she left the car and hurried into the house. The convertible pulled away.

Now Barrett would run up the stairs to Eddie's room, throw herself on the bed, and gush all about her evening.

Eddie waited.

She heard Barrett on the stairs. Barrett passed Eddie's door, went down the hall, entered her own room, and shut the door very quietly, as if she didn't want anyone to know she was home.

As if she didn't want to talk to anyone. As if this date, this evening, was private.

Eddie understood. She'd been away for two years. Barrett would be out of the habit of reviewing each date with Eddie. Still, this must have been a very good date. Barrett had been gone for five hours.

Good grief, Eddie thought, what had happened to her that she was sitting in her bedroom like an eighteenth-century spinster aunt, longing to live off someone else's romance?

It was better, she decided, to wonder about Barrett than to imagine what would happen when Jeff returned tomorrow to start building the bins for her father's books.

She brushed her teeth and crawled between her sheets and knew she wouldn't be able to sleep, and fell asleep at once.

Eddie woke early in the morning, before the others were up. Pulling on a loose shirt and ripped jean shorts, she slid her feet into sandals and crept down the stairs. During the year she'd lived here, two years ago, before she went to work for Dinah, when the island was new to them and the house was unfamiliar and their lives sparkled with sea air and hope, she had often made coffee and brought it out to the back porch to sit and watch the morning arrive. The air was always fresh, carrying the scents of ocean salt and flowers.

It was comforting to be back, making coffee and sitting on the porch again. Duke was already here, lying on the warm boards in a patch of sun, snoring. Birds called. Duchess stood at the fence nuzzling the grass. Eddie called out a greeting. Duchess snorted.

Behind her, the door opened. Barrett stepped out to the porch.

"Good morning!" Barrett almost sang the words.

"Good morning," Eddie answered. "You seem awfully cheery. How was your date?"

Barrett wore an ancient sundress that once had belonged to Eddie. She sank onto the wicker swing, cradling her coffee in her hands.

"My date was fine," Barrett said. "Drew's nice. And handsome."

"Wow. You really like him."

"He's a distinct possibility," Barrett said, using her really bad British accent.

Eddie asked, "Have you seen Dad?"

Barrett stretched. "Yeah. He's already in his study, deep into his book."

"Let's leave him there. I don't want him freaking out when we start working in the barn."

Just as Eddie spoke, a truck came rumbling down the drive all the way to the barn. A load of boards lay in the bed of the truck. Jeff stepped out from the driver's side. Another man jumped down from the passenger side. He looked vaguely familiar to Barrett but she couldn't remember his name. He had black hair and sky blue eyes rimmed with thick black lashes.

"Why are carpenters always so hot?" Eddie whispered to Barrett as they went down the back steps to greet the men.

Before Barrett could reply, Jeff said, "Hello, ladies. I've convinced Paul to help me. I know you want to get this bookstore started ASAP."

"Thanks, Jeff." Eddie tried to be casual even though she almost couldn't look at him. He made her feel bewitched. "Hi, Paul. I'm Eddie and this is my sister, Barrett."

Paul nodded. His eyes rested on Barrett. "Hey. Barrett, I think I've seen you at some beach parties now and then in the summer."

"Me, too," Barrett said, blushing. "I mean, I think I've seen you there."

Duke barked and wagged his tail.

Barrett reached down to pat the dog. "This is Duke. He's our watchdog, as you can see."

"Hey, Duke." Jeff stroked Duke's fur. "Sorry, but we're on the clock here. We've got more jobs than we can handle."

The guys walked off. The women stood watching as they unloaded the lumber from the truck.

"Look," Eddie whispered. She nodded her head toward the fenced field.

The horse was standing nearby, watching everything.

Barrett cooed. "Aw, that's sweet, to see her be curious. Maybe she likes those men."

"Maybe *I* like those men," Eddie said, only half-joking.

Jeff came toward them, a laptop in his hand. "I've made a prelimi-nary sketch of what the book bins should look like." He stood between the sisters, holding the open laptop so they could see his drawing. "They'll be thirty-nine inches tall, sort of general waist level. Books are generally about seven inches wide and eleven inches high, so if you want eight bins, we'll make thin plywood dividers, and build the over-all cabinet forty-five inches wide. Does that sound okay to you?"

"I guess." Eddie looked over at Barrett. "We have only a general idea of what we want, but that sounds okay."

"It's not going to take us long to build four or five of these," Jeff told them. "If you want them stained, Paul said he could do it in the evenings. How are you doing with sorting books?"

"We've got several bags full . . . and we've only started. We can sort more today, right, Barrett?"

Barrett nodded. "I've got to get to my shop, but I'll work here for an hour or two."

As Jeff turned toward the barn, he said over his shoulder, "I brought some cardboard boxes for you to carry the books in. I'll drop them on the porch. We'll help you carry them out when you're ready."

"Great!" Eddie headed toward the house.

Barrett was turning to follow her sister when Paul asked, "What kind of shop are you opening?"

His question was serious. She studied his face. He wasn't flirting. He was asking for information. She realized that Paul was an *island* guy, and she wanted his approval. "It's a kind of gift shop. I've called it Nantucket Blues. It's in the little mall next to Aunt Leah's Fudge."

Paul grinned. "So you sell bluefish?"

"Right." Barrett smiled back. "No. No fish. Sweaters made by Louisa Sheppard. Framed photos of the island by Barbara Robinson. Some island jewelry by local artisans."

Paul crossed his arms over his rather magnificent chest. "Do you have a quarterboard?"

Barrett shrugged. "I couldn't afford that. I made a wooden sign, painted it dark blue, and stenciled the store's name in pale blue. The Historic District Commission has approved it."

"I could make a quarterboard for you," Paul offered.

Barrett shook her head. "Oh, I couldn't possibly pay for that."

"How about I do it for nothing?"

Barrett's goosebumps got goosebumps. The way he was looking at her . . . he was *hitting* on her. *Hitting on me with a quarterboard,* she told herself, laughing. She'd remember to tell Eddie that when they were in the house. "That's . . ."

"Think of it this way, it would be good advertising for me."

Oh, Barrett thought. Of course. He was networking.

"Don't you have lots of work scheduled?"

"I do. But I can fit this in." Reaching out, he put his hand on her arm near her elbow. His touch was light and warm. "I'd like to do this for you. I know how important it is to get all the business you can in the summer. We islanders should help each other."

Barrett stammered, "I . . . I'm . . . not an islander, really."

Paul shrugged. "I've noticed you're here in the winter."

He *had?* Barrett knew she was glowing with pleasure. "I've only lived here three years. To be honest, I thought islanders resented newcomers."

"Only the arrogant ones," Paul told her. "I'll make a quarterboard for you. If you like it, you can take me out to dinner at Crosswinds."

Barrett laughed. "It's a deal."

"Paul," Jeff yelled from the barn. "Are you planning to work today?"

"I'm on it!" Paul shouted back. To Barrett, he said, "I'll have it for you in a couple of days." He walked off to the truck to heft a stack of boards onto his shoulder.

Eddie approached. "We can't stand here watching their muscles flex. Let's get busy on the books."

"Eddie," Barrett whispered, "I'd like to get busy with Paul."

Eddie laughed and linked her arm around Barrett's neck. "Let him get the work done first."

They returned to the dining room and seated themselves on the floor in front of the piece of furniture they still referred to as "Grandmother's china cupboard."

"Look at these!" Eddie cried. "All these children's books. *Cat in the Hat. The Runaway Bunny.*"

Barrett picked up *Where the Wild Things Are* and ran her hand lovingly over the cover. "Mom used to read these to us every night and when we were sick."

Eddie said, "Well, we don't need them anymore. Hand me that cardboard box."

Barrett flinched. "We can't get rid of these books! We'll read them to our children."

"I'm not having children, remember?" Eddie put some books into the box.

"You'll change your mind," Barrett argued.

"No, I won't." Eddie bit her lip. "I refuse to be the kind of mother our mom was."

"You wouldn't be like her, Eddie," Barrett protested. "You're totally different." She smoothed the book cover. "You'll change your mind someday."

Eddie ignored her. She moved over to the books piled on the dining room chairs. "Let's look over here," she called. "They're not in categories, so we have to go through them individually."

Barrett rose and joined Eddie.

"Now here's a winner!" Barrett held the book up for Eddie to see. "*How to Avoid Huge Ships.*"

Eddie grinned. "I know. Jimmy Fallon talked about it on his show. It's a serious book for yachtsmen. Although Dad's never been interested in boats. That can go."

Barrett bashed open a brown paper bag, dropped the book in, and picked up another. "*How to Make Macrame Dresses.*"

"That was Mom's," Eddie said. "I remember it."

For a moment, both sisters gazed at the book, as if it were some kind of message from their mother.

"Well, she's not here, so the book is going." Barrett was decisive. She stuffed the book in.

They worked together all morning, disagreeing, agreeing, laughing. By the time they were done, most of the chairs were empty of books.

"So many chairs! We could have a dinner party!" Barrett crowed.

Eddie snorted. "We haven't even cleaned off the table."

In the kitchen, they made chicken salad sandwiches and a large pitcher of iced tea. Eddie took lunch to her father. He was in his study, bent over a notebook, deep in thought. Eddie quietly put his lunch on the only open spot on his desk.

Together, Eddie and Barrett went down to the barn to take lunch to the guys.

The air smelled of sawdust. Three long plywood boxes stood next to the piles of boards.

"Wow," Barrett said. "You've done so much!"

"What do you think?" Jeff asked.

"This is amazing." Eddie walked around the bins, running her hand over the edges of the wood. "Smooth."

"Absolutely." Paul looked pleased with his work. "It wouldn't do to have your customers get splinters."

"We made lunch, if you'd like it," Eddie said, holding out the plates.

"Thanks." Jeff took his sandwich and glass of tea, then scanned the area around him.

The barn was full of sunshine. Dust danced in the warm light.

Barrett said, "Oh, gosh, there's no place to sit. Want to come up on the porch with us?"

"If that's okay," Jeff replied, looking at Eddie.

Eddie couldn't hold back her smile. "It's okay."

They settled in the wicker chairs to eat.

Barrett swallowed a bite of sandwich. "Paul offered to make a quarterboard for my store."

Eddie brightened. "Oh my gosh, Paul. That's wonderful!"

"It's not going to be a real quarterboard," Paul told her. "I mean, I'll use a stained teak board left over from outfitting a yacht, so it looks good, but it's not as heavy. Plus, I can't make shells or designs on the ends. Real quarterboards have five or six coats of paint or stain on them, but I can't get that done by Memorial Day."

"Damn, man," Jeff said. "I hope you've got a power tool."

"Definitely. I want to get a laser engraver someday, but I need more money for that." Paul turned back to Eddie. "It will be three-D and from the ground it will look great. But I want to do a better one . . . for later."

After the men had gone back to the barn, Barrett and Eddie carried the plates and glasses in to the dishwasher.

Eddie sidled close to Barrett. "You've made a conquest."

"I've made a *friend*," Barrett insisted. "Anyway, you've made a *conquest,* too. Jeff can't take his eyes off you."

Eddie leaned against the sink and folded her arms over her chest. "Let's not go there."

Barrett checked her watch. "Actually, I need to leave right now. I've got new deliveries I have to unpack and inventory to do. Are you okay here?"

"I'll be fine. Go."

All afternoon, Eddie roamed the house, reading book titles, selecting some for the barn, leaving others, and often sitting on the floor, reading a paragraph or a page, allowing memories to surround her. So much of who she was came from reading these books, as if *The Great Gatsby* had made her dream of attending riotous parties and *Bridget Jones's Diary* made her want to live in a city and smoke, and *Little Women* made her wonder why her own mother wasn't as patient and loving as Marmee, and what would have happened to the March family if they'd had a brilliant, challenging brother. She wanted to be as gorgeous as Scarlett O'Hara, as clever as Nancy Drew, and as madly in love as Juliet, although she didn't want to die young.

She took a break to make another pitcher of iced tea, then chastised herself for wasting time and returned to the living room to pile more books in more bags.

At five, Jeff knocked on the kitchen door.

"We're taking off now," he said. "We'll see you tomorrow."

His T-shirt was damp and the enticing aroma of hot male and cut wood made Eddie dizzy.

"Would you . . . like some iced tea before you go?" she asked.

"No, thanks. I'm going to grab a beer and finish up another job in Shimmo."

Jeff waved a hand and walked away.

Eddie made a note to stock up on beer.

The next evening, Eddie and Barrett sat in the TV room, eating from their very own cartons of Ben & Jerry's Phish Food. Their father had made himself a sandwich earlier and sat with them now, wielding the remote control. The Boston Red Sox were losing to the Yankees, which was infuriating.

"Dad," Eddie said. "Go to YouTube. Jim Gaffigan. Nate Bargatze. They're funny. You always get grumpy when the Sox lose."

Before William could speak, Eddie's phone chimed. Barrett's phone chimed. William's phone buzzed.

Eddie looked at the caller ID. "Oh, golly. It's Dinah."

"Dinah's calling me, too," Barrett said.

"She's calling me, as well," William told Eddie. "How does she know my number?"

"She must have gotten it when we synced phones. Sorry. She's afraid. She thinks a man is stalking her. She has a doorman and an alarm system, but she keeps seeing this guy. I have to admit, I've never seen her like this before."

"Be kind," Barrett advised.

The phones kept signaling.

"How can I be kind to her and stay on the island?" Eddie asked. "I don't want to go back to the city so soon."

"Well, Eddie, ask her to come stay with us," Barrett said. "We have enough bedrooms. She'd feel safe here. Dad's usually at home, plus we have a dog."

"I don't want to have to work . . ."

"You're working part-time for her remotely, aren't you?" William asked.

Eddie hesitated. "Barrett, this summer is supposed to be all about your store and spending time with the two of you."

"That's sweet, Eddie, but I know you care about Dinah and I wouldn't want her to be miserable."

Eddie looked at her father.

"It's fine with me," he said. "I'll be in my study writing all the time."

Eddie hesitated. "Barrett, tomorrow is Sunday! Your shop opens! We need to focus on that."

"Eddie, I'm *so* ready. I've done everything I can. I'm super-organized and super-nervous. Besides, once my shop opens, I'll be crazy busy, or at least I hope so."

"She's right, Eddie," their father said. "Go ahead and invite your writer friend."

"You guys." Eddie squeezed both their hands. "I love you." She stood up. "Hi, Dinah. What's up?"

"Oh, Eddie," Dinah cried, "I'm so sorry to bother you, but the stalker's across the street. He's looking up at my windows. I'm frightened."

"Okay, Dinah. It's all right. Who's the doorman tonight?"

"That's just it. He's a substitute. I don't even know his name."

"Regardless, he won't let the guy into the building," Eddie said.

"But the doorman doesn't know who the guy is! He might think the guy lives here!" Dinah was sobbing. "Eddie, I'm frightened. I'm really frightened."

Eddie took a deep breath and wondered if this was a really bad idea. Then she said, "Listen, Dinah. Why don't you come visit us in Nantucket?"

"Really?"

"You could stay with us. We have a guest room. I'll just have to move some books. And someone is almost always here, plus we have a dog."

"But what about your father? Your sister? Won't I be an intrusion?"

"Dad's writing his book and Barrett's opening her shop and I'll be doing a hundred other things, so I won't be able to, um, be your cook and everything, but you'll have a safe place to live and the island's got lots of great takeout."

"Eddie, thank you! I can never thank you enough! I won't bother you. I promise. I'll just stay in my room and write. I know you're busy with your family."

"I really am, Dinah. I've got to help my father and my sister. This is my first vacation in two years, and *you* will have to take care of yourself."

"Oh, I will, Eddie. I completely understand. You won't know I'm there. Eddie, I'm really grateful. I'd better hang up. I'll pack a few things and fly there tonight."

"Wait, Dinah! I'm not sure any airlines are flying from New York to Nantucket at night."

"I'll take the private jet. Heaven knows I pay enough to be in the consortium. I can be on Nantucket in an hour."

"Dinah. Slow down. Think. You need to get in touch with the admin and see if a pilot is available. They need to have some kind of advance warning. You need to pack. You'll need warm clothes, not winter clothes, but some sweaters—"

"Ooooh," Dinah wailed. "You always pack for me. I don't even know where my suitcases are."

"You can do this. First, you need to get in touch with the jet admin. They're open twenty-four hours a day. The number is on my phone. You should have it, too."

"I'll find it. I'll text you my information. And, Eddie, thank you. More than I can say, thank you. I love you, Eddie."

"Love you, too," Eddie said and ended the call. She turned to her father and sister. "Okay, I've done it. I invited Dinah to stay with us. She'll be here tomorrow."

Her phone buzzed again.

It was Dinah, sending a text message. *Can't get a plane until ten tomorrow morning. Will pack tonight. I've got to write a scene that just hit me. If I don't have time to pack, I'll just buy stuff on Nantucket.*

Barrett rose early, knowing the carpenters would be here soon. She pulled on white cropped jeans, a blue tank top, and flip-flops, made herself a cup of coffee, and sat out on the porch to ease into the day.

The morning air was fresh, almost sparkling in the sunlight. Birds were hopping from twig to branch and singing about their little bird lives. The horse came to the fence and tossed her head. Barrett walked down to the fence and scratched Duchess behind her ear. Duchess snorted and walked away.

Barrett knew Eddie was awake—she heard her taking coffee up to her room—and she had a pretty good idea what Eddie was doing.

She'd bet fifty dollars Eddie was writing in her journal. Eddie had kept a diary on and off all her life, especially during difficult times. When Dove's family moved away and Dove disappeared, Eddie had stayed in her room writing for hours. When Stearns died, Eddie wrote in her journal deep into the night. So many times, Barrett had seen the light under Eddie's bedroom door and wanted to go in and talk with her, but she stayed in her room, knowing Eddie's writing was therapeutic, and wishing she had the habit of journaling, too. But for her, the words would never come.

The kitchen door opened and Eddie leaned out. "Hey! Have you had breakfast?"

"I was waiting for you. I made coffee."

Barrett went into the house. Eddie, in jeans and an old T-shirt, her hair caught up in a leaf-green bandana, was putting slices of Portuguese bread in the toaster.

Barrett set two plates on the table, added a jar of Aunt Leah's cranberry honey, knives, spoons, and napkins.

"Beautiful day out there," Barrett said as the toast popped up.

"I hardly slept. I'm nervous about Dinah being here. She's pretty high maintenance."

"I'm nervous about Nantucket Blues," Barrett said.

"It will be amazing, Barrett! You're amazing. And once I get Dinah settled here, I'll do whatever you want me to do."

"Thanks, Eddie."

The sisters slathered the toast with butter, spread the cranberry honey, and munched in contented silence.

"I could eat this all day," Eddie said.

"Me, too," Barrett agreed.

Barrett put two more slices in the toaster. "So, Jeff will be here today."

"I know. I wonder what he'll think of Dinah." Eddie glanced at the kitchen clock. "She'll be here at eleven. I've got to put that bedroom in order."

"I'll help," Barrett mumbled as she chomped on her toast.

They set their plates in the dishwasher, washed the runaway honey off their hands, and went up to the guest bedroom. All the furniture was in the middle of the room, surrounded by stacks of books.

Eddie ran her hand along one shelf. "Whose books are these? *How to Knit with Dog Hair? Does God Ever Speak through Cats? How to Poison Your Husband with Natural Plants?* This is insane!"

"Are there unnatural plants?" Barrett mused.

Their father startled them. He stood in the doorway, dressed in khakis and a blue rugby shirt. He'd shaved and slapped on aftershave lotion.

Barrett raised her eyebrow at Eddie. It meant: *Are you thinking what I'm thinking?*

Eddie grinned and nodded. Dad was dressed to impress.

"Those books can all go," he announced. "I meant to get around to sorting them. When the library had its book sale, your mother and I took the leftovers home. Otherwise, they would have gone to the dump."

"And you brought them across Nantucket Sound and unpacked them and put them here?" Eddie shook her head. "You know that's crazy, right?"

Barrett held up a book. "You might want to keep this one, Dad. It's called *How to Write a Book in Ten Days.*"

William rolled his eyes. "That ship has sailed."

Eddie's phone buzzed.

"I'm boarding," Dinah yelled. She had a tendency when she was in an airport to speak loudly, thinking the connection was bad because of all the plane supercomputers. "I'll be there in an hour."

"I'll be waiting for you at the airport," Eddie told her. Ending the call, she gave her sister and father a helpless look and said, "I don't think we have time to get this room in shape."

"Nonsense," her father said. "I'll help you."

"Here come Jeff and Paul," Barrett cried. She went out to the porch and waved at the men. "Hey, guys, come help us move books."

Ten minutes later, they were all working together. Eddie carried a box from the bedroom, handed it to Barrett in the hall, who took it to her father in the kitchen, who took it out to the porch where Paul took it out to the barn and Jeff stacked it near a bin. Paul put his phone on top of the refrigerator and blasted out his classic rock playlist. In twenty minutes, most of the books were out of the bedroom. William made coffee and they all stood on the back porch, huffing and puffing.

"You guys are the best." Eddie noticed a spot under Jeff's chin that he'd missed when shaving. She wanted to kiss it. What? She shook her head. "I'd better finish the room."

"We'd better get to work," Jeff said.

Paul caught Barrett's eye. "If you need any more help, let me know."

Barrett said, "Thanks," and wanted to say more, although what she would say she didn't know. Paul's presence threw her mind into such a jumble. She picked up the coffee cups and went into the kitchen.

"I'm going up to finish the bedroom now," Eddie called.

Eddie returned to the bedroom, shoved the dresser and armchair into place, vacuumed, and made the bed with fresh sheets.

Barrett came into the room. "Didn't you say you had to pick her up at eleven?"

Eddie checked her watch. "Good grief, it's already ten-thirty." She started to race from the room, but stopped in front of her sister. "Thank you for helping this morning. I couldn't have done it without you."

"I know," Barrett replied, smirking. "Now you owe me big-time."

Eddie kissed her sister's cheek, grabbed her keys from the hook, and hurried out to her car.

Barrett went into the kitchen. Her father was there, his computer case in his hand, reaching for *his* car keys from the hook on the wall.

"Dad? Where are you going?"

"To the library. I need to focus on my book, and it's going to be noisy here."

Barrett watched him go, then called Eddie. "I think Dad's nervous about meeting Dinah. He's gone to the library to work."

Eddie had her phone set in the dashboard mount. "That's so funny. I never imagined this, but I bet Dinah's going to rock his world."

Barrett heard a loud thud. "The guys have started hammering. See you later."

She walked to the barn, allowing herself to check Paul out while he was intent on pounding nails into a board. He wore work boots, canvas carpenter trousers with a loop for a hammer, and a white T-shirt. When Barrett entered the barn, Paul noticed and walked toward her. He was tall and muscular, and his dark hair spouted up in the opening of the baseball cap he wore backward.

When he smiled down at her, Barrett completely forgot what she'd intended to say.

"I'll bet you want to know how the quarterboard's going," Paul said.

"Yes! Yes, that's what I was wondering." She took a breath, regaining her composure. "I'm headed into the shop now to get it ready for tonight. The grand opening. Maybe you could hang the sign this evening?" She took another breath.

"I'll be there," Paul told her. "I think we should make a big deal of it. Like, I'll hang the quarterboard and you invite Eddie and your friends and we'll all toast with champagne. Lots of photo opportunities for your social media. You're taking online orders, aren't you?"

"I am, but I hadn't thought of a grand opening with champagne. What a wonderful idea!"

Paul grinned. "I'm full of wonderful ideas."

Her knees went weak. Was he hitting on her? Because she was way overheated. She managed to say, "Oh, good."

From the barn, Jeff yelled, "Paul! You've got to hold this end!"

"See you later," Paul told Barrett, and walked off.

Barrett watched him walk. He had slim hips, long legs, wide shoulders.

This summer promised to be interesting, she thought, as she got into her Jeep and drove into town.

Memorial Day was late this year, at the very end of the month of May. Summer people were already arriving to open their houses.

Barrett parked her car near Commercial Wharf and walked to Lower Main Street and her small rented shopfront. DogCatLove, with treats, brushes, water bowls, leashes, and even a few dog bikinis, was open. The owner, Kari Golden, was polishing her window to a shine. She waved at Barrett. In the sunglasses shop, the lights were on and the owner, an older man wearing a plaid bow tie, yelled into his cellphone. The door to Aunt Leah's Fudge was thrown wide and irresistible scents drifted out into the fresh spring air.

Barrett stopped to study her window. She needed to place the small nautical paperweights higher on the glass shelves. She'd put a blue straw sun hat and a necklace of seashell earrings on the foam mannequin's head. She'd tied a blue scarf around the neck. Cashmere sweaters in shades of azure, turquoise, and sky blue lay against one another. All very Nantucket summer.

And her quarterboard would go up above the door tonight. She checked the weather on her phone. Miraculously, the weekend forecast was for dry, clear, and mild.

"*Yes!*" she said.

"Good morning!" The UPS deliveryman was at her door, his arms full of boxes.

"Hi, Arnie!" She unlocked her door and followed him to the room at the back of her shop, which was full of cardboard boxes, tissue paper, price tags and stickers, a broom and dustpan, a supersize bottle of Windex, rolls of receipt paper, and a cornflower blue tray holding matching cups, a sugar bowl, and a milk pitcher. Eddie had sent her the set months ago when Barrett told her she'd signed the papers renting the space.

Arnie set down her boxes and left. Barrett just stared at them for a moment. The stack was almost as high as she was. She felt like it was Christmas in May, even though she'd ordered all the merchandise.

Maybe, Barrett thought in a burst of optimism, just *maybe* it would work out nicely to have Eddie's boss staying with them. What if their father liked Dinah? That was not beyond the realm of possibility. Barrett imagined the two of them kayaking side by side in the inner harbor, lying on the beach, reading each other's work and discussing it. And Eddie could go to a play or a party or somewhere with Jeff, and Barrett could date Drew . . . or Paul. Drew *and* Paul?

Plus, her dream was coming true. She was about to open her very own shop!

She couldn't stop smiling.

Eddie parked her car as close to the airport entrance as she could get. Today, the last Sunday in May, crowds were descending on the island to open their summer houses. A Cape Air plane from Boston landed a few minutes before Dinah's.

Dinah arrived in a sleek Citation Bravo jet that carried only seven passengers. She descended from the plane looking like a flower among a clump of weeds.

When she sold her first romance novel, Dinah Lavender had decided to base her image on Barbara Cartland, the British romance writer who had been an English debutante and, rumor said, had been friends with the Queen Mother. It was a style that hugged Dinah's curvaceous body. Red was her favorite color; it suited her glossy black hair. Today, she was very restrained in a lavender dress (lavender was her other favorite color) with a matching cape, and she looked very Elizabeth Taylor. Her hair was held back by a wide headband, and her sunglasses were large. She carried a small handbag and had her lavender quilted computer case slung over her shoulder.

Dinah spotted Eddie and eased her way through the other passengers toward her. She threw her arms around Eddie.

"Oh, Eddie, thank heavens, you are an angel from paradise, you have no idea what this means to me. I've been so frightened, so terribly worried. I've actually lost weight!"

Eddie hugged Dinah tight. "You'll be fine here. Come on. Let's find your luggage."

"Of course! I've brought only three suitcases."

Three Louis Vuitton suitcases sat alone in the baggage bin. Eddie wrestled them onto the floor. They were small, but heavy. That didn't necessarily mean Dinah was planning to stay for the summer.

"You drove, right? Or do we have a limo waiting? Where are the porters?"

"I drove, Dinah. No porters here. We can manage." Eddie coaxed Dinah into pulling one of the suitcases. Eddie pulled the other two.

"The flight was so restful," Dinah said. "The other passengers were all businessmen who made no attempt at conversation. I mean, they had no who idea who I am, which was slightly insulting. But at least the stalker didn't follow me."

"I know you're safe here." Eddie beeped the Jeep's hatch open and lifted the three suitcases inside. As Dinah settled into the passenger seat, Eddie noticed her Manolo Blahniks. "Dinah, I hope you brought some sensible shoes. I think I've mentioned that the sidewalks are brick and the streets are cobblestone. The easiest way to sprain an ankle is to get a heel caught between bricks."

"I brought several pairs of flats and sandals," Dinah replied, tucking her flowing skirt in around her.

"I'm taking you home so you can get settled," Eddie told her. "Remember, my family is eccentric and every room is stacked with books."

"That sounds absolutely heavenly to me," Dinah answered.

"My sister has already gone into her shop. You'll meet her later. She's getting ready for the grand opening tonight."

Dinah fastened her seatbelt and smoothed her skirt. "I've seen posts of Nantucket Blues on my social media. Brilliant idea!"

It took only fifteen minutes, much of it spent bumping over dirt roads, to wind through the back streets to the Grant farm off Hummock Pond Road. As she entered their driveway, Eddie was pleased with what she saw. Trees fluttered fresh green leaves and dozens of tulips embroidered the front of the house.

Dinah stepped out of the Jeep and looked around. "Oh, my. It's certainly not the city out here."

Eddie couldn't tell if that was a compliment or an insult, but before she could decide, Dinah cooed, "Who are *they*?"

Eddie followed Dinah's gaze. Dinah had spotted Jeff and Paul, working in the barn. Of course she had.

"They're carpenters." Eddie beeped the hatch open and lifted the suitcases onto the gravel drive. "They're building book bins for the used bookstore we're persuading our father to open."

"Where is he getting used books?" Dinah asked. She fluffed her hair and smoothed her dress. Without waiting for a response from Eddie, she carefully stepped through the gravel toward the men.

Little Lavender Riding Hood, Eddie thought, *hoping those men are wolves.*

Jeff noticed Dinah. He set down his hammer and walked out toward the women. He wore a T-shirt, canvas pants, work boots, and around his hips, a tool belt, one of the sexiest pieces of apparel on earth.

"Hi," Jeff called. "Hey, Eddie, who's your friend?"

Dinah didn't wait for Eddie to speak. She minced her way up to Jeff and said in a breathy voice, "I'm Dinah Lavender. Eddie might have mentioned me to you. Eddie is my assistant."

Eddie couldn't hide a grin when she saw Dinah's face. Jeff was straight out of one of Dinah's books, her hardworking, tough-talking, rough-living hero with a heart of gold.

Dinah held out her hand.

Jeff hesitated.

"I'm kind of dust-covered. Sawdust, but still."

"Oh, I never mind a little dust," Dinah said, and shook his hand.

Paul joined the group. Dinah patted her chest as if trying to slow her heart.

"Hi, Ms. Lavender. I'm Paul. I'm helping Jeff build the book bins."

Paul wasn't wearing a tool belt, and he was a good two inches shorter than Jeff, but he had pirate eyes.

"Oh, I'm so glad you men like books, because I *write* books!" Dinah batted her eyelashes.

Behind her, Eddie rolled her eyes.

"I'm coming to stay with Eddie because . . . Oh, well, never mind, we won't dwell on scary things out there and no one is going to stalk me with you two big men around."

Feeling mischievous, Eddie cooed, "Maybe you big strong men would like to help carry Dinah's luggage to her room?"

"Absolutely," Jeff said.

Eddie led the way, up the slate walk to the steps to the porch and into the house. She paused in the front hall.

"A word of warning," Eddie said to Dinah. "This house is crowded with books. My father's writing a book about the English Romantic poets, and he does a lot of research."

Dinah nearly fainted. "Romantic poetry! I can't wait to meet him!"

"Let's go to your room," Eddie suggested.

She led the writer and her big strong men up the stairs and down the hall, their passage punctuated by the sounds of the luggage hitting the books piled everywhere. When they arrived at the room, which looked spacious now with all the books removed, Dinah walked around, appraising her surroundings.

"I don't mean to be picky, and I'm so grateful to you, Eddie, but why is the closet so small?" Dinah asked.

Eddie nodded, noting how the New York Dinah was being replaced by the Southern Belle Dinah. "When Dad bought the house, he had carpenters cut out part of the closet to put in an en suite bathroom." She quickly added, "You could always go to a hotel . . ."

Dinah waved her hand dismissively. "I don't want to go to a hotel.

I'm so grateful to be here, Eddie. This room is perfect." She opened her purse and attempted to hand money to Jeff, who stepped back, shaking his head, and then to Paul, who kept his hands in his pockets and blushed.

"You don't have to pay us," Jeff said. "We were happy to help. We've got to get back to work now."

The men hurried away, their work boots clomping on the floor as they went down the stairs.

"Sit down a minute, Dinah," Eddie said, wrenching the writer's attention away from the men. "I want to tell you what's going on here. Dad and I are going to the grand opening of Nantucket Blues tonight. Barrett's going to hand out little gift bags to anyone who shows up. I'm going to go into town early to help her prepare. If you want to join us tonight, you're welcome, but don't feel you have to come. Barrett and I will probably be busy this afternoon. So, you're on your own. The refrigerator and pantry are stocked if you get hungry. If you need to go into town, call an Uber or a cab. Don't ask Jeff—"

"He seems sweet on you," Dinah interjected.

"You think so?" Eddie lost her train of thought for a moment. "Anyway, let me show you around the house."

As Eddie led Dinah into the living room, dining room, and kitchen, Dinah stopped to scan the shelves of books. Eddie tried to hurry Dinah along because she wanted to go help Barrett. She was relieved when Dinah confessed that she was tired and wanted to take a little nap.

"I had to wake up so early today. I had a limo waiting to take me to the airport, but you know how congested the traffic is. I feel like I flew here on my own wings. Remind me to hire a helicopter if I ever want to come here again."

Back in Dinah's room, Eddie assured her boss that the sheets were clean, the bureau drawers empty, and the closet held plenty of hangers. Dinah sank onto the bed with a sigh. She eased off her shoes, pulled the mohair blanket up over her shoulders, and closed her eyes. "Thank you, Eddie. I haven't felt so safe since you left."

"I'll be back this afternoon."

"That's fine. And I've got those big strong men working out there to make me feel secure."

"Yes, you're totally safe," Eddie assured her.

She left the house, jumped into her Jeep, and drove quickly to Lower Main. Because it was late May, Eddie easily found a parking spot. She opened the door to the backseat and took out the gift she'd been hiding beneath an old sweater. The large package, beautifully wrapped, held a cappuccino machine and a box of pods and packets of sugar. She carried it with both hands and used her elbow to knock on the door of Nantucket Blues.

Barrett opened the door and screamed with delight when Eddie gave her the machine. They set it up on the counter in the back, near the sink. Barrett made a cup for each of them and they drank and chatted as they filled Nantucket Blues bags with white tissue paper and blue gifts: a tiny blue glass whale, a blue swirled bangle bracelet, a blue ballpoint pen with blue ink, and individually wrapped blueberry lollipops. Eddie shot lots of photos of the store, the shelves piled with shawls and sweaters, the gift bags, and posted them on social media.

As they worked, Barrett said, "I just had a thought. Do you think Dad will feel funny around Dinah?"

"No. She's charming. Why would he?"

"Because she turns out three books a year and he's been working for years and still hasn't finished his. Plus, her books make money."

"We'll see. Let's focus on your shop."

It was almost three in the afternoon when Barrett decided everything was ready for the grand opening.

"Let's go home and get beautiful!" Barrett said.

eight

They arrived back at the farm to find Dinah in her room, wearing full war paint and a sky blue skintight sexy-bodice dress.

Dinah swooped down to hug Barrett. "Look at you! Such a beauty! Thank you for allowing me to stay with you for a few days. I'm *so* grateful."

Barrett was dazzled by Dinah. "We're glad you're here."

"If I may break into this lovefest," Eddie said, "Barrett, we have to shower and change."

"Just one question, Eddie. Will I be allowed to accompany you? Should I call a limo?" Dinah blinked her long eyelashes and made a dimple.

"You can ride in with me," Eddie said. "Barrett will take her own car. She'll probably stay longer than we will, or go out for drinks with friends."

"Lovely. I'll wait for you in my room. I found a book by Georgette Heyer and believe it or not, I've never read her. You don't mind if I borrow the book to read, do you?"

"We don't mind if you eat the book," Eddie joked.

"Yes," Barrett agreed. "Have them all."

They took turns showering, then got together in Barrett's room to dress. When they looked out the window, they noticed that Jeff and Paul had closed the barn doors and left for the day.

Barrett was giddy. "I'm shaking, Eddie! I can't wait for Paul to bring my quarterboard."

"He must have worked fast and late to get anything resembling a quarterboard done." Eddie leaned close to the bedroom mirror to put on her eyeliner and mascara.

"I know. Isn't he nice?" Barrett put on a pair of blue topaz earrings.

"He's not just nice, Barrett. He likes you. And he seems like a really good guy."

"Gosh!" Barrett held up her phone. "Drew texted. He's coming to the island this evening to be at my official shop opening!"

Eddie grinned. "You have admiring men all around you."

"Well, wouldn't *that* be nice!" Barrett said.

When they were finally dressed and ready, the women went out to Eddie's car and settled in. Barrett wore a simple blue linen dress with her blue topaz earrings and had to pull her skirt up in order to step up into her Jeep. Eddie wore a Lilly Pulitzer dress with swirls of blues that swirled even more as she got in. Dinah had added a heavy necklace of turquoise and matching earrings to her sky blue dress.

Dinah said, "Aren't we all a perfect bundle of blue publicizing Barrett's shop?"

"Yes, Dinah," Eddie agreed. "We'll have you walk up and down the street. People will follow you as if you were the Pied Piper."

Dinah shivered. "I always hated that children's tale. It's creepy."

They were fastening their seatbelts when William's tan Land Rover turned in to the drive. He drove past the women and parked.

Jumping out of his vehicle, he called to Barrett, "I'll clean up and be at your shop in time for the grand opening."

Barrett waved at her father. "Thanks, Dad!"

"See you there," Eddie yelled.

William strode into the house without responding to Eddie or glancing at her passenger.

"That was your father?" Dinah asked. "Oh, my. No wonder you girls are so gorgeous."

"You'll meet him later," Eddie assured her. She started her Jeep, backed out of the driveway, and headed for town.

The summer season hadn't started, so Lower Main had a few empty spaces. Together the three women walked across the street and up the brick sidewalk to the shop with a window as blue as a summer sky.

Barrett unlocked the door to Nantucket Blues and they entered.

Dinah stopped in the doorway. "This is fabulous! Like an underwater grotto! Why, look at this ring! I want to buy everything in the store!"

Barrett flicked on the lights and the small electric oil-filled heater. "Just to get it warmed up a bit," she told the others.

"Ohhh," Dinah breathed, "here comes Paul! And Jeff! Hellll-loooo!" she called, waving.

Jeff carried a ladder and a toolbox. Paul carried the quarterboard at his side. He was three yards away when he turned the wooden sign around so the women could see it.

"Wow!" Barrett exclaimed. "Paul, you're wonderful!"

It was ten until five when Jeff set up the ladder and held it so that Paul could attach the sign above the door to the store. He swiveled on the ladder, smiling down at Barrett.

"Okay? Is it straight?"

"Wait! Wait!" Eddie snapped photos on her phone.

"Oh, goodie!" Dinah clapped her hands. "I was afraid they'd arrive too late."

"Who?" Eddie asked.

Three handsome caterers wheeled a small table toward them. Covered in a white linen tablecloth, it held two buckets of champagne on ice, dozens of plastic glasses, and platters of blue cheese, crackers, and blueberry muffins. Blue balloons filled with helium bobbed from the table.

"Congratulations!" one of the caterers said, stationing the table against the shop, just below the picture window.

"What's this?" Barrett asked, completely puzzled.

"Something in honor of your grand opening," Dinah declared, looking very pleased with herself.

Eddie was shocked. "How did you manage to arrange this?"

Dinah gloated. "I'm not completely without computer skills. I did it all on my little phone."

"Dinah, thank you!" Barrett said.

Paul came down the ladder and stood next to Barrett, looking up at the sign. "Do you like it?"

"It's wonderful, Paul! Thank you!" Barrett threw her arms around him in a quick hug.

"Barrett, look this way!" Trudy Ellison, a local photographer, snapped shots of the crowd, the table of champagne and munchies, the sign, and lots of shots of Barrett.

Dinah sidled close to Jeff. "You were so helpful, holding that ladder. It would have been awful if Paul had fallen. Why, I could just hug you."

Before Jeff could respond, Dinah threw her arms around him and kissed his cheek. "Oooh," she cooed. "You're all bristly."

The waiters opened the champagne. A small crowd gathered on the street, obviously curious.

Dinah noticed them. "Hello, everyone! Welcome to the opening of Nantucket Blues! Please come join us for our little celebration! The champagne is free and so are the delicious munchies." She popped one in her mouth and moaned her appreciation.

Several women approached the table and accepted glasses of champagne.

"I love your headband," Dinah told a pretty brunette. "It's such a pretty blue. Would you mind if we took a photo of you inside the shop? We'd use it on Nantucket Blues's Facebook page."

"Cool," the brunette said.

She and her friends entered the shop. Dinah bustled around, placing them strategically in front of the wall of blue scarves as she snapped photos. The women went wild over the scarves and Dinah subtly directed their attention to the jewelry case. Barrett slid into the shop. She went behind the counter and began taking credit cards, wrapping purchases in pale blue tissue, and tucking them into elegant bags with the Nantucket Blues name on the sides.

Eddie waited outside the shop, offering champagne to passersby. Women were bustling out of the shop with Nantucket Blues bags on their arms. As they came out, more women went in.

A handsome man with blond hair and Nantucket blue eyes approached. He wore chinos, a blue button-down shirt, and leather loafers without socks.

Eddie stepped forward to greet him. "Hi, there! You must be Drew. I'm Eddie, Barrett's older and wiser sister."

"Nice to meet you, Eddie," Drew said. "Quite a crowd Barrett has for her opening."

"I know. I'm so proud of her. She said you were her first customer." Eddie wondered how she could ease Drew through the mob and into the shop to have his photo taken with Barrett. "Oh! You should meet Paul. He made that gorgeous quarterboard for Barrett."

Paul heard his name and walked over. "It's not a real quarterboard."

"Whatever it is, it's eye-catching." Drew held out his hand. "Drew Fischer."

"Paul Folger. I'm an islander. Born here. I'd guess you're from the mainland?"

Drew grinned. "I look like it, don't I. I work in Boston, but I've summered here all my life. I've been here for holidays, too."

Paul said, "You have the best of both worlds. The winters can be long here. I usually go skiing at Tahoe or down to Costa Rica."

"Smart man."

Eddie pretended to watch the crowd while she listened in on their conversation. Drew sounded pleasant enough, not arrogant or patronizing. He seemed slightly older than Barrett. He was handsome. But so was Paul, and Paul was a normal person, and Barrett needed normal. Her sister didn't need a romantic disaster now that she was starting her own business. Drew might be more complicated than Barrett needed right now.

She faced the men. "If you're hoping to see Barrett, you'll have a long wait. It's amazing that she has so many customers. It's a great start for her shop. Maybe you should come back and see her tomorrow."

Paul looked at his watch. "That's a good idea. I'm starting early tomorrow. I'll head off now."

"Thank you so much for that amazing sign!" Eddie hugged Paul tight.

Jeff joined the group. "Do I get a hug, too?" he asked Eddie.

"Absolutely." Eddie stood on tiptoe, put her arms around his neck, and pressed against him.

Oh, it felt good.

"I could use some more of this," Jeff whispered in her ear.

Eddie's heart melted, just a bit. "I need to concentrate on Barrett now." She quickly stepped away from Jeff and pasted a smile on her face.

Eddie saw some Nantucket women Barrett's age joining the crowd and her heart lifted. In a way, this felt like the year Eddie walked Barrett into kindergarten. Their mother had been busy elsewhere, or still asleep, so Eddie had been the one holding her little sister's hand when they rode the school bus and they entered the big hallway bursting with laughing, shouting children. Barrett had huddled close to Eddie. And when they got to the door of her classroom, Eddie had reassured Barrett she would have fun, and watched her enter the room, her little shoulders tense with worry and hope.

Barrett had been fine then, more than fine. And she was certainly doing well today. Her cheeks were rosy with excitement.

The crowd was thinning out when Eddie spotted her father. He'd put on his faded Nantucket red slacks and a navy rugby shirt. He was tall and slender, with thick caramel-colored hair that all his children had inherited. Eddie was pleased and somewhat startled to catch all the admiring and even flirtatious glances several women were giving him.

He has no idea, Eddie realized. She'd known he lived in his own literary world, and she'd known he hid there after that terrible year, but she hadn't realized he was still sequestered there. How could she coax him out into real life? She needed him to understand that he could have a rich life in the real present without dishonoring the events of the past.

"Hi, Dad!" Eddie waved at him, beckoning him toward her. She set her champagne glass on the table and squeezed through the chattering women.

"Oh, my, you must be the brilliant William Grant."

Eddie stopped dead as she watched Dinah saunter up to her father. *Ah,* Eddie thought. *If Dinah can't entice Dad into the present, no one can.*

As Eddie watched, her father froze. It had been a long time since he'd been near a living, breathing, smiling, sexy woman, and it seemed like her father didn't know quite what to do.

Dinah didn't seem worried. She held out a plump hand. "I'm Dinah Lavender. Your lovely, brilliant daughter is my assistant, and she is beyond fabulous."

Totally out of his depth, but knowing he had to respond somehow, William asked, "Is your last name really Lavender?"

Dinah laughed. "Why, of course it's not. I think Dinah Lavender just sounds so pretty that people want to read my books. Just like William Grant sounds so historical and intelligent that people want to read *your* books."

William turned red and made a choking sound and coughed. "I'm writing a comprehensive criticism of eighteenth-century British poets. My name isn't . . . a selling point. And I certainly won't have a large readership. Excuse me. I want to say hello to my daughter."

Eddie hurried over to Dinah as her father escaped into the shop.

"Dad didn't mean to be rude," she explained. "He's just out of practice with socializing."

"He did look like a rabbit caught in a hole," Dinah agreed. "I'm thinking he might be the perfect new project for me." She twinkled her fingers at Eddie and headed for the drinks table.

Eddie watched the writer chat with the waiters who manned the table. It was such a relief to see Dinah back to her normal self, not paranoid because she thought a man was stalking her. This relaxed, stress-free Dinah enjoyed flirting with any and all men. She glowed and glimmered like a star, and men just naturally smiled back. Dinah turned even a brief meeting into a memorable moment. Like her books, Dinah was radiant and sensual and addictive.

Eddie glided away from the crowd. She walked around to the brick sidewalk overlooking the first boat slip and sat on a wooden bench, looking out at the water. The sun flooded the harbor with light. A few gulls stood on the pilings, arranging their feathers. Cormorants bobbed in the water. A fishing boat with its high tower was slowly sliding into the harbor, its gentle wake rippling toward shore, rocking the ducks.

She put on her sunglasses and relaxed. Dinah was having fun this evening, but she would probably grow bored with the quiet and return to the city before two weeks were up. Eddie would bet on that. Her father was, so far, okay with the boxes of books that left the house and went into the Book Barn, and the book bins were almost done.

She needed to think whether she should ask Jeff to build some kind of counter for a cash box and a credit card machine. Who would run the Book Barn? Not Barrett. She would be right here, in her own store. Maybe Eddie could convince their father to man the barn bookshop on the weekends. People wouldn't be stampeding down the driveway to buy used books. Yes, it was a good idea! William could spend Saturday and Sunday in the barn, selling his dusty old books, and he would also be talking to people, people who liked books. It would be a kind of therapy for him.

Eddie would stay for the summer, she decided. They'd only made a start in decluttering the house of books. Eddie could get the Book Barn business launched. Eddie could spend some time with Dinah, helping her plan the next few months.

Laughter from Barrett's opening party drifted across the cool evening air. Eddie smiled. She was so glad her sister's store was working out.

"I thought I'd find you here."

Jeff sat on the bench, not too close to Eddie, but not too far away, either. He held a plastic glass of champagne and handed it to her.

"Thanks." Eddie took a sip. Wow. Dinah had splurged on the champagne. "Barrett must be thrilled by the crowd."

"She should be. People are still coming in."

Jeff stretched, sending an alluring scent of testosterone and shaving cream past Eddie. She remembered this aroma even now, after two years away. It had been pure Jeff, when he kissed her on the beach.

"The bins for the barn are almost done," Jeff told her. "I'm thinking it would be cool if we built a few tables, for coffee-table books laid face up."

"That's a wonderful idea." Eddie turned to study him. His face and hands were already tanned from working outside, and scars from working stitched across his hands.

Jeff caught her gaze. "So. Life in the big city."

Eddie nodded. He was so near, she felt too hypnotized to speak.

"From time to time, while you were gone, I ran into Barrett. She told me what an exciting life you were living. Paris. London. Meeting novelists. You were moving in the fast lane."

Eddie found her voice. "I was. I've had an amazing time. It's what I'd always dreamed about."

He studied her. "You think you want to live that way for the rest of your life?"

"I thought I did," Eddie told him. "Now I'm not so sure." She met Jeff's eyes and the moment of honesty they shared took her breath away. She wanted him to kiss her like he had on the beach. After more than two years away, that was the kiss she remembered.

"Hi, kids!" Dinah swooped down on them, glittering with excitement. "A bunch of us are going to Le Languedoc for dinner. I called and made reservations. It's getting late and Barrett is closing the shop. The boys have taken the goodies away. The champagne was completely gone, so we decided we should go, too. Come on!"

Well, Eddie thought, no chance of privacy with Dinah here.

And that was probably a good thing. Eddie was so close to embracing Jeff, kissing him like they'd kissed before, and promising things she'd regret.

She smiled at Jeff. "Come with us."

Jeff stood up and addressed Eddie and Dinah at the same time. "Sorry, ladies, but I've got some work to do."

"I understand, but we'll miss having you," Eddie said, trying to hide her disappointment.

The three trooped back to the shop. It was quiet on the wharf now, even though the sun hadn't set. People were at dinner or enjoying cocktails.

"I'll see you tomorrow," Eddie said to Jeff, who saluted her and walked away.

"I'll meet you there," Dinah called to Eddie. She joined a group of brand-new friends and walked up toward town.

Barrett came out of her shop and carefully locked the door. Paul and Drew were gone. Their father had left as well.

The two sisters stood together in the sudden quiet.

"It's happening," Barrett whispered. She leaned against Eddie. "It's really happening."

"Congratulations, sis," Eddie said. "You did it."

"I'm doing it," Barrett agreed. "And it's a dream come true."

nine

Memorial Day flew past in a blur of backyard barbecues, flags flying from shingled houses, a parade with veterans of past wars, people flocking to the beaches to start their summer tans and later, rushing to the pharmacies to buy ointment for their sunburns. The wind was mild, the sun was high, and during the clear nights people went to movies, plays, restaurants, and beach parties or sat on their porches to watch the stars in the summer sky.

For the next few days, Jeff and Paul dropped by for an hour or two to work on the book bins, shelves, and tables. Barrett worked in her shop. William was never around, leaving the house early, eating breakfast at the Downyflake, and working in the Atheneum in the middle of the town. In the mornings, Dinah wrote in her room, while Eddie culled books from the house. The horse ate the new green grass and raced around the field, obviously loving the new season. In the evenings, Dinah called an Uber and went into town, returning home late.

Dinah and William had met, officially. They'd shaken hands and used their best manners, but they never spent time together. Just the opposite. They seemed to be trying to avoid each other.

One afternoon, a storm with gale force wind swooped down, shrieking and bellowing and streaming rivers of rain. Jeff and Paul shut the wide barn doors and took off. Dinah lay on the living room sofa, calling her city friends, getting caught up on the gossip. Eddie made a beef stew and chocolate chip cookies, while singing along with her playlist.

Barrett closed her shop at five, because no one was daring to come out in the downpour. She was completely soaked from running from her shop to her car. The tide was high and flooding the island's lower streets. Two boys were canoeing down Easy Street. She drove home through the torrent, glad for a break from work. She ran into the house, called hello, and raced upstairs to shower and dry her hair. She pulled on sweats and moccasins and joined Eddie and Dinah in the living room.

The three women were trying to decide which movie to stream when William came home.

They heard him remove his raincoat and cap—he'd checked the weather report that morning and been prepared. With his briefcase in hand, he walked into the living room.

Dinah was there, in leggings and a lilac-colored sweater. She was curled up at one end of the sofa, her toes with their pink polish flashing as she moved.

She gestured to the seat next to her.

"Come join us," Dinah said. "We'd enjoy the company of the famous father!"

William took a step back. "No, thanks. I have to work."

"You can't work all day," Dinah told him. "Has your publisher put you under a deadline?"

William's face reddened. Eddie and Barrett knew he didn't have a publisher yet.

"I haven't decided on a publisher yet. Several literary houses are interested, but it's taking longer than I thought. Excuse me." He turned on his heel and walked out of the room. They heard his study door slam.

Dinah smiled winsomely at the sisters. "I don't think he likes me."

"Don't worry about him," Eddie said. "He's becoming a hermit."

"He's really a nice man," Barrett told Dinah. "He'll be nicer when he gets a little more work done. Plus, it bothers him that we're moving so many books out of the house."

"Writers are very protective of their fiefdoms." Dinah sank back onto the sofa. "Now. Which movie are we going to watch?"

For the next few days, Eddie drove Dinah around the island, showing her the Sankaty lighthouse, the 'Sconset Bluff Walk, the old mill, and in town, the Nantucket Historical Association. In the evenings, after Barrett closed her shop, the three women dined at Galley Beach or Le Languedoc, Topper's, Brant Point Grill, or American Seasons. Dinah insisted on paying for it all, which was just fine with Eddie and Barrett. The sisters both texted their father, asking him to join them. He always replied that he was busy.

One morning, Eddie woke to find that Dinah was already up and out. Eddie poured herself a cup of coffee and went out to the back porch to watch. Dinah, in a sundress and espadrilles, was in the barn, chatting with Jeff and Paul. When she noticed Eddie, she waved and came up to the porch.

"Good morning," Eddie greeted her.

Dinah said, "Darling, I've been checking out your bookstore and really, it's so dreary, too *bare*. It needs some color, some comfort. You're not selling old books, you're selling the vision of curling up in an armchair to read an old favorite or a new book you've only heard about and aren't sure you want to buy in hardback but don't mind spending a few dollars on. You need to make the shop a place where people want to relax, stroll, dream."

What we want is to get enough books out of the house so it looks like sane people live there, Eddie thought. She asked, "How do we do that?"

Without pausing, Dinah said, "I've made a list. Two lists, actually. This list is what we need to acquire. A big old rug, Persian, if possible, some armchairs, some standing lamps. Jeff and Paul are going to ask a friend to put in a new electric circuit breaker with lamp cords taped to the floor and covered with rugs so that there will be enough light for people to read by."

"Dinah." Eddie was no longer amused. "We can't afford an electrician in the summer."

Dinah waved her hand. "Never mind. I promised to pay the bill as a thank-you gift for allowing me to be your guest. Also, the men are going to build a special bookcase and paint it lavender with gold trim, and I'm donating an entire set of my books to draw people to your shop."

"Wow, Dinah, that's incredibly kind. But they'll disappear quickly."

"I know. So, I'll send more. You know I have boxes in storage. Now. Here is my list of tag sales happening on the island. I've marked the days and places on my calendar. In the meantime, we'll go to the Seconds Shop and the Thrift Shop to see what we can find."

Eddie shook her head. "Dinah, this is so kind of you. Aren't you planning to return to New York?"

"If you don't mind, I thought I'd stay a little longer. I'm enjoying myself so much. Harriet Lancaster—she was at Barrett's grand opening—invited me to speak at her book club. Also, I've noticed several important writers are coming to the island to give talks for fundraisers, and I don't want to miss those." Dinah checked the lists on her phone. "Oh, one other thing. Could you drive me to the airport? I've rented a car for the summer."

Eddie swallowed. "You rented a car for the summer?"

"If you don't mind."

Was that anxiety making Dinah's voice tremble?

In a flash of comprehension, Eddie saw how her family must seem to Dinah. Three people living together, working together, arguing together, sharing meals together. Dinah felt safe here, but also knew clearly that she was not part of the picture.

Maybe beneath all that glamour, Dinah yearned to belong to a family.

Eddie quickly hugged Dinah. "This is so cool! You'll be here for the summer!"

Blushing, Dinah said, "Well, maybe not for the entire summer. We'll see."

"All right, come on then. Let's go rent a car."

At the airport, she accompanied Dinah to the rental counter. Dinah signed some papers, was given some keys, and walked out with the clerk to find her car in the rental lot.

It was a silver Mercedes.

Eddie grinned. Of course it was a silver Mercedes. She was surprised Dinah hadn't specified one in pink. She got into her Jeep and waved to Dinah, who followed Eddie back to the farm.

During the first two weeks of June, families arrived on the island with their cars, housekeepers, chefs, and assistants. Other summer people arrived with an ever-changing cast of grandchildren. The luggage carts for the ferries held golf clubs, tennis rackets, boogie boards, paddleboards, fishing poles, and kayaks. The sun stayed high in the sky and the wind took a nap.

Eddie sorted through books in the mornings while Dinah wrote. In the afternoon, they drove around the island looking for treasures at tag sales. Jeff and Paul stopped by to put the finishing touches on the standing bookshelves Dinah required. Most evenings, Dinah took Eddie and Barrett, and sometimes Jeff and Paul, out to dinner. Eddie kept insisting they could cook at home, but Dinah loved being around people, and actually, it was very nice to enjoy delicious meals, fine wine, and good conversation. Eddie admitted it was also very nice not to have dishes to wash.

The more books Eddie and Dinah took out to the Book Barn, the more they found. Not just on top of sofas and bureaus, but under them.

The more they found, the more they wanted to keep.

Bunnicula. The Celery Stalks at Midnight.

One day, just for a change, they decided to check out the attic. They climbed the steep stairs to the large dusty room. Light shone in from windows on each end.

The first things they found were cardboard boxes marked: SABRI-NA'S BOOKS.

"Your father will want to keep these," Dinah said. "In case your mother comes back."

Eddie snorted. "They're divorced, Dinah. She's never coming back." She unfolded the flaps on the top box. "Good grief!"

"But *look!*" Dinah clasped her hands in front of her as if she was praying. "Victoria Holt!"

"I've never read her. I didn't know Mom read her. She's, like, out-dated. We can toss all of these."

"Are you *kidding?*" Dinah snatched several books from the box and held them to her chest. "*The Shivering Sands? Mistress of Mellyn? The Demon Lover?* Eddie, truly, you need to read her. Start with this book." She handed Eddie *Bride of Pendorric.* "Just disregard your preconceptions and surrender to her."

Eddie laughed. "You sound like a romance writer."

"I *am* a romance writer, and proud of it!" Dinah sneezed. "I've got to get some tissues. Shall I bring us both a bottle of sparkling water?"

"Good idea."

While Dinah carefully went down the steep stairs, Eddie opened the book Dinah had handed her. She wasn't going to read the silly thing, but it was like opening a secret door into her mother's life.

She read the first line of the novel.

I often marveled after I went to Pendorric that one's existence could change so swiftly, so devastatingly.

Well. Eddie thought of Stearns.

She thought of her mother leaving them.

When Dinah returned with the water, she found Eddie on the floor, leaning against a tower of boxes, reading.

Eddie smiled at Dinah. "This certainly isn't a self-help book."

Dinah handed Eddie a bottle of Poland Spring. "All books are self-help books," she said, with a smile. "Actually, I just remembered a small scene I wanted to put in my new book. I'd better go down and write before I forget it. I'll be back up in a while."

The summer deepened. They came and went according to their own schedules. After an hour of doing emails for Dinah, Eddie drove out to Bartlett's Farm to buy farm-made casseroles, pies, and vegetables, and over to the Nantucket Meat & Fish Market to buy steaks or fish, returning to fill the kitchen with all kinds of possible meals. Barrett came home at nine and wanted to eat alone while reading a book. She'd spent the day talking with people and craved solitude. Dinah wrote in the morning and drove into town to eat and drink at one of her favorite restaurants. Most of the time, she struck up conversations with strangers. It was simple to do. She'd prop a paperback of hers up against her wineglass and read. Often, a woman stopped as she passed by.

"Oh, I love that book!" she'd say.

"Thank you," Dinah would reply. "I wrote that book."

The woman and her friends would join Dinah at the table and talk and drink until the moon was high.

———

One afternoon, Dinah drove her rented Mercedes convertible into town for an appointment with a hairdresser, a masseuse, and a manicurist.

Eddie went to the dining room with several wicker baskets with handles, which were easier to carry than cardboard boxes. She was determined to purge a great shadowy clump of books from beneath the table.

This seemed to be her father's history nook. Fat tomes about the Tudors leaned against biographies of Thomas Jefferson. *The Big Book of Iceland* lay on top of a three-volume set about ancient Rome. Eddie gave each book a careful scrutiny. The pages were yellow, the publication dates decades old, the covers soft with dust. If she found a book about England, she kept it. Her father might want it for research.

It was just after four o'clock when she carried the first basket of books out to the barn. Jeff and Paul were there, removing the sheets and tarps that protected the furniture and rugs from dust.

Paul's phone buzzed. He went out to lean against his truck to talk.

Jeff and Eddie were alone in the large open space.

"You guys are really done," Eddie remarked, looking around.

"I'm not so sure. The way you keep bringing more books out here makes me think we'll be here for eternity."

"Would that be so bad?" Eddie asked, only half teasing.

Jeff moved toward her. His T-shirt was stained dark with sweat. He caught her gaze and held it. "You sure you should be saying things like that?"

She wanted to touch him. A shiver of pleasure ran down her back at his words. "I've been gone for a while," she reminded him. "We can't be who we were."

Jeff's voice grew husky. "Fine. Imagine how we *could* be."

"How we could be?" Eddie dropped her hands. She stepped closer to Jeff. "You mean, like lovers?"

Jeff reached out and took Eddie's hand. "I mean, like everything in the world."

His hand was so large, and strong, and warm. If he took it away, Eddie thought she would faint. She was almost hyperventilating, and that was terrifying, because her body was surging way ahead of her mind.

She knew he'd never want to live in New York. She knew what was happening right now was purely physical.

Eddie stepped away. "Could we . . . could we just be friends for a while? I don't think I'm ready for a serious talk."

Jeff's face closed down. "Eddie, I'm certainly not trying to trap you into a *serious talk*. For one thing, Paul will be back here in a minute. But I can't be your good *friend*." Heat radiated off Jeff.

Gravel crunched as Paul returned from his phone conversation.

"Hey, guys," Paul said. "Am I interrupting something?"

"Not at all," Eddie announced, more loudly than she'd intended. "I've got to bring out some more books." She did an about-turn and went toward the house, realizing that hope as much as fear made her heart race.

There was a momentary lull at Nantucket Blues. No customers in the shop, no potential customers looking in the window. Barrett took the opportunity to Windex the shelves and place new merch where former objects had been taken down and bought. She was exhausted. Her shop was doing better than she'd expected, and she worked at night after she closed, finishing orders and catching up on paperwork. Drew had called, wanting to see her, and she'd had to refuse, promising she'd see him once she caught her breath.

She'd just gone behind the counter to straighten the bundle of bags beneath the cash register when she saw Drew walking toward her shop. A lovely young girl was with him. Too young, Barrett was sure, to be his girlfriend.

They entered the store. The girl went *ooooh*. Most women did when they entered the paradise of blue.

Barrett smiled. "Drew! How are you?"

"I'm good. I've got a week off and frankly, I can't stop thinking of you. Could I take you out somewhere? Maybe a day at the beach, maybe dinner." Before Barrett could answer, he said, "I know you've been busy. I brought you the solution to your problem. Janny, come over here." He put his arm over the shoulders of a girl who looked much like Drew. "Barrett, this is my sister, Janny. Janny this is Barrett."

"Hi, Janny. Nice to meet you." Barrett couldn't understand how Drew's pretty sister could be the solution to her problem. What problem?

Drew said, "Janny is nineteen years old. She's a sophomore at Wheaton. She has worked in retail several times. She has a résumé and references from her former employers."

Barrett frowned. "Okay."

Janny spoke up. "What Drew means is that I could work for you part-time. He said you're in this shop eleven hours a day, at least, and you haven't had one solid hour to go to the beach with him. Or dinner. I was going to look for a job on the island anyway, and I'd love to work for you. I'm good with customers, and I know my way around a cash register."

Barrett's eyes widened. This might actually be the answer to her prayers. She liked the look of the young woman. If she worked only part-time, Barrett certainly had the money to pay her and Barrett would have more time to focus on orders and spreadsheets. "Could you work in the evenings?"

"Absolutely," Drew said.

"Hey!" Janny laughed and punched her brother's shoulder. "Absolutely," she agreed.

ten

At last, they were ready.

Paul had made a handsome wooden sign to hang over the barn doors.

BOOK BARN.

Inside, track lighting hung from the rafters, to be used when it rained. Old-fashioned standing lamps had been set around, near the bookshelves and bins, their soft golden glow illuminating book titles. Two ancient, cracked leather chairs rested on a threadbare Persian rug with a low table between them and a fake Tiffany lamp on the table, illuminating piles of books. An old lectern had been placed near the door, so the shopkeeper—whoever it was on any given day—could greet customers, and slightly behind the lectern was a table holding a computer and a cash box. From the back of the barn, an electric fan rested on a pile of books, its hum adding to the general sense of comfort and rest. Paul and Jeff had hung framed scenes of the ocean and the town above the bookcases and bins. Against one wall of the barn stood a long bookcase, painted lavender, with gold embellishments, and this held Dinah Lavender's books. Along the opposite wall were low book bins with children's books and two small chairs for reading, a low table, a pile of coloring paper, several sticker books, and coloring books to keep kids busy while their parents browsed.

With the barn doors open and the sun slanting in, the spines and covers of all the books glowed like precious stones.

The hardest part had been pricing the used books. The sisters spent days squabbling. Should paperbacks be fifty cents? Who even *remembered* fifty cents? Everyone used their phones to buy things, or they had some paper money in their pockets. Also, should some books be more expensive than others? Surely a hardback of *The Fondue Cookbook* should cost more (or less?) than the paperback of James Michener's *Centennial*.

It was Dinah who stepped in to solve the problem. "The idea is to get rid of the books, not to make money, correct? Eddie, you'll be running the store and I'll help. Barrett has to be in Nantucket Blues. All we have to do is get rolls of quarters from the bank. Price the paperbacks fifty cents and the hardbacks one dollar. Easy."

"Good idea. You're so smart, Dinah!"

"Let me make a sign," Dinah decided. "I'll use the crayons." She slid into one of the small chairs at the children's table and set to work.

Eddie had been busy on social media. Finally, she announced, *The Grand Opening of the Book Barn, book signing with romance author Dinah Lavender.*

The bookstore opened on a Saturday morning, at ten o'clock. Barrett had already gone to her shop. Eddie wore a cute sundress and Dinah was sensational in a lavender sundress and Hermès sunglasses. William kept out of sight, but Eddie glimpsed him from the kitchen window. Poor Duke had to be shut inside. The dog would have been so excited he'd have barked himself into a coma. But the horse was curious, running up to the fence, neighing, snorting, tossing her head in disdain, and running away again.

At ten minutes till ten, Eddie opened the wide barn doors. The shop looked like the set of an especially interesting play.

By ten-thirty, not one person had come down the gravel drive to check out the barn.

"It's all right," Eddie reassured Dinah. "People move slowly on the weekends."

"It's *not* all right," Dinah complained. "Readers should be lining up to meet me and get my autograph."

At ten thirty-five, Dinah stood up from her chair carefully situated in front of her gorgeous bookcase of Dinah Lavender books and put her special lavender (purple, really) Sharpie on the small table in front of her.

"This is a waste of time. Buzz my cell if anyone comes." She tossed her head and started to leave.

As if by a signal, a parade of cars came crackling down the drive. Three; no, four; no, five cars.

Dinah went back to her chair.

Together Eddie and Dinah watched women of all ages step out of their vehicles. They wore full-press makeup and frilly sundresses. They tittered and giggled as they approached the barn.

"They're here to see you," Eddie whispered.

"Of course," Dinah said.

The women, glowing with expectation, went straight to Dinah, and she did not disappoint. As Eddie watched, it seemed that a light went on inside Dinah. If it was the readers' dream to meet their favorite romance writer, it was Dinah's dream to meet the women who read her books. They chatted and laughed and browsed through Dinah's books, and Dinah bent her head over the table and signed books with a lavender flourish.

A white delivery van pulled up next to the cars. A man stepped out with an enormous bouquet of lilacs, iris, and pale purple tulips.

"Is Dinah Lavender here?" he asked.

"Right here," Dinah said.

The man brought the bouquet, already thoughtfully placed in a vase of water, to Dinah's table. The women sighed with delight and snapped photos on their phones.

"Thank you," Dinah said. "Have a book for your wife."

"Oh, I'm not married," the deliveryman told her.

Dinah didn't miss a beat. "Give this book to your girlfriend and you will be." She handed the man a book. "I've included a special bookmark. Thank you so much for driving all the way out here."

The man glanced at the book with a fifty-dollar bill tucked inside.

"Thank you," he said. "Wow."

Eddie left her post to help Dinah place the flowers on the low table between the two leather chairs. The bouquet was so huge, it would have hidden Dinah's face.

"You didn't have to give him *fifty* dollars," Eddie whispered to Dinah.

"Publicity," Dinah whispered back, and winked.

Dinah removed the gift card from the flowers. She opened it, glowed, and whispered, "*Oh, my*. Eddie, look who sent me flowers."

Eddie leaned over Dinah's shoulder. The card read *Love, your secret admirer.*

"Who is that?" Eddie asked, afraid it was Dinah's stalker.

"It's fine. I'll tell you later," Dinah told her. She tucked the card into her bosom and turned to smile at her readers.

By noon, the Book Barn was full of customers, mostly women and children, but a few men, too. Sales were brisk, but quarters and one-dollar bills didn't add up to a fortune. Still, Eddie thought, as Dinah had reminded her, the important thing was that they were clearing out the towers of books.

By early afternoon, the rush was over. The summer people were at the beach. The year-rounders were working.

After twenty minutes of no customers, Eddie wandered over to Dinah.

"Could you stay here for ten more minutes while I run into the house and make a sandwich? Then I'll take over for the next few hours and you can write or do whatever you want."

"Of course." Dinah rose. "Take your time. I'll wander around and straighten the shelves."

"Thanks. Want me to bring you a sandwich?"

"No, but a glass of iced tea would be lovely."

"Before I go," Eddie said, "who sent the flowers?"

Dinah twinkled. "I did."

"You did? Okay, but how? If you'd used your phone or email, the florist would know you were the one ordering them."

"I asked Paul if I could borrow his phone. He let me use his credit card, and I reimbursed him in cash."

"That's wild, Dinah! Pretty clever."

"I have my ways," Dinah said, and winked.

Eddie grinned. She went into the house, used the bathroom, stretched her arms, and headed for the kitchen. She took out a bottle of sparkling water, tilted her head back, and drank deeply. She took out the pitcher of iced tea and found their summer plastic glasses.

Her father came into the kitchen. "I see you've had some customers."

Eddie snorted. "Yeah, Dad, we've already made thirty dollars and fifty cents." She set the pastel glasses and the pitcher on a tray.

"That's actually more than I thought you'd make," William said.

"And we've only started!" She picked up the tray and handed it to her father. "Would you carry it out for me? It's heavy."

To her surprise, William froze. It was as if he'd forgotten how to walk. He wore an expression she had never seen on her father before and it took her a few seconds to name it.

Was her father actually *shy*?

During the weeks Dinah had been here, William had never spent much time around her. He'd become even more of a hermit, tucked away in his study or slipping out the front door to his car and driving away. Of course, the entire household was coming and going, but still . . .

Was it possible that her father had a crush on Dinah? Why hadn't Eddie realized this was possible? Dinah was a gorgeous woman and Eddie's father was a living, breathing man.

"Come on, Dad," Eddie said. "Let's go out and enjoy the day. The humidity is low for once, and it's cool inside the barn." Was she babbling? Eddie felt the urge to laugh hysterically, but managed to tamp it down.

She held the kitchen door open for her father as he walked out on to the porch and down the steps and over the lawn to the barn.

Dinah was putting more of her books on the shelf. She turned and saw Eddie's father.

"Oh, William," she gushed. "You've brought tea. How marvelous!"

"Here, Dad," Eddie directed. "Put the tray on the table. Sit in that nice old leather chair."

"I'm not staying," William replied, bending to set the tray down. "I've got work to do."

"Oh, please stay," Dinah said. "I've been wanting to talk with you about your book."

William perched on the edge of the chair. "I don't think my book would be interesting to you. It's a critical exploration of the British Romantic poets."

"Yes, Eddie told me." Dinah poured a glass of tea and handed it to William as she quoted, "*And there I shut her wild wild eyes with kisses four.*"

What? Eddie wondered if Dinah had lost it.

Her father cleared his throat. "I admit I'm surprised that you know Keats."

Dinah poured another glass and handed it to Eddie, who was leaning against a book bin, silent with shock.

"How could I not know 'La Belle Dame Sans Merci'?" Dinah sank down in the other leather chair and crossed her long legs. "I write romantic novels."

William spoke with his eyes pointed at his tea, as if unwilling to face Dinah. "Yes. Your books are called romance novels, but they're different from what I write. Your books, for example, have a wide audience."

"That's true," Dinah said sweetly. "I have hundreds of thousands of readers."

William's face went pink. "My book isn't meant for so many people. It's based on research. It's meant to be intellectually stimulating."

"I see." Dinah's words were honey-covered as she asked, "Whereas my books are *physically* stimulating?"

William's face went red. "I couldn't say," he replied. "I've never read one."

Dinah lit up like the sky on the Fourth of July. "Oh, William, I'd love it if you'd read one of my books. And I'd love to read yours!"

At those words, all color drained out of William's face. *Good grief,* Eddie thought, *is he having a heart attack?*

"I-I-I don't think it's ready for anyone else to read." He stood up. "Um, nice talking to you." Without looking at Dinah again, he stalked toward the house.

After he entered the house, Eddie said, "Dinah, I don't think he meant to insult you."

Dinah smiled. "I didn't take it as an insult at all."

Before Eddie could reply, a car pulled into the driveway and four women got out. They hurried toward Dinah. Dinah returned to her signing table and chatted with the women.

Eddie took out her phone and called Barrett.

———

When Eddie called, Barrett was laughing with Janny about a TikTok of a cat stealing a dog's food bowl.

"I'd better take this," Barrett told Janny.

She slipped into the back room and answered. "What's up?"

"I think Dad has a crush on Dinah," Eddie whispered.

Barrett laughed. "Why do you sound worried?" She heard her shop door open as someone entered.

"Because, Barrett, Dad is *Dad* and Dinah is *Dinah*."

"Right. Dinah is gorgeous and Dad is handsome. What's the problem?"

"Dad was nervous in the barn today. Dinah plays with men like a cat with a mouse. She's going to seduce and abandon him and break Dad's heart."

Barrett heard voices and peeked around the corner to see if Janny was helping the customer. To her surprise, the man who walked in was Paul. He'd changed out of his sweaty work clothes into a classy striped button-down shirt and chinos.

"Barrett?" Eddie asked. "Are you there?"

"Give me a moment," Barrett said into her phone. She leaned against the wall, listening, wondering why Paul had come in. She heard Janny's sweet welcoming voice.

"Hi! I'm Janny. Barrett's new assistant."

"Hi, Janny. I'm a friend of Barrett's. I brought some of my mom's chocolate pecan cookies. I thought Barrett might enjoy them."

"Oooh," Janny cooed. "Those look delicious."

"Help yourself," Paul said. "I'm Paul Folger. I helped Jeff build a bookstore out in the family's barn."

"I know. Barrett's told me all about it. I hope it works out for them. Mmmm, these cookies are mouthwatering."

"Barrett?" Eddie called.

With effort, Barrett pulled her attention away from Paul and Janny. "Still here. But listen, I've got a customer. Let's talk about it when I get home. Don't worry so much."

Barrett ended the call and stepped into the front room. "Paul! Hi, sweetie." She went around the counter and kissed his cheek. Paul was surprised by the kiss. Actually, so was Barrett.

"Paul's mother made these delicious cookies," Janny said, holding out the plate as if it belonged to her.

"Wow. Thanks." Barrett nibbled a bite. "So good. Paul, I should be bringing *you* cookies. I can't thank you enough for the quarterboard."

"It looks great. Listen, I was wondering—"

Barrett's phone buzzed. "Sorry, I have to take this. Crisis at home."

She returned to the back room and answered. "Is everything okay?"

To her surprise, Drew was speaking. "I certainly hope so."

"Oh! Sorry. Hi." Barrett was torn, wanting to talk with Drew, and oddly wanting Janny to leave Paul alone.

"I'm coming to the island Saturday. Could I take you out to dinner? I know your shop is open, but maybe Janny can handle it. She's working out okay, right?"

From the other room came the sound of Janny and Paul laughing.

Why was Janny's laugh so irritating?

Barrett concentrated on Drew's voice. "Yes, Janny's great. And yes, I'd love to go out to dinner with you Saturday night."

"Cool. I'll call you when I get there." He paused.

"Oh. Good."

"I can't wait to see you," Drew said.

Now she had to say *something*. "Me, too."

Barrett slid her phone into her pocket and returned to the showroom. No customers, only Janny and Paul leaning over the counter to talk.

Was Janny flirting with Paul?

Why should she care? After all, Paul was just a friend. So why did Barrett suddenly feel possessive of Paul? What was wrong with her? A moment ago, she'd been on the phone flirting with Drew. How many emotions could a person have in three seconds?

How many men could she like at the same time?

Whatever. Barrett gently elbowed Janny so she could lean on the counter, too. "Paul, thanks for the cookies. Tell your mother we love them!"

"Will do." Paul winked at Barrett and left the shop.

"Was that my brother who called you?" Janny asked.

Barrett was recovering from the wink. "It was."

Janny folded tissue into a bag, ready for the next customer. Carelessly, she asked, "Do you like Paul? I thought you liked my brother?"

Barrett answered evasively, "Who *wouldn't* like your gorgeous brother?"

Before Janny could answer, two women came in. Barrett had babysat for both their children years ago, and she was glad to see them again.

"Cath! Rosalind! How are you?"

"We wanted to check out your shop," Cath said. "It's absolutely dreamy."

Barrett chatted with them as an older man came in and spoke with Janny about a blue sweater. Now the small shop was crowded. Two more customers came in, and as she helped them, she forgot about men and lust and romance. Well, she *almost* forgot.

Barrett made a plan to talk to their father that evening. She brought pizza home even though it was after nine o'clock, so her sister and father had probably had their evening meal, but who could resist a slice of pizza no matter the time of day?

Eddie had been watching for her. She held the door open as Barrett carried the unwieldy pizza box inside. While Barrett set plates around the kitchen table and took three beers from the refrigerator, Eddie went into their father's study and talked him into joining them.

It was a comforting, bonding few moments as the three settled into their normal places and sipped their beers and took their first glorious bites of pizza.

"Dad, we need to talk," Eddie began. "Dinah has gone to dinner with friends. She won't be home until midnight, probably, so we can speak openly. Dad, is something bothering you?"

William hesitated. "I suppose I'm not happy about the Book Barn."

Barrett spoke up. "Dad, look around. Haven't you noticed how much more space there is in the hall now that some books have gone? Before we took them out, we couldn't put on a coat without knocking over a pile of books. Now we can actually see the table with the bowl where we put the mail."

"And the mirror, so we can do a last-minute check of our hair," Eddie added. "Dad," Eddie said, putting her hand on his. "We won't ever take out books that are important to you. It's just that over the years, all of us, Mom and Stearns included, brought books into the house and no one needs them."

"A lot of them are outdated," Barrett added. "I miss Mom and Stearns as much as you do, but honestly, Dad, there's an absolute *wall* of books in the upstairs hall that are all about coding on computers, and not only can we not code, these books are already obsolete. Stearns would throw them out if he were here."

Eddie took up the argument. "And the den is still piled with boxes of Mom's woo-woo séance, Tarot, spiritualist, fortune-telling stuff. She had *three* different Ouija boards! We've been checking every single item in her boxes, and honestly, we have no idea why you bothered to bring them here to Nantucket."

Barrett continued, more softly, "Dad, I've met a really nice man. I think you'd like him. I want to bring him home. I'd like to invite him to dinner. But our house still looks cluttered and hoardy. We don't want to get rid of *all* the books. But maybe thirty percent of what is left."

Eddie knew how much her father hated statistics. "We're living in such a beautiful place. You were the one who moved us here. You wanted to start over."

"I suppose," he conceded.

"And about Dinah," Eddie said, sweetening her voice. "Does she make you feel uncomfortable?"

William gave a half-hearted grin. " 'Uncomfortable' isn't the right word. She's so—*much*."

"She is," Barrett agreed.

"Our worlds are so different," William admitted. "People bought so many books of hers and I haven't even finished writing mine. I can't compete with her."

"Dad, you don't have to compete with her. And you and Dinah are more alike than you realize. You both need time in isolation to write. Plus, you're strong, Dad, but Dinah's fragile. This house, our family, are her safe harbor."

William ran his hand through his thick sandy hair. "I take your point, Eddie, that we do have some things in common. But the truth is, Dinah' s rich and famous, and I'm a struggling intellectual."

"Daddy, that's crazy," Eddie said. "You two write for different audiences. Plus, you have two fabulous daughters, and a farm—"

Barrett cut in, "And a Duke and a Duchess living on the farm."

That brought a smile to William's face. "You're right. I'll try to be less . . ."

"Defensive?" Eddie suggested.

"Attractive?" Barrett said teasingly. She stood up, kissed her father on the forehead, and put her plate in the dishwasher. "I'm exhausted, and tomorrow will be busy. I'm going to bed."

William stood up and checked his watch. "I'm off to bed, too."

Eddie said, "I'll just tidy the kitchen. Good night, family."

"Good night, Johnboy," William said.

His daughters glanced at each other. They never had understood why their father said good night to Johnboy. They'd decided it must be something from Wordsworth.

———

Eddie showered, slipped on a clean T-shirt and leggings, and settled herself in bed with both pillows behind her. She lifted her journal from the drawer in her bedside table, chose a pen from the cup holder she'd made in seventh grade, and took a deep breath.

Dinah is so smart. It seems she knows everything. Dad knows almost as much, but he can't seem to finish his book. A person must need some kind of insane self-confidence to write a book to release out into the world for other people to read.

Dad has the desire to write a book, but maybe not the ability? I worry for him. He puts so much importance on the book that no one has asked for.

That makes me think I could not write a book. I love words. I love stories. I love the rhythm and astonishment of sentences. I'm obsessed with books and one thing I know for certain is that if you have children, it is wrong to care for something more than for the children. I don't know if I'll ever be ready to lose sleep, listen to wailing children, wade through a world of dirty diapers and constant demands. The idea of loving a child terrifies me. My deepest desire is to write, but when I watch Dinah, who seems to summon words from the air like magic, and my father, who tortures himself over words, I fear I don't have it in me to become a writer.

Saturday, Drew flew in from Boston and took Barrett to dinner at the Chanticleer. As they wound along the Polpis road to 'Sconset, Drew set the radio to the big band channel, and Barrett leaned back in the luxuriously soft leather seat and relaxed.

She'd chosen to wear a simple little navy dress with only a hint of cleavage. Her hair had been bleached by the sun from caramel to blond, and she wore small emerald earrings that brought out the green of her eyes. A touch of lipstick. No blush, no eye shadow. Everything simple, elegant. Drew wore a madras blazer and no tie. Leather loafers without socks. Barrett had sworn she'd never date a man who wore loafers without socks, but she quietly changed her mind.

Barrett felt people looking at her and Drew as they walked beneath the rose arbor and into the restaurant's garden. She felt a slight shiver of pleasure, knowing that the two of them were the perfect summer couple, young, good-looking, well-dressed, sexy. She was delighted that their table faced the rose garden, and it was sweet to sit in the handsome room after all her days and hours of working.

"Let's have a glass of champagne to start," Drew suggested.

Barrett said, "Lovely," and stifled a gasp when he ordered a champagne that cost forty-five dollars a glass.

"An excellent choice, sir," the waiter said.

"We'll have wine with our meal," Drew told Barrett, looking deep into her eyes. "First, I want to celebrate meeting you."

Barrett smiled, even though she knew she'd tell Eddie and they'd fall all over laughing because, wow, that was such a cheesy thing to say.

But Drew seemed sincerely interested in Barrett. He asked her about her shop and how Janny was doing. Over their scallops and salmon (and sinfully expensive white wine), Barrett told Drew about her family, making them all seem eccentric in an intellectual and amusing way, not mentioning her brother. Drew told her she was lucky to have such an interesting family.

Drew talked about his parents, always traveling to their houses off the coast of Greece or in Jackson Hole. He was very close to his sister and considered himself her protector because they so seldom saw their parents.

"I'm really glad," Drew continued, "that Janny's working with you. You're a good role model for her. She's doing well, right?"

"She's great. She's great with our customers."

After dinner, they walked up and down the charming small-town streets of 'Sconset. Everywhere, roses were blooming, tumbling in the hundreds over the low roofs and along the picket fences. When they came to a private grassy lane between two obviously empty cottages,

Drew gently pulled Barrett into his arms, kissing her slowly and thoroughly. She leaned back against the shingled wall, closing her eyes and—and seeing *Paul's* face.

What? Barrett thought.

Drew stopped kissing her. "Are you okay?"

Reluctantly, Barrett pushed him away. "Drew, I have to go home. I have to get up early tomorrow."

He nuzzled her neck. "I know. I know." He cradled her face in his hands. "You're so delicious."

She accepted another heated kiss before easing away from him. "I really have to go now."

They returned to his car. He held her hand as he drove, and when they reached her house, he hugged her against him.

"Soon," he whispered in her ear.

"Soon," Barrett echoed, not certain of what that even meant.

eleven

From the Fourth of July on, the population exploded from twenty thousand people to sixty thousand. The sun was bright, the beaches were golden, the bars and restaurants packed, and anyone who worked fell onto their bed, exhausted.

During the hot summer days, Eddie was busy in a slow, luxurious way. She spent hours proofreading Dinah's latest draft. She wasn't working full-time for the writer, but they both agreed that Dinah needed a proofreader and she was coming up to a deadline.

Eddie also ran the Book Barn. When no customers were around, she hurried into the house, snatched up a pile of books, and carried them back outside to fill the gaps.

Because there were gaps. People bought the most amazing books. A biography of Hegel. What? Who was Hegel? Who cared? And how did you pronounce his name? *Whistling While Whittling*. Eddie actually checked inside the wide, flat book, thinking the title was some kind of code for spies or pornographers. Nope. It was for real. Four versions of *Little Women*. She kept one but put three out for sale, even though it made her sad. One had been her mother's, one someone gave Eddie, one Eddie gave Barrett, another one Eddie had given Barrett that Stearns had scribbled all over with crayons. Eddie knew she should just throw it away, but she didn't. It sat on a shelf in the barn, where she knew no one would buy it, but it reminded her of Stearns.

Hours went by when no one came to browse. During those quiet times, Eddie prepared that evening's dinner, or tidied the house, or sat in the barn and read.

One evening, Barrett was still in her shop, Dinah was at dinner with friends, and William was at a lecture at the library.

Eddie was lounging on pillows on the wide wicker porch swing, reading a book. She heard a noise, glanced up, and there was Jeff, walking around the corner of the house, with Duke following, wagging his tail.

"Hey," Eddie said. She sat up and set her book on the small side table.

"Hey, yourself. I hope I'm not disturbing anything. I was on my way home and thought I'd stop by and see if you'd like a beer." He held up a six-pack. "Don't worry. I'm here strictly as a friend."

"Nice," Eddie said. She was slightly flustered—no, she admitted to herself, she was very flustered, almost *giddy* to see Jeff. He wore carpenter's pants and an ancient Rolling Stones T-shirt. He had wood dust in his hair and a cut on his hand and a sensational sunburn on his cheeks and nose. An odor of wood and sun and cinnamon drifted away from him, and when he smiled, his teeth were snow white against his sun-chapped lips.

"Have a seat." Eddie gestured to the chair next to her.

Jeff set the six-pack on the table, wrestled a couple free from the plastic rings, handed her one and popped open one for himself.

"Man," Jeff said. "I'm tired."

Eddie studied him. The urge to step off the swing and throw herself on his lap was strong, but she stifled it. "Your lips are chapped."

"Ha!" Jeff laughed. "Do you want me to apply a little tube of lip balm while I'm carrying a two-by-four up the ladder?"

"Maybe not my best idea," Eddie agreed. "How's *your* house coming along?"

"I'm ahead of schedule with it, actually. These long summer days allow me to hammer a few nails early in the morning and again after work with the crew."

"You look tired," Eddie told him.

"Really?" Jeff smiled and cocked his head. "I look *tired*? What do you think, is it a good look for me?" He flexed his arm.

"I have to admit, your biceps are impressive." Eddie wanted to reach out and hold his hand. Her brain flashed: *Get hold of yourself, girl.*

Jeff's eyes darkened. Eddie was washed over with desire.

She grabbed the first safe topic she could think of and blurted, "Barrett's shop is doing really well!"

Jeff gave her a sideways, knowing smile. "Tell me."

Eddie talked about her sister, and then about her father, and then about Dinah. Jeff talked about his co-workers and his parents. Duke sat at his feet, gazing up at him with adoring eyes. Duchess approached the fence and muttered sweet nothings at Jeff.

Honestly, Eddie thought, *does the man give off a* come kiss me *scent?*

After that, Jeff came over at the end of every day—*his* end of the day was after nine o'clock when the sun set and the builders couldn't see to work—and they sat on the porch drinking beers and talking. There was always something to talk about. For some mysterious reason, this summer cars and SUVs were slamming into trees and buildings and flipping on their sides, or upside down, like turtles helpless in their shells. Were people going too fast? Was that even possible on Nantucket, where the highest speed limit was forty-five miles per hour for about ten miles? Drew Barrymore had eaten at Millie's in Mada-ket. Bill Belichick had hired Captain Tom for a day of deep-sea fish-ing. Sharks were circling the island.

Sometimes Dinah would join them on the porch for a chat. She spent much of her day at the library, writing, and she often ate lunch and dinner at one of the many restaurants in town. She scraped her hair back in a bun, wore no makeup, and walked around town in a T-shirt, sneakers, and a baseball cap, and it worked. No one recog-nized her, and she found it amusing and slightly disconcerting. Occa-sionally, she would agree to speak at the library or at a local book club, and then she wore one of her summer dresses and "just a few" diamonds in a necklace or hair clip.

William and Dinah seldom crossed paths. William woke early, with Barrett. They had breakfast, Barrett left for her shop, and William secluded himself in his study to write. Eddie and Dinah woke at seven-thirty, had breakfast, and went their separate ways, Eddie to the Book Barn, Dinah to town. In her rented Mercedes convertible, she zipped into town, often returning home with bags filled with fruit and expen-sive cookies for everyone.

Saturday night, Jeff didn't come over. He didn't text her to let her know he wasn't coming over. He'd come every night for the last two weeks and Eddie felt hurt by his absence, even though she knew she shouldn't.

She made a meal of cold sandwiches and salad but wasn't hungry. She felt so down, so bored. She decided she could use a little playtime. Their father was in his study. Dinah was eating dinner out with a new friend. Barrett had closed her shop for the day and lay on the sofa with her feet on a pillow.

"Let's go to the Box," Eddie suggested.

Barrett yawned and stretched her arms. "Really? I don't know if I have the energy to stand up."

"Maybe not, but I'm sure you have the energy to dance." Eddie tickled her sister's bare feet. "Come on."

They quickly slipped into jean shorts and tank tops, pulled their hair up into high ponytails because they knew the bar would be hot, left a note for their father, and raced out the door.

The place was booming when they arrived. They walked into a pulsing wall of noise, went straight to the bar, and ordered margaritas. A country-western band was playing. Everyone was dancing, shouting, flirting, laughing. Barrett was quickly surrounded by people who'd met her at the dress shop or the restaurant. Eddie was ordering her second drink when Barrett pulled her out on the crowded floor.

"You're the one who dragged me here," Barrett yelled. "You have to dance!"

"Let's do this!" Eddie shouted back, and let the music take her.

The cover band was playing Aerosmith, music that was impossible to stay still to. Eddie and Barrett danced, screaming, letting go. Eddie felt Jeff's presence before she saw him. The hair on her arms stood up like an early warning signal.

"Hey." Jeff wore jeans and a T-shirt that read NANTUCKET OR NOWHERE.

"Hey," Eddie said back. It was too loud on the dance floor, so they didn't talk.

Barrett disappeared into the crowd. Jeff took Eddie's hand.

"Are you here with someone?" Eddie asked.

"Why?" Jeff pulled her to him.

"You didn't come by this evening!" She bent her head back to see his face. He was so tall. She'd always loved it that he was so tall.

"So, you missed me?" His smile was mischievous.

Eddie struggled to think of a witty comeback, and gave in to the truth.

"I did."

Jeff's eyes darkened with emotion.

They moved together naturally, a perfect pair. By the end of the evening, her arms were around his neck, their bodies were touching, and she nestled her face into his shoulder. They started kissing, and they couldn't stop kissing until someone knocked Jeff's shoulder.

"Hey, you two, take it outside."

They held hands as they elbowed their way through the crowd to the door. Outside, they leaned against the wall and kissed hungrily until Jeff pulled away.

He said, "Eddie. We need to talk. Let's go to my car."

They ran to his truck and climbed in. Jeff reached for Eddie, but she pushed him back.

"Wait, Jeff. What are we doing?"

His eyes were dark, intense. "I don't know but I don't want to stop."

"But I'm probably returning to New York with Dinah. This summer with my father is temporary."

"Don't think about later. Think about right now."

Jeff's voice was low and solemn. Outside, it began to rain, thunder cracking through the sky, rain suddenly spilling out over the truck, the parking lot, the island. It enclosed them in their own small world, and already the windows were steaming up.

"Right now," Eddie whispered, and moved toward Jeff.

Right now was all that mattered.

Rain flooded down around them, blanking the outside world from them as they kissed and touched and pressed into each other. It was urgent, intense, instinctive.

It was Jeff who pulled away.

"Not here," he said, his voice hoarse. "Not in a truck in a parking lot."

Eddie shivered. "Jeff, why do I want you so much?"

Jeff was quiet as he organized his clothing. When he turned to face Eddie, his eyes were serious. "Because I want you so much. We should be together."

"What do you mean?" Eddie slid the strap of her tank top back up to her shoulder.

"I mean stay here. Marry me. Let's have a life together."

"Oh, Jeff . . ." Eddie's heart was so full it almost prevented her breathing. "Jeff . . ."

"I know. I know. You don't want to have children."

Eddie listened carefully to his words. When she replied, it was as if a mysterious code came clear to her.

"It *has* been all about that, Jeff. It *was* what I needed. Or what I thought I needed. But it's also been about helping Dinah, and no, I certainly don't see her as a mother substitute. She's a writer, and *that's* what interests me. Books, and writing."

Jeff nodded. "Okay. Let's keep going with that. You spent a year in New York, working for a publisher. Then you spent a year here, on the island."

"Right." She spoke slowly, and felt strangely anxious—or was she excited?

"You've spent the last two years working for a writer."

"Right."

Jeff asked, "What do you want to do next?"

She couldn't look at him. She had never said it out loud before. She whispered, "Maybe I want to write a novel?"

Jeff smiled. "Maybe you do."

Eddie took a deep breath. "Well, that was a terrifying moment."

"Why?"

"How can I write a book? I mean, I know I can do that, but there's no guarantee it would get published."

"No one can guarantee anything," Jeff countered quietly. "That doesn't mean you can't try. If we were married, you could write. You could give yourself, let's say, one year, to do nothing but write."

Eddie gave him a wary look. "Could we be together, married, in New York?" She knew she was being contrary. "We could get an apartment together, and I could work part-time for Dinah, and spend, let's say, the morning, writing. You could work in construction there."

Jeff frowned. "I hadn't thought of that. Damn, Eddie I don't want to live in New York, or any city. I want to stay on Nantucket. I thought you knew that."

"I do know that," Eddie said. She pulled her hands away from him and turned to face the front. The rain was slowing now. She could see other people running out from the Box to their cars. It was after one in the morning.

She waited for him to say he'd consider living in New York.

Jeff didn't speak.

Eddie said softly, "I should go home."

"Okay." Jeff started the truck engine and pulled out of the parking lot. "I guess we have a lot to think about."

Eddie nodded. "I guess we do."

Barrett's shop was quiet in the morning. She restaged her windows, setting out cool blue jewelry and a set of glasses, pitcher, and matching ruffled apron all in turquoise with white polka dots. Sunburned island guests drifted inside. She and Janny were busy receiving, unpacking, and checking invoices for blue sun hats, sunglasses, bracelets, and flip-flops patterned with seashells.

While they worked, Janny chattered away cheerfully, mostly telling Barrett how wonderful Drew was, such a kind, caring big brother who had always helped Janny out of a tough spot. Whenever Janny got into an argument with their parents, Drew took Janny's side, stood up for her, argued with her parents until they finally gave in or gave up. When she almost drowned at Surfside, Drew had rescued her. When she'd got deathly drunk the first time she tried alcohol, Drew had taken care of her.

Barrett thought it would have to be a saint who looked like Ryan Reynolds to compete with Drew for Janny's love.

Barrett saw little of Drew because she was working twenty-seven hours a day in her shop. At least it seemed that way. Drew was in Boston during the week, sometimes coming to the island late Friday or Saturday night. When he couldn't come on the weekend, he sent small, tasteful presents—to help her remember him, he said. A box of Godiva chocolates. A copy of Ann Patchett's latest novel. A box of multicolored paper clips. The gifts made her laugh.

One Sunday Drew did get to the island for the day. He brought a picnic basket from Formaggio Kitchen in Cambridge, and they spent the afternoon on the beach. They walked, collected shells, swam, lay in the sun, and kissed, but casually, because so many other people were around.

"I don't want to leave you," Drew said that evening. "Come with me."

Barrett laughed. "I have my shop, remember?"

"Janny's running it today. She could open it tomorrow. We could spend the night together and I'd fly you back to the island tomorrow morning." His eyes were dark with desire, and the invitation was tempting. "Or, she could be there for the weekend, and you and I could do anything we want."

Barrett was irritated by Drew's suggestion. She was making her living by running a shop that she hoped she'd have for years. Even decades. She had customers and friends and new objects to put out. And really, Janny couldn't run the shop by herself.

Yet Drew was making puppy eyes at her. She smiled at him. "Stop it."

"Tell me you'll come with me someday."

"Someday," she whispered. *Someday* could be weeks, months, years away.

———

In the middle of July, Barrett invited Drew to dinner at her house. She wanted to explain to Drew that this didn't mean she was getting serious, and it didn't mean that it had a "meet the family" kind of importance, but actually, she did want Eddie to get to know him, because she valued Eddie's judgment. Plus, she needed Drew to see how her family lived.

Eddie volunteered to make dinner. Barrett asked Janny to run Nantucket Blues alone until closing time at nine. She gave her a key so she could lock the door, feeling uneasy about this extreme measure of trust, even though Janny was over the moon because Barrett was going to be with Drew. Still, Barrett decided to phone Janny just after nine to be sure the girl had remembered to lock the door.

That night, Barrett raced home at five-thirty, took a shower, put on a cute sundress, and flew down to the kitchen to help Eddie.

Eddie was in the kitchen, wearing jean shorts and a halter top. Barrett winced when she saw Eddie's clothes. She wanted her sister to look just a little more *covered,* but she knew if she dared say anything, Eddie would probably stalk out of the house and drive away.

"He's coming at six-thirty, right?" Eddie asked.

"Right," Barrett said.

"We're having a summer meal," Eddie told her. "Grilled swordfish, potato salad, green salad, and strawberry shortcake."

"That's perfect!" Barrett peeked in the refrigerator.

"I actually made the shortcake for the dessert," Eddie told her. "But I can't improve on Reddi-wip."

"What can I do?" Barrett asked.

"Set the table. Slice some limes for drinks. Put out a bowl of nuts. I'm going up to change." Eddie noticed Barrett's look of relief. "You thought I was going to meet him like this, right?"

"Of course not," Barrett lied. "How many places shall I set?"

"Five, I guess. Me, you, Drew, Dad, Dinah."

"Dinah's eating here tonight?" Barrett tried not to wince.

"Do you have a problem with that? Would you prefer that I take her dinner on a tray so she can eat in the bedroom?"

"Don't be silly, Eddie. It's only that she usually eats out in the evening."

"She wouldn't miss this for the world. She's eating here tonight so she and I can thoroughly discuss your new beau afterward." Eddie flicked a dish towel at Barrett and went out of the room.

Barrett set the table with their everyday china, so she wouldn't seem like she was trying too hard to impress Drew. She picked some vibrant zinnias from their backyard and set them in her favorite white ironstone pitcher, the one her grandmother had used. Their bright colors gave the table a homey, festive look. Or did they? Barrett stood studying the flowers, almost in a trance of anticipation, when her father came out of his study and Dinah came down the stairs and Drew knocked on the door, and Eddie raced to open it.

Eddie was wearing a plain linen dress in a light sand color and no jewelry. In one glance, Barrett realized this and knew Eddie was allowing Barrett to be the one to shine.

"Hello!" Eddie pulled the door open. "You must be Drew! Come in. I'm Eddie, Barrett's older and much wiser sister."

"Hi, Eddie," Drew replied, stepping into the front hall. He wore khakis and a blue button-down shirt and he held a bouquet of sunflowers wrapped in the special paper of Flowers on Chestnut.

Barrett stepped forward. "Hi, Drew. Oh, thanks for these. Come in and meet everyone else."

They gathered in the living room. Barrett made the introductions. Her father looked normal, in chinos and a plaid shirt with the sleeves rolled up. Dinah looked—well, Dinah *never* looked *normal*—like an actress trying out for the part of a forty-year-old Barbie. Her dress was pink, swirly, and extremely low cut. Actually, she looked fabulous. Eddie offered to put the flowers in water while Barrett got the drinks, and for a moment they were together in the kitchen whispering just like they had a thousand times before.

"He's handsome," Eddie said. "But what are you going to do with these sunflowers? They're so big, and there are so many of them. They make your zinnias look pitiful. But if you put these on the table, no one will be able to see anyone else."

"Thank you for pointing out the painfully obvious," Barrett snapped. "I'll put them in a vase on the bureau. I'm taking Drew's G and T in to him, and I've got the same for Dad. You can handle the rest."

"I'll try not to make a mistake." Eddie curtsied and replied in one of her downstairs *Downton Abbey* accents.

Barrett served the drinks and settled in the living room.

"Our pharmaceutical company is relatively small," Drew said, speaking to William.

"I'm surprised anything about you is small," Dinah said, blinking her lashes like a starstruck teenager.

"Dinah, stop it," Barrett hissed.

Eddie saved the conversation by asking if Drew followed the Red Sox. After that, their father and Drew engaged in a hearty conversation about sports. Eddie and Barrett slipped away to put dinner on the table. They made Dinah come with them.

"What do you want me to do?" Dinah asked when they entered the kitchen.

"I want you to stop with the flirty talk for the rest of the evening," Barrett ordered.

"Barrett!" Eddie put her hand on her sister's arm, trying to calm her.

"Barrett, I apologize," Dinah said. "It just slipped out. I mean, look at the man. But I promise I'll be good now."

And she was. The rest of the evening went smoothly. Eddie grilled the swordfish steaks to perfection. Everyone had a glass of cool Chardonnay, and no one drank too much. Eddie and Drew bonded over the mixed joys of having younger sisters. William and Drew talked about the Patriots.

Only one other difficult moment marred the dinner.

Drew said to Dinah, "Barrett tells me you're a novelist. What kind of books do you write?"

"I write romance novels," Dinah said. "That's how I met Eddie. She took a job with me as an assistant."

"Romance novels? Like with the naked man on the cover? Where do you sell your, um, romance novels? I mean, could I find one at the grocery store? Or maybe Walmart? Or would I have to go to a, um, specialty shop? Or could I buy one directly from you?"

Before Eddie could intervene, Dinah said, in a tone that could create glaciers, "You'd find them in bookstores. But they're not the sort of book *you* would ever read. They're about beautiful women and elegant, *classy* men."

To everyone's surprise, William spoke up. "*All* books and *all* writers deserve respect," he said in his most serious professorial tone.

Barrett, Eddie, and Dinah stared at him, shocked.

William continued, "I'm *also* working on a book. I was a professor of English literature at Williams College. Now I'm writing a critical study of the British Romantic poets."

"Really?" Drew looked confused as he turned his attention to William. "That sounds impressive."

"Maybe, Drew, but it won't ever make the kind of money Miss Lavender makes, and I'm sure it's the *financial* aspect that is of interest to you."

Their father was defending Dinah? Eddie and Barrett made googly eyes at each other.

Drew nodded politely. "That's not quite true. I read a lot. I don't believe I've read any Romantic British poetry, but please tell me about it."

"I'd be glad to." William leaned forward. "I'm sure you've heard of Wordsworth, Coleridge, and Keats, but did you know they regularly indulged in opium?"

"No, I didn't know that," Drew admitted, glancing around the table to see if anyone else wanted to enter the conversation.

No one else spoke. William launched into a long and colorful speech about poets and drug usage. He continued while Eddie and Barrett cleared the table and dished the strawberry shortcake into bowls.

"Was Dad actually coming to Dinah's defense?" Barrett whispered.

Eddie replied, "Well, Drew was being kind of a dick."

"I know," Barrett agreed. "And I'm sorry. But I don't think that Drew meant to be rude. He's just so interested in the financial aspect of everything."

Eddie snorted. "If you say so."

They carried the desserts out to the table. Conversation quickly turned to pleasant subjects. Favorite desserts. Funniest Facebook posts. Chickens adopting puppies, dogs adopting kittens.

"This was a wonderful dinner," Drew said, looking around the table. "Thank you all, for the delicious food and the fascinating conversation."

"You're welcome," Eddie told him. "Maybe Barrett can show you the Book Barn before you go."

"I'll help you in the kitchen," Dinah told Eddie. She didn't bother to say goodbye to Drew.

"I've got some emails to answer," William grumbled, disappearing into his study.

Barrett took Drew's hand and led him through the kitchen and out to the porch. Night had fallen, but a radiance lingered in the sky. The horse appeared at the fence, as if checking out the newcomer. She snorted, tossed her head, and galloped to the far end of the field.

They stepped into the barn. Before she could speak, Drew embraced Barrett, kissed her long and hungrily.

When Drew pulled away, he said, "I apologize if I displeased anyone in your family."

Barrett laughed. "You sound so old-fashioned."

"Can you blame me? You have an . . . unusual family." Quickly, he added, "I enjoyed them. Now show me this barn enterprise."

Barrett turned on the overhead light and they walked around the shop. She pointed out each category—mystery, children's, fiction, textbooks.

"You're pricing these at fifty cents?" Drew asked. "How can you make a profit?"

"Oh, it's not about making a profit," Barrett assured him. "It's about clearing the house of all the books our family has acquired over the years. Our father's a bit of a hoarder, only of books, but still . . ." Feeling embarrassed, she asked jokingly, "See anything you like? I'll sell them to you for a quarter."

"Let me get this straight. You're bringing all these books out of the house to this barn, and someone remains here to sell them?" Drew walked around the charming room they'd put together. "It doesn't seem like a very good use of personal time. Does Dinah sit out here? Or your father?"

"Oh, no, they're busy writing their own books. Eddie is out here mostly, but it's not like we have a steady stream of customers. Probably at the end of the summer we'll end up donating the books to a thrift shop."

"Why don't you go ahead and do that now? This means you have to carry the books at least twice. Eddie could get a job that makes real money. This seems a waste of time."

"It's not, really," Barrett protested. "We've had . . . a lot of changes in our lives, and this process is sort of therapeutic."

"Okaaay." Drew seemed amused.

Barrett changed the subject. "But hey, it's a gorgeous night. Want to drive me out to the beach to look at the stars?"

"Sorry. I'm catching an early plane back to Boston tomorrow." Drew wrapped Barrett in a warm hug and whispered in her ear. "I wish I could *look at the stars* with you, but when we do, I want to do it right."

Before the meaning of his words came clear in Barrett's mind, Drew kissed her long and firmly, pressing her against him, all up and down. She was uncomfortable. She wanted to explain that she actually meant *look at the stars* when she said "look at the stars," but the moment passed. She walked Drew to his car, kissed him goodbye, and watched him drive away.

twelve

Barrett had just opened her shop for the day. She was dusting and windexing her glass shelves when Paul came in, carrying a small cardboard carton. He was wearing work boots and his T-shirt was already damp with sweat. July could be hot on the island, and humid.

She gave him a big smile. It always made her happy to see him.

"Hi, Paul. What's up?"

Paul gently placed the box on her glass countertop. He was flushed. He cleared his throat. "I thought you might be interested in these."

He lifted out a small object: two bluebirds sitting on a branch. The entire piece, about eight inches long and eight inches high, balanced perfectly on the shelf. The birds had been carved from wood and painted a deep mesmerizing sapphire, with shiny black eyes and beaks.

"Did you make this?" Barrett carefully picked up the carving and turned it around, inspecting it. "Paul, this is amazing. So beautiful. So detailed. And the tilt of their little heads toward each other is ador-able. I want it!"

Paul laughed. "It's yours. But I brought another one for you to sell in your shop, if you want to. You wouldn't have to pay me. I don't know how much they would go for."

"But how did you do this? You're a carpenter!"

"I have a woodworking shop set up in a garage I rent. This is what I prefer doing, but carpentry pays a lot better."

He lifted a box out of the carton. It was large enough to hold some jewelry or mementoes. It was turquoise, its lid embellished with silver arabesques.

Barrett ran her fingers over the box. It was as smooth as silk.

"Open it," Paul said.

Barrett gently opened the box. "Oh, Paul."

The entire interior of the box was gleaming silver. While Barrett gazed at it, Paul brought out another box, this one deep azure, its in-side gold.

"Wow," Barrett said softly. "These are gorgeous, Paul." She turned the box over. A tiny star was stamped in the corner. "Is this your sig-nature?"

"It is."

Barrett looked at Paul with renewed admiration. "I thought you did such a great job with my shop quarterboard, but I had no idea you could do this kind of work."

"That sign isn't really a quarterboard," Paul reminded her. "The real quarterboards are works of art, and they take patience and skill."

"These took patience and skill." She turned them around, wonder-ing how much to price them. "Paul, this is beautiful."

Paul shrugged. "I like carving. I never got hooked on video games, and I don't find television relaxing or even interesting after a hard day's work. Plus, don't hate me, but I'm not much of a reader. So, I do this in the evening."

Barrett turned the little box this way and that. It called to her like an icon, a magic charm. She studied Paul as he stood there near her, with sawdust in his hair. He wore shorts, a dark T-shirt, and work boots, with a tool belt around his hips. Paul was sexy, and fascinating, with his macho exterior and his artistic secret side.

"Do you think I could ever watch you carve?"

He seemed surprised by her question. "I don't know. I mean, I've never thought of having anyone watch me carve. It's kind of personal."

"I understand. Can you make any more of these? Does it take you a long time? Could you do, I don't know, a fawn or a rabbit or whales, island animals?"

Paul ducked his head, as if embarrassed. "I'll bring you some other things." He quickly changed the subject. "Have you heard about the new head of Safe Harbor?"

"No. Tell me."

She leaned on her counter, talking about the town with Paul. He knew everyone—he'd been born on the island—and working with a crew of carpenters, he heard everything. He was kind with his gossip, and she liked that. She liked his smile, his big shoulders, his—what was the word? Was there a word? His openness, honesty, and willingness to bring her his carvings, obviously the work of his heart, and if these small and beautiful objects were what he produced, she knew somehow that she could trust him.

Eddie decided she'd had enough with the lugging books from the house in boxes or bags or baskets or her arms. She dragged one of the family's old wheelie suitcases, filled it with books, and bumped it out of the house, down the steps, over the drive, and into the Book Barn. In the past few weeks, she'd learned what hours and days brought the most customers and what kinds of books people bought. Of course, anything by Dinah Lavender went fast, and Dinah was having a few cartons of her books sent from her storage unit. It was fun to watch people getting excited over a book, and as the house emptied out, it was opening up like a flower in the summer.

For most of the day, Eddie was alone in the barn, and she'd developed a very enjoyable habit.

She read. She read for hours, as if each book was a passport and opening the book meant entering another country.

Some were duplicates of her father's. Some had been her mother's. *Summer* by Edith Wharton. *A Mother and Two Daughters* by Gail Godwin. *September* by Rosamunde Pilcher. Eddie kept a cooler by the counter, filled it with ice each morning, and set a pitcher of iced tea inside, along with an egg salad sandwich or a few bars of chocolate. During the heat of the day, when most people were at the beach, Eddie curled up in the old leather chair, opened a book, and read while shadows slowly moved across the room. When anyone drove up the driveway, the shells crackled beneath the tires, and Eddie would lift her head and be slightly surprised to see what was around her: the old barn, cases of books, her cellphone. The world she inhabited while she read the book would quickly vanish, not all at once, but slowly, like the pupil of an eye shrinking shut, like a door slowly closing.

Jeff often stopped by during his lunch break. He'd bring takeout from Faregrounds or a food truck, and Eddie would make a cold pitcher of iced tea with sprigs of mint. It was always good to sit in the barn with him, casually talking about their day as they ate and relaxed, but it was magical when it rained. Eddie would have pulled the barn door mostly closed. No one would come out in the rain to look at used books. Jeff would run from his truck to Eddie, the rain soaking his shirt and arms so that when he entered the barn and pressed Eddie against the wooden wall and kissed her, the cold made her shiver and she would cling to him until they were both warm.

They didn't make love in the barn. They didn't want a customer, or worse, Eddie's father, to rush in out of the rain and catch them wrapped around each other. But those moments together led to a different kind of making love. As they talked, an intimacy grew around them, so powerful that often, after sharing a secret, they sat in silence for a long time, giving each secret its worth.

Eddie was the one with the saddest confidences. One day she talked truthfully about her mother, and as she described her to Jeff, she felt the sadness lighten.

"No families are perfect." Jeff smiled ruefully. "Jared, my older, perfect brother, the Army Ranger, was crazy mean when he grew up. If something made him angry, he'd slam his fist into the wall. Broke several walls that way. He's four years older than I am, and about seventy pounds heavier. We fought all the time. He was bigger, but I was slippery. Our parents called us the Gorilla and the Eel. The thing is, even though our parents told him to leave me alone, *I* couldn't leave *him* alone. I wanted to win just one fight. So, I started fights all the time." He grinned at a memory. "We broke the coffee table."

Eddie had to ask. "Did you ever win?"

"Are you kidding?" Jeff broke into a laugh. "I was Winnie-the-Pooh to his Godzilla. They had to send him away to high school. He was on the football team, and my parents thought he'd be an athletic coach, but Jared also made straight As in all his classes. That's why he was accepted into the Army Rangers. It was a perfect fit for him. When he comes home, he's nicer than he ever was when we were kids."

"I told you that my brother died," Eddie said, and her chest tightened as she spoke. "I didn't tell you everything. Stearns was part of our gang when we were kids. We were close, all of us. Barrett and me, and our next door neighbor Dove, who we loved, and Stearns. Stearns was super smart and didn't even finish high school, but went to work for a computer company in Troy." Her voice cracked as the grief returned full force, as heavy as when he first died, even heavier, because she had gone through so many days of life without him. "I miss him so much."

Jeff didn't speak. He kept his hand on her arm, being there for her, being a witness, understanding her sorrow.

Eddie wiped her face. "And Dove had his baby, but we've never seen him. It was all so complicated, it happened so fast."

Jeff said, "Tell me."

Eddie nodded. She told him about Dove, her father going to prison, Dove's drinking, Stearns rescuing her, Stearns working at a computer company, the baby, the motorcycle accident.

Eddie gulped back her tears and tried to calm down. But the sorrow broke through. "Why hasn't Dove ever brought the baby to see us? For us to see him? His name is Bobby."

"Where is she?" Jeff asked.

"She's living with her aunt and uncle in Colorado. She sends a photo at Christmas. Just a photo, and the little boy is three years old."

"Could you call her and ask her to visit?"

"I don't know. I really don't know." Eddie faced Jeff, knowing she looked ragged and wretched, and no one had ever seen her this exposed before, and if this made him leave her, then he was meant to leave her, because her sorrow and fear were part of her and always would be.

Jeff said, "I love you, Eddie."

She pushed herself away. "No, wait. You know I read all the time, and you know I might even write a novel, or try to. I think I spend so much time in books because it's the only way I can control my world, even for a while. I'm not sure I'm cut out to be a wife and mother. Look at my mother. She ran away. And my father hides in books, too. He ran away, too, kind of."

Jeff said, "No. Your father moved here to give his daughters a new world. New friends, new hopes for the future. He gave up so much, a teaching position at a prestigious college, your beloved home and town and friends. He didn't run away. He helped you both start over. Look at Barrett and Nantucket Blues."

Eddie caught her breath, absorbing his words. "Barrett is brave," she said.

"Yes, Barrett is brave, but she's also clever, energetic, and sure of herself. And you went into one of the most complicated cities in the

world and worked with a world-famous writer. That took some courage, too."

"I suppose . . . I never thought of it that way."

"Eddie, I'm honored that you confided in me. I'm sorry you've had
so much grief in your life. And I can't promise I'll give you a life without grief, but I'm willing to try. I want to be with you." He paused,
then added, "And you don't have to answer now."

One evening, Jeff left early. He was exhausted from working all day in
the hot sun and he had to get up at five. Eddie kissed him, waved to
him as he drove away, and went into the house.

Barrett was waiting for her.

"Want a beer?" she asked Eddie.

"No, thanks." Eddie walked across the room. "I think I'll chill with
some television."

Barrett said, as pleasantly as she could, "Well, *I* would like to talk."

"What about?" Eddie sat cross-legged on the sofa.

"How can you be so casual about Jeff?"

Eddie looked confused. "Excuse me?"

"Eddie, be real. You know you're going to break Jeff's heart when
you return to New York. You'll break your own heart, too."

"What about your heart?" Eddie countered. "Does Drew care
about you? Have you met his parents?"

"No, but his sister, Janny, helps me in the shop. She would tell me
if he was seeing someone else. Besides, he's in Boston most of the
week."

"I don't trust him, Barrett. He's too smooth, too rich, too summer
person."

"Don't worry about me," Barrett said. "I'm a big girl now."

Eddie paused, then smiled. "We need some *Gilmore Girls*. Bring
the ice cream."

———

One morning, when Barrett took inventory in her shop, she was astonished at how many items had been bought during late July. Expensive items, too. She'd priced Paul's boxes at two hundred dollars, and they were gone in a day. So were the bluebirds, priced at three hundred dollars. And five more of Louisa Sheppard's sweaters had sold, not to mention a few pieces of fine jewelry, gold with pearls in a deep blue shell and a silver mermaid pendant.

She opened her door to let the fresh morning air in. She sat on her high stool behind the counter and skimmed the list of recent sales.

Janny came to work at noon, and stayed until five, three days a week. She was patient and charming with customers, and many of her friends dropped by, purchasing some of the most expensive items. When Barrett and Janny were alone in the shop, unpacking or dusting, Janny would talk about her wonderful brother, and sometimes she'd mention one of Drew's former girlfriends.

"Ariadne is beautiful," Janny would say, "but she's kind of dim, and Drew needs an intelligent partner or he'd get bored. Besides, the children. I mean, he wants someone with a decent IQ, not just because he's so smart but because he wants his children to be smart, too."

Once, when it was raining and Janny was driving Barrett mad with her chatter, Barrett said, "I don't know why he's dating *me*. He hasn't asked me about my IQ once."

Janny hadn't realized Barrett was being sarcastic. "Oh, Barrett, I'm sure he can tell you're really smart."

Also, Janny flirted with *Paul*. He stopped by the shop often, bringing iced coffee, asking how their day was going. Even though he clearly wanted to talk with Barrett, Janny crept in, batting her lashes, biting her bottom lip, leaning forward to show the view down her dress. It bothered Barrett because she knew Janny was only playing around. Janny would never love some working-class guy like Paul. She didn't want Paul to get hurt. It was almost funny, how Barrett didn't want Janny to be with Paul and Janny wanted Barrett to be with Drew.

But Janny was, if not invaluable, certainly helpful. Without someone else at the counter, Barrett could never take a break to use the bathroom or eat a sandwich or talk on the phone. On rainy days, she and Janny worked in sync, talking to customers, making sales, wrapping and boxing up purchases. Janny could be funny, too, and that lightened the days.

Janny was with Barrett Friday afternoon when Paul entered the store.

Before Barrett could speak, Janny leaned over the counter, her breasts bulging, and said sweetly, "Hi, Paul! Have you brought more of your gorgeous artwork for our shop?"

Our shop? Barrett wanted to tell the younger woman to peel herself off the counter so Paul could set down the box he was carrying.

"Hi, Janny. Hi, Barrett." Paul smiled at them both. "Right. I've brought in a few more things."

He brought out picture frames of different sizes, the wood carved into rising and falling waves and painted blue. Curvaceous mermaids shaped into bookends. A wooden bird's nest holding three robin's-egg blue eggs.

Janny cooed, "These are lovely, Paul."

A woman entered the store just then, and Barrett could have kissed her.

"Janny, will you help our customer, please? Paul, let's take this box to the back room. It gets so crowded in here."

Her worktable was piled with boxes, bags, heaps of tissue paper, and her store laptop. Barrett shoved them aside. While Paul held the box, she carefully brought out each carved piece and set it on the table. The back room was smaller than the shop area, and as she moved, Barrett was aware of Paul's body so near to hers. Her hand accidentally touched his arm, and goosebumps rose all over her body. She wanted to tell Paul how perfect it was that he worked with wood, because he was so sturdy and strong himself, like a tree. And his carvings showed he could also be gentle and patient.

"How would you like to price these?" she asked him, her voice hoarse.

"I'll leave that to you. You know better than I about such matters. I've got some more in my workshop."

She studied Paul. He was tanned. His hands were blistered and scraped from construction work.

"Your nose is sunburned," she told him. "You should wear a cap."

"It's too hot for a hat," Paul told her.

"Your nose is going to peel." Who was she? Barrett thought. His mother? She didn't feel maternal toward him. She felt uncomfortably attracted to him. What did that mean about her relationship with Drew?

Reaching out, she took one of Paul's hands in her own, opening it, running her fingers over the calluses. How would these hard, rough hands feel against her body?

"Hey, listen," he said. "I know it's short notice but someone gave me tickets to the museum gala tomorrow night. It will be a big deal. The tickets sold for three hundred fifty dollars each. Want to go with me?"

"I'd love to," Barrett told him. "What time is it?"

"Great! It's six to nine but we can go anytime. It's casual. Well, as casual as these galas can be."

"Tomorrow's Saturday," Barrett said, thinking. "Let me see if Janny can work late."

She was surprised to see Janny standing at the door, watching.

"You know we agreed that Saturday nights I never work," Janny said, before Barrett could even ask.

Barrett sweetened her voice. "But could you, just this once?"

"No. I'd rather go to the gala with Paul." Janny grinned and put her finger between her lips, looking like a mischievous child.

Barrett felt like she'd been slapped in the face. Her voice shook slightly when she asked, "Well, *could* you work tomorrow night?"

Janny countered, "But what about Drew? Doesn't he get here tomorrow? Don't you have plans with him?" She peeked up through her eyelashes at Paul. "I would *love* to go with you."

Barrett felt Paul's entire body shift away from her.

"Oh, right, Barrett's got Drew," Paul said. "Sure, Janny, I'll take you."

Barrett wanted to tell the girl she was fired *right now*.

But Janny was right. What about Drew?

Saturday, Nantucket Blues was busy, and Barrett was glad. Janny came in at noon and worked until five. Barrett was uncomfortable around Janny, wondering why Paul so easily agreed to take her to the gala. Drew hadn't called her. Usually he called in the morning, to tell her what time he'd arrive. She'd meet his plane and they'd go off for a late dinner or a long quiet evening on the beach.

In the afternoon, when the store was in a lull and Janny was at the counter, Barrett slipped outside to take a walk up and down the wharf. The day was delightful, sunny and not too humid, and the mega-yachts on the outer, private docks were amazing, like boats out of a Liam Neeson movie. Children were running, laughing, buying balloons, kites, and candy, their parents strolling behind, licking ice cream cones.

Life was beautiful! She should stop whining. She should be brave! She sat on a bench beneath a tree and impulsively called Drew.

"Hey, babe," he answered. "What's up?"

"Hey, you. I'm just wondering what we're doing tonight."

"Oh, damn. I meant to call you . . . I've got to go to some stupid fundraiser gala with my parents tonight. They bought tickets. Plus, it's a good opportunity for me to network."

Barrett blinked, confused. Drew was going to the gala and he hadn't invited her to go with him?

Drew continued, "You wouldn't like it, Barry. It's all old farts and old cheese with damp crackers." He laughed at his own joke.

She had to say something. Forcing good humor into her voice, she said, "Janny will be there."

"I know. She told me. She's going with that carpenter."

That carpenter.

Paul was so much more than that. Barrett felt as if she were on an iceberg, breaking away from the continent.

When she didn't speak, Drew said, "But I'll try to be there early tomorrow. We can spend the afternoon together tomor— Oh, right. Do you have to be at your shop? Can't you forget it for one afternoon?"

Barrett was so shocked, she couldn't speak.

Drew continued talking. "Never mind, let's get together Sunday evening. I'll call."

"That sounds nice, Drew." Her mouth was dry. Her hands trembled. She felt like a foreigner in her own life. "I've got to get back to work."

She ended the call and began walking again. Drew didn't want to take her to a party where his parents were. She hated it that Eddie had been right, that Drew wasn't interested in something real. She hated it more that Janny had weaseled her way into an evening with Paul.

Eddie had many sexy and sophisticated dresses in her closet, but Jeff was taking her to have dinner with his parents tonight, and Eddie wanted to look pretty for Jeff and sweet for his parents, although they had to know by now that their son was a grown man who didn't date women only for their sweetness. She settled on a simple blue cotton dress with low-heeled sandals.

She had butterflies in her stomach when Jeff picked her up at the house. Why was she so nervous, or was she excited? She knew why! Because "meeting the parents" was a big deal. It was a test she wanted to pass and she didn't know all the rules.

She was certain she'd met Jessie and Howie Jefferson sometime during that first year she'd lived on the island. Howie was treasurer for the town, a demanding and admirable job. Jessie loved to cook and channeled that love into running bake sales for the local churches and charities. Jessie was, in her own way, famous.

The Jeffersons' house was off Milestone Road, down a tree-lined driveway to a small ranch house settled in a paradise of flowers.

"Mom takes bouquets to the Saturday farmers' market in town," Jeff explained as he helped Eddie from the truck. "She donates the proceeds to A Safe Place."

Jessie was at the door. "Hello, hello, come in!"

Jessie was a pretty woman in jeans and a floral shirt. Her dark hair was twisted up and held by a silver barrette inset with glittering stones. She was barefoot, and her toenails were painted deep purple.

"Lovely to meet you, Eddie." Jessie kissed Eddie's cheek and gave her son a hug and ushered them into the house, past the open-plan room with a TV and sofas at one end and a kitchen at the other, and out the door to the deck.

Jeff's father was busy at the grill, but he turned and greeted Jeff and Eddie with a wave and a question. "You eat meat, right? Steak?"

"I do," Eddie said.

"Sit, sit," Jessie said, indicating two canvas deck chairs. "How are you? Have you had a good day? Eddie, I want to hear *all about* Dinah Lavender!"

"You should come by the Book Barn sometime. I know she'd love to autograph a book for you."

"Thank you for the invitation! I belong to a book club that meets once a month. My friends are very excited that Jeff has met the writer, and they want an up close, firsthand account, because Jeff is hopeless, he just says she's pretty and she's *nice*." She caught her breath. "Would you like a beer? That's what the men are drinking. I'm having a sparkling pink wine. It's called Mimi, a perfect name, don't you think? All the women I've met who are named Mimi are sparkling."

While Jessie went into the kitchen for the drinks, Jeff said quietly, "I was going to warn you, but I thought I'd let you get the real Jessie, full force."

"She's amazing," Eddie whispered.

When Jessie arrived with their drinks, Eddie sat back in her chair and relaxed. They ate sliced tomatoes topped with mozzarella, the tomatoes from Jessie's plants, and tender steaks, potato salad, and a green salad with arugula and Bibb lettuce that Jessie had grown in her garden. Jeff's father was not a conversationalist. He obviously left that to his wife and sat happily listening to her, adding sharp remarks now and then.

"Tell me about your father," Jessie urged. "I've noticed him here and there. He's a terrifically handsome man. I've heard that he's divorced. Is he seeing anyone? Because I have several friends who would be over the moon to go out with him, to dinner or a play. One of my friends, Darcy, has a boat. Do you think your father might enjoy a sail this summer?"

"Leave her alone, Jessie," Jeff's father said gently. "The man doesn't need you prying in his life."

"Oh," Jessie said sweetly, "I'll bet he does." She jumped up from her chair. "I'll get dessert."

Jessie brought out Klondike bars.

"I can't get enough ice cream in the summer," she announced. "I hope you aren't insulted that I didn't make something special."

"This is perfect," Eddie said. "What a marvelous summer meal."

"The corn isn't ready yet. It will be a few weeks more before it's sweet." Jessie caught her husband's glance. "I know, I know, I'm such a chatterbox. Eddie, how do you like being back on Nantucket?"

"It's beautiful here," Eddie began.

"Summer in the city can be so hot," Jessie said. "And I could be wrong, but it seems that during summer in New York, the sidewalks become even harder than usual. Maybe the molecules shrink or expand? And I've often wondered how any breeze can get to the street between all the tall buildings."

As if showing off especially for Jessie, a cool, sea-scented breeze slid around them, making the trees at the back of the Jeffersons' land dip and sway.

Jeff ate the last bite of his Klondike bar, crushed the wrapper in his hands, and stood up. "Sorry, Mom, but I've got to work tomorrow."

Eddie rose, too. "Thank you so much for this wonderful evening." She smiled at Jeff's father. "My steak was delicious. Thank you."

Before she could say more, Jeff took her hand and led her away, down the steps from the deck to the driveway and his truck.

Once they were settled in with their seatbelts fastened, Jeff grinned at Eddie. "Well, now you've met my mom."

"She's wonderful," Eddie said truthfully. She wondered how her life would have been if she had had a mother like that.

Saturday evening, Barrett locked up her shop and headed home, going out of her way to drive past the Fischer house on the cliff. It was an amazing property. Tommy Hilfiger had once owned it. Flowers bloomed everywhere. Lights shone from the many windows like beacons. This was Drew and Janny's summer residence.

When she pulled into her own driveway, she sat for a moment, considering. The old farmhouse her father had bought was not a mansion, but it was sturdy and welcoming. The Book Barn was closed and the horse had trotted up to the fence to check out her arrival. She knew Duchess would race away if she tried to pet her, so she only called a hello as she left her car and walked toward the house.

Two tubs of glossy begonias with bright pink flowers stood on the porch at either side of the steps to the front door. This was Eddie's touch, Barrett realized, and as she entered her home, she walked through it slowly, noticing for the first time all the small changes Eddie had made.

On the front hall table, an antique blue and white porcelain basin held all the mail that was usually scattered. The windows were open in the living room, letting the cool evening air drift in and gently stir the vase of roses on the coffee table. Eddie had bought them, probably at the local grocery store, and three bunches had been gathered together, brightening the room. The dining room cupboard held several bottles of good wine, brought home by Dinah, and Barrett walked into the kitchen, knowing that if she opened the refrigerator, she would find several tempting desserts. Tiramisu. Blueberry pie. Chocolate chip brownies.

"Hello?" Barrett called.

Duke barked once in reply, but was too comfortable on the living room sofa to jump down.

"Hello, handsome," Barrett said, petting him.

Her father didn't respond, but the light was on in his study, shining out beneath the closed door.

Barrett took a piece of pie, wandered into the den, collapsed on the sofa, and clicked the remote control. Someone, probably Dinah, had been watching *The Borgias*. Barrett was tired. She'd worked hard all summer and had more work to come. Her father stuck his head into the den to say hello and went off to bed at ten.

She yawned and relaxed and gave herself over to the complicated world of fifteenth-century Italy.

It was nearly eleven when her phone buzzed. The caller ID read *Drew*. Barrett hesitated. Why wasn't he at the gala?

She muted the TV and answered her phone.

"Hey, aren't you at a gala?" she asked.

Drew's voice was low and sexy. "I was. I went with my parents, and we left early. I thought you might be up for a moonlight walk on the beach."

Barrett hesitated. He hadn't taken her to the gala, but that was because of his parents, right? Did this call mean he really liked her?

"That would be nice," she said.

"I'll pick you up in ten minutes."

Barrett raced up to her room, took off the blue sundress she'd been working in, pulled on a T-shirt and shorts, brushed her teeth, and hurried down to the porch, arriving just in time to see the headlights of Drew's car as he turned in to the drive.

Drew leaned over and opened the passenger door. Barrett left the porch, ran to his car, and slid inside. Drew touched her face lightly and kissed her.

He said, "I'm so glad to see you."

"Me, too," Barrett replied, keeping it light.

Drew smelled like alcohol and a high-end men's cologne. He'd changed into a wrinkled T-shirt, board shorts, and loafers.

"Did you have fun tonight?" Barrett asked him.

"Not really. My parents still like to show me off as if I were five and had just starred in a school play."

"That's nice," Barrett said. "You're lucky. Not everyone's parents are so admiring."

"It's not admiration," Drew told her, sounding serious. "My sister and I have always been acquisitions, possessions, enriching their portfolio."

"Somehow," Barrett said, "I'm not feeling sorry for you."

"I get you." Drew steered onto the Cisco road. "I'm not doing the poor-little-rich-boy bit. I'm lucky and I know it. I would just rather have spent tonight with you."

Drew parked the car at the barriers to the beach.

"How cool is this?" he asked. "No other cars here. It's all ours! Let's walk."

They kicked off their shoes, left the car, and walked and half slid down the dune to the wide beach. It was a sultry night with a crescent moon blurred by haze and humidity. The ocean hid its shades of blue and silver beneath a deep expanse of black. Beneath their feet, the sand was still warm from the sun.

"It's hot," Barrett said.

Drew stopped walking. He took Barrett in his arms. "*You're* hot."

He kissed her softly. Sinking onto the sand, they lay back together, side by side. Darkness covered them, with only enough light from the moon for them to see each other's faces. Drew slid his hand up her thigh and beneath her shorts.

Barrett said, "Drew, *no*."

In a low voice, Drew said, "Barrett, you're all I think about. I'm crazy attracted to you and I think you feel the same."

"Drew." She rolled away from him, putting space between them. She didn't think she'd ever been so confused. This was the guy romances told her she should want, this wealthy, handsome, urgent suitor. And he was attractive. But something wasn't right and she couldn't figure out what it was.

She said, "It's late, and I have to work tomorrow, and I'm sorry, but I think I need to go home."

Immediately she sensed his disappointment. It seemed as if anger was steaming off him like the summer's heat.

Then Drew took a deep breath. "Yeah, you're right." He stood up and held out his hand. "We should go home."

As they walked toward his car, Barrett said softly, "Drew, don't be mad."

"I'm not mad," Drew muttered.

Still, when Drew sat behind the wheel and started the car, Barrett noticed how tight his lips were, almost thin, and his jaw was clenched. Or maybe it was a trick of the moonlight.

Eddie was writing on her laptop. Her bedroom window was open to allow the cool night air to drift in with its alluring scents of salt and honeysuckle. She'd turned off her bedroom lights as she always did, so that people would think she was asleep. She needed privacy for what she was doing. She knew she was being paranoid and even ridiculous, but she didn't want anyone else to see what she was writing. After all, not one, but two writers were in the house now, and her efforts were nothing compared to theirs.

What she was writing was a journal in a way, but really, it was more than that. Was it the beginning of a *novel*? From the first page, the first line, she'd embroidered and reordered the events of her own personal day with the events, emotions, and dreams of a woman much like her, but different, and it was only as she sat at her desk, typing words into her laptop, that this other woman was becoming clearer, as if she were telling Eddie her own story, which was like Eddie's but also very different.

It was about a woman named Edie who had come to the island to run her sister's shop while her sister and her sister's new husband were on their honeymoon, and were kidnapped. Her sister's husband was from a wealthy family, and the kidnappers wanted ransom and his parents were stalling about paying . . .

Writing this novel or whatever it was made Eddie's brain wake up. She could almost feel all the little brain cells light up like fireworks as she wrote. She was only halfway through, and she knew at some point she wanted someone else to read it, but who could she trust to read it and still love her and respect her afterward? What if she was deluded that it made any sense at all?

Her computer chimed to alert her to a new email. It had to be junk if someone was sending it so late, but she was stalled at a scene, so she opened her email.

And almost fell off her chair.

It was from *Dove*.

Hi, Eddie, I'm coming to the island this summer, with Bobby. I have a lot to tell you and Barrett but I'll wait until I see you all in person. So much has changed in my life. I hope you and Barrett and your father are well.

Love, Dove

"*What?*" Eddie threw her hands up in the air. She hit *Reply*. The email address was @coloradocybercafe.com.

"Dove," Eddie said aloud. "I don't believe this!"

In a barely controlled frenzy, Eddie typed, *OMG Dove, I'm so*

happy to hear from you! I can't wait to see you! Call me. Here's my
cell number. Plus, here's Barrett's cell. We will be SO HAPPY to see
you and Bobby! Love, Eddie.

She clicked *Send* and sat with both hands pressed to her heart while
she waited for Dove's reply. She realized Colorado was two hours behind Nantucket, and maybe Dove wasn't at the Coloradocybercafé
computer. Maybe she wasn't waiting for a reply. Surely she knew they
would want to see her.

Should she wake her father and tell him? Was Barrett home from
her date with Drew?

Barrett would turn cartwheels!

Eddie stared at her mailbox. Nothing new arrived. Eddie tapped
her fingers on her desk.

Nothing new.

She stood up and paced the room. It was so easy to get supersti-
tious with internet communication, because the entire system was so
mysterious and even unbelievable that entire words and manuscripts
could pass from one state to another in an instant—really, it was impossible, but it happened, so why wasn't it possible that her messages
could pass instantly, mysteriously from her mad hopes into Dove's
mind?

The laptop chimed.

Eddie flew back to her desk and plonked down in her chair.

Email not deliverable.

"Come on!" Eddie yelled at the computer.

She opened Dove's email again and wrote her own message again
and clicked *Send* again.

She went to Facebook, Instagram, Threads, X, Yahoo, and Google
and searched for *Dove Fletcher* and *Dove Grant*. Nothing.

She wanted to throw her laptop out the window. No, she wanted to
throw it on the floor and jump up and down on it in a frenzy of frus-
tration.

Rationally, she knew that wouldn't help. She knew that computers could make human beings insanely angry beyond all logical limits. She wanted to tell someone, anyone, that she hated the internet.

Was there anything she could do?

Her computer chimed. *Email not deliverable.*

Eddie closed her laptop. She wondered how many people had died of heart attacks because of the cold, uncaring, incomprehensible unresponsiveness of computers.

She really did want to break something. Maybe Bill Gates's nose.

It was after one o'clock. Eddie went downstairs and roamed through the dark house. The hall light was off, which meant Barrett was home and in bed. Duke was on his back, snoring, looking ridiculous, by the kitchen door. She stared out the kitchen window. The spotlight on the barn illuminated the backyard. Everything was still. Everything quiet.

Everything except her brain.

She returned to her room, got ready for bed, wondering if she should tell Barrett and her father about Dove's email, or if it would make them as frustrated as she was.

But she hadn't imagined it. Dove had contacted her, and she and Bobby were coming to the island to see them.

Barrett was lifting the white sheet, preparing to slide into bed, when someone knocked on the door, and without waiting, Eddie entered.

"Barrett," Eddie said. "I have to tell you something."

"Okay, but why be so drama queen about it?" Barrett sat on her bed. She was tired and she had to work tomorrow.

Eddie sat at the other end of the bed. "I just got an email from Dove."

"You're kidding!" Barrett shivered. *Dove.*

"Not kidding. It was really odd. She found my email address, and she said she's coming to Nantucket this summer and bringing Bobby."

"Really? Why didn't she write me? Dove isn't just yours!"

"Simmer down," Eddie said. "I know she's not all mine. Here, read her email." She handed her phone to Barrett.

Barrett read the message. "This is wonderful. Did you reply?"

"I *tried* to email her back, but it wouldn't go through. I've tried so many times. It's as if Coloradocybercafe.com doesn't exist, because the email is undeliverable."

"I don't understand."

"I don't, either. It can't be fake or a scam or a bot. But her email address simply does not exist."

"Have you tried—"

Eddie interrupted. She rose and paced the room. "Yes. I've tried Dove Grant, Robert Grant, Rob Grant, Bob Grant, Stearns Grant, StGrant—"

"Okay, okay. If Dove contacted us once, she will again. She says she's coming to the island, so she'll come."

"But she doesn't say when," Eddie said. She plunked down on the bed again. "I didn't want to get your hopes up. I mean, what if she changes her mind? Do we just have to *wait*?"

"What else can we do? It's good that she wants to come here, Eddie. She's had a lot to deal with. Maybe she had to sort of crawl behind a rock and heal and now she's well enough to see us."

"Should we tell Dad?"

"Not yet. Let's wait and see if you hear from her again."

Eddie said, "I don't know whether to be happy or worried about this."

Barrett was pleased that for once she got to give advice.

"Be happy," she said. "Now go to bed."

thirteen

Sundays were lazy for most people, but Barrett, like all the other merchants on the island, opened her shop. Janny didn't work on Sunday, because business was slow then, and really, Barrett enjoyed her time alone. No famous, glamorous romance writer was here, making Barrett feel boring and, in comparison, flat-chested. No beautiful, brilliant older sister was around, taking care of their father and Barrett, wishing she were really back in the city, *any* city like New York or London or Paris or Rome. No unhappy father trudged through life, writing his seven-hundredth version of a book that no one needed.

No, this was Barrett's place, one she'd created with her own money and dreams. She was really living in Nantucket Blues. As she gently dusted and polished her blue souvenirs, she thought about what blue meant to her. It was the color of the sky and the color of the sea. In the dark universe, the earth was a globe of blue. Blue was breath and breathtaking. Blue held the ships as they crossed the ocean and blue was the essence of the sky that carried the planes. When she had been a little girl, she'd decided that as long as she could see the sky, she would be happy. A simple, innocent thought, Barrett knew, but not the worst motto to live by.

Laughter and music drifted over the water from the boats moored in the harbor. Chocolate and coffee scents rippled through the air. Today it was hot and super humid. Clothes were damp and sticky and hair that was set to be straight went frizzy and hair that was set to be curly hung flat. Barrett wore no bra and a sundress that hung loosely around her body. She twisted her hair into a whale's spout on top of her head.

Most days Barrett didn't turn on the air conditioner, because she thought that keeping her door open invited more people in to browse and buy. But today she turned it on and hung an extra sign in the window: AIR-CONDITIONED.

A man came in and bought a present for his wife. Two women came in to buy mementoes of their island vacation.

Eddie called. "You close your shop at six on Sundays, right?"

"Right." Barrett watched a man, holding hands with a little girl whose braids bounced as she skipped, come toward the shop.

"I'd better go," Barrett said.

"Okay, but don't eat dinner out. I'm fixing a great dinner here."

"Wonderful!" Barrett clicked off.

"We're buying a present for Mommy!" the little girl called out.

"That's so cool!"

Barrett had placed the breakable items above the reach of small children so pieces wouldn't get accidentally broken, but of course the objects the girl wanted to see were little. Barrett was kindness itself as she reached for a tiny blue glass whale and a miniature porcelain birdhouse. She happily showed ten different pieces before the little girl decided she wanted the blue T-shirt with an image of the island on the front. As they left, a group of women here for the weekend came in, chattering and twittering like robins on the first day of spring. They bought all of Paul's work, and some T-shirts, and all the blue baseball caps, even the ones with the smiling sharks across the front.

Eddie told everyone to come for dinner at six-thirty, and everyone came, even Dinah. Eddie took one end of the table and her father sat at the other end. Barrett and Dinah would face each other across the table. Eddie sensed that Barrett was brooding about something, but that would have to wait. Eddie was serving lasagna, garlic bread, corn on the cob, and a green salad.

Dinah was the last to arrive. She made a grand entrance, carrying a bottle of champagne.

"What's the occasion?" Eddie asked.

"Being with all of you is the occasion," Dinah said. She certainly looked festive in her lavender sundress. Her long black hair was swept up into a twist at the back of her head. An amethyst pendant hung from a gold chain, pointing directly down to the space between her swelling breasts.

Sweetly, she said, "William, could you please open this bottle? I'm sure I can't do it. And the bottle is so cold, the glass hurts my hands."

Before he could refuse, she handed him the bottle. He focused on opening it as if he were defusing a bomb. Dinah settled into her chair with a rustle of her dress. Eddie noticed that her father had showered and put on a clean shirt.

Good for him, she thought. *Maybe he's reentering real life.*

William uncorked the bottle perfectly. He rose and went around the table, pouring champagne for everyone, which was nice of him, although just possibly he was trying to sneak a look down Dinah's bodice.

"Here's to summer!" Eddie raised her glass in a toast and everyone joined.

The champagne tasted like sunshine.

They chatted lightly as they ate, describing their days, pausing to moan with pleasure when they ate the fresh, butter-covered corn on the cob.

Barrett asked Dinah, "How do you like it on Nantucket?"

Dinah smiled, her lips shining with butter. "More than I can say. I've been reading all the Nantucket history and Nantucket fiction I can get my hands on. I'm dreaming of writing a Nantucket romance."

William shifted uncomfortably in his chair. "We're both working on what we call romances. I think our ideas are very different."

Dinah turned to him with a beautiful smile. "Oh, yes, of course. *My* idea of a romance involves men, women, and love. Your English Romantic poets were very British in their inability to talk about love between men and women."

Oh, here we go, Eddie thought.

William couldn't take his eyes off Dinah. "I'm not sure you're right about that."

Dinah focused on William. "From what I know of the British Romantic poets, and, William, *you* are undeniably the expert on them, it seems they wrote about skylarks, clouds, and daffodils. Rainbows. Deep chasms, and that wasn't a metaphor for part of the human body. The most famous are about nature. Not *human* nature."

"What poems do you consider the most famous?" William asked, obviously skeptical but interested.

"'The Rime of the Ancient Mariner,' of course. 'Kubla Khan.' Wordsworth's daffodil doggerel."

Eddie wiggled her eyebrows across the table at Barrett. They waited quietly as the other two talked, and when their father pulled his chair around so he could face Dinah directly, they widened their eyes comically at each other.

"A woman also wrote poetry at that time," Dinah said. "Have you ever heard of Charlotte Turner Smith?"

"Of course," William answered.

"Are you including her in your book?" Dinah asked sweetly.

William cleared his throat. "Probably not. She wasn't that important."

"Really? Have you read her poetry?" Dinah leaned toward William.

"Not all of it," William admitted, slanting toward Dinah as if she were a magnet.

Dinah spoke alluringly. "Have you read her biography?"

Eddie locked eyes with Barrett. Was Dinah trying to seduce their father?

"We'll get dessert," Eddie said quietly and nodded to her sister.

They carried their dishes into the kitchen.

"What's going on?" Eddie whispered to Barrett.

"I can't even guess!" Barrett hissed back. "I think Dinah is hypnotizing Dad."

"Let's get back there!" Eddie ordered.

They brought out the platter of Bartlett's desserts.

"Dinah, Dad, what would you like?" Eddie asked. "We have a blueberry pie, chocolate mousse, or tiramisu."

"Can we have two desserts?" Dinah asked.

"Of course!" Eddie replied.

"You have a sweet tooth," William remarked as he helped himself to blueberry pie.

Dinah had chocolate mousse on her plate and a spot of whipped cream on her lips. She smiled at William. "I certainly do." She licked her spoon, closed her eyes, and moaned quietly.

William blushed.

Eddie looked at Barrett, who read her mind. Their father had *blushed*.

William wrenched his focus onto his pie. He took a bite, swallowed it, and said to Dinah, "You seem to have an impressive knowledge of the Romantic poets."

"I love romance," Dinah told him. Leaning closer to him, she said, "I would love to read the book you're working on."

William looked absolutely terrified.

He choked out, "It . . . it's not ready for anyone else to read."

"But *I'm* not just anybody," Dinah reminded him. "I have no connection with anyone in your very exclusive intellectual circles but I do, as you say, know a lot about the Romantic poets." She leaned even closer to him, her creamy bosom swelling. "I'd let *you* read one of *my* books."

William looked stunned. "I don't . . . I don't have time to read contemporary fiction."

Eddie cried, "Oh, go on, Dad! It will do you good to lighten up!"

"Yes, Dad, go on," Barrett echoed.

William gazed around the table at the three women. "I'll think about it. Now, if you'll excuse me, I have work to do. Eddie, thank you for the dinner. Good night."

He quickly left from the room.

Barrett waited until her father had shut his study door before speaking.

"Dad's always been defensive about his work."

Dinah nodded. "Yes, of course he has. As have I. For some reason, the literary world scorns romance. Yet any and all of those critics want romance in their lives. *Need* romance."

"Why?" Barrett demanded. "Why?"

Dinah spoke gently. "Because romance stirs up our endorphins, and we always need little hits from the chemicals that are released when we fall in love. When we fall in love, we float on our pleasure into marriage, where we love profoundly, if we are lucky. But in marriage, reality comes stomping in like a smelly old warthog, crushing us with rent, mortgage, accidents, toothaches, difficult relatives, babies who won't sleep through the night. We lose our sense of romance beneath the problems of everyday life. Reading a romance novel wakes up our endorphins, relaxes and releases us from the grip of necessity to the pleasure of being with another person. It makes you remember how it felt when you were in love and your lover was sitting next to you and he simply touched your hand. Just one light touch, and you're happy." She smiled and nodded to herself, as if remembering.

"Is that why you never married?" Eddie asked.

Dinah's smile was gentle, wistful. "Yes. That's why. And I got to enjoy many romances, and I intend to enjoy many more."

"Me, too." The sisters spoke at the same time and the three women laughed.

"Let's go to Madaket," Eddie suggested. "If we go now, we'll be there for the sunset."

"I don't know," Barrett said. "I've got to do laundry, and help clean the kitchen, and I'm already bushed from working seven days a week."

"Then you really need to go to Madaket," Eddie told her.

Dinah spoke up. "Your sister is right. We should go to Madaket now. Tell your father to clean the kitchen."

Barrett stared in shock. "I thought you were all about romance."

Dinah lifted one perfectly shaped eyebrow. "There is nothing romantic about a messy kitchen and something very sexy about a man who can do the dishes."

Eddie laughed. "That sentiment should be printed on dish towels." She tugged Barrett's arm. "Come on. Let's go."

Eddie led the way. William's door was shut. She knocked on it.

"Dad, we're going out to Madaket. Would you clean the kitchen? Thanks. Bye."

Before he could speak, the three women hurried out the door to Eddie's Jeep.

Eddie flicked on the radio as she drove and Meghan Trainor's "All About That Bass" blasted into the air. When they arrived at the west end of the island, they discovered the Madaket sunset was no secret. Dozens of cars were parked in the small parking lot.

"Never mind," Eddie said. "We'll walk."

They parked on the side of the road and walked to a giant dune blocking the view. Eddie was their trailblazer. They climbed the dune and stood at the top, catching their breath and gazing out at the long stretch of perfect beach stretching out to the horizon. Laughing, they half slid down the dune and hurried to slip their feet into the water.

The sea was calm, the tide drifting up to shore and whispering *sssssh* as it receded. They slowly walked west, not speaking, as if listening to what the ocean was telling them. When the sun was close to the horizon, they sat cross-legged to watch the light play over the sky and sea, and the view was so vast, the water turning amber, brown, gold, so it seemed that if they ran into the water now, they would come out with their own skin magically flickering with sunlight.

Eddie cleared her throat. "Dinah, remember when I told you about our brother, Stearns? And Dove, who was our friend? Before Stearns died, Dove had a baby, a little boy, Bobby. Stearns died, and Dove took Bobby to Colorado with her. Well, um, I've had an email from Dove. They're coming to visit us, here, on the island. I don't know exactly when."

"How nice," Dinah said. "I look forward to meeting them." She continued gazing at the sky.

It took a long time for the sun to sink below the horizon. When it did, a group watching from the top of a cliff applauded. At once, the air was cooler and the world was a darkening gray.

Dinah broke the silence. "My hair is frizzing."

Barrett laughed and Eddie said, "It's part of Nantucket's charm."

As if sent by the sun, a breeze came up, and they shivered.

"Time to go home," Eddie said.

They walked down the beach, back up the dune, down to the road. This time, as Eddie drove home, she didn't turn on the music. No one talked. They were lost in their own thoughts.

When they returned to the house, they discovered that William had cleared the table, cleaned the kitchen, and started the dishwasher. Eddie and Barrett did a high five.

Barrett buzzed with good energy as she opened her shop. She should walk by the ocean every evening, or at least several times a week. She unpacked deliveries, set out more stock, dusted, and polished.

She was surprised when Paul came in, carrying a box of carved pieces.

"Oh, good," Barrett said. "We've sold all of your boxes and only one songbird is left."

Paul put the box on the counter and brought out several paperweights, carved into orbs, except for the flat bottom, and painted to resemble a blue ocean with a gold Nantucket Island curving over the top. They were stunning.

"Wow, Paul. These are amazing. This is your best work yet," Barrett told him.

They discussed the pricing, and Barrett gave him the proceeds from his sales last week, and she offered him coffee, and he said he'd rather buy two very cold iced coffees from Provisions.

"It's almost noon," Barrett realized. "The wharf is deserted. Anyone with any sense is at the beach now. Let's sit on the bench outside."

"Agree. I'll be right back." Paul left the shop.

Barrett sat on the bench. Thank heavens, it was in shadow now, cooler than the other side of the wharf. She watched Paul coming back with the cold drinks. He was wearing work boots, cargo pants, and a white T-shirt. He was tall and muscular and sunburned.

"Thanks," she told him when he handed her the iced coffee. When he had settled next to her and they had both sipped their drinks, she asked, "Why are you wearing your work boots today?"

"Because I've been at work." Paul rolled his shoulders.

His very big, very handsome shoulders.

"But you're here now?" Why couldn't she keep her eyes off of him? When he moved his arm to drink his coffee, she saw the ropes of his veins over the swelling muscles. She wanted to put her hand on his arm, to feel its strength, its sturdiness. She'd always thought Paul was sexy, but this felt like more.

She was confused in so many ways.

"I started work at five," Paul told her. "I wanted to take an hour off to come see you."

Was it hot out here? Barrett wondered. *Why am I so hot?* "Oh, right. To bring me your paperweights."

After a moment, Paul agreed, "Right."

"How is it going?" she asked. "The building, I mean."

"Good. We're working from sunup to sundown, with only a half hour lunch break. But I get it. Everyone wants a fancy new house on the island so they can live here for two weeks and brag about having a place on Nantucket when they're in the city."

"I'm amazed at how much money everyone has," Barrett said. "The island's changing."

"It will be fine," Paul said. "I grew up here. Change happens, but the island is still here. Still the island." He changed the subject. "How are the sales at the Book Barn?"

"Slow. Still, enough books are getting sold so that Eddie can cull more from the house to put on the shelves," Barrett said.

"Good. That's good. Let me know if you need anything else. Like more shelves."

"Thanks. Oh, how was the gala with Janny?" Barrett was surprised at how her pulse quickened when she mentioned his date. Was she jealous?

"It was okay. Lots of good champagne, great food."

Barrett couldn't keep herself from pressing, "Did you have fun with Janny?"

"I guess. She's young. I met her brother and his date." Paul took another swig of iced coffee. "Well, I'd met Drew before, here at your opening."

"So," Barrett said slowly, as if figuring out a puzzle, "you and Janny and Drew and *his date*?"

"You know." Paul turned to Barrett as he spoke. "I didn't want to take Janny. I wanted to take you."

Barrett sat there, confused and elated. *Paul wants to be with me.*

"I'm going to another gala in a few weeks," Paul continued. "A benefit for the Nantucket Safe Harbor for Animals auction. It's at the

Nantucket Yacht Club this year. Cocktails, lots of hors d'oeuvres, live music, and a silent auction. Starts at six, goes till eight. Would you come with me?"

Barrett heard herself reply almost before she thought of her answer. "I'd love to," she said. "If Janny can't work for me that night, I'll close the shop."

After Paul went back to work, Barrett was glad to be busy. Her emotions were in turmoil. Drew had taken another woman to the gala and then had picked up Barrett after the gala for a booty call? She needed to talk to Eddie. And really, she needed to talk with Drew.

Eddie was enjoying the summer more than she'd imagined possible. She held the fort at home. She bought groceries, made crockpot meals so anyone could eat at any time, stocked the refrigerator with watermelon, seedless grapes, and lemonade. Some evenings, she accompanied Dinah to dinner and a concert or play and on a rare occasion, she coaxed her father into going with them. She ran into old acquaintances—could she call them *friends* if she'd only been on the island for one year?—and went to their barbecue parties. Some evenings she spent with Jeff, and those were the loveliest times of all.

During July, the island reached its peak population of summer people as well as its fiercest heat. The island's narrow and often one-way roads were crowded with Mercedes SUVs, Range Rovers, Toyota Land Cruisers, and every kind of van known to mankind. Summer people without helmets steered bikes in and out of traffic, disregarding stop signs, or strolled in front of moving cars as if cars didn't exist on Nantucket. People honked, yelled, and cursed. The valiant drivers of UPS and FedEx delivery trucks rumbled along the streets without plowing into the convertibles that ignored the signs and zipped in front of them.

And yet, Eddie realized she was happy. This traffic was nothing compared to New York. Once she turned off Main Street or went around the rotary onto Milestone Road, she headed for secluded places, like the moors in the middle of the island. Here, the dirt paths winding between green fields were bumpy and curvy, and surrounded by heath, ivy, beach plum bushes, and flowers so small they could make a bouquet for a doll. She often ate her lunch sitting by the "Doughnut Pond," a hidden round pond with a round island in the middle. There it was so quiet, she could hear birds calling and watch iridescent blue dragonflies flitting near her. Rare, endangered wood lilies, their orange petals speckled with black dots, grew for only a few weeks a year, mostly hidden in the high grass and blueberry bushes.

This was an area she hadn't known about during her first year on the island. She hiked up and down the low hills, surprised at all the various shades of green and the enticing wink of blue water from small nearby ponds. This was an island of peace in the middle of Nantucket, and it spoke to her, it enchanted her.

Best of all, at night, when the others were in bed, Eddie sat at her computer and spent time with her secret love. As she wrote, her worries and hopes for her life disappeared. As she struggled to delve deep into her heart to find the words she needed for this fictional life, she sensed she was creating new possibilities for her real life. When she wrote, it was like finding her way through a dark tunnel toward the light, and it changed, brightened, clarified, how she was finding her way through her own life. Also, what she wrote was becoming its own separate thing, as if she was weaving with words and creating something that hadn't existed before.

Today, she opened the Book Barn and picked some of her zinnias to put in the barn and another bunch to put in the kitchen. Barrett was at her shop, Jeff was working. Her father was standing at the kitchen counter, eating peanut butter and crackers.

"Is that your lunch?" Eddie asked him.

"Mmm." William drank a sip of water. "I'm thinking."

"Dad, let me make you a sandwich."

"Thanks, but this is good. I need to get back to work." He gave her a rare smile and returned to his study.

Eddie strolled out to the mailbox at the end of the drive. Duke was lying in the shade of the porch and only thumped his tail as a greeting. The mailbox was stuffed. Eddie realized that she and her family had gotten lax about checking it. Everyone sent emails or texts these days and Eddie paid bills online.

She carried the pile of catalogs and envelopes into the house, set it all on the dining room table, and started sorting it out. It was mostly junk, but one envelope was addressed by hand. Eddie's heart stopped.

It was a letter, addressed to Eddie and Barrett, from Dove.

Eddie couldn't wait until Barrett was home to read the letter. She ripped open the envelope.

Hi, Barrett and Eddie, I hope you got my email. Bobby and I are on our way to visit you. I'm not sure when we'll get there. I have a health problem that will slow me down. But Bobby's very healthy. I can't wait to see you all and especially for you to meet Bobby. He is a little Stearns.

Remembering the happy times we had when we were kids.

XO D

"What!" Eddie yelled. She stood up, then sat down again. She was thrilled and furious and excited. She felt like she was going to explode.

What should she do? What *could* she do? She'd tried Instagram, Threads, Facebook, even Google, but she couldn't find any mention of Dove Fletcher. Eddie had also tried Dove Grant, in case her brother and Dove had gotten married and hadn't bothered to tell them. It was the sort of thing Stearns would have done. But no Dove Grant showed up.

She needed to talk this over with Barrett. Should she tell her father now? Eddie knew she was too emotional. She returned to the kitchen just in time to see a carload of people headed for the Book Barn. Eddie stuck the letter in the cloth napkin drawer and went out to the barn.

Eddie decided to make a special meal for Barrett when she returned home after closing her shop. She wanted Barrett calm and relaxed before she showed her the letter Dove had sent. Barrett loved having breakfast for dinner, so Eddie made blueberry pancakes and piles of perfectly browned bacon and poured Vermont maple syrup from a can into a small glass pitcher.

Barrett walked into the house, dropped her bag on the front hall table, and entered the kitchen.

"What smells so good?" she asked.

Eddie couldn't help it. She was very pleased with herself.

"Sit down. I've made a special dinner just for you."

Eddie slid two pancakes onto a plate, added a pile of bacon, and set it in front of Barrett. "Butter and syrup right here. What would you like to drink?"

"Oh, my God, Eddie! You did this for me?" Barrett burst into tears.

"Hey, hey, Barrett, what's wrong?"

"Oh, nothing, really. I'm just tired. This is just so great of you, Eddie."

Eddie sat at the other end of the table, idly folding napkins, chatting about nothing important, watching Barrett eat like a starving woman.

When Barrett had done everything but lick the plate clean, Eddie rose to get her sister a glass of cold water.

"Now," Eddie said. "Did you have a bad day?"

Barrett sipped her water and sighed as she leaned back against her chair.

"Not really. I mean, the shop was really ticking over today. And people were so complimentary. It's just . . . oh, you know, man trouble."

Eddie set her elbow on the table and cradled her chin in her hand. "Tell me."

Barrett blurted, "Drew took another woman to the gala!"

Thank heavens she hadn't told her sister about Dove's letter. "How do you know?"

"Paul told me. He took Janny, even though he asked me first. In front of Paul, Janny reminded me that I had a date with Drew that night. She slimed her way into getting Paul to take *her*. Then when I thought Drew was taking me, he told me he had to go with his parents. But today I learned that Drew *had* a date!"

"Oh, Care Bear, that's awful." Eddie wanted to race out of the house, find Drew Fischer, and slug him in the nose.

"It gets worse. Saturday night, Drew called me *after* the gala and asked me to go to the beach with him, and he wanted . . ." Barrett choked on her words.

Eddie prompted, "And did you?"

"No! I'm not an *idiot*. Or maybe I am. We were at the beach by the Creeks, and he kissed me, and he tried to . . . and I pushed him away."

"How did he react?"

"He was annoyed. It was awkward. But, Eddie, I'm angry at Drew, but at the same time, I want him to like me." Barrett shook her head. "I *am* an idiot."

Eddie was puzzled. When they were younger, she could always comfort Barrett with something sweet. A lollipop. Ice cream. But nothing sweet would taste good after the pool of maple syrup Barrett had devoured.

And Barrett was no longer a child, Eddie reasoned. "Barrett, it seems to me that Drew is pretty much playing around with you. I mean, how sleazy is he to take someone else to the gala and then try to mess around with you?"

Barrett sniffed back her tears. "I think he's just really busy."

"And you believe that."

Barrett's mouth bunched up like it did whenever she was arguing.

"I don't know what to believe." She carried her plate to the sink. "Thanks for the dinner. I'm going to shower and go to bed. I'm exhausted."

"Okay," Eddie said to the empty room. She didn't show Barrett Dove's letter, and maybe that was a good thing. Barrett had enough to deal with today. Eddie rinsed Barrett's dishes and put them in the dishwasher, and checked the kitchen.

That was the thing about family, she thought as she climbed the stairs to her own room. Eddie was afraid Drew would break Barrett's heart. And Eddie could do nothing about that.

fourteen

Tuesday Barrett left early for her shop. She didn't wait for breakfast—
she'd had breakfast last night. It was quiet in town, the world just
waking up. The farm trucks carrying leafy lettuces, heirloom tomatoes, and little potatoes were parked on Main Street. A few people
ambled into the Hub and came out with a newspaper and a coffee.
Restaurant workers biked into town, jolting over the cobblestones.
The low hoot of a ferry horn announced that it was coming around
Brant Point. Seagulls patrolled the boardwalk on Straight Wharf,
waiting for crumbs. The sun was strong. The day was hot. Maybe too
hot for people to go to the beach?

Her shop was an oasis of freshness. She congratulated herself on
naming it Nantucket Blues, because blue signified cool, and she knew
people would flock to her shop today.

At noon, Janny showed up, carrying an iced mocha cappuccino for

Barrett. They chatted and unpacked new deliveries, and as Barrett had expected, they spent the day waiting on customers who lingered in the shop and bought several things, as if they could carry the icy air home with them.

During a lull, Janny asked teasingly, "Well, how are things going with my brother?"

Barrett had been placing a blue glass starfish on a soft bed of white cotton. She didn't react immediately, turning the starfish this way and that to catch the light.

"Fine," Barrett replied.

Just then, two women entered the shop. Thank heavens, Barrett thought. She was in no mood to talk to Drew's sister.

The day had grown cloudy, with a feisty west wind that sent people's bags, caps, and toys flying. Barrett was pleased to be crazy busy in the afternoon. A mob of teenage girls came in, cooing and giggling about the jewelry. A flustered young mother holding a small cranky child by the hand bumbled around, picking up things and putting them back in the wrong place. Barrett nudged Janny to get out on the floor and ask if she could help the woman. Men came in to buy their wives and daughters gifts and wanted them wrapped with a great big bow.

In the midst of it all, Drew called.

"I'm hoping you could close early so I could see you. I've got to fly back to Boston tonight. Couldn't you close your shop at seven? Just this once? Please?"

A spark of anger flared in Barrett's chest because Drew considered his work more important than hers.

"I'd really like to see you," Drew continued, his voice low and compelling.

She might as well go, Barrett thought, and her emotions were all over the place.

———

Eddie walked around the Book Barn, filling in the empty spots on the shelves. An older couple came, purchased a few old science books, and left. A young mother with a baby in a back carrier and a three-year-old tugging on her hand arrived. The three-year-old was obviously hot and bored. Instead of sitting on the small child's chair by the children's books, he ran past the shelves, pulling the books to the floor and yelling like a banshee. When the mother told him he could choose one book, he flung himself onto the floor in a tantrum of resistance. He wanted *more*!

The kid could use a cold shower, Eddie thought, but she had great sympathy for the mother, who was trying to calm down her son while her baby woke up and screamed.

The woman's eyes were wild. "I . . . I have to go to the car to nurse my baby," she told Eddie.

"Sit in that chair," Eddie told her. "No one else is around. I'll help your little boy choose books."

The woman collapsed in the chair with the baby at her breast. Eddie sat on the floor next to the child who had gone quiet at her presence.

"What's your name?" she asked.

"Timmy," he said.

"Timmy, you see all these books you've pulled on the floor?"

Timmy's eyes welled. "Sowwy."

"Here's the deal. Do you see that house over there with steps to the flowers in a pot? If you can run there and back in the time I count to ten, I'll give you two of these books to take home."

Before she could start counting, Timmy raced off and back.

She made the bargain three more times, and when Timmy returned, panting, Eddie leaned toward him and whispered, "See those pretty red flowers in the pots? Pick off two to give to your mother. Don't worry. More will grow."

So the family left with a well-fed baby snoring in the back carrier,

Timmy with eight children's books in his hands, and the mother holding two geranium stems with bright red flowers.

"This is the best rest I've had this year," she told Eddie. "How can
I thank you?"

"It was fun," Eddie told her, and she meant it.

A few days later, Eddie turned on the HVAC, to hell with the electric
bill. She worked in the house, choosing more books to put in the barn.
Duke lay asleep on the back porch, knocked out by the heat. The arrogant horse spent the day nibbling the grass in the shade of the barn
and Eddie was diligent about filling the horse's water trough.

Her father was secluded in his office, Barrett was in her shop, and
Dinah was at the library, when Eddie heard the crackle of shells and
peered out the window to see a car she didn't recognize coming up
the driveway. She went out the back door and walked to the Book
Barn.

The car was an ancient Volvo, so dented and scraped Eddie was
amazed it still ran.

A woman stepped out of the car. For a moment, Eddie thought it
was Dove . . . She hadn't seen her since before Bobby was born and
Stearns died.

A child climbed out of the backseat and went to stand with his
mother, holding hands.

"Eddie," the woman called. "Hi."

"Dove? Is that you?" Eddie walked toward the woman, and it was
as if she were walking through a garden, as if joy, grief, love, and guilt
were petals brushing against her skin.

"It's me."

Dove came closer, still holding the child's hand. The little boy was
three years old and looked like Stearns. Goosebumps broke out all
over her skin.

Eddied summoned up all the courage she possessed to ask lightly, "And who is this?"

"This is Bobby," Dove said. She grinned. "Like Robert Frost, only younger."

Eddie dropped to her knees so that she was on eye level with the child. "Hi, Bobby."

Bobby clung to his mother's hand. He wore a striped rugby shirt, blue shorts, and sandals. His hair was the color of caramel, and his eyes were pale green, like Stearns's, like Eddie's and Barrett's, like William's. But the child's face had his own beauty. She didn't know if she could ever stop looking at him.

A sob rose in Eddie's chest. She swallowed it, pretending she was sneezing, and forced the tears back. She faced the child with a smile.

"Bobby, I'm your aunt Eddie. I'm so happy to see you."

The little boy looked up at his mother. Dove squatted down.

"That's right, sweetie. I've told you about Aunt Eddie, and here she is."

Dove had told Bobby about Eddie? She'd told him Eddie was his aunt?

Duke woke from his deep sleep on the back porch to lazily saunter down to the driveway to investigate.

Bobby yelled, "Dog!" and ran toward Duke.

Dove cautioned, "Be careful, Bobby. Just hold out your hand."

"It's all right," Eddie assured him. "His name is Duke. He won't bite. He's curious. Your mommy's right. Hold out your hand and let him smell it."

Bobby screeched to a halt two feet from Duke and held out his hand. Duke came nearer, stretched out his neck, and sniffed. He wagged his tail and did something astonishing. He moved right up to Bobby, sat down next to him, and leaned against him.

"Wow," Eddie said softly. "Bobby, Duke likes you a lot."

Eddie took a moment to study Dove. She had always been slender, but now she was almost emaciated. She had dark circles beneath her eyes and no color in her cheeks—she was so pale beneath the strong light of the sun.

Eddie said, "Hey, Bobby, we have a big bunch of children's books in the barn. You might like to read some of them. They're free, and there are chairs just your size. Let's go into the barn and your mommy and I can talk and you can look at the books."

The little boy looked up at his mother. Dove nodded, and they all went into the barn. Bobby sat at the table. Duke lay at his feet.

Eddie gestured to a chair for Dove to sit in—it was one of the old leather chairs, soft and enveloping. Dove looked like she could use something soft.

"Dove," Eddie began to speak, but emotion broke through and she knelt before her old friend and hugged her tight. "Dove, I've missed you so much."

Dove hugged Eddie back, hard. "Me, too."

Eddie released her and went to sit in the other leather chair. "Barrett and Dad have missed you, too. So much has happened. We don't understand why you left like that, why you didn't stay with us."

"I'm sorry." Dove's voice quavered. "I'm so sorry. That was such a horrible time."

"Mommy!" Bobby hurried to his mother with several books in his hands. "Read!"

Dove quickly flicked tears from her cheeks and smiled at her son. "I'm talking to Auntie Eddie right now—"

Eddie watched Dove. Something was wrong. How could she help Dove? Maybe she and Bobby wanted to live with them?

Eddie stood up. "Hey, Bobby. I have some lemonade in the house. And some cookies. I'll bring some out."

Bobby nodded his head. "Okay," he said.

Dove whispered to Bobby, "What did we talk about?"

Bobby nodded quickly. "Yes, pwease."

"Good. I'll be right back." Eddie headed for the house.

She heard Bobby say, "Read." *Bobby's part of our family for sure,* Eddie thought.

Her head was spinning. Should she tell her father? Should she interrupt his work? Would he have a heart attack when he saw Dove and her child?

As soon as she entered the kitchen, she called Barrett.

Janny answered the phone. "Nantucket Blues," she trilled.

Eddie rolled her eyes. Janny sounded so sweet and so fake on the phone. But today she was glad Janny was in the shop.

"Hi, Janny. I need to talk with Barrett."

"Okey-dokey."

When Barrett said hello, Eddie said urgently, "I need you to come home. Now. Dove is here with Bobby and he looks just like Stearns. Dove looks *terrible,* skinny and jaundiced, and I don't know what to do. We're in the Book Barn. Should I bring Dad out here?" Eddie finished, her panic easing as she talked.

Barrett was decisive. "Don't tell Dad yet. I'll come right away."

Eddie made a peanut butter and jelly sandwich for Bobby, piled Oreo cookies in a bowl, poured lemonade into three plastic tumblers, set it all on a tray, and carried it out to the barn.

Dove said, "Bobby, look. Auntie Eddie is bringing us lunch."

They settled Bobby with his sandwich, cookies, and lemonade at the small child's table. Eddie and Dove took tumblers of lemonade and went to stand just inside the barn doors, out of range of Bobby's hearing.

Dove sipped her lemonade. Her hands trembled.

"He's beautiful," Eddie said. She couldn't take her eyes off the little boy. It hurt to see Dove so thin, so fragile. Their old best friend, their almost-sister, the woman Stearns had loved. What had happened? Tears welled in Eddie's eyes. "Oh, Dove, Dovebug, are you okay? Why did you go away? Why didn't you keep in touch? We wanted to be with you. We would have taken care of you and your baby."

"I know that." Dove bent her head, speaking softly. "But I needed to leave. Look around, Eddie. Look at all you have. Your father, and Barrett, and a home."

"Dove—"

"What if it all disappeared? Your home, your family, the man you have loved all your life . . ." She flicked tears from her cheek. "I lost it all, Eddie. I lost my parents, and the feeling of being a good person from a good family—"

"You *are* a good person, Dove!"

"You have no idea what it was like to live in that town with everyone hating my parents. Those cheerleaders gossiping together about how my father was a thief. I couldn't stay, Eddie. Especially not with you and your perfect family."

"God, Dove, we were never perfect!" Eddie protested.

"Yeah, right." Dove sniffed. "You had Barrett. She had you. You never had to walk down the hall at school and hear someone say, 'Watch out that she doesn't steal your bracelet. Her father's a crook.' On Instagram people called me a criminal, criminal girl, jailbird. You saw those posts."

"We did, Dove, and remember, Barrett and I stood up for you! We told them they were lying, being stupid. But you disappeared—"

"—and became the town drunk." Dove knocked her head against the wall. She breathed deeply, trying to get in control. "The night they took my father to jail? Mom went to her friend's house and I was alone, the last night I would ever sleep in my house. And I—"

"You should have come to our house!" Eddie cried. "I can't believe you didn't come to our house. Or at least called us. We could have come to be with you."

Dove shook her head. "I knew something was going to happen. I heard my parents talking. You can't understand, Eddie. What my father did—those men in suits coming to our house—I felt ashamed. I wanted to hide. I didn't want to be *me,* the Criminal's Daughter."

"But, Dove—" Eddie cried, holding out her hand to touch her old friend.

Dove moved out of reach. "I didn't feel like I was good enough to be with you."

Before Eddie could speak again, Barrett tore into the driveway, scattering the shells. She turned off the engine, jumped out of the Jeep, and ran toward Dove.

Barrett smashed into Dove, crushing her in a hug, crying, "You're here! You're really here!"

Dove let Barrett hold her as the two women cried together. Eddie watched, tears running down her face.

"Mommy?" Bobby had left his coloring and come close to his mother. He looked worried. Even frightened.

"Oh, *wow*!" Barrett fell to her knees to face the boy. "You're Bobby. You're really Bobby."

Bobby edged closer to his mother. He reached out and grabbed a reassuring handful of her jeans.

"Calm down, Barrett," Eddie said softly. "You're freaking us out a little bit."

"Sorry." Barrett took some deep breaths. "Bobby, these are happy tears. Because I'm *so* happy to meet you. I'm so happy to see your mommy." She stood up. "Dove. Dove, sorry to manhandle you. I'm just so thrilled to see you after all this time."

"I'm happy to see you both, too." She cradled her tumbler of lemonade to her chest and clutched the wall with her free hand. "I have to sit down."

Eddie exchanged a worried glance with Barrett.

"Yes, of course. You must be tired after your trip. Let's go in the house. Do you let Bobby watch TV?"

"*Pete the Cat,*" Dove said. "Bobby loves the book."

Eddie walked over to Dove and put a bracing arm around her, helping her stand. With a swift nod to Barrett, she signaled for Barrett to take care of Bobby.

"Bobby," Barrett said. "Would you like to come into the house and watch *Pete the Cat*?"

"YES!" Bobby shouted. He caught his mother's reaction and spoke more softly. "Yes, pwease."

"Go on with Auntie Barrett," Dove said. "I'm coming, too. You know sometimes I walk more slowly than you do."

Bobby took Barrett's hand. They crossed the yard, climbed the steps, and stood on the porch. Bobby turned back to see his mother.

Barrett stifled a gasp. Dove was walking slowly, and it looked as if she wouldn't be able to walk without Eddie's help.

"It's okay," Bobby said. "Sometimes Mommy gets tired."

Barrett tried to sound calm. "Let's wait and open the door for your mommy and Eddie."

Barrett and Dove struggled up the steps to the porch and through the open door into the kitchen. Barrett followed, holding Bobby's hand.

Dove collapsed into a chair. "Thanks, Eddie. Bobby, Auntie Barrett will take you to watch *Pete the Cat*."

Barrett took the child to the family room and settled him in front of the television. She streamed *Pete the Cat* and handed the remote to Bobby.

"You can adjust the volume, but don't touch any other buttons. Aunt Eddie and I get confused with those buttons."

Bobby giggled. "So does Mommy."

Barrett returned to the kitchen. Eddie sat next to Dove, holding her hand.

"Bobby's happy with Pete," Barrett announced, trying to sound upbeat.

Still holding their friend's hand, Eddie said softly, "So, Dove, you look terrible. What's going on with you?"

Dove lifted her head. "I'm dying," she said.

fifteen

For a moment, the sisters sat in stunned silence.

Eddie asked softly, "Dove, why would you say something like that?"

Dove smiled weakly. "Because it's true. I have end-stage cirrhosis of the liver."

"But how?" Barrett demanded. "Why?"

Eddie moved her chair closer to Dove's. "Tell us."

Dove closed her eyes. She seemed infinitely weary. "It was hell when my father went to jail. I was an outcast, and Curt took care of me. That was my first introduction to the bliss of being drunk. I drank until I blacked out. Slept, woke up, drank some more. Stearns saved me. He helped me get sober. He *rescued* me. But when Stearns died . . . when Stearns died, I lost everything. I had always loved him, and of course I had always loved you two, but Stearns, Stearns was *everything* to me." Dove leaned toward the sisters. "I promise you, when I got pregnant with Bobby, I wasn't drinking. I hadn't had a drink for months. And I didn't drink during my pregnancy. I loved Stearns so much, and we were going to have a child and a home and a family. I would never have endangered that. And Bobby was born. We were so happy. But the motorcycle accident . . ." Her breath hitching, Dove went quiet. After a moment, she asked, "Could I have a tissue?"

Barrett jumped up, got the box, and set it before Dove. "Go on."

Dove wiped her face. "I was lost. Confused. I didn't want to return to Williamstown, where my father was sent to jail and my mother abandoned me. I called my uncle in Denver. My father's brother. I told him that Stearns had died, and I had a baby. They sent me a plane ticket. My aunt Ruth and uncle Howard met me at the airport. They gave me a room in their house. They took care of me and Bobby. They knew about my father, about my mother taking off to Florida with another man. They didn't know I'd had a few months of drinking myself silly. After Stearns died . . . even in Colorado, even with my beautiful little baby . . . I didn't want to live. I was like a ninety-seven-year-old shut-in. I never left the house. I took care of Bobby and slept."

Eddie stood up, filled a large glass full of water, and handed it to Dove.

"Thanks." Dove stared down into the glass. "They suggested I get a job. They thought it would do me good to get out of the house. Aunt Ruth was crazy about Bobby. So, I took a job at a grocery store, putting stock on the shelves. And I met some people, and had some friends to hang out with after work . . . and I started drinking again."

Dove paused to drink water. Suddenly, she smiled. "In the mountains in the winter, there are so many stars in the sky, you can't believe it."

Barrett took a moment to go into the hall to check on Bobby.

"He's still watching TV," she reported.

"He's an angel, isn't he?" Dove's smile was anguished. "Here's the deal. I spent the past two years drinking heavily. Passing out. Once I start drinking I can't stop. Add the months I spent out of control with

Curt and his gang when my father went to jail. Add the nights when we were kids and I helped myself to my parents' gin so I could fall asleep."

"We didn't know you were drinking!" Barrett cried.

"It was only late at night. And it was a lot . . . It's why I have end-stage liver cirrhosis. Also, hep B."

"You can have a liver transplant," Eddie suggested.

Dove shook her head. "I'm not a good candidate. Believe me, I've seen doctors. I've had tests." She made a circle with her hand over her torso. "You don't want to know what's going on in here."

"Dove, this is horrible." Barrett put her hand on Dove's. "I'm sure doctors here can do something. We'll take you to Boston. There are first-class hospitals in Boston."

Dove gripped Barrett's hand. "Please, listen to me. I'm not here because I want to be cured. I *can't* be cured. Look at the color of my skin. Look at how thin I am. It took all my energy to get here. I came because of Bobby. I want you to have Bobby."

"Dove? Is that really you?"

William stood in the doorway. He'd gone white with shock.

Dove smiled. "Hi, Mr. Grant. Yes, it's really me. Or what's left of me." She laughed and stood up and trembled all over and collapsed back into her chair.

"Dad," Eddie said. "Bobby's in the family room, watching *Pete the Cat*. Maybe don't go meet him right now. Dove has some . . . news for us all."

William joined them at the table. He listened to Dove tell him how sick she was and how it had happened. And what she was asking of Eddie and Barrett.

"Good God, Dove," William said. "I'm so sorry. Okay, so do we have a timeline?"

"Dad!" Barrett was shocked.

William ignored Barrett and spoke to Dove. "How can we help you? How can we make you comfortable? What have you told Bobby?"

"Thank you, Mr. Grant." Dove smiled at the sisters. "He's asking the right questions. The necessary questions. No, I don't have an exact timeline, but I probably won't last through the year. I'd like to be connected with a doctor here. The last few days . . . whenever they come, won't be easy. I was hoping I could stay with you for a few weeks, get Bobby feeling safe with you, help Bobby realize he's part of your family. He's very young. After a few years, he won't remember me."

"Mommy?"

They all jumped a little when they heard Bobby's voice. He was standing in the doorway, looking around.

"Mommy, *Pete the Cat* is over."

Dove held out her arms. "Bobby, come here. I want you to meet your grandfather."

Bobby ran to his mother and climbed on her lap.

William bent down to face the child.

"Hello, Bobby," William said. "I'm your grandfather. You can call me Pop."

Bobby's eyes went wide. "I've never had a grandfather before."

William kissed the boy's forehead and managed to smile, although the rest of his face was scrunched up as if he were in pain.

"Cheese and crackers," William said, blinking away tears.

"Helloooooo!" Dinah's greeting carried to them as she came in the front door. "My darlings, I've had such a wonderful day."

Dinah swept into the room, all frills and perfume. Her lips were pink, her cheeks were rosy, her white summer dress was very low-necked.

Bobby's jaw dropped. "Are you an angel?"

Dinah didn't skip a beat. "No, but *you* are." She came close to Bobby and Dove. She put out her finger and gently pressed Bobby's arm. "Oh, wow! You're real! I thought you were an angel, but you're a real little boy. Would you like to test me?"

Bobby gently touched Dinah's arm. "You're real, too."

"Extremely real," Dinah told him. She pulled a chair up to the table. "You must be Dove. I'm so happy to meet you and your son. I'm Dinah Lavender. A friend of the family."

"Bobby," William said, "I want you to meet Dinah. She writes wonderful books."

"I like books," Bobby said.

Barrett sniffed loudly.

"Good grief," Eddie said. "What a day. I'm going to heat up a pan of mac and cheese."

"I'll make a salad." Barrett went to the refrigerator to take out lettuce and vegetables.

The sisters worked side by side, listening to the conversation at the table. Eddie took the large pan of homemade mac and cheese from the freezer and pre-heated the oven. Barrett tore up the romaine with shaking hands.

Dinah said to Bobby, "Your grandfather is writing a book about men who write poems."

Bobby crinkled up his nose. "Does it have monsters like *Shrek*?"

William glanced at Dove.

"He likes monsters," Dove said.

William stuttered, "Monsters . . . well, let me think."

"He's writing about Lamia," Dinah whispered. "Lamia is a woman but she's also a snake."

"Cool!" Bobby yelled.

"And sweet old Wordsworth called his wife a *phantom* of delight." She explained, "A phantom is like a ghost."

"You've been reading my book," William said.

"Yes, of course," Dinah replied. She winked at William. "Have you been reading mine?"

Barrett muttered to Eddie, "Dinah winked at Dad!"

Dinah focused on the little boy. "Bobby, do you like poems?"

Bobby blinked and shrugged.

"*Twinkle, twinkle, little star.*" Dinah recited the short poem.

Bobby didn't look impressed.

Barrett began to quote, "*The Owl and the Pussy-Cat went to sea /
In a beautiful pea-green boat.*"

"But wouldn't they fight?" Bobby asked.

The sisters laughed and told him that was a very good point. William and Dinah were involved in their own conversation. Dove sat
gripping the arms of her chair, struggling to stay upright, but manag-
ing to smile.

The buzzer rang. Eddie dressed the salad and set out plates and
silverware. Barrett brought the mac and cheese from the oven and
went around the table, giving everyone generous helpings.

Dove told her son to eat some lettuce.

Bobby obeyed. "It tastes like toilet paper!"

Dinah leaned toward him, her jewelry glittering, a whisper of her
perfume drifting over him. "How do you know? Have you ever eaten
toilet paper?"

"No, silly," Bobby replied, laughing.

He finished eating before everyone else, so Dove said he could
watch television again. Bobby shrieked with joy. Eddie took him into
the den and settled him in front of cartoons. She returned to the
kitchen, took a platter of grapes, plums, and peaches from the refrigerator and set it in the middle of the table. Now Dinah was arguing
with William about a poem called "Lamia." Barrett was telling Dove
about her shop.

We're almost like a real family, Eddie thought. A slight disaster of
a family, but still a family.

That evening, Eddie gave her bedroom to Dove and Bobby, and Barrett
and Eddie made a little parade as Eddie moved her clothes into Barrett's room and brought Dove and Bobby's luggage in from the car.

When everything was arranged, Dove said to Eddie and Barrett, "I
want to tuck Bobby in. I'll be down in a while to talk."

But when half an hour had passed and Dove didn't appear, Eddie went upstairs to check.

She found Dove deeply asleep next to her son.

She returned to the family room to tell her father, sister, and Dinah that Dove and Bobby were asleep.

"Could we please watch television?" Barrett begged. "I need to zone out."

Together, they watched *Father Brown*, a gentle British mystery set in the 1950s. Barrett was delighted by Mrs. McCarthy's hats, Dinah was thrilled every time Lady Felicia appeared, Eddie kept hoping that Bunny would fall in love with Inspector Sullivan, and William said they were all delusional.

"Those aren't real people," he reminded the others.

"And what a shame that is," Dinah told him.

After three episodes, they all went to bed, knowing that tomorrow would require clear minds and strong hearts.

After breakfast the next morning, Barrett was in her shop, unpacking new inventory, when Eddie called.

"She's awake. Dad's taking Bobby to Children's Beach so we can talk."

"I'll come home right away."

Barrett drove carefully, obeying the stop signs, wanting to keep the edges of the world straight. She found her sister and Dove in the kitchen. Eddie was at the sink, filling the ice cube tray. Barrett kissed Dove on her forehead and then, for no reason at all except that she felt like it, she kissed Eddie on her forehead, too.

"Eddie's been telling me about your shop," Dove said. "I'd love to see it."

"Of course. But first . . ." Barrett hesitated. "I mean, I can't stay here too long today, and since Bobby's at the beach and we can talk freely—Dove, you're staying with us for, um, a while, right?"

Dove made a sound that was half laugh, half cough. "I am. I can't be specific, but we do need to map things out. I've seen doctors, had tests run, trust me on this, I have gotten second and third opinions. I've been informed that I will basically be getting sicker, and weaker. And that the end could get pretty ugly. I'm hoping you two and your father will be able to keep Bobby distracted."

"When should we take you to the hospital?" Eddie asked.

"I don't want to go to a hospital. I want to be here. I've seen doctors. I've been in hospitals. I know I can't be cured. I came here—" Dove bent her head, choking on a word, struggling for breath. "I came here because you two are the only ones I can count on to take Bobby."

"Of course, we'll take Bobby," Eddie told her.

Dove held up her hand. "Wait. I also came here because I can trust you two to trust my judgment and my decisions. I want to die in my bed in my sleep."

"But what do we tell Bobby?" Barrett cried. "I mean, Dove, think of him."

"He's *all* I think about," Dove insisted. "I have prepared him. I've already told him that I'm going on a long trip soon. I told him he'll stay with you while I'm on my trip, and many, many years later, he'll see me again."

"What?" Eddie said. "Aren't you giving him a promise you can't keep?"

"I'll see him again. Just not on this earth." Dove summoned up a smile. "That's what I want you to tell him."

"Dove," Eddie protested.

Dove said, "That's what I believe."

"Good grief," Barrett said. "This is too hard."

Eddie moved a chair closer to Dove and sat down. "If that's what you want us to tell him, that's what we'll tell him. We'll do everything the way you want us to do it, Dove."

Dove reached out and took Eddie's hand. "I want you to adopt him, Eddie. Barrett, don't be insulted—but you just started your store,

I've been reading social media about it and the photos you've put on Pinterest are gorgeous. And Eddie is the oldest and she could work at home with her proofreading or whatever she does for Dinah, and when you have time, Barrett, you can help, if you want, and of course your father could be his real grandfather, I mean, he is his real grandfather."

"What about your mother and father?" Eddie asked.

"I haven't been in touch with either of them. They don't even know about Bobby."

"Oh, Dove," Barrett said. "That's so sad."

"Barrett," Dove responded, "when was the last time you spoke with your mother?"

Barrett rolled her eyes. "That's different."

Dove lifted an eyebrow. "What was that quote you used to repeat whenever you were mad at your parents?"

"Oh, right!" Eddie said. "The Khalil Gibran one."

"I remember," Barrett said. "Something about how your children come through you but they don't belong to you . . ."

Suddenly, Dove was crying. "Weren't we so cool? All the times we sat in the family room, talking about death and life and children and sex and—"

"—and we'd go crazy in your room, dancing to 'Hollaback Girl' and we wanted to be Rihanna—"

"—and we'd put on fabulous makeup and false eyelashes and fake tattoos—"

"And when we were real little, we'd dress up like fairies and have our little fairy hideaway and your mom bought us all fairy costumes—"

"And your mom gave you a fairy birthday party and she gave us all wands and light sticks!"

Dove winced and turned her head away from them. She struggled to get her breath. "I'm tired," she gasped.

"Do you want to go back to bed?" Eddie asked.

"Please."

"I'll help you." Eddie lifted Dove from the chair and waited as Dove steadied herself.

"Can I bring you anything from town?" Barrett asked.

"Actually, it would help a lot if you went to a drugstore and bought some disposable incontinence bed pads."

"Oh, damn, Dove, *really*?" Barrett sounded horrified.

Dove burst into laughter. "I know, right? Incontinence bed pads wasn't a game we ever played."

Because Dove was laughing, Eddie started laughing, and Barrett couldn't help herself. She laughed, too. For a moment, there in the kitchen in a farmhouse on an island, they were three friends again, sisters more than friends, and they laughed because they were terrified and heartbroken but they were together again, and they would laugh as long as they could.

Dove went upstairs to sleep. Barrett returned to her shop. Eddie put together a casserole and went up to Barrett's bedroom, shut the door, and sat on her bed, leaning against the headboard. She opened her journal and began to write. It was odd, she thought, how the only place she could be honest about her feelings was in the journal. She could write, *this is too hard,* and *maybe Dove won't really die,* and *how can I be Bobby's mommy?*

After a while, she went to her Web browser and looked up the poems of Khalil Gibran.

At nine o'clock, Barrett closed her shop and drove home. She entered the house, carrying a white pharmacy bag filled with bed pads and boxes of chocolate, which she hoped Dove could eat.

"We're in here," Eddie called from the family room.

William sat in one overstuffed chair and Dinah had kicked off her sandals and was curled up in the other one. Eddie and Dove were seated on the sofa in front of the television. Eddie had the remote in her hand and had obviously paused the TV.

"We're watching John Mulaney," Dove said. "He's so funny."

Barrett said, "Hi, everyone!" and sat next to Eddie, trying to hide the pharmacy bag by stuffing it beneath the sofa.

"Barrett." Dove leaned forward to look past Eddie. "You don't have to hide those. We've told your father and Dinah about it. About me."

"Also," Dinah said sweetly, "I think I see a box of Ferrero Rocher sticking out of the bag. I think our little group would be cheered up by a bite or two of chocolate."

Barrett was speechless. How could Dinah think of chocolate when Dove was right there, so ill and thin?

"That's a wonderful idea," Dove said. "Dinah's had a difficult day. Her stalker is on the island. He sent a message through her website that he's here and would like to see her, at her convenience."

"What are you going to do?" Barrett asked.

"We were just discussing that," her father said.

Barrett glanced at Dove. How could anybody think about anything with Dove so sick?

Dove seemed to read her mind. "I realize I'm the most important person in this room, Barrett, but we've spent enough time moaning about my problems. It cheers me up to hear what's going on with everyone else."

Eddie elbowed Barrett in the side. "What about those chocolates?"

Barrett drew out the white paper bag and passed the chocolates around. She watched as Dove took one, but then only held it in her hand, fiddling with the gold wrapper.

The new Book Barn family developed their own routine.

In the morning, Barrett rose and zipped off to her store. Eddie, sleeping in the other twin bed, would yawn and dress and head down to the kitchen to make coffee. Bobby would leave his sleeping mother, tiptoe down to the kitchen, eat the cereal and drink the juice Eddie gave him, and hurry off to the den to watch television. Dinah would enter, talking softly to her iPhone, plotting the next chapter of her novel. She'd make a piece of toast and a cup of coffee and wander back to her room to write. William would come down the stairs fully dressed in khaki shorts and a striped rugby shirt that he'd purchased of his own accord from Murray's Toggery, so that when he took Bobby exploring for the day, he would look casual, less like a stuffy old professor.

Eddie would tidy the kitchen, pack a picnic lunch, and go off with her father and Bobby to look at the boats in the harbor and hang out at Children's Beach, or if it was raining, visit the Whaling Museum. They'd pick up books from the library and sometimes stay for story time. They'd visit Barrett in her shop if it wasn't too busy. The Maria Mitchell aquarium was always fascinating to Bobby and the secret candy room at the back of Force Five was a kid's idea of heaven.

Sometimes Eddie and Bobby would stop to watch Jeff and the crew building a new house. In spite of the noise of the hammers and saws, Bobby was fascinated. Often, when Jeff took a moment to come to their Jeep to say hello, Bobby would almost explode with excitement. The little boy adored Jeff, especially when he was working. One late afternoon when a storm with torrential rain and gale force wind hit the island, Jeff came over with a present for Bobby, a child's wooden workbench set. He sat on the floor with Bobby and showed him how to hammer down the pegs and work the pliers. Bobby was entranced; Eddie thought he wouldn't notice if Santa Claus himself walked into the room. If Jeff was too whipped to stop by, he would always call Bobby and ask how his day went. Later, he would call Eddie.

"Bobby and I are head over heels in love with you," Eddie told Jeff.

"Me, too," Jeff said.

Dove would remain in her room, sleeping. Eddie woke her in the afternoon, appearing at her bedside with a strong cup of sugary coffee and a chocolate croissant. Dove would shower and dress and slowly make her way to the back porch. Bobby would take a nap up in the room that was now their bedroom. Afterward, William sat with Bobby in the Book Barn. Sometimes William read to Bobby, and just as often, William worked on his laptop while Bobby, who was a champ at playing by himself, sat at a smaller table, coloring or reading or building with the carpenter set or the Lego set William had bought him, talking and singing to himself.

Dove said she was feeling better, stronger. Sometimes she went for a short walk, but it was brutally hot and humid, and she always returned quickly and went to her room to rest. Eddie would take Bobby and sometimes Dove for a swim at one of the beaches, and then to Bartlett's or Stop & Shop for groceries. Even though Dove hardly ate, there were five people to feed, and Eddie enjoyed trying new recipes, especially if she could coax Bobby into eating something new.

One day Dove, seeming energetic, even hopeful, took Bobby to an afternoon showing of *Rally Road Racers* at the Dreamland. William and Dinah were both in town, and Barrett was at her store.

Eddie sat in the Book Barn for a while, but no one came, and people seldom did in the hot afternoons. She went into the house and was seized by the need to clean up and make order. Wearing headphones playing her favorite mix, she zoomed through the house, changing sheets and towels, vacuuming, dusting, moving what seemed like dozens of glasses from tables and bureaus.

Eddie finished cleaning, took a glass of iced tea out to the back porch, and sat in the wicker rocker. She thought about how she had returned home, and then Dinah had come, and now Dove and Bobby, and it seemed that this house, like the island itself, had a kind of mystical, invisible allure that pulled people to it, and kept people wanting to stay.

She closed her eyes and listened to the quiet. Did she miss the city and its frenetic glamour? Was she sad not to wear expensive dresses and glitzy, painful heels? Maybe she was just in a summer mood, listening to the sparrows chirp from their hiding places in the lushly leaved trees. Maybe she was different, more relaxed, here with the salty ocean and the rose-scented breeze cooling her bare, tanned arms.

She'd planned to stay a month and she'd been here over two months. Barrett's shop was doing well, and Barrett was ecstatic about that, Eddie was deeply happy that she was helping her sister by taking care of their father, and in a way Dinah. She was glad Dinah was here, feeling safe, writing every day, and often having dinner out with friends.

And now, Dove and Bobby.

Barrett's shop was doing better than she'd ever dreamed. It kept her furiously busy and the only reason she stayed sane was Janny working afternoons five days a week and until nine on Friday. She was charming with customers, efficient with paperwork, and always glad to run an errand or buy Barrett an iced mocha cappuccino. When the shop was quiet, she helped Barrett dust and organize the shelves, and she'd chat about her various boyfriends and how she was never going to get married, because the wedding would be great, but after that, where was the fun?

How different this young woman is from Dove, Barrett thought. *How fortunate Janny is.*

One afternoon, Janny said, "You know, Barrett, my brother really likes you. I mean *really*."

"I like him," Barrett answered, keeping her tone pleasant.

Janny continued, "He'd like to come down here more often, but work is killing him. I mean, you can't imagine."

"I don't even *try* to imagine," Barrett said dryly.

Once in a while, Barrett would steal a quiet afternoon when Janny was working. She and her father took Bobby and Dove somewhere special, kayaking in the shallow waters at the end of the harbor, building sandcastles at Surfside, swinging and climbing on the playground at 'Sconset. In the evenings, when Eddie arranged for everyone to have dinner together, Barrett insisted on helping in the kitchen, not only because she felt guilty with her sister doing so much work, but because it was a pleasure to talk while working side by side. It would be heaven, she thought, if Eddie moved back to the island for good.

Thursday evening, Barrett was finishing a sale when Eddie walked in.

"Thanks," Barrett said to her customer. When the woman left, Barrett said, "Well, this is a surprise."

"I know." Eddie handed Barrett a cookie. "I made these today. Had to hide a couple so Bobby and Dad didn't eat them all."

Barrett rested against the back wall. "Umm. Delicious. What's the occasion?"

"Nothing, really." Eddie crossed her arms on the counter. "I was just feeling the need for a little sister time. So much is happening. We haven't had time to talk."

Barrett nodded. "I know. But it will be calmer when summer's over."

"Will it?" Eddie gestured around the shop. "Look at this, Bare! You've made your dream come true. You've created your own world. And it's only the beginning. You could have this shop for years."

"I know. I mean, that's what I hoped would happen, but I haven't had a chance to think past tomorrow."

"You really like living on Nantucket."

"I do. It was hard when Dad moved us here and Mom was gone and of course Stearns . . . I don't think I'll ever have one day when I don't think of Stearns. And Dad was getting odder and odder. As if he was trying to hide from life behind all those books. Eddie, when you came here, it was as if you changed gears for us, from *idle* to *go*. Like you reset our lives. Like now we are truly starting over. God, Eddie, what will we do when you're gone? Plus, you can't go with Dove and Bobby here."

Eddie said softly, "Oh, Barrett." She looked at her phone. "It's four forty-five and it's starting to rain." She went to the door and turned the sign from OPEN to CLOSED. "Let's go in the back room."

"Want an iced tea?" Barrett asked. "I keep bottles in the refrigerator." Barrett unfolded a canvas chair for herself and another for Eddie.

Eddie seated herself, opened her tea, and smiled at her sister.

Barrett sat, too. "*So*. When are you going back to the city?"

"I don't know about going back to New York. Dinah hasn't mentioned it. She told me she's getting a lot of good writing done here, she's more easily concocting complicated plots and characters."

Barrett's eyes lit up. "Maybe she wants to live here?"

"I don't know. She never swims or goes to the beach, but she's always in town, shopping—I'm sure she's bought thousands of dollars' worth of new clothes and jewelry. She's made friends and she told me—this is the only thing she's told me, we haven't made any plans—she wants to stay on the island until January to enjoy the cranberry harvest and stroll." Eddie laughed. "She told me she likes the *air* here."

This was wonderful, Barrett thought. More than she'd hoped for. Eddie might stay through Christmas? She kept the lid on her reaction. "We do have some fine salt air."

"But you're right about Dove and Bobby. I don't want to leave them here, with Dove so ill, and . . . with everything so unsettled."

"And what about Jeff?" Barrett asked.

"I know." Eddie looked pensive. "What about Jeff? I haven't had a chance to talk to him privately about Bobby. I mean, it's nearly September, and we're all working our butts off. Contractors have their crews working long hours. So many people wanted new houses. New mansions. Guesthouses. Air-conditioned and humidity-controlled squash courts. Screening rooms like those in movie theaters, complete with seats that recline and cup holders for their drinks. Jeff is whipped at the end of the day."

"I know. I'm straight out, too. But it's kind of a good thing, really." Barrett hugged herself as she spoke. "I never dreamed my shop would be so successful."

———

Eddie missed seeing Jeff, but she understood. He was working long hours in the broiling sun. Usually he'd head home, take a shower, drink a beer, and eat whatever his mother left for him on the counter or in the refrigerator.

But their phone conversations lasted longer every day, until Jeff was yawning with exhaustion. Their conversations were loose, wandering talks, about all the little things, how their day went, how crazy the traffic was in the summer, how people cut cars off if they thought they were driven by summer people, how frightening it was when a family on bikes crossed the intersection without stopping to check right of way. Or they discussed the newest movie review by Anthony Lane in *The New Yorker,* the one magazine they both took, and yes, it was true, they had become hoarders, too, because the days weren't long enough for them to read all the reviews, fiction, and op-ed pieces every week, so the magazines piled up on their bedside tables. Maybe someday they'd be moved to the Book Barn. They talked about movies they wanted to see again, like *My Cousin Vinny,* especially to see the courtroom scene with Marisa Tomei, or *Armageddon,* especially to see Steve Buscemi on a nuclear bomb, or Christopher Walken in anything, especially his dance video, and why it was that some people were just *cool,* and other people could never be cool, no matter what they did. They talked about Barrett and her store, and Dove and Bobby, and her father and Dinah, who often spoke with each other at length at the kitchen table, until William looked embarrassed and went *harrumph* and left the table, walked into his study, and firmly shut the door.

Eddie understood how she and Jeff were like teenagers, not wanting to hang up the phone, to say good night, to separate, to lose the sweet slight sounds of breath and the mysteriously profound pleasure of the other's voice.

Jeff never nudged her into thoughts of the future, but Eddie would wonder into the night: What *were* her thoughts for the future? She was almost thirty. She'd always balked at the thought of having children.

She'd loved her crazy, super-busy city life with Dinah. But Dinah had changed. She often took her laptop to the Book Barn to work, and if customers came in, Dinah would help them. Dinah also had never put on a bathing suit and swum at Surfside, or anywhere. She hadn't gone walking on the winding paths through the moors or in the slightly soggy trails through Squam Swamp. But she was happy with life on the island, Eddie thought. Dinah went to all the plays, movies, concerts, and galas she was invited to, and she was invited to them all, once the organization realized who she was and how much she could give.

But her life shouldn't depend on Dinah, Eddie thought. What did *Eddie* want to do? Where did she want to live? How did she want to live her life?

Right now, it all depended on Dove. Some days Dove rallied and everyone was optimistic. But more often, Dove spent the day in bed.

Eddie wrote in her journal every day. She knew she was finding escape and even solace in writing, but her thoughts raced through her mind and her heart was overflowing with emotions.

sixteen

Saturday evening, Barrett went home early to shower and dress for the gala. Eddie did her hair and makeup, and Barrett wore a sleek slip dress in turquoise with turquoise and diamond earrings that Dinah had loaned her for the evening.

Paul arrived, looking amazing in a navy blazer that pulled at his wide shoulders, a white shirt, and white ducks. He was all cleaned up and shaved, more sophisticated than she'd ever seen him.

The yacht club was crowded. Beautiful people in fabulous clothes drifted through the high-ceilinged rooms and out onto the grassy lawn leading down to the water. They drank icy vodka tonics and cut through the crowd to view the auction items laid out on long tables covered with immaculate white tablecloths. In the background, a live jazz band played. Waiters passed through the crowd with platters of crab cakes and tuna tartare. The very air they breathed was special, spicy from sea salt and expensive perfumes.

Barrett and Paul recognized some of the crowd. Connie Higgins, recently retired from the Nantucket Select Board, and Martin Malcolm, new member of the board, were there, Connie looking serene as always, Martin looking as brilliant as he was. Heather and Miles Hunter were there with Kailee and Ross Willette. Barrett caught some of the crush studying her and Paul, and she gave a moment of mental thanks to Dinah for loaning her the jewelry and to Eddie, who'd insisted Barrett wear her Christian Louboutin high heels.

Barrett leaned against Paul and asked, "How many billions of dollars are walking around this room right now?"

Paul smiled. "None of them is as happy as I am, here with you."

She couldn't take her eyes from him. "Oh." She drew closer to him, almost pressing herself against him. "I'm happy, too."

Annie Gardner, a small blonde in a red dress, and a friend, brushed Barrett's side. "Behave," she teased as she passed by.

Barrett laughed and detached herself from her date. "Let's go look at the auction items," she suggested, holding Paul's hand.

The silent auction was laid out on long tables running the length of two walls. People could write their bid on a pad next to the article, adding the number they'd gotten when they entered the gala. Some of the donated items were in place. A gold lightship basket from Jewel in the Sea. An indigo silk shawl from Vis-a-Vis. A rainbow fleet men's belt from Murray's Toggery. Other donations were virtual. Two nights and days at Greydon House. Dinner for four at Le Languedoc. A twilight cruise on the tall ship *Lynx*.

A spectacular, foot-high, topaz-hued statue of Poseidon rising from the sea.

"Oh, look!" Barrett said, nudging Paul. "That's almost as beautiful as the statues you make."

"That's because I made it," Paul told her, trying to look cool.

Barrett gasped. "Really?"

"Really."

"*I'm* going to bid on it!" Barrett told him.

She squeezed through the mob to stand in front of the statue.

The paper tablet in front of the statue held a list of bids already made. The largest was for three thousand.

"Three thousand dollars?" Barrett was stunned.

A woman standing next to her said, "I think it's worth that much, if not more. Look at the detail work. The waves parting as Poseidon rises. And his beard." Gently nudging Barrett aside, she bent and bid three thousand five hundred.

Paul whispered, "Let's get some air."

He led her through the throng out to the lawn and along the brick walk down to the benches overlooking the harbor. The buzz of conversation and a few notes from the jazz band drifted down to the water.

"Paul," Barrett said. "Good Lord! I had no idea."

"I've been carving since I was a kid. I'm fascinated by the figureheads on ships. It's been done for centuries, in all countries that sail the seas. They bring luck and protection. Someday I want to do large-scale carving."

"How would you do something as large as a figurehead?"

"I'd need a studio, of course. I rent a garage now."

"But the beautiful carvings you bring to my shop. You could sell them for so much more in art galleries."

"No. I want them to be sold only in Nantucket Blues. This way I get to see you."

Barrett nudged him. "You can always see me."

"Not the way I'd like to see you. Not with any privacy. I live with my parents. Lame, I know."

"Why? I live with *my* parents. Well, my father. But it's good for both of us. Someday I'll be able to buy a small house, or have one built on our property. Half the people I know live with their parents. How can we afford to buy a house when doctors and teachers can't? This island has been taken over by billionaires."

Paul shrugged. "Yeah, but not its heart. Not its soul."

Barrett gazed up at Paul, flooded with emotion, deep desire, crazy lust, joy mixed with terror. She whispered, "That's lovely."

He turned toward her, pulled her close, and kissed her for a long time.

"Okay, boys and girls, let's move this show somewhere else."

Barrett glanced up. Her friend Annie was coming down the path toward them.

"Who made you the party police?"

Annie sat down on the bench, squeezing Barrett closer to Paul.

"Look at this view. Amazing. Several people are wandering down this way to see it, and I thought I'd better warn you before *you became* the view."

Before Barrett or Paul could respond, voices drifted through the warm night air and a small crowd arrived, some with drinks in their hands, some chattering like parrots, and one woman complaining about her daughter-in-law's lack of manners.

"Thank you," Barrett said to Annie.

"Yeah, thanks, Annie." Paul leaned across Barrett. "Where's Marcus tonight?"

"Over on Tuckernuck," Annie said, mentioning a wild island west of Nantucket. "He hates these parties. I came with Linda. It's fun to get dressed up. Plus, the finger food. So good."

The three sat together companionably while the crowd around them buzzed and chortled.

"Why is it," Barrett asked, "that when you're alone or with one special person instead of with a group, the night seems more mysterious, more . . . magical?"

"I think it has to do with that one special person," Paul told her.

"He's right." Annie kissed Barrett's cheek. "You look gorgeous tonight. Have fun." She headed back to the clubhouse.

"Let's walk," Paul suggested.

Holding hands, they left the party and strolled down to Children's

Beach. For a while they didn't talk, but simply sat on benches, watching the boats come and go.

Paul kissed her again.

She pulled away. "Paul, wait. I think I need to tell you something . . . I don't know how to say this . . . it's just that . . . well, maybe you know, I've been . . . seeing Janny's brother. Drew. I've been . . . I only met him this summer . . . and I've seen him . . . but I haven't . . ." She didn't know how to say it.

Paul nodded. "I understand. I've been seeing other women. Not Janny, though. I went to the gala with her, but that's it. I'm working hard this summer. I know *you* are." He paused. "Barrett, I'd like to stop *seeing* anyone else. I'd like to be with you. Just you."

"I'd like that, too." Barrett had trouble catching her breath.

"Don't worry," Paul told her. "It's summer. We're slammed. We won't be able to do much more than work and sleep. But September isn't far away."

Barrett laughed, from nervous energy and excitement and embarrassment. "Oh, Paul, I sound like a child. I promise I'm a grown-up. I'm just . . . What I feel for you is so huge I can't really deal with it, I mean, not now."

"I know," Paul said. "Me, too. But we've got all the time in the world."

Sunday morning was hot and sunny, with only a light breeze. Barrett gave Eddie a quick report on her night with Paul and went off to her shop, smiling all the way. Eddie spent some time with Dove, who was having a good day and wanted to go to Children's Beach with Bobby. William and Dinah said they'd drop off Dove and Bobby, buy the *Times* and the *Globe* at the Hub, pick up sandwiches at Something Natural, and share a picnic lunch with Dove and Bobby.

Eddie drifted out to the Book Barn. The air shimmered with heat.

The horse was on the far end of the field with her head stuck into a bush. Eddie assumed that made her, or at least her head, cooler. She wouldn't mind sticking her head into a bush, too. The shadowy barn was cooler than the open air, but still warm.

She went into the house, found a small electric fan, and brought it out to the barn. It moved the heavy air in a rotating breeze. She returned to the house and crawled behind the sofa in the living room. Her father stored some of his older books here. *The Tao of Physics* by Fritjof Capra. Three heavy tomes by Simon Schama. *Ulysses* by James Joyce. *The Complete Works of Lord Byron: Including His Suppressed Poems.* The books were lined up the length of the sofa, and they were all covered with dust. Eddie whipped out her phone and snapped a photo. If her father complained, she'd have proof that he hadn't even looked at them recently.

She carried them out to the barn and shelved them wherever she could find a gap. Few people had stopped by in the past week. Eddie thought they were either working or cooling off on the beach. She checked the special section of Dinah Lavender's books. Eddie had read some of them, but Dinah had published over a hundred, so Eddie had a lot to choose from, and right now she needed something light and frothy to occupy her mind.

She'd just settled in with *The Seduction of Sadie* when a truck came down the drive. It looked like Jeff's truck. It *was* his truck. She ran her hands through her hair, hoping to shake out any dust from the books, and went out to meet him.

"Hey. I brought you something." Jeff held out an iced mocha cappuccino from Espresso to Go. "I thought you might need it."

Eddie reached both hands out, grabbed Jeff's T-shirt, and pulled him to her. She kissed him thoroughly. "I need *you*."

"You've got me, Eddie." Jeff released her and pulled her into the shade of the barn. "Vinnie gave us the day off. What's up?"

"Do you have a moment to talk?"

"I do."

They settled on the chairs and sipped their coffees.

Eddie spoke all in a rush. "I-I told you Dove is here, with Bobby. I told you that she's really sick. She says she's dying, and she won't see a doctor, and some days she's better than other days, but Jeff, she wants me to adopt Bobby."

"And you," Jeff said very quietly, "you'll be moving back to New York with Dinah." Before Eddie could respond, he said, "I get it. Dinah's wonderful. She's nice and lives a fabulous life."

"I don't know, Jeff." Eddie couldn't meet his eyes. "I haven't talked it over with Dinah, but of course I would stay *here* with Bobby, no matter what Dinah does. It's Bobby I'm worried about. I don't how to be a mother, Jeff. You know how I feel. It's why I moved away."

"Can you imagine staying on the island?" Jeff asked.

"Oh, Jeff," Eddie said. "I'm afraid."

Jeff set his coffee on the table between them. He reached over and took her hand. "Can you leave the barn for a while? I want to show you something."

Eddie walked with him to his truck, her heart pounding.

She knew he was taking her to Tom Nevers Head, to see his house.

The traffic was congested at the rotary, with lines streaming down Old South Road and Milestone Road in both lanes. Once they were near the turn to Tom Nevers Head, the road cleared and they were in a lane of lush green grass and the glossy jade of tupelo trees. Eddie hadn't seen all the new houses and roads in this area. The landscapers had been careful to leave the mature trees and bushes, so the houses were set back in their own private forests. She caught glimpses of handsome new houses, small, large, and huge, behind the trees and shrubbery.

Jeff went down a dirt road and arrived at a house. Two-story, gray shingled, with a chimney at one end and a cupola at the top, it was perfect New England architecture.

"You have a cupola," Eddie said.

"Yeah. Come see."

Jeff led her through the patchy grass, up the steps to the front door, and into the house, which was finished inside with hardwood floors and six-over-six windows. They went up the stairs to the second floor, and up another, steeper set of stairs. The top step widened to become the floor of the small, six-sided space with a floor large enough to sit on and walls tall enough to stand by, and six windows.

"Jeff!" Eddie was breathless. "You can see the ocean from here!"

He nodded. "Nice, right? I looked at architectural designs and chose this one because it would make a perfect hideout for a kid."

Eddie turned away from him, pierced through with longing and regret. She composed herself. "Show me the rest of the house."

"Sure." Jeff started down the steep steps. "You have to go down backward."

Back on the second floor, Eddie strolled through the three bed-rooms and two bathrooms.

"Look at all the closets!" She sighed.

The primary bedroom had a fireplace with an elegant carved wooden surround and a marble mantel.

"Does the fireplace work?" she asked.

"It does."

Jeff stood behind her. She could feel his breath on her neck. Every cell of her being longed for him. He put his hands on her shoulders. She leaned back against him. He wrapped his arms around her and held her tight.

She knew she belonged here, in this house, with Jeff. Her very soul was at home here.

She thought of Bobby, and she pulled away.

"Jeff . . . please." Tears streamed down her face. "I do want this. I love you. I love this house. But, my God, we would be taking such a risk." She wiped her cheeks with her hands. "I need to think of Bobby."

Jeff said simply, "Bobby could live with us."

Nantucket Blues was busy. Janny and Barrett were both waiting on customers until five, when Janny took off and customers disappeared for drinks and dinner.

Barrett walked around her shop, putting things where they belonged. She went to the back room to open a new shipment of hair accessories.

She heard her door open. She smoothed her hair and went to the front counter. "May I help you?"

"Just looking," the man said.

Her new customer was tall, lean, and good-looking. He wore board shorts, a Kansas City Chiefs baseball cap backward over curly dark hair, and a short-sleeved shirt in a gaudy Hawaiian flower print. He wore a heavy gold link bracelet on one wrist and what seemed to be a Rolex on the other. He kept his hands in his pockets and constantly jiggled the change, at the same time whistling tunelessly. He didn't have a tan, so he didn't look like a summer person. She couldn't figure him out.

When her phone buzzed, she answered.

"Hey," Paul said. "What are you up to in your air-conditioned paradise?"

"You can join me anytime," Barrett told him.

The man slipped an expensive bracelet off the display and, holding it with both hands, brought it close to his eyes to study it.

"Paul, I have to take care of a customer now. Let's talk later."

Barrett ended the call and gave all her attention to her customer. She didn't get many men in her shop, but usually they bought a nice present for a woman. This bracelet was *really* nice.

The man set it back, gently, on the counter. "How much?"

"It's six hundred dollars," Barrett told the man. "Tanzanite is a rare gemstone, and the bracelet is made of gold."

"It's small. Do you have something bigger?"

"How do you mean? Wider? A bigger stone?"

"Yes, I guess."

"We're not a fine jewelry shop. I suggest you go to Jewel in the Sea for something more spectacular. They're an excellent shop, beautiful stones, reasonable prices. Just up the street."

"No, I like it. I'll take it." He pulled out his credit card.

Barrett smiled and bent down to take a small white gift box from the lower shelf.

"Hey, do you know this writer woman who lives around here?" the man asked.

Barrett froze. Could this guy be Dinah's stalker?

She tried to relax her face as she stood up. His credit card was on the counter. She ran it through the machine, noting that his name was John Henderson.

"I'll just put it in this box." Her voice and hands shook slightly as she handed him his card. "Would you like this gift wrapped?"

"That would be great. Thanks."

Barrett carefully packaged the bracelet in a small white box and tied blue ribbon around it, adding a bow. "Here you are."

"About that writer. I think I've seen her come in here."

"We have several well-known women writers on the island," Barrett said as pleasantly as she could.

"Her name is Dinah Lavender." He looked uncomfortable. "Odd last name, Lavender."

Warily, Barrett said, "Why, yes, she's been in. I think she bought a scarf. If you'd like to leave your name with me, I could tell her if I see her again."

The man frowned. "I really need to see her. In person."

Barrett stood her ground. "If you give me your name, I'll give it to her if she comes into my shop again."

"It's important."

"Yes, I understand."

He reached into his shirt pocket and pulled out a business card. Heavy stock, dark print. He was John Henderson, of Henderson Brokerage, Wichita, Kansas.

Barrett smiled. "Mr. Henderson. Wow, you've come a long way from home."

"As I said, it's important."

"I promise that if she comes into the shop, I'll give her your card and tell her you stopped in asking about her. Will you be on the island long?"

"I'm staying at the White Elephant," he said, mentioning an upscale hotel. "I'll be here as long as I have to."

"Okay, then," Barrett said. "If I see her, I'll tell her."

John Henderson looked as if he were going to cry.

"And I'll pass the word along. I'll tell other shopkeepers to look for her."

"That's very kind," John Henderson said. "Thank you."

In large letters, Eddie wrote: *Make your own dinner. Sandwiches inside.* She stuck it to the refrigerator with magnets. She asked Bobby to help her by putting the magnets on the bottom of the sign. He liked trying them in different configurations and shapes, and that kept him busy while Eddie set a light dinner out for her and Bobby and Dove.

Bobby finished with his magnet art and sat at the table long enough to eat a cheese sandwich and seedless grapes. Dove slowly ate some of her tuna salad.

Barrett called. "Is Dinah there?"

"Out on the porch, talking with Dad. Why?"

"I think I met her stalker today."

Bobby accidentally knocked his glass of milk over.

"Bare—we're eating dinner. Tell me when you get home." As she talked, Eddie picked up a dish towel and mopped up the milk.

"I'm sowwy," Bobby said.

"That's okay," Dove told her son. "I knock things over sometimes, too, don't I?"

"Me, too," Eddie said as she poured Bobby another glass of milk.

She could see how Dove was struggling to sit up in her chair, and her heart ached.

Eddie really wanted a nice cold beer or a glass of dry white wine, but she didn't want to drink around Dove. She could tell that Dove was tiring, and soon she helped Dove upstairs to undress and slip into bed.

Afterward, Eddie took Bobby's hand and led him outside to run off his energy while she organized and closed the Book Barn. The sun was dropping behind cotton ball clouds, making every color imaginable streak the sky.

The horse came to the fence and nickered at them. Bobby climbed on a rail and reached over to scratch her nose.

"Why is she named Duchess?" Bobby asked.

"Because she acts like she thinks she's royalty."

Her explanation seemed to make sense to Bobby. Eddie moved close to the boy, ready to catch him if he fell off the rail. The evening light made the child's face glow. His perfect skin. His bright eyes. His quick smile.

She could love this little boy. Maybe she already did. Could she love him enough to accept whatever pain that love might bring?

"What would you name the horse?" she asked Bobby.

"Duchess is a good name," Bobby said at once. "Because she's so bossy and she acts like she's better than everyone else."

The horse snorted, tossed her head, and raced to the other end of the field.

It was almost dark when Eddie took Bobby into the house for a quick bath and a bedtime story. Dove was still slumbering, her face as fragile and innocent as a little girl's. Bobby fell asleep the moment his head hit the pillow, a talent Eddie envied. She tucked the covers around him, turned off the light, and quietly left the room.

She found Barrett waiting expectantly in the living room.

"We have to talk," Barrett said.

"Wait for us," Dinah called.

Dinah came into the living room, slipped off her sandals, and curled up on the sofa. Their father sat next to her. *What?* Eddie thought. When did they start sitting near each other?

Barrett perched on the ottoman. "Listen, guys. A man named John Henderson came in to the shop today, looking for Dinah. He asked specifically for Dinah Lavender. He gave me his card and told me to pass it along if I saw her."

Barrett handed the card to Dinah. Dinah read it, with William peering over her shoulder.

"He's from Kansas?" Dinah asked, shaking her head. "I don't know anyone from Kansas or recognize this name."

"Could he be your stalker?" Barrett suggested.

William looked alarmed. "He's still on the island?"

Dinah put a calming hand on his arm.

Barrett flinched in surprise. Dinah touched Barrett's father so easily. *Barrett* never touched her father so easily.

"Maybe," Dinah told William. "But probably not. Since I've been here, I haven't seen any signs of anyone following me. I'm fairly sure this Henderson fellow isn't the stalker."

"Well, why is he looking for you?" William growled.

Barrett laughed. "Dad. Come on. She's *Dinah*."

William turned, muttered, and looked the other way.

Dinah said, "In my own way, I'm famous, William. A little bit famous." She read the card aloud.

"John Henderson," Dinah read. "Henderson Brokerage."

"Let me see it." William slipped the card from Dinah's hand and read it. "I don't like this at all," he muttered.

"What should we do?" Barrett asked Dinah.

"I'll call him and make plans to meet him for coffee tomorrow," Dinah said. "I'm sure I'll be safe at a restaurant in town with so many people around."

"Would you like me to accompany you?" William asked.

"Thank you, William. I don't think that will be necessary. You should keep working on your book."

William looked crestfallen.

Eddie laughed. "Dinah, I think you're collecting material for a new book."

"Of course I am," Dinah agreed with a toss of her head. "I like living with a group of people. I feel safe here, with you all so close. I feel safe enough to sleep at night." She cast her beautiful gaze at William. "It would be even better if I didn't have to sleep alone."

Their father blushed a deep crimson.

"I think I'll go up." Dinah rose, and in a rather Scarlett O'Hara move, sashayed to the door, stopped, and looked back over her shoulder. "Please don't worry about this man. I'm sure I'll be fine." With a swish of her skirt, she walked away.

"I'm going into my office for a while." William stood up and left the room.

Eddie and Barrett stared at each other, both of them covering their mouths with their hands to hide their laughter.

"What is going on with Dad?" Eddie whispered.

"I think he might have a little crush on Dinah," Barrett said. She stood up. "I'm going to bed. I've got to get up early tomorrow."

"I'll be up soon." Eddie rose and stretched.

"We have a full house," Barrett said.

"I know. The weird thing is, I like it."

Barrett hugged Eddie. "I like it, too. I think you belong on Nantucket, Eddie." She hurried away and up the stairs, before Eddie could disagree.

Eddie picked up the glasses and plates. She took them to the kitchen and set them in the dishwasher.

"Come on, Duke," she said to the dog. "Last time."

Duke wagged his tail and followed her out the kitchen door.

The day's heat had lessened, and the air felt cool and dry. Eddie sat on the top porch step and breathed in deeply. The moon was almost full, lazily rolling along in the sky, lighting up the fluffy clouds and showering the world in silver light. Duke sniffed around until he found the perfect bush. Duchess came to the fence and tossed her head. Honeysuckle trailed over the fence and the porch railing, sweetening the air. Eddie thought she could almost see those infinitesimal light particles called photons streaking down in their constant secret rain.

"Come on," Eddie called the dog. "Bedtime."

Duke padded along pleasantly up the steps and into the house. Eddie locked the kitchen door and checked that the front door was locked. Her family never locked the doors here on the island, but Eddie had adopted the habit when living in the city.

She got ready for bed and quietly peeked in at Bobby and Dove. They were both sleeping peacefully. The house was full of people, and the moon was high, lighting a path in the upstairs hall. Her journal waited for her on the desk in Barrett's room, where Eddie would sleep after she wrote. Maybe she was where she belonged.

seventeen

Barrett had trouble concentrating on her customers that morning. Her mind raced.

When she'd left the house, Dove was still sleeping. Eddie was in the kitchen eating breakfast with Bobby.

Would Dinah and Eddie really stay on Nantucket until January? If they didn't, who would run the Book Barn? It had solved one problem, and the house looked more civilized, more normal, but Barrett would have to close it on Labor Day. She couldn't keep it open and run her shop, too, and her shop was more important. She had to talk to her father. *He* had to stop mooning around in his study, obsessing on a book he'd never finish.

And *Paul*. She loved being with him, she might even be in love with him, but Nantucket Blues was her first priority. She'd been planning on this shop for years, and she had made it happen. She couldn't give it up. But Paul wasn't asking her to give it up. She'd read that no matter the question, love was always the answer, but how far could love stretch?

But how would she feel if Eddie tried to take Bobby back to New York with her?

The door opened. Thank heavens, she thought. A customer. That would knock her thoughts out of their circular worry path.

But no. It was John Henderson.

"Good morning!" He took off his Kansas City Chiefs cap and held it in his hands, like an old-fashioned gentleman. "I wondered whether you managed to speak with Miss Lavender."

"I did, actually. I gave her your name and phone number. She said she'll try to get in touch with you today."

"Thank you so much," Henderson said. "That is very kind." He took his phone from his pocket and checked. "She hasn't called yet. I'll wait at my hotel. Thank you again."

Then two women entered the shop, cooing and raving over all the beautiful sweaters, statues, soaps, and jewelry.

John Henderson left.

Barrett breathed a huge sigh of relief and smiled at the women.

Still, after they left with bags full of purchases, Barrett was unsettled.

Barrett phoned Dinah, Eddie, and her father. She was sent to voicemail on all the numbers, so she left messages. Then she stood at her counter and worried. She had so many things to worry about.

Eddie had brought her laptop down to write while the house was still sleeping. Barrett had already left for her shop. She thought she'd have half an hour before the others woke.

Bobby finished his breakfast and asked Eddie if he could watch TV.

"Fifteen minutes," Eddie told him, her mind focused on her journal. She closed her laptop.

Then, surprisingly, Dove showed up. She'd showered, and dressed in a swimsuit and beach cover-up.

"You look good," Eddie told her.

"I feel good." Dove kissed Eddie's cheek. "I had such a good sleep."

"I scrambled you a couple of eggs for breakfast," Eddie said.

"Thanks, Eddie." Dove sat at the place nearest the stove and carefully nibbled at the buttery yellow eggs. "Oh. Delicious. Yum."

Eddie put a glass of water next to Dove. "What are your plans for the day?"

Dove carefully chewed and swallowed before answering. "I'm taking Bobby to a special beach."

"Want me to pack some snacks for you?" Eddie asked.

"That would be nice."

Eddie found the bread, whole wheat but not seedy, because Bobby hated seeds. "Do you want me to come with you?"

"Not today. Maybe another time we can show you and Barrett. I want it to be our special place."

"You'll take your phone?"

"Yes, Mom, of course I will."

Bobby raced into the room, excited. "She's not your mom, she's my aunt!" he yelled. "Are we going to the beach?"

"Let me finish my eggs," Dove said. "Can you find your bathing suit? And your special towel?"

Bobby raced away.

"If only I could siphon some of that energy," Dove remarked.

Eddie found two pears to add to the peanut butter sandwiches. "Are you sure you feel well enough to go to the beach with him?"

"I'm sure. I don't know how many more good days I'll have, so I want to make the most of this. I'm taking him to Miacomet. I googled it on my phone. It's got a long pond and a big dune and on the other side, the ocean."

"Oh, yeah. It's beautiful out there."

"I'm hoping it will give Bobby the idea of transition. How thin the barrier is between one place and another. Between fresh water and salt."

"That sounds a bit metaphysical for a little boy."

"Silly Eddie, I'm not going to lecture him. I want him to learn it the way three-year-olds learn things. He's too young to understand concepts like transition or even death and heaven. I want him to feel it, hear it, breathe it. He'll learn it through his body when he runs from seashore to freshwater pond, through swimming in both waters and sensing how the earth connects them."

Eddie wrapped her arms around Dove and nestled her chin in Dove's hair. "You are an amazing person."

"Don't make me cry," Dove warned playfully.

"I wish you weren't sick," Eddie said.

"Not as much as I do," Dove replied. "Now let me eat my eggs."

William came into the room smelling of the racy aftershave he'd started wearing after Dinah arrived. For once he wasn't carrying a book. Bobby was prancing along behind him.

"Those eggs look delicious," William said. "Hello, young man. Can you eat those eggs? Good. Fist bump." William held out his fist and Bobby bumped it with his own small fist, giggling with delight.

Eddie scrambled more eggs. Dove and Bobby went upstairs. Soon they were noisily returning down the stairs, Bobby wearing a swimsuit and T-shirt. They had towels thrown over their shoulders, beach bags in their hands. Eddie handed out sandwiches and water bottles and tried to kiss Bobby goodbye, but he was too excited to stand still. He pattered barefoot to the door.

"Mommy! Come on!"

Dove waved at Eddie and left with her son.

Dinah came into the kitchen. She wore the most modest sundress Eddie had ever seen on the writer. "John Henderson called," she announced. "I'm going into town to have coffee with him."

"What? Dinah," Eddie said, "don't be silly. This guy could be your stalker."

"I think he very well might be. He said he was trying to find me in New York earlier in the year. He said he contacted my publisher but they wouldn't give him my number. He has a very important task he needs my help with. It involves books. He wasn't actually clear when he spoke—his voice shook. He sounds very nice. He was so grateful that I said I'd meet him. He said his wife loves my books." Dinah returned to the hall and critiqued herself in the hall mirror. She put on more lipstick and fluffed her hair.

Eddie said, "I'll go with you."

Dinah shook her head. "You don't need to, Eddie. Really. I'll be back this afternoon. I want to get some writing done." She walked away, then did an about-face and put her hand on Eddie's cheek. "You're sweet to worry about me. But I know I'll be fine. And I need to grow up a little, don't you think?"

"You'll call me if you need help?" William asked. "You should be careful."

"You worry too much," Dinah told him with a smile.

"Even so," William retorted.

"No one talks like that anymore." Dinah laughed.

What is going on with them? Eddie wondered.

"I'll definitely call you, whatever happens," Dinah promised.

Dinah went out the door. They heard her silver Mercedes convertible purr as she steered it out of their drive.

"I'm going to follow her," William announced. "Eddie, come with me."

"Dad, that's crazy. Dinah's right. She'll be fine. She'll be in the middle of town."

"Well, I'm going whether you come with me or not."

"Oh, Dad!"

Exasperated, she followed him out to his car. As he drove into town, she had a quick text conversation with her sister.

They're meeting at Born & Bread, Eddie texted. *Dad insisted we follow.*

Good luck! Barrett replied. *Gotta go. Customers.*

"There she goes, into the café!" William leaned toward the windshield, as if being a few inches closer gave him long distance vision.

"Dad." Eddie gently hit her head against the back of her seat.

"There's a parking spot!" William announced, swerving sideways toward the curb. He squeezed between two cars in three jerky motions. "Come on."

"Slow down, Sherlock." Eddie put her hand on her father's arm. "Give it a minute."

"Fine. But be ready to jump out of the car."

"Stop with the drama," Eddie begged. "Dad, I've lived with the woman for two years. I know she'll be on red alert, and I know *she* knows what she's doing."

"Look, Eddie. She came here because she was afraid of her stalker. Are you telling me not to worry? Because I'm confused."

Eddie cocked her head sideways and scrutinized her father. "What do you care, anyway, Dad?"

Her father ignored her. "I think they're coming out, I think . . . *look.* She's getting in his car."

"He doesn't look dangerous," Eddie muttered, but now she was worried, too. Why would Dinah go *anywhere* with this man?

William started the car and cursed under his breath as he tried to angle out of the small space without hitting the other cars.

"Watch where they go!" he shouted.

"I'm watching." Eddie didn't know whether to burst into hysterical laughter or to scream. "He's going down Broad Street. He's turning left onto South Beach."

The traffic was crazy. People were leaving the beaches because of the erratic wind, and driving into the small town to eat or visit museums. The intersection at Broad and Centre was especially bad, with lines of cars rushing forward only to slam to a stop as a gaggle of giggling tweens idled across the street, unaware of the cars.

"Watch out, Dad," Eddie said. "There's a family on bikes." As her father slowly drove past the mother, father, and two children, Eddie zipped down her window, stuck out her head, and yelled, "HELMETS! You should all be wearing helmets!"

The father glared at them and almost lost his balance.

William chuckled. "I would think you were used to congested traffic after living in New York."

"This is Nantucket," Eddie told him. "And it's reckless to bike anywhere without a helmet."

John Henderson turned right onto Easton Street and then left into the parking lot for the White Elephant. William slowly drove past the hotel. Eddie unclipped her seatbelt so she could turn around and watch where the couple went.

The hair at the back of Eddie's neck stood on end. "They've gone into the hotel, Dad."

William swerved into another open spot on the street and parked. "Hurry."

"Don't run," Eddie advised. "We'll get all sweaty."

They crossed the circle drive, walked up the steps, and entered the hotel.

At the reception desk, they waited impatiently for the clerk to finish speaking with another couple. Eddie checked the name on the clerk's badge.

"Deep breaths, Dad," Eddie whispered. "Don't have a heart attack."

Finally, the clerk turned to them. "How may I help?"

"What room is John Henderson in?" William demanded.

Eddie slid in front of her father. "Hi, Lisa, it's so cool to see you again!" Eddie had never seen her before, but with a constantly changing summer workforce, it could be true.

"Oh, hey." Lisa clearly didn't remember Eddie, but politely tried to fake it. "How are you?"

"I'm good," Eddie answered. She spotted the large engagement ring on Lisa's fingers. "Are you still with . . . oh, gosh, I've forgotten his name."

"Andy Gardner!" Lisa held out her hand. "We're engaged!"

"That's *awesome*! Congratulations!" Eddie took Lisa's hand and gazed at the ring. "It's so beautiful."

William cut in. "Excuse me, but we'd like John Henderson's room number, please."

"Oh." Lisa retrieved her hand and blinked. "We don't usually give . . . but since it's *you* . . ." She glanced at her computer. "He's in Room 201."

"Thank you," William said.

"When is the wedding?" Eddie asked.

"Oh, not until next February. It will be a destination wedding. In Aruba."

Eddie made a girlish squeal. "Awesome!" She twinkled her fingers at Lisa and followed her father to the elevator.

"What the hell was that all about?" William muttered as they rode to the second floor.

"We got the room number, didn't we?" Eddie asked pertly.

It took only a minute to find Room 201. William pounded on the door.

"Settle down, Dad," Eddie hissed. "You're not the gestapo."

They heard the door handle turning and saw the glitter of the gold chain from the door to the wall.

"Yes?" He was tall, slender, and maybe forty years old. A tired forty years.

Eddie stepped in front of her father. "Hello, I'm Eddie Grant. I work for Dinah Lavender. We have an urgent message for her."

"Oh," John Henderson said, and took off the chain. "She's right here. Come in."

Eddie almost pushed the man aside as she went through the door. Her father followed.

"Why, Eddie, William, what are you doing here?"

Dinah was sitting at a desk with a stack of books near her. On the floor next to her rose five cardboard boxes. The top box was opened.

"What's going on?" William demanded. "Are you here of your own accord, Dinah?"

Dinah smiled beatifically. She rose from her chair. "Are you worried about me, William?"

Her father's face turned red. "You are in a strange man's hotel room," he blustered. "You came to Nantucket because you were afraid of a stalker. How can we *not* worry about you?"

Dinah stepped close to William. "I think that's the nicest thing you've ever said to me."

"Dinah." William struggled to control his voice. "What are you doing here? What is *he* doing here?"

Dinah said, "I'll let John explain."

William and Eddie turned expectantly to John.

"It's my wife," John said. "Bea. She's ill. She has to have surgery. And well, she adores Dinah Lavender's books. I want to give her something to look forward to. To give her hope. Something magic. So, I bought all of Miss Lavender's books, and I asked her to sign them to Bea. She will be thrilled to have them. You've got to understand how it is when a book is signed. I mean not for everyone, but for some of us. I mean, she has a couple of Dinah Lavender's books, and only one has been signed, and she holds it and carefully touches the signature. She says that even so far away in reality, when she touches the signature, she's somehow magically in contact with the author. With the essence of the author . . . Bea's not a spiritually gifted person. But she does get some kind of strength from touching Miss Lavender's signature."

Dinah continued, "John did the most remarkable thing. He found one hundred and twelve of my books in good shape, and he's brought them here, and asked me to sign them."

"One hundred and twelve books?" William huffed. "That will take forever. He can't expect you to—"

"Dad," Eddie said. "Chill. Dinah signs more than one hundred and twelve books at her talks."

"Well, are you the one who's been stalking her?" William demanded.

John looked horrified. "Oh, I wouldn't say *stalking*. I did fly to New York. I rented a hotel room and tried to find where Miss Lavender lives, which is not that easy. It's a big city. I didn't want to barge into the building and knock on her door. That might alarm her."

"Plus," Eddie pointed out, "the building has a doorman."

"I went to her signing, but she had such an enthusiastic and, might I say, impatient crowd lined up, I couldn't take up her time to explain about wanting her to sign so many books. I had to go home for a while to be with Bea." For the first time, John's face brightened. "Be with Bea. We always like saying that. Anyway, I searched online, and I saw that Dinah Lavender was here on the island. I came here, and I saw her go into Nantucket Blues and I went in and talked with the owner. I gave her my card . . . and Miss Lavender has graciously agreed to sign the books."

William relaxed. "Do you mean you've been flying around the country with boxes full of Dinah's books?"

John straightened his shoulders. "I have. It's been my quest."

"Your *quest*?" William sank down on the end of one of the double beds, as if his legs wouldn't support him any longer.

To Eddie's shock, Dinah settled on the end of the bed next to William. She touched his arm lightly. "It's all right. It's wonderful. Knights of yore aren't the only people who can have quests. Living people can have quests, too." Dinah smiled at William and Eddie. "You see, I'm just fine. It won't take me more than an hour to sign the books. Eddie, you can go, but I'd love it if William could stay here with me and open each book to its title page, and then pass it to John to put back in a box. It would go more quickly that way."

"I can do that," William said.

"Thank you!" John held out his hand to William. "That will be a big help."

William smiled slightly. Rising, he shook John Henderson's hand.

Dinah sat at the desk. "Well, my dears, let's get started!"

"I'll go visit Barrett at Nantucket Blues," Eddie said. "I can walk down. Give me a call when you're ready to go home."

The best part of today, Eddie thought, would be telling her sister about everything.

eighteen

Barrett was finishing an online order when Eddie burst in, bright-eyed and laughing.

"You won't believe this!" she told Barrett.

"Lock the door," Barrett said.

Eddie locked the door and followed Barrett into the back room.

"So. First of all, Dad, *our father,* went all Sir Galahad on Dinah." Eddie found two paper plates and set pastries on them as she described that morning's amazing adventures. Her father rushing to rescue Dinah from her stalker. Actually tailing her like a stalker himself, and then practically breaking into the hotel room to find Dinah and John Henderson, who had traveled all the way to the island with two suitcases of books for Dinah to sign so that John could give them to his wife.

"That is the sweetest story I've ever heard," Barrett said.

"Yeah," Eddie said, "almost as sweet as our father bursting into he-man mode to rescue Dinah."

"Eddie! It does seem like Dad is . . . *interested* in Dinah. And she seems to be attracted to him."

"I know. But don't get too excited yet. She flirts with any male within sight." Eddie waved her hand. "Listen. Let's forget about Dad for a minute. Forget about Dove and Bobby."

"Forget about Dinah?" Barrett challenged.

"Yes! Forget about Dinah!" Eddie grinned. "I want to tell you about me. About me and Jeff. Barrett—we're in love. I'm going to stay on the island."

Barrett frowned. "Oh, Eddie. Are you sure?"

"Absolutely. He showed me the house he's been building for us. And we're going to be Bobby's family if . . . if necessary."

Barrett studied Eddie's face. "Are you kidding me? You run away to live a fancy, fabulous life, and you think I'll believe you're giving all *that* up to stay here on this little island?"

"I love Nantucket. And I love *Jeff*, Barrett. Maybe I had to leave him to learn just how much I love him. How much I want to be with him."

Barrett fretted. "Well, then, what about Dinah? You'll have to tell her to hire another assistant. She won't want you to leave her. She'll offer you a zillion dollars, and you won't be able to turn that down, and you'll break Jeff's heart again and Dad's, too, and mine, too, not that you care about me."

Eddie slid off the stool and stood face-to-face with Barrett. "Where is all this coming from? I thought you'd be happy for me. Happy that I'm going to stay."

Barrett nibbled her lip, wondering how to phrase it. "I don't know if I can trust you. And what about Bobby? What if Dove really does . . . die? How do I know you won't leave again?"

Eddie reached out, trying to pull Barrett into her arms.

"Barrett, honey, I'm not going to do that. I'm not going to leave Bobby, or you, or Dad, or Jeff. I promise."

Barrett leaned on Eddie's shoulder. "Why are things so messy?"

Eddie held her sister tight. "I know you're afraid. I'm afraid. We're all taking chances. It's the only way life can be lived." She kissed Barrett's cheek. "Otherwise, we'd all just be hiding under our beds. Remember when we were small? We watched a scary show on TV and it frightened us so much we both hid under my bed until Mom enticed us out with grape Popsicles."

"I remember," Barrett said, half-smiling. "Grape was my least favorite flavor. Okay, you're right. Sorry to be so freaky. I've got to get busy. I've got stuff to organize. Bills to pay. Hopefully, I'll have more customers."

Eddie asked, "Do you want me to hang out with you for a while?"

"No. Thanks. I'm fine. I'll be better if I get some work done."

Barrett walked to the front of her store. Blue surrounded her, and she saw two women lingering at her window.

"Okay, then." Eddie slung her bag over her shoulder. "I'll see you at home tonight."

A young woman hurried into the shop. "Thank heavens you're open! I've got to buy a present. I forgot today is my mother's birthday and she loves your stuff."

Her words worked like a magician's wand on Barrett. She lit up. She smiled. "Sure. Let's find something and I'll gift wrap it."

Eddie grinned. "See you later." She left the shop.

Barrett turned to her customer. "What sort of thing are you looking for?"

"Oh, I don't know. You have so many beautiful things in here. I want them all!"

Eddie pulled into the driveway. Duke ran out to greet her, tail wagging. The horse stood next to the barn, in the shade near the fence. As Eddie approached, she stood firm, waiting, and when Eddie reached over the fence to stroke her long soft muzzle, the horse extended her neck and closed her eyes, surrendering to the touch.

"You're getting to like me, aren't you?" Eddie said sweetly.

The horse snorted and tossed her head. Duke squeezed below the fence rails and ran up to the horse. Together, the two animals strolled to the back of the field.

Eddie opened the Book Barn and stepped inside. She scanned the eccentric shop, assessing the shelves. Dinah's books were all gone, no surprise there. Good old Hegel and Nietzsche were still hanging out on the lowest shelf, next to the quilting books. Most of the children's books were gone.

She walked around, straightening shelves, folding the afghan on the back of the chair. August was melting to an end. Eddie guessed there would be a lull for a few days, and then the newlyweds and the almost-deads crowd would arrive, and some of them might like looking at used books.

Eddie climbed on the high stool and leaned on the counter. She opened her computer to the shop page, then closed it. She had to face it. She had to stop putting it off. She had to decide how and when to tell Dinah she was staying on the island. Her fear was that Dinah would be hurt. Eddie genuinely loved her, and thought Dinah loved her back, in her own self-centered way. Eddie could almost predict what would happen. Dinah would fall apart, weeping that she couldn't go on without Eddie, Eddie was the only assistant she'd had that really made a difference, and why couldn't Eddie come back just for a month, to help Dinah get settled in the city again?

But Bobby was the most important person in the mix. At some point, probably within the next few months, Dove would die. She was failing faster than she'd hoped, and she had agreed that for the last few days she would go into the hospital. She would tell Bobby she was going on a trip.

Eddie's heart ached at the thought of Dove and her "trip." She couldn't imagine how it would happen. But they would help Dove, and mourn her, and take care of her son. Eddie and Barrett and Bobby would stay in the farmhouse while Jeff finished building his house. At some point she and Jeff would make wedding plans. They would formally adopt Bobby.

What a terrifying thought. Eddie had to be a good mother. That was what she *had* to do, and she was scared.

As if summoned by her thoughts, Dove returned home, parking her ancient Volvo near the house.

Eddie walked out to help her carry in the beach stuff, the picnic basket, the umbrella, the damp and sandy beach towels.

"How was it?" she asked.

Dove released Bobby from his car seat straps. Bobby hurtled out of the car and raced around the yard.

Dove leaned against the car, obviously exhausted, watching her boy run.

"We had a great time," Dove said. "We both have sunburns here and there, and Bobby must have a bucket's worth of sand in his bathing suit. I'll make sure to take it off before we go into the house."

"Don't worry about that," Eddie said. "Go on in, take a shower, take a nap. Whatever. I'll hang with Bobby."

"Thanks, Eddie." Dove pushed off from her car and walked slowly to the house.

"Hey, Bobby!" Eddie called. "Come to the backyard with me so I can rinse the sand off your legs."

Bobby ran up to Eddie, grabbed her hand, and pulled her toward the barn. "Read me a book!"

"First, let's get you into some dry clothes."

Eddie stripped his bathing suit off and used a long hose to wash sand off Bobby. He giggled and jumped in the force of the spray. She found clean underpants and dry shorts and a T-shirt in Dove's beach bag. She dressed Bobby.

"Go in the barn and choose a book," she said. "I'm going to rinse off your sandals and swimsuit, and then I'll come in to read."

She took the sandy clothes to the clothesline at the side of the house. She shook out the towels and beach clothes, pegged them to the line, and sprayed them with the hose until they looked reasonably sand free.

"Okay, Bobby," she called. "Let's read."

As she spoke, she saw Bobby crawling under the fence.

The little boy stood up and walked toward Duchess, who was standing maybe twenty feet away. Bobby was talking so softly Eddie couldn't hear the words.

What should she do? The horse had never bitten anyone before. Had never reared up and whinnied and come down, hooves striking a person. But clearly Duchess was on guard. Her ears were back. She was bobbing her head and huffing.

Eddie's heart jumped to her throat. Should she call out to Bobby, tell him to come back? Would that scare the child and make him scream and frighten the horse? If Duchess hurt the child—and she was so huge, standing there towering over the little boy!—if she hurt the child . . . Eddie told herself not to panic.

She climbed over the fence. She crouched down, making herself small so she wouldn't frighten the horse, and took a few steps toward the child and the horse. Her presence might be enough to make Duchess run to the other end of the field. Usually, it was. Duchess would only tolerate an adult's touch if there was a fence between them.

Now Bobby was next to the horse. Talking to her.

"Bobby." Eddie spoke in a normal tone, as if what was happening was also normal.

Bobby whispered to Duchess. The horse dropped her head down and made nibbling motions with her huge rubbery lips. The little boy giggled. He patted the horse on her head, near her mouth. He stroked the horse's muzzle. The horse held very still. She closed her eyes.

Bobby continued to pet the horse, until the huge animal snorted softly and walked away.

Eddie whispered, "Wow."

Bobby turned, a big grin on his face. "She likes me."

"Yes, she does, Bobby. But maybe don't get into a yard with a strange animal unless you have an adult with you. I mean, this horse usually isn't very friendly. I was afraid she might kick you, or bite you."

"I'm not strange to her," Bobby said. "She likes me."

He was so sweet, his cheeks and the tip of his nose pink from the sun, his hair stiff with salt, standing out in every direction, his face chubby, his eyes bright with youth. He looked like Stearns as a three-year-old.

She would be more careful. More watchful. She would protect this child with her life.

"Let's go in the barn and read," Eddie said, holding out her hand.

Bobby took her hand. Eddie climbed over the fence and watched him squeeze through. The barn was shady and cool. The quiet comforted them both like a soft breeze on a hot day. Eddie sat in one of the old armchairs, pulled Bobby onto her lap, and opened a book from the table. There was a frog and a toad, and the little boy nestled his head against Eddie's chest and fell asleep.

By late afternoon, Barrett was exhausted. The shop had been swamped all day. Janny had been helpful, but she kept answering her phone and shooting mean looks at Barrett.

"Is something wrong?" Barrett demanded after the last customer left.

Janny picked up her clutch and got ready to leave the shop. "You should look at your phone more often," she said. "You're being kind of rude."

After Janny left, leaving clouds of anger behind her, Barrett checked her phone.

She had three messages from Drew, asking her to get in touch.

"Hey, babe," Drew said when he answered her call. "I wanted to take you out to dinner, but you never called me back."

She should tell him, Barrett thought. She should let him know she was committed to Paul.

Would it be wrong to do it over the phone? It wasn't as if they had a long-term relationship.

"Sorry, Drew. It's been busy here today, and—"

He cut her off. "Look. I'm at the Brotherhood. Come meet me. I'll buy you a drink."

Barrett hesitated. It was after six. No customers were around.

"Okay. I won't be able to stay long. But I'll be there soon."

She texted her father and sister and went back out the door to her car.

The restaurant was crowded. As Barrett entered the historic brick building, she heard the shouts of laughter from the men at the bar and felt, for just a moment, that she was in the nineteenth century, and the bar was full of hearty sailors returning from exotic voyages. Dinah would love this place.

Drew was seated at a table in the corner. Barrett threaded her way through the crowd and joined him. He rose and kissed her, and she turned in time to receive the kiss on her cheek.

"I've ordered already," Drew said. "Sorry to be rude, but you never got back to me. I'm having the fish and chips. I ordered a glass of red wine for you, and if you want food, too, that's fine."

"I can stay only a short while." She sat in the chair across from him. "I've had a crazy day—"

Drew interrupted her. "Tell me about it. I'm trying to put out five fires at the same time. We've got a lot of things going on. I'm exhausted. First, our number one bookkeeper, she's been with the company forever, says she's retiring. I'll be damned if I'm going to give a retirement party for someone who leaves us when we're struggling to

hold things together. I've had three Zoom meetings with three different banks, and thank God I could record them, because one of the
bankers put his foot into some shit and I can call him out on that—"

The waiter brought Barrett a glass of red wine and set the fish and
chips in front of Drew.

"Another beer," Drew said to the waiter.

Drew ate a bite of the chips.

Good, Barrett thought. While he was eating, she had the opportunity to talk.

"Drew. I'm sorry to tell you this when you've had a difficult day, but
I need to let you know that I can't see you anymore. I'm in a relation-
ship with another man. Paul. You met him at the opening of my store.
We—"

"*That* guy?" Drew sat back in his chair, shocked. "You can't mean
that . . . that *carpenter* fellow."

"I do mean that carpenter fellow. He's also an artist, he sculpts
wood, really beautiful pieces—"

Drew snorted. Shaking his head at her in a kind of patronizing
pity, he said, "You won't have much of a life if you marry him. You're
better than that, Barrett. I mean, go look at his home and then look at
my parents' house here on the island—"

Barrett reminded him, "You've never invited me to meet your parents."

Drew swatted her words away. "I was going to, Barrett. We've been
so freaking busy. Plus, I haven't known you very long. I didn't want to
do anything prematurely."

"Inviting me to your house would be premature?" Barrett knocked
back a big swig of wine before she said anything rude.

"Barrett, come on. You know who I am, who my parents are. I
didn't want you to get the idea that . . . I mean, some women I've dated
get dollar-bill signs in their eyes once they've seen our house, our an-
tiques, our art."

Barrett was angry and somehow amused. She took a deep breath and managed to speak in a civil tone of voice. "I didn't know a woman had to be vetted before meeting your parents."

"Well, come on, be honest," Drew said. "I don't think you were ready for the meet-the-parents bit. I mean, you wouldn't even have sex with me."

Shocked, Barrett burst out laughing. "What? Do you have a checklist a woman has to complete before you issue a coveted invitation to step inside your family's summer home?"

Drew stopped eating. He gave Barrett a solemn stare. "I didn't know if you were serious. Summer affairs usually end, and not nicely. But I really like you, Barrett. You need to give me more time. Plus . . . how can I feel close to you if you won't have sex with me?"

Barrett took another sip of wine. "This has got to be the strangest conversation I've ever had, and I've had some doozies."

"Barrett—"

"Seriously, Drew? I think you've got some kind of mental problems. But anyway, I don't want to see you again."

Drew shook his head. "You don't know what you're missing out on."

"Oh, I think I do." Barrett stood up. "Goodbye, Drew."

Drew reached across the table, snatched up her glass, and tossed the last of the red wine down his throat, as if winning an argument, taking what he wanted.

Barrett didn't bother to speak. She walked away from the table, and she was almost giddy with relief.

Barrett drove home, thinking about her talk with Drew. She was glad that it was over. She felt her emotions clearing up like the clouds drifting away from the summer sky. She wasn't sad at all. She felt *free*.

At home, she found Eddie in the kitchen, tearing romaine for a salad.

Barrett asked, "Where's Bobby?"

"He's eaten. Now he's watching television. Dove's still sleeping."

Barrett held up her phone and snapped some photos.

"Hey!" Eddie said.

"I want some shots of you all mom-ish in an apron," Barrett said. "Wow, something smells good."

"I made lasagna." She looked over her shoulder. "I've invited Jeff to join us for dinner."

"Cool. I'll call Paul."

"How did your talk with Drew go?"

"Actually, it was easy. But he's so arrogant, it's going to take him a while to believe I dropped him."

Barrett ran upstairs to call Paul. She left a message on his voicemail, took a long hot shower, and pulled on dry clothes. She peeked in on sleeping Dove and went downstairs and began to set the table. Paul called back to say he'd be there soon.

The front door opened and Dinah and William walked in.

Eddie hurried in from the kitchen.

"Everything okay?" Barrett asked.

"Everything's fine." Dinah beamed up at William. "We drove him and his box of books to the airport. He's on his way home."

"So that was your stalker, Dinah," Eddie said.

Dinah smiled like a cat with a bowl of cream. "Yes, and here is my hero." She leaned against their father and put her arm around his waist.

Eddie and Barrett locked eyes. *He was her hero?*

Once more, the front door opened. Jeff and Paul came in, carrying a blueberry pie from Bartlett's and a carton of vanilla ice cream.

Barrett set more plates at the table, lit a candle, and carried in the salad as Eddie was serving the lasagna. They sat at the table talking about this amazing day, and no food had ever tasted better.

When dinner was over, Barrett, William, and Dinah helped clear and do the dishes. Paul and Barrett walked out to lean on the fence, sweet-talking Duchess. Eddie and Jeff went into the den and found Bobby asleep on the couch in front of *The Loud House*. Eddie turned off the television and watched as Jeff gently lifted the little boy into his arms and carried him upstairs to bed. Eddie followed, and watched as Jeff laid Bobby next to his sleeping mother.

They turned off the light and pulled the door almost, but not quite shut, so if the child woke, he wouldn't be in complete darkness.

Eddie sat on the top step, her feet on the step below. She patted the space next to her.

"Sit with me a minute. I'd like to talk."

Jeff sat. "You're worried about Bobby?"

"Yes." Eddie reached over and took Jeff's hand. "If we . . . if you and I are going to adopt Bobby . . ." She didn't know how to say it.

"We have to get married," Jeff finished for her. "And we have to decide where to live until I can finish our house."

"How long will it take you?"

"After Labor Day, things will slow down. A little. Kick Gordon has penciled me in for installing plumbing during the month of September. I'll finish the dry wall, and the painting . . . I'll need to furnish it . . . if I'm lucky, we can move in around Christmas."

"That's amazing, Jeff." Eddie leaned against him. "Just think of it. You and me waking up together . . ."

"And Bobby, don't forget."

"Oh, I won't forget him. Ever. But we have to see a lawyer with Dove to make everything legal."

"And you have to tell Dinah that you won't be working for her anymore."

"I know. It's going to be hard. And I'm going to miss the income."

"Don't worry about money. I'll take care of us."

"I suppose, but I want to do my share."

"We'll sort it out," Jeff said. He put his arm around Eddie's shoulders. "We can do it all."

———

The house was quiet. Eddie checked that the doors were locked and went upstairs to bed. As she passed by Dove's room, she heard coughing. She hesitated by the door, wondering what she should do.

"Eddie?"

She opened the door and looked in at Dove. The other woman was sitting up in bed, holding tissues to her mouth.

"Dove. What can I get you?"

"Mommy's coughing," Bobby said, and Eddie realized the little boy was still awake, and frightened.

"It's just a cold," Dove assured him. "But, Eddie, I wonder if Bobby can sleep with you tonight. I need to take some cough medicine, but I don't know how soon it will act, and Bobby's so sleepy."

"I'd love to have Bobby sleep with me tonight." Eddie went to the bed and sat down next to Bobby. She was surprised when the child reached out his arms to her and easily moved with her when she pulled him onto her lap. She held him close.

Dove coughed, caught her breath, and said, "I've been telling Bobby that you love him as much as I do. And I have this bad cold. Maybe Bobby should sleep with you from now on."

Sorrow tugged at Eddie's heart. She managed to say, "I think that's a wonderful idea. Is that okay with you, Bobby?"

Bobby nodded his head, yawned, and rubbed his eyes. "Okay."

"Can I get anything for you?" Eddie asked.

"No, thank you," Dove said. She held up a prescription bottle. "I have what I need right here."

Eddie said, "Good night, Dove."

She stood up, cuddling Bobby close to her. His head was heavy and hot. She managed to leave the room and pull Dove's door shut. She slid into Barrett's room.

"Sssh," she said to Bobby. "Barrett's sleeping."

She laid the child down on her twin bed and carefully slipped in beside him, snuggling him close. She was surprised at how little room he took. Grateful for the air-conditioning, she pulled a sheet up over her shoulder and tucked it around Bobby. She tried to stay awake, but the sweet sound of his deep breaths, accentuated by an occasional little snore, lulled her into sleep. When she woke, it was morning.

nineteen

Eddie was taking homemade cinnamon buns out of the oven when she heard footsteps on the stairs. Skipping and jumping—that was Bobby. Progressing more slowly—that was Dove.

"Oh wow, cimmamom buns!" Bobby yelled.

Eddie smiled. She was beginning to see why women liked to cook and bake.

"They're still hot, so you have to wait a minute," Eddie told the little boy.

Bobby threw himself on the floor and cuddled with Duke, who vigorously licked Bobby's face.

"Is that okay?" Eddie whispered to Dove.

Dove nodded. "The experts say it's all okay for little kids. It gives them immunities."

Eddie made coffee for them all, put out plates and knives, and they sat at the table.

"How do you feel?" Before Dove could speak, Eddie said, "Tell me if you get tired of hearing me ask how you feel."

"I slept really well," Dove told her. "I'd like to go out to Miacomet again today, and Eddie, I'd love it if you could come with me."

"We can absolutely do that."

"Also . . . I wish Barrett could come with us."

"Where are you going?" Barrett entered the room, dressed for her shop in a navy dress with white trim.

"I want to take Bobby out to Miacomet again. He loves the pond and it's not so crowded as other beaches. I think it will be a good place to talk."

"I can talk anywhere!" Bobby informed them.

"I'd like to go, too," Barrett said. "Let me see if I can get Janny to work this morning."

Janny answered her phone by screaming out, "Are you kidding me?"

"Janny?" Barrett flashed an amused look at Eddie and Dove.

"Who do you think you are, dumping my brother like that? I'm never coming near your pathetic little shop again."

Barrett held the phone out so the others could hear Janny ranting about how wonderful her brother was and how fortunate Barrett had been to have him even *speak* to her and she was not spending one more minute in that stupid little shop.

When Janny stopped to catch her breath, Barrett said, "Do you want to pick up your last paycheck?"

Janny burst into full force sobbing. "How can I care about money when you've broken my brother's heart?"

"Janny, I haven't broken Drew's heart. Maybe I hurt his pride, but you know he's going to find another woman, someone of his . . ." Barrett remembered the word Janny would appreciate. ". . . *caliber*."

"I don't care. I hate you." Janny clicked off.

Eddie poured her sister more coffee. "Goodness, Barrett, I had no idea that you and Drew were so involved."

"We weren't *so involved*," Barrett said. "Whatever, I have to open the shop this morning. I'm sorry to miss out on going to Miacomet with you all. Can we all talk again this evening?"

"Of course," Dove said.

"Of course!" Bobby echoed.

Eddie, Dove, and Bobby arrived at the beach in the middle of the morning, so only a few families were there. They made their small nest near the freshwater pond. Bobby allowed his mother to smooth sunblock over his pudgy little body. Then he took his red plastic pail and his blue plastic shovel and began to dig holes in the sand. Quickly he was lost in his own little adventure of exploration.

"Bobby seems content with his own company," Eddie remarked.

Dove agreed. "He can lie on his stomach, studying worms and bee-tles, or on his back, gazing up at the clouds and naming them."

"He's got a little Stearns in him," Eddie suggested.

"He's got a lot of Stearns in him."

Eddie scooped up a handful of sand and watched it trickle through her fingers as she spoke. "I've talked to Jeff about Bobby. Jeff is almost finished building his house, and there will be a bedroom for Bobby, if that ever becomes necessary."

"It's not *if,* Eddie. It's when. I'd like to have a talk about all this with you and Jeff and Bobby. This week, if possible."

"Well, *I'd* like to make a doctor's appointment for *you*," Eddie said. "Maybe you're being overly pessimistic."

"Eddie, look at me. My kidneys are shutting down. My liver is hardly functioning. I'll be lucky to last until October."

"Okay, then," Eddie responded, almost angrily. "Let's talk about *that*. When will you have to go into the hospital? Do you want hospice to come? Do you want to . . . to say goodbye to Bobby?"

"I'm experiencing signs that my physiological systems are shutting down. Eventually, I won't be lucid. After that starts, I don't want

Bobby to see me any longer. Not in that state. I've talked to him every day about how I'll leave soon to go on my trip. Before that happens, I want him to spend time with you and Jeff, as much time as possible."

Sobered by her friend's honesty, Eddie said, "Okay."

"And I will see a doctor. I need to make arrangements. Probably this week, if possible," Dove said.

Eddie grabbed Dove. "Oh, shit! Really?" She was shocked at how thin Dove's arms were.

They felt like bones without flesh or muscles. She carefully released her.

"Really." Dove remained matter-of-fact. "We need to see a lawyer, and we need to go to a bank. I need to transfer some money into your account."

"We don't need your money," Eddie protested.

"Children are expensive," Dove said. "Think of it as a college fund. Stearns created a video game called *Tag the Bag*. A company named Vegas Video bought it for five hundred thousand dollars. Your brother named me as the recipient of all proceeds, and there are a lot of proceeds. I'm going to sign it over to you and Barrett. I've done most of the paperwork. I just need to have it finalized."

"This hurts my head," Eddie moaned.

"I know. But I've done almost everything."

Eddie said, "Dove, how can you be so calm about this? If Bobby wasn't here, I'd be screaming and pulling out my hair."

Dove smiled. "I did plenty of that when I was first diagnosed. I've had months to accept it and I know why this is happening. I had almost a year of serious boozing after my parents lost their house. For two years after Bobby's birth and Stearns's death, I lived on Scotch, bourbon, gin, the hard stuff, while my kind aunt and uncle took care of my baby. They can't continue to do that. They have their own health problems. So yes, I have cried. I regret what I've done to my body, but honestly, I'm too tired to cry anymore. I only care about Bobby. I want him to be okay with this. He's young enough to forget me. I want him to feel completely at home with you and Barrett and Jeff, too."

"But what can I do?" Eddie implored.

"Exactly what you're doing," Dove told her. "In fact, I need to lie down for a while. Keep an eye on Bobby."

As Dove slept, more people came to the beach, with coolers of food and rubber doughnuts and fluorescent swim noodles and other beach toys. A little girl asked Bobby a question, and soon they were holding hands as they waded into the clear shallow water of the pond.

The next day the air hung around the island like damp gauze. The wind was gone, allowing the humidity to settle and stay. Eddie and Bobby carried more boxes of books to the barn and arranged them on the shelves. Then Bobby sat at the children's table in the barn while Eddie waited on the occasional visitor.

They were surprised when, around noon, Jeff drove up in his Jeep. Bobby ran out to greet him and insisted on carrying Jeff's backpack to the barn.

"What's in here?" Bobby asked as he set the pack on the table. "Can I see?"

"Let me catch my breath," Jeff said.

Duke came hurrying into the barn, tail wagging, and even the horse swung her head around as far as it would go so that she could watch them.

"What am I?" Jeff asked. "Santa Claus?"

Eddie grinned. "Sometimes."

Jeff sat on the big cracked leather chair and Bobby squeezed in next to him.

"Okay," Jeff said. Unfastening his pack, he reached in and pulled out a leathery pig's ear. Duke danced and whimpered with delight, gently grabbed the snack, and ran off to lie under a tree to gnaw on it.

Jeff took out an apple and handed it to Bobby. "Want to give this to the horse?"

"You're in a good mood," Eddie said as they watched Bobby and the horse.

"Max said to take the afternoon off. Brukacher, the silicon tsar, hasn't paid his bills for the massive amount of work we've done building his house. He keeps changing his mind. Now he wants a bowling alley in his basement, but he owes us a pant load for work we've already done."

"So, you dropped in with a bag full of apples and dog bones."

"Oh, more than that. You'll see."

Bobby returned, wiping horse drool onto his shorts. "She licked me!"

"Well, Bobby, I've got a couple of things in here for you." Jeff brought out a packet of Oreos. "Hang on, don't open them yet. I've brought you something else. Something every boy should have."

Carefully, Jeff lifted out a large, brightly colored box of Legos. He put his hand on Bobby's shoulder. "Bobby, you'll be living with Eddie and me now, in a house I'm building, and I'm a builder, and I'm going to teach you to how to build a house. Let's go over to the table and build something."

Bobby followed eagerly and they settled to play.

Eddie went to the stand to check her emails. It was all she could do not to throw herself on Jeff, telling him how wonderful he was to spend time with Bobby, to bring Legos to Bobby. She heard Jeff quietly explaining what to do, and she heard Bobby's giggle when he'd made a tower. Duke lay beneath the tree, gnawing on his treat. The horse stood at the fence, leaning her head over, keeping an eye on the action.

It can happen, Eddie thought. Misfortune, craziness, and madness could happen. But so could kindness, optimism, and courage. On the spur of the moment, she called her sister.

"Hi, Barrett, just checking in. Are you okay?"

Barrett sounded happy. "I am. Paul is going to call later. We're talking about other small sculptures he could make for the shop."

"Cool. Tell him I said hello. I'll talk to you later."

After a while, Eddie went into the house to make lunch, and brought lemonade and sandwiches out to the porch. Even in the shadow, the heat and humidity of the day was oppressive. Duke slept under the tree, one paw on his pig's ear. The horse had retreated to a shady spot and stood with her head stuck into the bushes.

"Eddie, can I go inside and watch television?" Bobby asked.

"Sure," Eddie said. "Take your plate and glass in, please. Put them by the sink." She watched Bobby make his way into the kitchen. "Jeff, is there anything else you want?"

Jeff looked at the window. He saw Bobby walking out of the kitchen toward the den.

"There's a lot I want," he said quietly. He angled his chair around so he could face Eddie. "I want to make a difference in that child's life. I want you to believe we could have a happy child ourselves. I want you to stay on the island. I want us to be a family. I want to marry you. Soon."

Eddie's heart flipped like a kite in the wind. She put her hand on her chest. "I want that, too."

Jeff looked solemn. "*But?* Do I hear a 'but' tagging along? But you don't want to leave Dinah? But you aren't sure you want to have children? But you don't like the thought of living on the island year-round?"

He looked serious, and worried, as if he expected Eddie to run away again. She flung herself off her chair, landing on her knees on the floor, reaching up to take Jeff's hands in hers.

"I want to be with you. I don't want to leave you or the island or Bobby. I want to marry you and I'll marry you as soon as you want."

Jeff smiled. "I think I'm the one who should be on my knees. But this way will work, too." Reaching into his pocket, he took out a small black velvet box and handed it to Eddie.

Inside was a small, perfect, brilliant diamond ring. Jeff took it from her and slid it onto her finger. Time stopped. The world vanished. Tears speckled Eddie's cheeks. She was here, with Jeff, and the universe was telling her she was exactly where she should be.

Jeff leaned down and kissed her gently. "I love you."

"I love you," she whispered.

The back door opened. Bobby popped out. "Can I have those Oreo cookies we left in the barn? Why are you crying, Auntie Eddie? Did you hurt yourself?"

"These are happy tears, Bobby," Eddie said. She stood up and held her hand out to the little boy. "Look! Look what Jeff gave me!"

Bobby glanced at her ring. "Pretty. Can I have some Oreos?"

Eddie felt like saying, *Sweetheart, I'll give you an Oreo factory!* Instead, she said, "Bring the bag here. We'll give you a few cookies, but not all of them at one time. You'd be sick."

Before she could finish speaking, Bobby hightailed it to the barn, quickly returning with the cookies. Eddie took the bag, carefully opened it, and gave Bobby a handful. Before the child could get into the house, Duke appeared, as if a bell had rung, sitting up prettily for Bobby, asking for a cookie.

"If the horse shows up wanting a cookie, I'll know I'm in a dream," Eddie said.

"Bobby," Jeff said, "no chocolate for dogs. If you want, you can eat the chocolate sides and give the middle to Duke."

Bobby looked at his cookies thoughtfully. "The middle is the best part," he said. And then he broke open the cookie, scooped a large piece of creamy sugar onto his finger, and held it out to Duke, who happily licked it off.

"I like that idea," Eddie said. "The middle is the best part."

Later, Jeff's boss called him to come work on another job, and Bobby fell asleep on the sofa, and in spite of the heat, Eddie felt energized, so she zoomed around the house picking out more books to take to the Book Barn. She closed the door—no one had come to the barn all day. She hurried back into the house to shower and wash her hair. Did anything feel as good as a cool shower on a hot day? She put on a pretty sundress, because she wanted to look good when she and Jeff made their announcement. Bobby woke up and she played hide-and-seek with him, giving him a chance to use some of his little boy energy without going out in the clingy dampness of the day. After a while, she sat down at the kitchen table with him to work on a sticker book.

Only occasionally did she experience a sting of worry, a little bell of alarm reminding her that she was going to have to break Dinah's heart when she told her she couldn't return to the city with her, that Dinah would have to find a new assistant.

But Eddie was determined. No amount of money or glamorous travel could lure Eddie away from Jeff this time.

Barrett was glad to close her shop that evening. It had been a difficult day. Her suppliers sent two boxes of the wrong product and Barrett had to email the company for the right product and prepare the return boxes for UPS to pick up. In the afternoon, a gaggle of teenage girls came in, giggling, picking up jewelry and dropping it anywhere, and taking off with two blue bracelets without paying for them, so Barrett had to call the shoplifter hotline for Nantucket's shops. Eddie had stopped by that afternoon to tell her about her conversation with Dove, leaving Barrett sad but also jealous that it was Eddie who got to spend precious time with Dove, and ashamed of herself for being jealous. Paul had called, but she'd had several customers and said she'd call him back, but she'd never had the chance. People kept coming into her shop, and Janny wasn't there to help.

Now she stood outside Nantucket Blues, locking the door, when her thoughts made her stop and look at her window. A silver and turquoise necklace lay against a blue silk shawl. A suncatcher made of spangling blue stars and planets dangled over a pillow silk-screened with blue waves.

What was wrong with her? She was upset because *people kept coming into her shop*?

Of course she had hard days and difficulties, but who didn't? She had created this blue world, and it was surprisingly successful. Most businesses took three years before making a profit. She was already turning a profit, and she hadn't even had time to devote to her online shop. She loved her family, and in a different way, she loved Paul, but right now, for better or worse, she loved this eccentric little shop, and she wasn't ready to give it up for anything.

Barrett caught her reflection in the shop window and had to laugh. She looked like a short, slender, bad-tempered bluebird.

"You should be ashamed of yourself," Barrett told her window-self. Poor Dove was dying, and Bobby was about to lose his mommy, and here she was grumbling around because she was tired. She tested the door to be certain she'd locked it, and started walking to her car.

Her phone buzzed. Automatically, she said, "Nantucket Blues."

"Hi, is this Barrett Grant? I'm Olivia Jayce, a contributor to the magazine *Cape Cod Life*. I've heard so much about the shop and I'd love to do a feature about it for our next issue."

Really? Barrett refrained from squealing like a little girl. In the most professional and friendly tone she could summon, she said, "That's great."

"It won't come out until October," Olivia said, "but Nantucket seems almost as busy in the shoulder seasons, and this should bring you some business."

Barrett sat right down on a bench overlooking the boat basin. "That's wonderful. What do I need to do?"

"Let me interview you," Olivia said. "I'll take a few good photos, too. Would next Monday work for you?"

"Absolutely," Barrett said.

They talked some more, then ended the call, and Barrett still sat on the bench, gazing out at the harbor. White sails against blue water. Puffy white clouds floating in a pastel blue sky. A pretty young woman leaving Peter England's clothing shop in a blue and white striped dress.

The thing was, Barrett thought, how amazing the timing had been with that phone call. As if the universe itself was encouraging her, supporting her. She was going to be interviewed! A photo of her shop would be in a magazine! She couldn't wait to tell everyone, and she hoped that Dinah would be so excited she'd treat them all with another bottle of expensive champagne.

Eddie was going crazy waiting for Barrett to come home, and finally, at nine-fifteen, she saw the headlights of Barrett's Jeep flash across the drive.

Eddie raced out to meet her sister.

Barrett stepped out of the car. "I have so much to tell you!"

Eddie squealed, "I have so much to *show* you!" Taking Barrett's hand, she led her toward the back of the house.

"Are you nuts?" Barrett asked.

"Sssh," Eddie whispered.

"Where is Dove? Where is Bobby?"

"They're in bed. Duh. It's after nine. Now, you and I are going to calmly walk up the steps of the back porch."

Barrett followed Eddie around to the back porch.

In the gentle light of the moon and the bolder porch light, their father and Dinah were sitting side by side on the wicker porch swing. They were holding hands.

"Get out of town," Barrett said.

"I know, right?" Eddie agreed.

"Girls," their father called. "We can hear you."

"Come join us," Dinah said.

Eddie and Barrett went up the steps and settled in the white wicker chairs across from William and Dinah. Duke, lying near the door, thumped his tail in greeting.

"You two are holding hands," Eddie commented, as if reporting the weather.

Their father smiled. It had been years since they'd seen their father smile like that.

"We're making plans," their father said.

Dinah fluffed her hair and scooted closer to their father. "I hope this doesn't upset you, Eddie, but I've bought a house."

Eddie was speechless.

"Where have you bought a house?" Barrett asked.

"On the cliff," Dinah told her.

Barrett almost fell off her chair. "On a *Nantucket* cliff?"

Dinah laughed. "Yes, darling. I've become very fond of this island, and also very fond of Bill."

"Bill?" Eddie echoed.

"William. Your father. I like to think of him as Bill."

"No one ever calls our father Bill," Barrett declared.

"I know," Dinah purred. "That makes the name special to me. To us."

"You and Dad are an *us*?" Eddie asked.

William, aka Bill, spoke up. "Dinah and I have become very close. We've decided to work on a book together."

Dinah leaned against him. "Yes, a book about romance."

Their father explained. "Dinah is talking about *romance*. That doesn't mean we're not also talking about love."

"And I've rather fallen in love with Nantucket," Dinah declared. "I've bought a house. My next few books will be a series of historical novels. I'm doing research at the Nantucket Historical Association, and I've already composed a timeline. Also, I'll be working with Bill on *our* book."

Eddie clutched the arm of her chair. "What about New York?"

"I'll keep the apartment. We'll probably go there occasionally to see the theater and so on."

"By *we,* you mean Dad, right?" Eddie clarified.

"Yes," Dinah replied sweetly. "Although you can use the apartment whenever you want to have a little city time. As for Nantucket, I've started the paperwork for the house. Eddie, you can live with me, or you can remain here with your family."

"I don't know what to say." Eddie looked to her sister for help.

"I'm stunned," Barrett said. "Does that mean Dad will be living here sometimes?"

"Yes," their father said. "But this house is your house, and Eddie's house, and eventually, Bobby's house, and of course, Dove is invited to stay here as long as she wants."

"Have you spoken with Dove about this?" Eddie asked.

"Not yet. I know things are complicated for her."

"More than complicated, Dad. She's dying. She's asked us to adopt Bobby—"

William interrupted. "By *us,* who do you mean?"

"So many us-es," Dinah interjected lightly.

Eddie began, "She means me and Jeff, because Jeff and I are getting married."

Dinah clapped her hands. "How wonderful, Eddie! I'm so happy for you. And hasn't it worked out well that I'll be here on the island, if you still want to work part-time for me."

Barrett held out her hands in a *pause* gesture. "You guys. This is a lot. And I haven't been able to talk with Dove about the future."

Eddie turned to Barrett. "We're not leaving you out, Bare. We want you to be with us, to help figure things out, but we know you need to be in your shop. Like yesterday was the first time Dove and I have gotten down to the real stuff, and we did that at Miacomet, and you couldn't come because of your shop. I'm not complaining, just stating facts."

"I get it," Barrett said. "I know it's difficult for us to get together. I'm always working, and now Janny has quit because I dumped Drew. I mean, I did it nicely, and things weren't serious between us anyway."

Dinah leaned forward, which gave everyone a lovely view of the pillowy tops of her breasts. "I think you are very serious about your shop, Barrett. Am I correct?"

Do they thinking I've been playing? Barrett wondered. She said, "You're right. I'm *very* serious about my shop. I don't have all the figures yet, and the summer isn't over, but I'm making an extremely healthy profit. And . . ." She paused dramatically. "*Cape Cod Life* magazine is going to do a feature article on me."

Eddie, William, and Dinah burst into such loud congratulations that Duke jumped up and ran around in a circle, barking. Duchess galloped up to the fence, whinnied, and raced away.

When everyone settled down, Eddie asked, "When is the interview?"

"Monday. Olivia Jayce is coming over from the Cape."

"What are you going to wear?" Dinah asked.

Barrett laughed. "I haven't even thought about that. I don't even know if I should keep the shop open when she's here. I won't want to lose customers, but I'll want to concentrate on the interview . . ."

William spoke up. "I have an idea. Allow me to hang out with you in your shop for a few days, and when you think I'm capable enough, you could take a few hours off here and there for whatever you need to do, and I could be in charge of Nantucket Blues."

Barrett was overwhelmed. "That would be *awesome*, Dad." *Also, terrifying,* she said to herself, but silently.

"Good. Good." William puffed out his chest and stood, ready to take on the world. "I think I'll watch the news now."

Dinah rose with him. "I'll go with you."

When Eddie and Barrett were alone, Barret whispered, "Do you think Dad can do it? Can I trust him to run my shop?"

"I'm sure he can," Eddie told her. After a moment, she added, "It makes me realize what enormous faith Dove must have in our Grant family to entrust Bobby to us."

"We're his family," Barrett said. "He belongs to us."

twenty

Barrett woke early, before her alarm sounded. Reaching out, she clicked it off. She didn't want to wake Bobby and Eddie, who were sleeping in the bed next to Barrett's. Eddie's arm was around the little boy, who was curled up against her.

She chose some clothes and slipped out to the bathroom. When she was dressed, she went down the hall to Dove's room and listened at the door. She thought she heard music. She opened the door and peeked in.

"Come in," Dove said.

"I don't want to disturb you." Barrett spoke quietly and went to sit on Dove's bed. She took Dove's bony hand in hers. "How are you?"

Dove took a deep breath. "Actually, I'm not good. I feel . . . really bad."

"What can I do?" Barrett asked.

"Just don't let Bobby see me this way. I don't want him to see me all swollen and pathetic."

"Oh, Dove!"

Dove clutched both of Barrett's hands. "It's okay. It's all okay. Eddie will be Bobby's mom and you'll be Bobby's amazing aunt Barrett. Plus, you have your own baby—Nantucket Blues. You've said you want to run it for years, maybe forever. Bobby can work for you someday."

Dove coughed. She struggled to sit up against her pillows, coughing, holding tissues to her mouth.

Barrett fought to hold back tears.

Dove gasped, "I think I'm going to have to go to the hospital soon."

Barrett hugged Dove, hoping she wasn't hurting her. "Oh, Dove, I wish you were okay."

Dove slumped against Barrett, her emaciated body astonishingly heavy. "Barrett, I have to rest now."

"I love you," Barrett whispered, trying not to cry.

"Love you, too," Dove responded, her eyes closed, sagging against the pillows.

"Do you want me to get someone? Eddie or Dad?"

Dove shook her head. "I have to rest."

Eddie roamed the kitchen. She'd heard Barrett drive away to open her shop. She'd checked on Dove, who was sleeping soundly. She'd given Bobby a bowl of cereal with a banana cut up in it. He was on the back porch, building towers with the colorful Legos, so she poured herself another cup of coffee and went outside to enjoy the coolness of morning. Duke was lying on his back in the shade of the wicker swing.

For a while, she simply sat, listening to the slight sweet tune Bobby was humming as he clicked the plastic blocks together. Duke snored. Duchess was at the far end of the field, her tail flicking at flies.

Eddie looked at her ring. It was as sparkling as the evening star. Soon she would start a new life, as Jeff's wife and Bobby's mother.

Before that, she had to tell Dinah she wasn't going to work for her anymore.

As if summoned by Eddie's thoughts, Dinah came out of the kitchen, a glass of iced coffee in her hand.

"Good morning, everyone!"

For a few minutes, Dinah sat on the floor and played Legos with Bobby. Then she rose and sat next to Eddie.

"Could we talk for a moment?" Dinah asked. "We haven't had a private conversation for days."

"Of course." Eddie wanted to act cool and slightly insulted, but instead she was achingly happy that Dinah was here.

"A lot has happened in the last few days. I'm taking Bill to view my new house today. I'd like to take you sometime."

"I'd like that. I think my father is happier than he's ever been." Eddie picked up a porch pillow and ran her fingers over the piping. She couldn't look at Dinah as she asked, "But what about you, Dinah? Do you really love my father?"

"Oh, yes. Please believe me." Dinah smiled contentedly. "He makes me feel safe. He makes me feel beautiful, even without my makeup. I love him truly, Eddie."

Before Eddie could respond, Dinah continued. "I know this is a huge change for you. I'm praying that you and I can still be friends."

Eddie swallowed her pride. "But I won't be your assistant anymore?"

"Oh, sweetheart, what a dear question. You are the best assistant I've ever had. I'll never forget your enormous kindness in inviting me to live here when I was afraid of the stalker. I'd love to keep you on part-time, for social media. Bill will take over my calendar, bookkeeping, and tax files. He's very capable with that sort of thing."

"He *is*?" Eddie asked. "That's the most shocking thing I've heard today."

"But what will *you* do, Eddie?"

Eddie felt herself blush. "Jeff and I will get married, but before then, Jeff and I must get his house ready for Bobby and me to move into. We're hoping to do that soon. Elementary school starts September sixth. Jeff and I have been talking with the school and a lawyer who will help us through the complications of adopting Bobby. It's going to be fairly streamlined since Dove has spoken to the lawyer and signed papers. Bobby seems happy to be with us. Jeff is working day and night to get his house in livable shape."

"May I see the ring?" Dinah asked sweetly.

Eddie held out her hand.

"It's beautiful."

"We'll have a wedding with all the trimmings, but we might need to get married in the courthouse first, so we can have Bobby live with us."

A tower of Legos collapsed on the floor with a crackling sound.

Bobby looked up. "Auntie Eddie, I want to go swimming. Can we go to the beach now?"

"Sure, Bobby. Let's go put our bathing suits on." She knew Dinah wouldn't want to join them, but Eddie asked, "Want to come with us, Dinah?"

"I'd love to," she said. "Let me put on a swimsuit and find my sunblock."

Eddie picked Bobby up and hugged him tight, kissing him all over until he giggled. She was so surprised and really thrilled that Dinah was going with them. She had to put her happiness somewhere, and as she held Dove's little boy, Eddie thought maybe that was what children were for.

twenty-one

Barrett sat in her car, sobbing into a soggy Kleenex. This was the one place she could be alone. The one place she could keep other people out. All she had to do was lock the doors.

Paul rapped on the window. "Barrett. Let me in."

He was the only person she wanted to be with, so she unlocked the door. Paul climbed into the passenger seat.

"Are you okay?" he asked.

"No. I'm not okay at all. Dove is dying and Eddie is going to marry Jeff and they're adopting Bobby and moving into the house Jeff built and Dinah is going to be Dad's girlfriend and live in a big house on the cliff and I'm going to be left all alone with a dog and a horse."

Paul reached over to pull her into his arms. "You've got your shop."

"I know, you're right, so why isn't that enough?" Barrett couldn't look at him, not now while her eyes were red and her nose was running and she felt like a human volcano.

"Maybe you need me," Paul said.

She was so surprised, she stopped crying. Stopped breathing even, for a few seconds.

She lifted her face to his. "What?"

Paul gently smoothed her tear-wet hair back from her cheeks. "Barrett, listen. I know this is the wrong time to say it, but maybe it's actually the right time. Barrett, I love you. I want to marry you. I don't have a house yet, but I want to live on the island with you, even if we live in a . . . a rented apartment in the attic of an un-air-conditioned house in August."

"Oh, Paul." Barrett laughed and cried at the same time. "That's the most romantic thing I've ever heard."

"I planned to wait to propose until I'd made enough money to make a down payment on a house. But I want to be with you now. I want to be *here* for you now."

Helplessly sobbing, Barrett pulled tissues from her pocket and blew her nose heartily. "Sorry that I'm such a mess. I think I'm transitioning from sad tears to happy tears."

"You're happy? Good. I want to propose to you, with a proper ring, but I don't want to rush things."

Barrett touched his face, his beautiful face. "Paul, I love you. I want to marry you. But you're right. There's so much going on, I can't keep it all in my head."

Paul said, "We don't have to hurry, although I'd like to live with you right away."

"So that we can wake up each morning and drink coffee together?" Barrett suggested.

"I wasn't thinking of coffee," Paul told her. He pulled her close to him and hugged her tightly. "You know, the garage I'm renting for my studio? I can stop renting and put that money toward a house of our own or at least for a nice apartment."

"Oh, no," Barrett said. "I don't want you to stop sculpting for a minute. We'll work things out. We'll find a way to be together." She put her hand on his face and gazed at him, and all at once her sadness floated away. "I want to be with you, Paul. And when I'm with you, you and I will be a family."

Saturday, Barrett was glad it was raining, a heavy, thundering, wind-driven rain that was flooding the streets and streaming along down-town sidewalks. On Facebook, the Nantucket Year-Round Community had posted videos of the rain-swollen waters surging over the piers and along Lower Main, where Nantucket Blues was. She couldn't safely open her shop.

And that was fine. It was the perfect day to spend like this, lazing around with family, making plans.

Eddie, Jeff, and Barrett were on the floor, playing Chutes and Ladders with Bobby. Or pretending to. Bobby sat on Jeff's lap. He spent more time gazing up at Jeff's bristle-covered jaw than he spent on the game. Dinah and William were relaxing in overstuffed chairs, doing crossword puzzles. Dove was stretched out on the sofa, her head resting on a pile of pillows, the rest of her snuggled beneath a down quilt.

It was clear to everyone that Bobby was fascinated by Jeff. Over the past week, the family had gathered at Children's Beach in different combinations. Sometimes Dinah would be there and leave, and then Jeff would stop by, and Barrett would take Bobby for lunch while William/Bill manned Nantucket Blues. To Barrett's surprise, her father was an excellent salesclerk and in turn it was providing some kind of therapy for him. He'd always enjoyed teaching. Now he enjoyed chatting with strangers, helping them choose the perfect gift. Once when Barrett had been in the back room, discussing an order with a supplier, she overheard her father talking to customers and realized with a shock that her father could be charming.

Barrett and Eddie had discussed their father whenever they had a moment by themselves. They'd decided that Dinah had somehow opened a portal into their father's personality that their mother had slammed shut. William also seemed enchanted by Bobby and often took him to the aquarium with the touch tank or to Squam Swamp on a hike.

It was odd, though, and frightening and sad, how quickly Dove was declining. Her face, feet, and ankles were swollen, the whites of her eyes were yellow, and although she was taking pain medication, Dove was uncomfortable and struggling.

One evening after dinner, their father had asked Dove for a brief conversation in her bedroom. After half an hour, he'd returned to the kitchen.

"Bobby, your mother and I were talking about this really fun place called Small Friends. I thought I'd take you over there to check it out."

"Will you leave me there?" Bobby asked.

William answered gently. "Not the first time. The first time I'll stay with you every minute."

"Because," Bobby explained carefully, "my mom is going on a trip pretty soon and she's leaving me here. She said Eddie will be my mommy and Auntie Barrett will be my aunt and you will be my grandfather."

"I am your grandfather and I'll be right here," William promised.

Bobby nodded. "Okay."

By eleven o'clock in the morning, Eddie was in the Book Barn, sending Dinah's work emails. Barrett was at her shop with their father. Dinah had driven her silver Mercedes into town to do research at the Nantucket Historical Association.

Bobby was with his mother at Children's Beach. Eddie had driven them there and planned to pick them up at noon, unless Dove called.

Eddie opened her journal. She hadn't had a chance to write in it for a few days. Well, she hadn't wanted to write in it.

She knew what she had to write would break her heart open.

Dove is dying. It will happen soon.

I am so afraid.

I don't know how people can stand this. Suddenly, and I can't tell anyone this, I'm weirdly grateful to Stearns because he died so quickly, efficiently, completely. We didn't have to watch him hurtle over the winding road, crash down the steep mountain, landing with a broken neck—the coroner said his neck was broken. His death would have been instantaneous. We didn't have to be with him as he died, we didn't have to witness him—was he terrified? Was he anguished for those few minutes when he realized he was losing his son and his wife? I hope he didn't even know. I hope he thought: Cool. I'm flying.

I don't think Dove's passing will go quickly. I promised her, and myself, that I'd stay with her in the hospital, and Barrett will join us if it's necessary for her to stay overnight. Dove doesn't want to die in the hospital, but it has come to the time when she needs help with her pain.

She says that she's not afraid to be dead. She believes once she is truly dead, once her body is dead, as Dove puts it, she will reunite with Bobby someday far into the future, she hopes ninety years in the future.

She says she's going to be with Stearns. She knows he is waiting for her.

I never disagree with her. If believing in life after death is foolish, then let her be a fool. And what do I know, anyway? What do we all know? Maybe she's right.

All I really know is that I'm watching a friend pass over a bridge that is blurred by clouds and will soon become invisible like this island is when mist and fog surround it. How will she know how to place her feet? I've asked her this.

Dove says that when she steps forward into the mist, the bridge will appear beneath her feet.

I've got to go pick Dove and Bobby up from Children's Beach.

———

The three friends were in a private room in the Nantucket Cottage Hospital. Their father and Dinah were home, taking care of Bobby. Dove was in a hospital bed with tubes going into her slight, shrunken body and nurses coming in to check on her every fifteen minutes. Eddie sat on one side of the bed, holding Dove's hand. Barrett was on the other side, holding Dove's other hand.

"How do you feel?" Barrett asked. Immediately, she corrected herself. "I know you can't talk but I hope you feel like you're floating on clouds of whipped cream." She flashed a glance at Eddie. "I sound idiotic. I hope she doesn't think I'm taking this lightly."

"It's okay, Bare," Eddie assured her. "The doctor said she can hear us, but may not understand what we say. Look at her. The pain medication is working. She's not grimacing in pain. That's the important thing right now."

Barrett nodded. "Hey, Dove, think of all the fun times we had together. Remember the time we made a fort in your backyard? Your mother flipped out because we used the good blankets and pillows."

"I remember," Eddie said. "We made spears out of sticks we found in the trees. We went hunting the monster. Once, we heard a noise near the forest, and we thought it was the monster and we screamed and ran back to our fort and huddled in there, shaking."

"Remember that Halloween when we went together and you were Rapunzel and I was the prince and Eddie had to be the witch?" Barrett cackled and made her hands into claws.

Eddie snorted. "I'll never forgive you two for that. I didn't want to be the witch. Who wants to be the witch? You two got costumes with sparkles and sequins. I had to wear a big black hat like the witch in *The Wizard of Oz*."

"Eddie," Barrett argued, "witches are good."

"Not when they wear the black hat," Eddie retorted.

Their eyes were fastened on Dove's face, but she showed no sign of comprehension.

Barrett said, "Remember when you got that karaoke machine for Christmas and we decided we were going to become a trio singing old-fashioned songs? We recorded us singing and when we replayed it, we fell on the floor laughing because we were so terrible!" She glanced at Eddie. "Is it okay to be silly?"

"Yes," Eddie answered. "But, Dove, we have serious things to tell you, too. We found your mother's phone number. She's still living in Florida with a guy named Archie. She's kept the last name, Fletcher. We called her . . . and left a message . . . but she hasn't called back so far." A surge of sorrow clogged Eddie's throat. She waved her hand to Barrett, telling her to take over.

"We can't find your father's address. The last person we spoke with said he'd moved to Costa Rica." Barrett paused. "You know, we haven't heard from *our* mother in years. We want to tell her she has a grandchild, but the last we heard she was in Amsterdam and we can't find her on social media or by searching."

"The three of us never had a perfect mother." Eddie felt tears beginning to well in her eyes. "But they did what was necessary, they kept us alive and healthy."

"Maybe it was the location," Barrett suggested. "Like a spell was cast over our neighborhood by on old witch who curses the area so that mothers didn't want to stay."

"But we'll be good mothers," Eddie promised. "We'll take good care of Bobby. Jeff and I will be the best parents we can be. And Auntie Bare and Grandpop will always be there for him, too."

"So the thing is, Dove, if you can hear us, we promise we'll take care of your little boy."

For a moment, it seemed as if Dove was speaking to them. Her breath was raspy, and her jaw moved. The doctor had said she would be in no pain because of the morphine drip.

"Is she going?" Barrett whispered to Eddie.

Eddie reached out and took Barrett's hand. They each held Dove's hand.

"Dove," Barrett said, "we're all holding hands, like we did when we ran and jumped into the swimming pool."

"The three musketeers," Eddie said. "And you get to go first this time."

A nurse came into the hospital room, put her hand on Dove's wrist, looked at a clock on the wall, and wrote something in a notebook.

Eddie was sobbing, standing bent double with her arms pressed into her belly.

Barrett's voice shook. "What do we do now?"

"Now you both go home," the nurse said. "Be glad you have each other. Be with your family. Drink a lot of water. Sit by the ocean. It's not going to stop hurting right away. You have to accept it, the pain. It's like having a baby."

Eddie choked out, "*This* is how it feels to have a baby? Well, give me a hysterectomy, because I'm never doing that."

"Me, either," Barrett said. She looked at Eddie. "I'll be a spinster, living with a dog and a horse."

The sisters smiled weakly. Barrett walked over to Eddie and hugged her, and they stood like that, crying and laughing and hurting.

"Is there someone you want to call?" the nurse asked.

Eddie nodded. "I'll call our father now."

By the time William arrived at the hospital, both women were numb. It helped, in an odd way, for them to have so much paperwork to deal with. Dove had efficiently left her strongly worded wishes. She wanted to be cremated. She did not want Bobby to know that she was being cremated. She wanted to be scattered in the ocean and she didn't want Bobby to attend.

Eddie closed the Book Barn and removed its presence from Facebook. Barrett closed her shop for a week. She added the words *Re-*

opening after Labor Day to her *Closed* sign, even though she couldn't imagine that would really happen.

Nothing seemed real.

When it did seem real, they went to one another and wept.

The hardest thing was telling Bobby that his mother had left on her trip. The first day he seemed happy enough, but by the third day, Bobby asked when his mommy was coming home from the trip. Several times he cried. Twice he went into a full-scale tantrum that left him exhausted and sad. They did their best to keep him happy. Bill and Dinah took him on the fast ferry to the Cape, played miniature golf with him, returned to Nantucket on the fast ferry, and bought him a hot dog and potato chips for the trip home. Jeff took Bobby for a ride in his truck one afternoon. They drove on the beach to Great Point, where Jeff held Bobby's hand tight as they looked at the hundreds of fat, grunting seals. Another day, Paul brought Bobby to his workshop to show him how he carved his wood into the shapes of boxes, bluebirds, and bookends. Paul gave Bobby a very small carving of an angel. He gave Bobby sandpaper and taught him how to smooth the wood.

In the evenings, the family ate comfort food—pizzas, chicken baked in cream sauce, twice-stuffed potatoes, tubs of ice cream.

After a week, they were notified that the urn was ready. The sisters waited until sunset. They stood on the beach at Cisco and looked at the calm, mysterious water sliding onto the sand.

"Take off your shoes," Barrett said.

"What?" Eddie looked confused, but she put the urn down in the sand and slipped out of her sandals.

Barrett unstrapped her own sandals. She held out her hand to Eddie.

Together, they walked into the water, which was still warm from the summer sun. Eddie carried the urn in her other hand, holding it tight against her chest. The sand shifted beneath their feet. With each step, they went deeper into the ocean, and they felt the water grow colder against their legs.

Eddie stopped walking. The waves were up to their chests. "More?" she asked Barrett.

"A few steps more," Barrett replied.

The cool ocean washed against their shoulders. Eddie held the urn out in front of them. Barrett took the lid off and held it while Eddie shook the ashes into the water.

"Goodbye, Dove," Eddie said.

"We'll see you in ninety years," Barrett said.

"Say hello to Stearns for us," Eddie said.

The sisters stood together as the sea surged against them and around them, touching them with the waters of all the oceans, carrying fish and shelled creatures and pebbles smoothed by millions of years of tumbling. Carrying the salt of tears, the whispers of secrets, the sweetness of dreams.

Carrying Dove's ashes.

Carrying Dove.

In September, when most of the summer people were gone, Dinah signed the contracts on her new house. She and Bill invited his family to come for a celebration.

Barrett and Eddie drove Bobby up the hill to the cliff overlooking Nantucket Sound.

Dinah and Bill were at the door, waiting for them to arrive. The house was large, with many high windows showing the blue waters and the ferries, sailboats, and yachts coming in and out of the harbor.

"Bobby," Bill said. "Come with me. I want to show you your room."

"He has his own room?" Eddie asked.

"Can we come see it, too?" Barrett asked.

Bobby took Bill's hand. Dinah and the sisters followed them up the stairs and into a large bright room with a captain's bed and sailboat wallpaper and a toy box that looked like a treasure chest, overflowing with toys. Best of all, in front of the windows overlooking the sound, a small, shiny brass telescope stood.

Bill knelt and showed his grandson how to use the telescope. "You'll get used to it," he promised. "You'll be able to watch boats coming into harbor and going out again. You'll be able to watch the birds flying and maybe you'll even spot a whale."

"Mommy told me she'd be in the clouds," Bobby said, looking hopeful and very serious.

Dinah knelt next to Bobby. "Do you understand that when your mommy floats past you in the clouds, she won't look like herself?"

Bobby nodded. "She said she might look like a pillow or a soccer ball or a bird. But she said I would know it was her. And she would know it was me."

"Your mommy is very wise," Dinah told him.

"Can I look in the toy box now?" Bobby asked.

"Of course."

The next morning, after breakfast, Eddie said, "Bobby, you're about to burst out of your shirt, and you need new clothes for preschool."

Bobby announced, "I want a T-shirt with a shark on it!"

"And that's what you shall have!" She was kneeling in front of the little boy, trying to fix a strap on his sandal. "But we'll get you some underwear and socks and pajamas, too. And we'll check out beds and sheets for your new room."

From the first floor, Barrett called up the stairs. "Are you guys ready?"

"Put on your backpack," Eddie told Bobby. "Yeah, we're on our way," Eddie yelled at Barrett.

"I don't want to be late," Barrett reminded them.

They hustled out to the car, slammed doors, fastened seatbelts, and Barrett drove quickly to town.

"Preschool starts tomorrow," Eddie announced. "New clothes time!"

"I used to love getting new clothes," Barrett reminisced. "And a new pencil case. New notebooks. I can almost remember how they felt, so soft and yet official."

Barrett dropped Eddie and Bobby at the brick entrance to the Hy-Line, drove around the block, and parked in her secret place. She walked against the flow of travelers headed for the ferry, and stepped into her shop. On these last days of summer, she was putting out new items for the coming fall and winter. Deep blue cashmere cardigans, blue wool and silk shawls swirling with violet and gold, clever hats made from turquoise felt and adorned with narrow gold hatbands. Throws and blankets in cobalt striped with white, hoodies patterned with smiling whales, and many pieces of Paul's work, carvings of a pale mermaid rising from blue waves.

Her father would have risen early and taken a cup of coffee into his study to work on his book. He'd arrive at the shop at noon to give Barrett an hour's break. Barrett would meet Paul in town or at the beach for lunch. It surprised her how much they had to tell each other when they'd just spoken last night.

Eddie and Jeff, Barrett and Paul, Dinah and Bill were all sitting on the back porch of the farmhouse on an early September evening. Everyone had prepared his or her own drink and Eddie had set out a bowl of chips. Bobby had climbed to the top bar of the fence and sat calmly having a conversation with Duchess, who hung her head low so that Bobby could scratch behind her ears.

Dinah announced, "Bill and I have discovered we enjoy living together, waking in the same bed, and so on. Deep breaths, darling," she told Bill as they all watched him turn crimson.

Eddie said, "Jeff and I are almost ready to move into the Tom Nevers house with Bobby." She glanced at her sister. "That will leave Barrett living alone in the big farmhouse, but we can't sell it. It belongs to Bobby. He has memories here. He feels safe here. Plus, he has his rituals with Duke and Duchess, and we're considering giving Bobby riding lessons when he turns four."

"Lucky boy," Barrett said, then caught herself. "Lucky in some ways."

"Anyway," Eddie continued, "Barrett, the farmhouse is yours."

"Wait. It's your house, too," Barrett argued. "It wouldn't be fair. I mean, financially. Should I pay you rent?"

Dinah threw her hands up. "My darling young women, you are straying into Agatha Christie territory where relatives fight about money and eventually murder someone."

Barrett laughed. "I don't think we're that bad!"

"You're right, Dinah." Eddie reached out and took her sister's hand. "Dad's going to sign the deed for the farm over to Bobby and you and me, and both of us as executors for Bobby until he's twenty-five. Jeff's house is perfect for us and Bobby, but we know Bobby wants to spend time with you and Duke and Duchess. You should remain in this house and have a bedroom for Bobby. If you want everything legal, we'll have our lawyer draw up a document saying that you're renting the farmhouse from Jeff and me for something like one dollar a year."

"May I suggest something?" Paul leaned forward.

Barrett wanted to go over and sit on his lap.

"Of course," Eddie and William said at once.

"I have accepted several expensive commissions for my carvings. The garage I rent is too small for what I want to do. Why don't I rent your barn for my studio?"

Barrett said, "What an excellent idea!"

"I agree," Dinah chimed in. "No one has come out in weeks. This

house looks fairly tidy, and the books that weren't bought this summer can go to the Take-It-or-Leave-It at the dump."

"Genius!" Eddie stood up. "This calls for ice cream. Barrett, come
help me."

The sisters hurried into the kitchen and opened the freezer. Several
pints of different flavors of ice cream were waiting. Barrett helped set
them on a tray. Eddie dug out big and small spoons. Barrett added
paper napkins.

They paraded triumphantly back to the porch. Bobby noticed the
ice cream. He climbed down the fence, got his Klondike bar, and returned to the fence where Duchess was waiting.

Everyone sat, hypnotized by the seduction of ice cream.

Barrett and Eddie watched Bobby carefully eat all the chocolate
before handing out the vanilla ice cream to Duchess. She took a bite,
whinnied, reared up, and galloped away.

Duke placed himself in front of Bobby, wagging his tail and begging.

"Okay," Bobby said. He gave the ice cream to the dog.

"Bobby," Barrett called. "Come get a new ice cream bar."

"And don't give any other human food to Duchess," Eddie added.

Bobby did as she suggested, and ran off with his treat.

"So," Dinah said, "Bill is going to live with me and we'll work together on the island and in New York. Barrett, you have your shop,
which seems to be doing well."

"It is," Barrett replied, scooping a big lump of Cherry Garcia into
her mouth.

"That's good. And we know that Jeff and Paul will be working."
Dinah let her gaze fall on Eddie. "Eddie, darling, what do you think
you'll do after the summer?"

Eddie took Jeff's hand. "We have a house to furnish."

Jeff added, "And a wedding to plan."

"And an adoption ceremony," Eddie said. "And we'll need to get
Bobby settled in preschool and so on."

Dinah leaned forward. "You know, Eddie, we can always help with Bobby."

Jeff put a protective arm around Eddie's shoulders. "We'll appreciate the help. Eddie has to plan a space in her day for writing."

"Writing?" Bill asked.

"Oh, just in my journal." Eddie met Jeff's eyes and was warmed by how he believed in her, how he championed her, how he loved her. "And maybe," she confessed, "maybe I'll try to write a novel."

about the author

NANCY THAYER is the *New York Times* bestselling author of more than thirty novels, including *All the Days of Summer, Summer Love, Family Reunion, Girls of Summer, Let It Snow, Surfside Sisters, A Nantucket Wedding, Secrets in Summer, The Island House, The Guest Cottage, An Island Christmas, Nantucket Sisters,* and *Island Girls*. Born in Kansas, Thayer has for nearly forty years been a resident of Nantucket, where she currently lives with her husband, Charley, and a precocious rescue cat named Callie.

nancythayer.com
Facebook.com/NancyThayerBooks
Instagram: @nancythayerbooks

about the type

This book was set in Sabon, a typeface designed by the well-known German typographer Jan Tschichold (1902–74). Sabon's design is based upon the original letter forms of sixteenth-century French type designer Claude Garamond and was created specifically to be used for three sources: foundry type for hand composition, Linotype, and Monotype. Tschichold named his typeface for the famous Frankfurt typefounder Jacques Sabon (c. 1520–80).